To Curti.

♡

Margy

Margaret Turner Taylor
March 2025

NO MORE SECRETS

MARGARET TURNER TAYLOR

LLOURETTIA GATES BOOKS • MARYLAND

Llourettia Gates Books, LLC
P.O. Box #411
Fruitland, Maryland 21826

Hardcover ISBN: 978-1-953082-33-6
Paperback ISBN: 978-1-953082-34-3
eBook ISBN: 978-1-953082-35-0
Library of Congress Control Number: 2025900666

Photography by Andrea Lõpez Burns,
Cover Judith Pattison – photographer, Sandra Mannakee – technical expertise
Cover and interior design by Jamie Tipton, Open Heart Designs

This book is dedicated to all those who sacrifice and work for freedom and to those who hope for freedom.

Contents

CAST OF CHARACTERS *for* *NO MORE SECRETS*

NORTH KOREAN LEADERS

Kim Il-sung
First Supreme Leader of North Korea 1948 – 1994. Founder of Democratic People's Republic of Korea. Made decision for North Korea to invade South Korea on June 25, 1950.

Kim Jong-il
Second Supreme Leader of North Korea. Assumed leadership when his father died in 1994 and ruled until his own death in 2011.

Kim Jong-un
Third Supreme Leader of North Korea. Ascended to leadership when his father died in 2011.

Jang Song-thaek
Brother of Kim Jong-il and uncle of Kim Jong-un. Murdered by KJU.

CHARACTERS IN *NO MORE SECRETS*

Kim Jong-nam
Son of Kim Jong-il and brother of KJU. Murdered by KJU.

Shin Jong-hui
Wife of Kim Jong-nam.

Kim Han-sol
Son of Kim Jong-nam and Shin Jong-hui

Kim Sol-hui
Daughter of Kim Jong-nam and Shin Jong-hui

George Alexander Thomas
Known as Thomas, he grew up in the KGB's Camp 27 for children. He came to the United States as Peter Bradford Gregory, a sleeper spy for the USSR, but while he lived in this country, he grew to love the USA. After the fall of the Soviet Union, he spent years escaping his past as a spy. Finally, he found his home in Skaneateles, New York.

Sergei Ivanov
Sergei also grew up in Camp 27 and was sent to Minot, North Dakota as a sleeper spy. After the fall of the Soviet Union, Sergei returned to Russia and became a priest in the Russian Orthodox Church. He reunited with his fellow Camp 27 brother of the soul in RUSSIAN FINGERS, the first book in this series.

Rhee Ji-su/Park Mi-na/ The Angel Twin
Chosen by the U Group to impersonate Kim Jong-un, Ji-su was born in North Korea. She escaped to South Korea after her parents were murdered by North Korean agents.

The Ri family
Ri Song-gi and his parents take Ji-su into their home near Wonsan, North Korea. Ji-su is escaping from the part she has played in the kidnapping of KJU.

Chapter 1

SKANEATELES, NEW YORK

At a summer resort, everything changes after Labor Day. The tourists and the renters are gone. The restaurants and stores are not as busy. It might be the angle of the sun that casts its light and its shadows at different times, in different places. The town settles back into itself... like a woman who has stayed dressed up all day and always has her make-up just so, then finally goes home and puts on her comfortable clothes and her bedroom slippers. Things are right again, back to normal. Those who are still here are the real people, not the summer interlopers who only came to kiss and tell and didn't stay.

Thomas was glad when the summer people left Skaneateles. He was wary of the vacation crowds who came from far and wide. He was afraid that someone might recognize him from another time, another place. He occasionally came to town and ate at the Sherwood Inn during the summer season, but after Labor Day, when the evenings began to grow cool, he felt safe and relaxed sitting at the bar, playing with his glass of pinot noir. He realized how much he missed Sergei, although they exchanged encrypted emails several times a day. He wished that Sergei were there to sit with him after dinner in front of the fireplace in the bar at the Sherwood.

Until he'd bought his properties in Skaneateles, his life had been the life of a vagabond. Once, when he'd lived his life on the run, he'd embraced that peripatetic existence. He was constantly in the process of moving on or thinking about moving on to the next place, to the next identity. He was always adjusting to the new place where he'd just landed. Or he was busy planning where he was going to go from where he was now and how he was going to get there from here without anybody noticing. He was forever thinking about the next place, the next move. He had found his security in being the nomad, an itinerant who never stayed in one place for too long.

At last, he'd settled down and made a home for himself. He loved his town, the town of Skaneateles, New York. He loved his house and his barn and workshop. He loved his ancient Italian motor scooter and his English sailboat. He loved the way he'd convinced everybody in town that he lived in the triplex. That satisfaction with his successful deception was the former spy and undercover agent in him, the boy who had been trained to fool others, to appear to be someone and something he wasn't.

Thomas had come to the United States as an agent of the Union of Soviet Socialist Republics. He'd arrived in California at age fifteen and enrolled as a freshman at Cal Berkeley. He was a brilliant student and double-majored in math and physics. Immediately after he received his summa cum laude undergraduate degree, he began working on his PhD in particle physics. After earning his doctorate, he worked for several years at the Lawrence Livermore Berkeley National Laboratory and the University of California at Berkeley

Department of Nuclear Engineering. He was positioned exactly where his mentors in the USSR wanted him to be. He'd always wondered why they had never activated him, why he had forever remained a sleeper spy.

At that time in his life, Thomas had been known as Peter Bradford Gregory, a man who had been created out of whole cloth in Russia at a place called Soviet State Project Camp 27. He had been brought to Camp 27 as a toddler and raised to be an American in this special school for spies. All of his fellow classmates at Camp 27 were in training to be Americans. They spoke nothing but American English and ate nothing but American food. They lived in American ranch-style houses and studied American history and geography in their American school. After classes ended for the day, they played golf, tennis, and... for the girls... field hockey. They studied football, basketball, and baseball. Peter learned to sail a small sailboat. These faux Americans were the finest creations of the KGB, their custom-made sleeper spy children who would be dropped into lives inside the United States and would fit perfectly into their American families and their American neighborhoods.

Peter had achieved everything his Soviet controllers had expected of him. He had performed impeccably in his role as an American, and he was where he was intended to be, at the forefront and center of U.S. atomic energy research. What his Soviet masters had never expected to happen was that Peter Gregory would fall in love with his adopted country. It started with his love for baseball. He became an ardent fan of the San Francisco Giants who played in Candlestick Park, and although he lived in Berkeley, he made the trip on public transportation across the bay, at least once every week during the baseball season, to watch his team play ball.

One night before the game, as he stood and began to sing *The Star-Spangled Banner*, the U.S. national anthem he'd had to memorize at Camp 27, he realized he loved this place, the land of the free and the home of the brave. He loved its people and the way that they had welcomed him and embraced him with honesty and respect. He loved the openness of the society. He loved the music and the shopping. He loved everything about the United States of America.

His predicament was that he was an agent of a foreign power, a spy who served the USSR, the archenemy of the country he had begun to love. He had been sent to the United States to destroy it from within, not to love it. His dilemma was excruciating, and he dreaded the day when he would be activated and expected to do something terrible to hurt this country which had taken him in and treated him with kindness.

Peter's salvation came in the early 1990s when the Soviet Union fell, and Communism and the KGB became rubble in the annals of history. It was as if he had been given a second chance, the chance to create a life for himself. The ersatz Peter Gregory set out on a quest to discover who really lived inside his handsome albino body, the body with ultra-white hair and skin and blue eyes. He was brilliant and wonderfully well-educated. He knew where his heart lay. He had to find his soul, his place in the world. His quest had taken him to Wheeling, West Virginia, to Philadelphia, Pennsylvania, to Wilmington, North Carolina, to Syracuse, New York, and to other places around the country. He'd finally ended it all in what he thought would be the last of his pretend lives when he feigned being a victim of the terrorists who took down the towers of the World Trade Center in New York City on September 11, 2001. The man who rose from the ashes of his past, George Alexander

Thomas built his new life on the shores of the magically beautiful Skaneateles Lake.

He was finally a happy man, and then he'd found a brother. Although Sergei was not a brother of the flesh, not a brother of blood, he was a brother of the soul. He was a brother who had lived through and survived his childhood in Soviet Camp 27, as Thomas had also survived it. Sergei had returned to Russia after the fall of the Soviet Union, and donning the robes of a Russian Orthodox Church priest, he had found his way to God.

Finally at peace with the world, Sergei was devastated when he had been abruptly taken from his monastery in Sergiyev Posad by Vladimir Putin's thugs and sent back to the United States. Bad Vlad's boys demanded that Sergei hunt down Peter Bradford Gregory and return him to his former masters, the neo-Soviets who were now threatening and intimidating their former satellite states. Vlad was trying to resurrect the old Soviet Union, and he wanted the former atomic scientist and wunderkind from Camp 27 to return to the fold and serve his Russian controllers again as a spy and secret agent.

But after the fall of the Soviet Union, Peter Gregory had become dust in the wind. He was no more. Early on, Sergei decided that his mission to find Peter Gregory was not so that he could conspire with the SVR to force Peter to do Russia's bidding. Sergei's real mission became a quest to find Peter in order to warn him that the Russian leader was hunting him. Sergei made it his goal to find Peter Gregory so that he could protect him. Sergei was a man of God, and he wanted to help the former genius and lonely child, the boy from Camp 27 who flew before the wind standing in an old wooden catboat on a Russian lake.

When Sergei returned to Sergiyev Posad after finding Thomas in the United States, he'd lived under a new identity for his own security. Sergei had submitted his report to the former KGB operatives who'd tried to force him to find Thomas and to enlist him in the service of helping to rebuild Vladimir Putin's dynasty. Sergei's report informed the Russians that Peter Gregory had died on September 11, 2001.

George Alexander Thomas had created an elaborate and completely false existence for Peter Gregory which showed that he'd been living in the U.S. under another name and had been on board American Airlines Flight #77 when it crashed into the Pentagon on that infamous September morning. Sergei and Thomas had labored over the deception and over the report. They created a totally convincing story that proved Peter Bradford Gregory was dead. The case was closed.

Sergei only wanted to return to his life in the church, and Thomas and Sergei had orchestrated a complicated ruse to make the old Sergei disappear. The two were able to convince the SVR that Sergei had vanished somewhere outside of Singapore, never to be seen or heard from again. As far as the Russians were concerned, the Sergei who had been at Camp 27 with Peter Bradford Gregory and who had subsequently tracked Gregory down, had disappeared forever. In fact Sergei had returned to Sergiyev Posad and his life as a cleric. Thomas had purchased, at great expense, a new Russian identity for Sergei. With Thomas's help and the help of his superior at the monastery, Sergei was able to resume his old life as a priest, but with a new name.

In fact, Sergei had never known what his real Russian last name was. He knew his first name was Sergei. But when he'd been taken from his family and sent to Camp 27, the last name of his birth family, as well as any details of his previous existence, had been hidden from him. Somebody somewhere had once known what his Russian last name was, but Sergei would never know that information. His past had been obliterated. The Union of Soviet Socialist Republics used its people as weapons, without any regard for their humanity. At Camp 27, Sergei was given an American name, Stephen Magnuson, and sent to Minot, North Dakota.

When Sergei returned to Russia after the fall of the Soviet Union, he knew his Russian first name had been Sergei, but he didn't have either a Russian identity or a Russian last name. Sergei was a real Russian. When he and Thomas had found each other in the United States, Thomas had provided him with a Russian passport and all the other documentation necessary for Sergei to prove he was a real Russian. His first name was still Sergei, that name being the only known remnant of his childhood. This first name was the one fragile link with his biological family, the only thing that remained from the time before he'd been taken against his will to Camp 27 and indoctrinated as a spy.

Sergei selected his own last name which means "God's grace" in Russian. He would be Sergei Ivanov. Ivanov was a common last name in Russia, but it was special to Sergei because it was a name he had chosen for himself. Sergei at last had an authentic, official, and verifiable Russian identity, and he was hiding in plain sight as Sergei Ivanov at the monastery in Sergiyev Posad.

Thomas had lived in Skaneateles for more than a decade, and many things had changed during that time. Thomas had convinced Sergei to temporarily leave the safety of the monastery and accompany him on a mission they both hoped would forever remain a secret. As a priest in the Russian Orthodox Church, Sergei was committed to God and to nonviolence, but Thomas had persuaded Sergei to join him, to sacrifice a few bad guys in order to save a lot of good guys. Some people had died, and both Sergei and Thomas had almost died. But Sergei's knowledge of the Russian language and the Russian culture, as well as his skill as a marksman, had in the end saved them both and saved thousands of others.

If the Russian government ever discovered what Sergei had been up to, he certainly would have immediately found himself on the list of those targeted for assassination. The tyrant Putin, determined to cast himself as the Soviet Napoleon, took out his enemies with polonium and by various other means. But Sergei and Thomas had been successful, not only in what they'd hoped to accomplish, but in keeping their identities and their participation off everybody's radar screens. Both Thomas and Sergei had been trained as the ultimate spies of the Soviet Union. They'd been taught from their earliest days how to deceive, how to live a lie. After their mission, Sergei had returned to his life at the monastery, and Thomas had returned to his life in Skaneateles. The bond between these two men was stronger than ever. They were in touch every day.

Sergei barely knew how to turn on a computer when Sergei and Thomas had been reunited in 2003, many years after they'd left Soviet State Project Camp 27. With more than fifteen years under Thomas's tutelage, and even though they were communicating electronically and half-way around the world, Sergei had become an expert hacker and a programming virtuoso. He was the go-to computer person at the monastery in Sergiyev Posad, which in every other aspect conducted its business as if it existed in the thirteenth century rather than in the twenty-first. The priests continued to wear the centuries old style clerical robes and observe the ancient rites and services, but those in charge at the monastery had decided that computers and the Internet were useful.

The clergy in Russia realized that, after a brief run of freedom and revitalization under President Boris Yeltsin, Vladimir Putin was really just an old Soviet guy, a former KGB spy with a few facelifts, who had no real love for the church. He was not actively out to destroy it, but he was either an agnostic or an atheist and regarded the Russian Orthodox Church as a pesky fly in his country. Putin's religion was power. He tolerated the church but had no fondness for it. As long as the church remained nonpolitical and didn't threaten his authority, he left it alone.

To survive, the Russian Orthodox Church decided that in form and facade it would appear to be just as it had always been, but behind the scenes, they would have to stay abreast of what was happening in Russia and what was happening in the world. Sergei was able to take a leadership role, as he attempted to move his fellow priests into the electronic age and educate these increasingly modern men, even as they continued to cloak themselves in their traditional clerical habits.

Chapter 2

SKANEATELES, NEW YORK

T*homas owned two exceptionally nice* properties in Skaneateles. He owned twenty-five acres on Skaneateles Lake, and this is where Thomas spent most of his time. The lake property included a large old-fashioned dairy barn, a solid structure that had been built to last. Thomas had renovated the barn and made it into his high-tech workshop. The barn was where he did his work as an inventor, and he was inspired by the view from his workbench that overlooked the lake. Located on this same property was Thomas's house, an older 1940s summer place that Thomas had enlarged and winterized and made into a luxurious and functional home. The library of his house was where he had his elaborate computer and TV networks set up. It was from this library that he made his virtual visits around the world.

Because Thomas was such a private person and because he would never be able to completely shake the fear that the Russians might come after him again, he kept his house on his acres beside Skaneateles Lake a secret. There was no visible entrance to his lake property. There was no mailbox, and the driveway that might have once announced that someone lived there, had been obliterated years earlier. No one could get on to Thomas's lake property, no matter how hard they looked for a way in. He was hiding in plain sight.

Thomas also owned an expensive triplex of two-bedroom, two-bathroom condominiums in the town of Skaneateles, and the locals all believed he lived in one of these condos. Thomas had lived in the triplex while his barn and house were being renovated. All of his bills and all of his mail went to the triplex. He kept his vintage Mercedes, which he drove only on out-of-town trips, in one of the condo's garages. When he wasn't driving his Range Rover, he rode his reconstructed Lambretta motor scooter around town. Thomas had been brought up to be a spy, so living in one place while everybody thought he lived in quite another place, kept his life obscured in exactly the way he wanted it to be.

Of course, everybody wanted to know who owned the twenty-five acres on the lake. It was owned by an LLC that no one would ever be able to trace back to Thomas. Real estate agents and developers and curious townspeople were always trying to figure out who owned the fabulous property. The dairy barn close to the road had been there for decades, so nobody paid much attention to the barn any more. Thomas's house, which was closer to the water, was nicely obscured by cliffs and trees and other vegetation. He could see out and had wonderful views, but no one could see in. Everyone knew there was some kind of a house there, but the consensus in town was that the house had been abandoned years earlier and nobody lived there anymore.

Still there was a great deal of curiosity about who owned the place. Thomas checked periodically with Sam O'Connor, the bartender at the Sherwood Inn, for the latest news on who the people of Skaneateles thought owned the property. Nobody, including Sam, knew the answer to that question... except for Thomas, of course. Thomas pretended from time to time that he was looking for a house on the lake.

The longest running story about who owned the acres on Skaneateles Lake was that it was still held by the family who had owned it for more than eighty years. The scuttlebutt for decades had been that it was held in a trust of some kind, and the heirs to the property couldn't agree what to do about it. They'd all sued each other over and over again, fighting over the various assets in their parents' estate. The property on the lake was thought to be one of those held in limbo by the litigious rich family.

Another favorite tale was that the property had been bought by a private conservation group to keep it from being developed. It was true that a great many wealthy people were buying properties on the lake and building huge vacation homes. The story was that someone who didn't want any more houses built on the lake and who had plenty of money had formed a nonprofit organization which was buying up real estate all over the Finger Lakes area so people couldn't build any more houses on the land.

The always popular and much more interesting gossip about who owned the property were the stories that attributed ownership to various famous, infamous, and shady characters. One story was that a Saudi princess spent a week or two at the house in the summer so that her daughter could learn English. No one had ever seen the woman or the daughter. Another intriguing person who might own the barn and house was a mafia don. Some said he didn't actually live there and only used the lakeside acres as a graveyard to bury the bodies. Speculation about other possible owners included a variety of movie stars, male and female, who used the place for secret trysts with lovers, as a refuge to dry out or get clean from their addictions, or as an investment they hoped to fix up and live in when they retired, etc. The legendary landowner was always reclusive and rich, and nobody in town had ever seen her or him or them.

Thomas loved the stories and always got a laugh out of what people could come up with when there was a vacuum of information. The unknown seemed to entice people to rush in to use their imaginations. Thomas had lived in Skaneateles for more than fifteen years. From time to time, he thought he might decide to confess that he was the owner of the property and give up his secret life on the lake. But he enjoyed the deception and the intrigue too much. He was always hugely entertained by the latest stories people invented to explain away what they didn't know anything about. He was having too much fun being the mysterious proprietor of the barn and the supposedly abandoned house on the lake to reveal himself.

Thomas was currently working on several inventions for fun. He knew his inventions would make him even richer than he already was. The unknown in his life was where he was going to go with his computer hacking. Thousands of new hackers appeared on the Internet every day. Years ago, Thomas had been able to identify the really good ones, but even as talented as he still was, there were now so many, he couldn't keep up with all of them. They were too numerous, and they were everywhere worldwide. The hacking game was a dangerous game, and Thomas knew that many of the new players were unscrupulous. The bad guys were either in it to steal other people's identities or money or to be destructive in other ways.

In the past, when he was able to identify major trouble makers, he'd tried to be an Internet policeman of sorts. Those days were over. Hacking had grown exponentially, and Thomas had no idea who the participants were anymore. It frustrated him that something in which he'd once been a master was now beyond his grasp. He could still insert a Trojan horse security program to protect certain sites from amateur hackers, but his extraordinary expertise in the area of cyber security was being challenged.

Philosophically, he thought there was a place for confidentiality and secrecy, but he also felt there was a place for something like WikiLeaks. If people didn't want others to know what they thought or what they said, they would have to learn that they couldn't send an email or a text over their non-encrypted cell phone or non-encrypted computer. If they wanted to be absolutely certain nobody knew what they said, they couldn't say it or write it down, let alone send it anywhere electronically.

In the past, spies, state-run intelligence services, and nosy people intercepted other people's mail. They steamed open letters, read them, resealed them, and sent them on their way. People listened through keyholes, and phones were tapped. As technology took over everyone's lives at an ever-increasing pace, listening devices and video cameras became smaller and smaller. Some had now become almost invisible.

The popularity of TikTok and Instagram and other social media sites was a testimony to the unfortunate fact that many people wanted others to know everything about them. Ego-driven technologies allow humans to broadcast their thoughts and actions to the world, almost before they have in fact had a thought or done anything. Taking a phone photo of what you were eating for lunch or dinner became a routine habit. The world was moving in the direction of full disclosure, and it would soon be a world in which everyone knew everything about everyone else. Thomas wondered how anybody learned to adjust, survive, and thrive in such a world. There were no more secrets.

Thomas had made his fortune as an inventor. The genius of Thomas's inventions was that he took something that was widely used and made a small improvement in it so that it worked much better. His inventions were used in businesses and industries of all kinds, and most were mechanical or electrical inventions or innovations. He had patents, and he had become very wealthy as he'd used his creativity and imagination to transform practical applications that made people's lives better. He eschewed any kind of attribution or notoriety. The patents on his inventions were owned by an LLC, and no one ever knew the name of the brilliant man who turned out so many remarkable and helpful gadgets.

The other part of Thomas was the man who was always at his computer and on the Internet. It was inevitable that, sooner or later, his two passions of invention and computer technology would collide. Thomas had long been fascinated with the philosophical questions and the ethics of hacking. His imagination couldn't help but lead him to wonder about a world where one could not only hack into another person's computer and look at their emails but could also hack into other people's actual lives as they were being lived, in real time. He had, after all, been trained to be a spy. What if it were possible to hack into another person's life, in real time anywhere in the world? That would be the dream and the ultimate accomplishment of any superspy.

In a way, live webcams, video cameras on construction sights and in day care centers, already made this possible, but these incursions were openly acknowledged and embraced by all parties who agreed to participate. What if your computer or your cell phone or your television set could be turned into a real time live web cam so that your daily life, both the audio and the video, could be hacked and observed by someone else? You could be under surveillance 24/7, as long as you were within range of your cell phone or your computer or your TV set. 1984 and the brave new world would finally have become a reality. There would be no privacy, except when one was inside a closet or in the shower and had left one's phone in the other room. Hardly anybody ever did that any more.

Thomas found this concept of real-time intrusion terrifying and abhorrent, and at the same time, he found it irresistibly intriguing. He knew that intelligence agencies around the world had many technologies that were way ahead of what they would ever reveal to the public. He knew that the stuff of spy novels was filled with imaginary, and not-so-imaginary, ways to take surveillance to new levels. What if Thomas were able to combine his hacking skills with his ability to invent new things? What if he could develop a video and audio gadget that gave him the ability to watch and listen in real time? What if the hacker could tune in and out at will, unbeknownst to and undiscovered by the subject who was being monitored? Who knows where that might take him? He knew he would never sell his discoveries to the government or to any business. He would never share his brainchild with anybody else, but he was always thinking about it and working on this puzzle in the back of his mind.

Thomas asked himself, if he could listen in on anybody in the world and find out what they were doing all day long, what person would he choose to watch and listen to? He was not much of a voyeur, but he'd always worried about what the despots of the world were up to and what kinds of trouble they would be getting into next. Thomas decided he would most like to know what the bizarre bearded guys in Iran were doing and what puff-boy Kim Jong-un was cooking up in North Korea. Both of these rogue nations had nuclear materials, were working to perfect their nuclear weapons, and were developing the means to deploy and deliver these weapons, with the ultimate goal of destroying their enemies. Both countries were ruled by fanatics and were characterized by secrecy and instability. The misogynistic Shiite theocracy of Iran had made the country an outlaw and a pariah in the world. Sharia Law, the mainstay of the cult of Islam, had been exposed as the handbook for evil that it was.

Kim Jong-un, the "baby boy" ruler of North Korea, was such a strange looking and incredibly fat little fellow. He was always strutting around and threatening everybody with his nuclear weapons. He touted his rockets that might or might not fly that day. Thomas was not trained as a psychologist, but he couldn't help but ask himself if the man was mentally ill. Or maybe the better question was, given that the man was entirely bonkers, how did he maintain his power?

When Thomas was at Camp 27, the Russians had imagined that their Americans in training would need to know about American folk music and other kinds of American music. These Americans in the making listened to big scratchy 33 LP American records on an old phonograph. Thomas remembered one record he'd especially liked that had several songs on it sung by Burl Ives. One song was about a little white duck and another was named "Lavender Blue." Thomas had listened to this record so many times, he'd learned all the words and the tunes to several of the songs.

His favorite was a song called "The Eddystone Light" about a man whose father was the lighthouse keeper. Thomas still liked the song, and as he grew older he realized why he'd liked it so much. The man in the song had a father, something Thomas had never had. The chorus said, "Yo, ho, ho, the wind blows free; oh, for the life on the rolling sea." This music and the idea of being on a ship at sea had exemplified freedom for Thomas, something he'd thought he would never be able to experience.

When someone at Camp 27 decided that he needed to learn to sail a sailboat, it was as if he'd been granted a chance to know, at least in a small way, what life on the rolling sea would be like. Even if he was only sailing an old wooden catboat around a Russian lake, the feeling of freedom he'd had when he was at the tiller was like nothing else he had ever experienced in his life. He'd sung "The Eddystone Light" while he was sailing the catboat. He still sang that song when he sailed his GP-14 on Skaneateles Lake. Sailing his boat and that song exemplified being free for Thomas.

In the back of his mind, he also vaguely remembered the name of another song that he'd heard at Camp 27, a song associated with an American television personality named Arthur Godfrey. Thomas only remembered the title to the song. He didn't remember the words or the music to that one, but he'd always remembered the title, "The Man with the Weird Beard." When he'd seen Kim Jong-un for the first time, he'd immediately thought of him as "The Man with the Weird Square Hair." Thomas was puzzled by the hair and wondered how KJU managed to achieve such a hairdo. Even if there wasn't a massive body of corroborating evidence publicly manifested by KJU's own words and behavior, Thomas thought anybody who would willingly choose to wear their hair in that way had to have a screw loose somewhere. It was "square hair" without question. It was so odd! Thomas wondered if he could possibly watch this person day in and day out and keep his own sanity.

If Thomas were to try to electronically spy on people in other countries, he realized he would have to enhance his surveillance program with a translation function, an interpreter app. Thomas didn't speak Korean or Farsi or Russian or Chinese or anything but English. He would have to build a translation program into his hack, if he was going to be able to understand what these people he was spying on were saying to each other. He began to work with voice recognition software and electronic translation software programs. It would be complex, and it would take some time, but he was sure that he could build a better mousetrap. His better mousetrap would catch the despotic rats around the world and expose their dirty little secrets and their evil intentions. Inventing gadgets was his profession and the means by which he had made his fortune. He liked to think of the time he was now spending on the computer as both his hobby and his community service work.

Since coming to the United States at age fifteen, Thomas had only traveled outside the United States during his mission with Sergei. He could afford as many sets of perfect papers, identities, and passports in other names as he needed. But having finally found his home, he didn't really want to leave the country unless it was for an unusually important reason. Going to England was one thing because it didn't present any language problems, but actually traveling to North Korea or Iran would be another thing entirely.

Thomas was without a doubt quite brilliant and had many skills, but he had never studied foreign languages. His years at Camp 27 had been focused completely on perfecting his American English. Sergei had spoken Russian as a small child before he'd come to Camp 27, but Thomas had never spoken Russian. He'd found out years later that his family was Hungarian, not Russian, and he had been too young when he'd arrived at Camp 27 to have remembered any Hungarian. He couldn't speak any language other than English, and he was afraid he would feel insecure depending on a translator in a foreign country. It would be best for him not to visit in person. If he could perfect his invention, he wouldn't have to worry about physically traveling to those terrifying foreign places.

First of all, no American in his or her right mind ought to be traveling to either North Korea or Iran. Of course, some did in spite of being forbidden to go there or cautioned not to do so. This often led to trouble, and sometimes, to tragedy. Thomas couldn't think of any place he'd less rather visit than North Korea, except maybe Iran. Thomas would be visiting those two countries only in a virtual capacity, and that suited him just fine. He could make electronic visits to Tehran and Pyongyang on a daily, even hourly, basis and still be able to eat dinner at the Sherwood Inn and sleep in his own bed at night. Traveling these days could be uncomfortable and exhausting, or it could be cybernetic.

Thomas encountered the U group quite by accident as he was watching the events in North Korea. He was working on a real time hack into Kim Jong-un's life, specifically a virtual tour of North Korea's imperial palace. Thomas happened to run into, electronically, the people of the U Group who were also hacking into the electronics and computer systems at the home of the despot, "Little Rocket Man." Someone else was spying on Kim Jong-un at the same time Thomas was spying on him.

At first Thomas didn't know the name of the group he'd encountered, but he was quite curious about who these people were and what these other hackers were up to. He was intrigued and wanted to know more about the organization he'd discovered which was also snooping around the North Korean royal palace. He wanted to know what their motivations were. Their software wasn't as sophisticated as Thomas's, and they didn't have the translation function. They could not possibly have that technology since Thomas had invented it. At least Thomas didn't know of anybody else in the world who had his invention.

The U Group was depending on translators who monitored what was being said in the North Korean royal palace. Thomas was impressed and fascinated that someone else was watching Kim Jong-un as closely as he was. The other hacker was not an individual. There were several members of a group who communicated back and forth with each other via texts and emails, and Thomas wondered why the group's written electronic conversations were always in English. The U Group's emails and texts were encrypted, but of course that was an easy thing for Thomas to overcome. Although he didn't know who they were working for or exactly what their objectives were, Thomas eventually found that they referred to themselves as the U Group. He wondered if the U stood for unknown or untraceable or if it stood for Un.

Chapter 3

NORTH KOREA AND SOUTH KOREA

T*he U Group's operation had* been in the planning stages for years. When Kim Jong-un came to power in 2011, intelligence services throughout the world realized he had some mental deficiencies and did not have a fully developed adult personality. At that time, a secret group had formed to work on a long-term plan to try to depose the North Korean dictator. It was against the law, for every one of the countries who had people involved in the project, to target and assassinate heads of state. Those who were committed to what they were doing knew that, if they were exposed at any stage of their planning, their own individual countries would deny any knowledge of what they were doing and would disavow them and their operation. That was the way it had to be.

Some or all of the group might die in the execution of their plan, and they all accepted death as a possible consequence of their involvement. If they were caught, they would be punished as criminals in their own countries or tortured and executed by those in power in the DPRK, the Democratic People's Republic of Korea aka North Korea.

The group, which became known over time as the U Group, believed so strongly in what they were doing that they were willing to take these chances and assume the risks. They could not allow a dimwitted and deranged little fuss pot who had nuclear weapons and was working to improve his ICBMs, to reach the point where he was able to deliver those weapons to the world. He had to be stopped. There had to be regime change.

At least one previous administration in Washington, D.C. had been burned badly by their forays into regime change. Saddam Hussein was a very bad man, but getting rid of the tyrant and toppling his rule had not produced the desired results. Muammar Gaddafi likewise had been a very bad man, but destroying his control in Libya had thrown that country into such complete chaos, it had never been able to recover. Putting Mohamed Morsi and the Muslim Brotherhood in charge in Egypt had been a huge mistake. Even with the consequences of these foreign policy disasters staring them in the face, the people of the U group were determined to pursue their goal of getting rid of Kim Jong-un. His erratic behavior and bad judgment put the entire world at risk, and he already had too many dangerous weapons.

The Korean Peninsula had been colonized by Japan in 1910. Occupation by the Japanese lasted for thirty-five years, until 1945, when Japan was defeated at the end of World War II. Korea, the former colony of Japan, was divided by the victors of World War II into north and south. The Soviet Union ruled North Korea after the country was partitioned in 1945, and the Communist USSR set up Kim Il-sung as the ad hoc and temporary leader of the Soviet puppet state. Subsequently, in 1948, Kim Il-sung anointed himself as the legitimate and hereditary monarch of the Korean people and as the permanent president of the Democratic People's Republic of Korea, the DPRK. North Korea would be communist and authoritarian, and South Korea would be democratic and free.

The Hermit Kingdom had been ruled since 1948 by a cult of personality rather than by a legitimate or elected government. The bureaucratic structure that functioned poorly but called itself a government operated entirely at the whim and at the mercy of the wishes and desires of its current leader. No one had ever been elected to anything. No one had even been chosen by anyone, except themselves. Their authority was self-imposed by a malignant and enduring tradition of narcissism.

The breed of nepotism that embraced three generations of despots as leaders in North Korea had begun with Kim Il-sung who had been the first of the family to set himself up in power in 1948. It was Kim Il-sung who authorized the invasion of South Korea in 1950, and as a result of this aggression by his troops, the United States became involved in another war. The ruler of North Korea wanted to absorb South Korea into his communist, authoritarian state. The U.S. led a United Nations force to protect South Korea and keep that struggling democracy alive. A ceasefire was signed in 1953, and the DMZ and the 38th parallel were established as the border between North Korea and South Korea. Kim Il-sung became one of the longest-serving non-royal heads of state in the twentieth century and illegitimately held his office for more than forty-five years.

North Korea had been, from its early days under Kim Il-sung, a nation shrouded in mystery, deceit, and punishment. Threats, torture, and death were the only way a corrupt and backward regime and society could possibly hope to keep its people in line. If North Korea's population had not been starving and sick as well as terrified of losing their lives, the succession of three petty tyrants, grandfather, father, and son, would never have been able to hold an entire country hostage decade after decade.

Until 2010, hardly anybody inside or outside the Democratic People's Republic of Korea had ever seen what Kim Jong-un looked like, either in person or in a photograph. Born in 1984, he made no public appearances, and everything about the heir apparent and his whereabouts was top secret information. He was Kim Jong-il's third son. His mother was a dancer, a Japanese-born ethnic Korean who was enormously ambitious for her boy. She promoted him with his father, and at the age of fifteen, Kim Jong-un was anointed as his father's heir apparent. Educated in Bern, Switzerland, his childhood was shrouded in mystery, and hardly anyone had ever seen him or heard of him.

There were no photographs in the media until an official photo was released in September of 2010. Kim Jong-un made his first public appearance on October 10, 2010, with his father, Kim Jong-Il, at a Workers' Party celebration. This "coming out" happened a little more than a year before the death of Kim Jong-il in December of 2011. Kim Jong-un was only twenty-seven years old when he succeeded his father and became North Korea's supreme leader.

In December of 2013, KJU ordered the murder of his own uncle, Jang Song-thaek. Song-thaek had been a key member of the North Korean first family since the days when Kim Jong-il, KJU's father, had been the supreme leader. When Kim Jong-il's health had begun to fail and he could no longer rule the Hermit Kingdom, Thaek had assumed de facto leadership for the ailing Kim Jong-il and governed for his brother. Before his death, Kim Jong-il had appointed Thaek as Regent for his son, the young KJU who ascended to power when he was in his twenties. KJU had been thrust into governing the country before he had been able to complete his training to be a leader.

Believing that his uncle was building a rival power base, Kim Jong-un declared in 2013 that Jang Song-thaek had committed treason against the DPRK and sentenced him to death. At age sixty-seven, Song-thaek was stripped naked and fed to a pack of hungry dogs. The dogs had been starved for three days before the execution, which lasted for an hour and was watched by hundreds of North Korean officials. Following this very public and very vicious murder, which had been intended as a warning to anyone who even thought of disobedience or revolt, KJU continued his purge against Jang Song-thaek's wife, children, and grandchildren. KJU had Thaek's entire circle of family, friends, and supporters assassinated.

In February 2017, Kim Jong-un had orchestrated another particularly public and heinous murder, the poisoning of his half-brother. Kim Jong-nam was Kim Jong-il's first born son and for years had been his father's designated successor. Jong-nam fell out of favor with his father. This was the point at which Kim Jong-il anointed his third oldest son, Kim Jong-un, as his successor to lead the Hermit Kingdom after he died. Since he had been passed over to succeed his father and was no longer in his father's good graces, Kim Jong-nam and his family left North Korea and chose to live in relative seclusion in Macau, a former Portuguese colony which had become a Chinese administered territory.

KJU's exact motives for the assassination of his half-brother are unknown. KJU had Kim Jong-nam murdered openly in the Malaysian airport of Kuala Lumpur. Two women suddenly attacked Nam, who was traveling under the name of Chol, with a chemical weapon. The women rubbed liquid substances on his face, and shortly after the attack, Kim Jong-nam died of VX poisoning on his way to a Malaysian medical clinic. The use of the weapon VX as a method for assassination would have been extremely painful. KJU may have believed that Nam was a threat to his leadership and purposely used this brutal killing to frighten his enemies and set an example for others.

KJU was not going to leave anyone alive whom he believed or even erroneously imagined was a threat to his power. The madman had set out to eliminate any other members of the Kim family who might be considered as replacements for himself. KJU's purges and brutality were well-documented, so no one was surprised whenever he ordered assassinations and other vicious reprisals against those he didn't like or didn't trust. His behavior was unpredictable and instantly changeable, and he gave orders to kill on a whim. KJU wanted everyone to know that he had the power to strike the innocent and unsuspecting, to kill anyone with impunity.

Living outside the country of North Korea did not provide any protection from KJU's cruel and spiteful wrath and arbitrary deeds. He could punish worldwide and kill whomever and whenever he chose to do so. From time to time, he liked to remind both his friends and his enemies that there was no place to hide. There was no place that was safe from the little man's long arm of death.

The plan of the U Group was multifaceted and complex. It required many things from many people, but the one person on whom the success of their entire operation depended was a young Korean woman, a girl who had escaped from North Korea when she was eleven years old. She had seen both of her parents and all of her siblings murdered in front of her eyes. She had escaped being killed because she had climbed a tree outside the hut where her family lived. She had hidden herself and watched as Kim Jong-il's henchmen slaughtered her family. They had even killed her baby sister who was only three months old. There was no reason for the murders. Her parents were not political people. They were simple farmers who were desperately trying to scrape together enough to eat from the poor soil of the tiny plot of land the government had allowed them to use to grow food. This part of the girl's story was not unique. There were many thousands who had been killed for no reason, and there were likewise thousands who had watched their families being arbitrarily murdered. Three things set this young woman apart from the others.

The first thing about her was that, after her family had been killed, she had escaped from North Korea. Many people want to escape from the nightmare, the hell hole of North Korea, but escaping from that place is an almost impossible thing to do. This child had, against all the odds, made her way to the 38th Parallel and thrown herself into the arms of the Americans who were stationed there. She was almost dead when she crossed into South Korea. When she collapsed on the ground near a U.S. Army base, she was so debilitated and dehydrated, she didn't realize that she'd finally made it out of North Korea and had arrived across the DMZ. She was finally safe in a democratic country. She hadn't eaten in days. The U.S. soldier who'd found her had fed her army rations. She thought these army rations were the best things she had ever put into her mouth. She was saved and she was free.

The second thing that set this young woman apart from others, who had also suffered from the repressive regime in North Korea, was how badly she wanted some kind of revenge for the deaths of her family members. After escaping from the North, she had been adopted by a South Korean family who raised her as if she were their own child. But she always remained absolutely committed, even obsessed, with her desire to retaliate against the North for executing her loved ones. Many who had endured terrible torture and hardship at the hands of the North Koreans would have liked to exact vengeance, but few were ever able to achieve it, even when they burned with passion to do so. The young woman joined the South Korean military as soon as she finished her education. Every day of her life, she thought about the possibilities for retaliating against the North.

The third and final thing this woman had was unique. Her face, although thinner and younger, resembled a more beautiful version of the face of Kim Jong-un. It was an uncanny likeness. As much as she must have hated to think that she was even remotely related to Kim Jong-un, there had to be some genetic throwback that linked these two who so closely resembled each other. She was from North Korea, after all.

As a member of the U Group, the young woman who had been born in North Korea was working outside the laws of her own country, and she was working outside the laws of almost all the countries in the world. She had a code name which was the name used by the people who worked with her. She was designated as the Angel Twin. The U Group referred to Kim Jong-un as the Devil Twin.

The U Group had two tiny, blurry candid black and white photos of a little boy they believed were of Kim Jong-un as a child, but nothing could be said with much certainty about anything that had to do with North Korea. These two small photographs were a guide to how the bloated freak, who was now in his early thirties, had looked when he was younger, before he'd been overfed with food and power. The photos from the despot's childhood confirmed that he had, when he was much younger and quite a bit slimmer, resembled the U Group's Angel Twin. The U-group knew they were starting with the right person. All they had to do now was transform their Angel Twin into the Devil Twin.

The young woman who became so important to the U-group had begun her life with a North Korean name. When Mi-na was adopted by the South Korean Park family, they had given her their last name of Park. Park Mi-na completed her university studies and her graduate work, and then she served five years in the Army of the ROK. She had been in military intelligence during her years on active duty and had decided to make the military a life-long career. Then she had been recruited by the U Group to become their protégée and key to the success of their elaborate plan to bring down the DPRK.

When she became part of the U Group's plot to destroy Kim Jong-un and the criminal regime in North Korea, the Group asked her to choose a cover name. She had chosen the name Rhee Ji-su as her cover name, because Ji-su meant determined and purposeful and the family name of Rhee was that of the first President of South Korea, Rhee Syngman, or Syngman Rhee as he was usually referred to in English.

The alternative cover name of Rhee Ji-su was for her own protection, to shield her ordinary identity as a citizen of South Korea. Adopting the cover name also protected the Park family. The Angel Twin was issued identity papers and a South Korean passport in her cover name of Rhee Ji-su.

Chapter 4

WHIDBEY ISLAND, WASHINGTON, USA

T*he U Group had debated* at length before choosing a site for their mission's central command. They had considered a number of places in Asia and in the United States. In the end they had selected Whidbey Island in Puget Sound, off the coast of Seattle, Washington. They'd located an isolated property on the island that was perfect for their needs. It was for sale. Everyone in the U Group spoke English. In the end, language had been the deciding factor. Negotiating life in Japan, Taiwan, or South Korea was too difficult if one didn't know the language.

Although many people in South Korea spoke English, South Korea was too close to the target location of the operation for the U Group's central command to be located there. As the U Group prepared the numerous facets of their complex undertaking, there would be a great many suspicious comings and goings. They needed space and isolation. There was too great a risk of discovery in the densely populated country of South Korea, and the U Group could not take the chance that there would be leaks. They realized they had to work on their preparations in a place that was far removed from North Korea. They did establish a safe house in South Korea close to the 38th parallel, and they also established a secret safe house in Dandong, China, across the Yalu River from North Korea.

The choice of Whidbey Island had worked out well. Many people on the island were artists and writers, fishermen and farmers. They marched to their own drummers and didn't think it was odd if others wanted to keep to themselves. The property the U group had chosen on the southern end of the island had eighty acres and a small cove with a dock that would allow sea planes to come and go. No one would ever need to know about who or what was flying in and out of the old farm.

The cover story for the U Group's existence on Whidbey Island was that they were a team of computer programmers from Cupertino, California who were working on a confidential international project for a Silicon Valley entrepreneur. The unit was ethnically diverse and made up of people with several different nationalities, as might be expected for a group working on a high-tech project out of California. The mysterious and unnamed entrepreneur, who was funding the secret project, wanted to keep the staff and operations for this particular venture far away from Silicon Valley. Nothing could be kept confidential any longer in the San Jose–San Francisco corridor.

The Bay Area's computer community had become incestuous in terms of everybody knowing everything about everybody. Security was a joke. If you wanted to be certain that what you were doing didn't become everybody else's business, you had to locate out of town, out of state, or even off-shore on an island. The story about the Silicon Valley entrepreneur was a convincing one because everybody knew that industrial espionage ran rampant in the world of high-tech innovation. Money talked, and greedy computer whizzes became double and triple agents in the spying game. The cover story for the U Group was totally believable.

The U Group's personnel went into town and socialized with the townspeople. They bought groceries, went out to dinner in Oak Harbor, and patronized the retail shops. Mixing with the local citizens was part of keeping rumors and suspicion at bay. The U Group wanted to show that they were ordinary, regular folks, that they weren't spooky or shadowy. The citizens of Oak Harbor got used to the people from the U Group being on the island. Enough information about what was supposedly going on at their remote facility was being spread around so that no one was curious about it anymore. It wasn't long before the people who were living and working way out on Cedar Cove Road were old news. That was the way the people of the U Group wanted things to be.

The long-abandoned Cider Mill Farm had been chosen for its isolation as well as for its cove where sea planes could land. The location was too far out of town for many people's tastes, and the buildings that were sold with the property were a sixty-five-year-old farm house that was a tear down and a huge old barn that had once held milk cows, horses, hay, apples, and a cider press. When the U Group had purchased the property, the barn still smelled like apples and horses. The orchards remained at Cider Mill Farm, and some of the trees still produced a few apples in the fall. No one had bothered to pay attention to the orchard for decades. The views of the sound were magnificent.

After several months of building, renovating, and repairs, the old farm had been transformed into a showplace and was more than comfortable as a home for the U Group. Because they would be selling the property after their mission was accomplished, they decided to turn the old barn into a wonderful and rustic Northwest-style lodge. The barn was made of stone and wood and was solidly build. Turning it into an elegant home took a great deal of money and more time than anybody wanted to think about. But in the end it was transformed into a magnificent space. There were enough bedrooms and bathrooms to keep everybody in the U Group happy and out of each other's hair. The U Group would be comfortable and productive there.

A housekeeper-cook was hired to live in and take care of the lodge kitchen. She ordered the groceries and prepared meals for the U Group. Good food had been the one definite and important specification which had been unanimously voiced by its members after the U Group was formed. All members had agreed that excellent food had to be provided and that they needed someone to do the cooking for them so they would be free to focus on their work. It hadn't been easy to find someone with the required qualifications who could also be vetted by their strict security protocols. They'd finally found a woman for the position. She was somewhat older than the group would have preferred, and she was a little bit cranky. But she passed all of the security protocols, and she was great with food. She got the job.

A new four-car garage was built to match the rugged stone and wood lodge former barn. The garage housed the group's cars and trucks on the ground floor. Below the vehicles, there were two underground levels, accessed by an elevator, which provided work space for the U-group's activities. Computer central was there. Satellite dishes and all of the necessary electronics their operation required were installed surreptitiously in discreet locations on the property to provide the workers in the bunker below the garage with the access to data they required. It was up-to-the-minute high tech built underneath the lodge garage.

No one who visited the property by car or boat or by flying over it would ever be able to tell that it was anything but a gentrified farm with a beautifully renovated barn and a new garage. Nobody ever drove out to that part of the island anyway. They were safe at the end of Cedar Cove Road, a dirt lane that had long-since disappeared from most maps of the island, a forgotten and unknown rural road that led nowhere except to some abandoned apple orchards.

Part of the tear-down farm house was able to be saved and repurposed into a one-story cottage and media center for Ji-su. There was a considerable distance between the renovated former barn and the cottage which had been built out of a remnant of the old house. Unkempt orchards stood between the buildings, and the area was wildly overgrown with many years' worth of untended bushes, trees, weeds, and other dense vegetation that obscured the cottage from the road, the barn, the driveway, and in fact from everything. Even the roof of the cottage was disguised with a camo design that resembled vegetation, so a plane or drone flying over the facility would never notice that the cottage was there.

A massive generator had been a requirement of the renovation. The farm had electrical lines that ran from the road to the buildings on the farm. These electrical lines had been installed many years earlier, compliments of the Puget Sound Energy Company that provided electricity to the residents of Whidbey Island. The U Group relied on electricity from the public utility some of the time, but they needed an industrial strength generator that could provide power to the entire compound if the electricity went out.

One red flag, which could raise suspicions about what was going on at the farm, would be an unusually high electric bill. Because they didn't want to draw attention to themselves, the U Group used the generator for its underground command center. The house used the electricity provided by the local utility. The generator ran on gasoline, and a large underground gasoline tank had been installed and was refilled on a regular basis. The compound had a new deep water well and a new septic system, making the U Group nearly self-sufficient.

The U Group had a helicopter pad and daily visits from a helicopter. Naval Air Station Whidbey Island was located on the island, so the local residents were used to hearing planes and helicopters taking off and landing at all times of the day and night. The helicopter pad at Cider Mill Farm was disguised as a tennis court. In fact, the helicopter pad was a tennis court. Members of the U Group played tennis on it if a helicopter wasn't parked there. The helicopter visited the compound every day but didn't stay on the island. It wasn't a stretch to believe that the Silicon Valley mogul, who was working on a secret project at the remote Whidbey Island farm, would fly in on his helicopter almost daily to see how things were going.

The helicopter flew in every day with the mail, groceries, and other supplies. It flew the garbage out when it left. Part of security was that the garbage that couldn't be incinerated or composted had to be disposed of privately so that no prying eyes could go through it and discover any of the U Group's secrets. The helicopter also brought in people who cleaned and did laundry at the lodge. A team of gardeners and grounds keepers came in twice a week. Repair people were brought in as needed. All of these workers had been carefully vetted.

Most of them were former military and law enforcement who didn't need to know a lot about what was going on at Cider Mill Farm and didn't ask a lot of questions.

Flying workers to the compound was smarter in terms of security than trying to hire local people. The locals would be full of questions and full of gossip to share with their neighbors. The helicopter was the U Group's lifeline. The pontoon plane didn't come as regularly and usually brought larger loads of supplies, people, and gasoline.

The water in the cove where the pontoon plane landed was clear and cold, and those who were brave enough to venture into it, swam there during the summer months. When she thought everybody else was asleep, Ji-su sometimes left her cottage in the middle of the night and walked down to the cove for a swim. Immersing herself in the cold water cleared her head and helped her to program her mind and focus on the preparations she was undertaking and on her future expedition into the treacherous unknown.

Chapter 5

WHIDBEY ISLAND, WASHINGTON, USA

When she was in the South Korean military, Ji-su had continued to visit her South Korean family, but when she had become a member of the U Group, she'd explained to the Parks that she wouldn't be able to visit them again for a long time. She had secret assignments that she couldn't talk about. She told them she would have to be away for months or even years at a time.

The Parks loved her and understood the depth of her commitment to seek revenge for the loss of her North Korean family. They'd known, when they had adopted the orphan who had escaped from the North, that she was special and had a damaged and tortured background. They did all they could to love her and help her heal, and then they sent her out into the world with their support to do what they knew she had to do. They wanted her to be safe, but they realized she had to follow her heart, even if that led her into danger.

Ji-su was secretly brought to Whidbey Island in the United States, to the central command headquarters of the U group.

She didn't have a visa or any papers that allowed her to be in the country. She didn't need papers because during her training, she would never leave the safety of the U group compound. No one, except a very few people connected with the U Group, would ever know she existed, let alone know that she was in the United States. The U Group itself was an exceedingly secret organization, and Ji-su was known to only a handful, even within the U Group. Ji-su lived in isolation because the U Group wanted as few people as possible to know of her presence on Whidbey Island. She was their secret weapon, their sine qua non, and they guarded her with absolute silence, a complete void of information about her very existence. Her cottage at the rear of the secure U Group compound was off limits to everyone, except the few who worked with her. Her tutors and instructors came to her. She ate alone and slept alone, except for her housekeeper.

Ji-su's housekeeper and cook lived with her in her cottage. The woman was Korean, and she did everything for Ji-su. She became almost a mother to the younger woman. She made special meals for Ji-su and reminded her when it was time to rest. She tried to keep Ji-su from pushing herself too hard. Ji-su spent hours each day on strength training and worked to improve her Krav Maga and other self-defense skills. She'd had extensive instruction in all these techniques before she'd joined the military, and her years in the South Korean Army had honed her expertise. She lifted weights and became exceptionally proficient in the many defensive and war-like martial arts. When the operation was finally activated and she was alone in the North Korean palace, she wouldn't have any weapons except her own body to defend herself and stay alive.

The cottage was a comfortable size, large enough for the electronic equipment, the large TV screens, and all the rest of the paraphernalia necessary for pulling off one of the most stunning and impossible impersonations of all times. Reruns from the old TV show *Mission Impossible* had been popular in South Korea, and Ji-su had watched them as a teenager. She joked with her instructors about how easy this mission would be if all they had to do was fit her with a perfect rubber mask of Kim Jong-un's face à la the television show, pump her up with some body stuffing, and plop her into the palace in Pyongyang. The irony was that, the scenario the U Group was proposing with Ji-su was not that far removed from being a "mission impossible" operation of their own.

Ji-su began the many months of intensive work necessary to make herself into the infamous Kim Jong-un. She studied his voice, and she studied the way he walked. She stuffed a specially-constructed, heavy weighted form under her oversized shirt so that she could be convincing as she learned to walk with the gait of this overweight, baby-faced little boy-man. She worked daily with an acting coach, and together they studied videos of Emperor Roly Poly when he appeared in public, strutting and reviewing his troops and looking completely silly.

Sometimes, Ji-su broke down in laughter when she was doing an exceptionally brilliant job of imitating "the un." He was such a little Napoleon, such a self-important prancer and preener. He reminded Ji-su of the fat black birds, the common grackles that strutted across the yard behind her cottage every morning as she was eating her breakfast. The grackles marched in a row with their protuberant bellies leading the way as they paraded across the grass.

Videos of North Korea ran all day long on one of the large TV screens in Ji-su's cottage. There were scenes of exterior landscapes, views of the sea, and photographs of everything a person who had grown up and lived in North Korea might be expected to know about. Because Ji-su really had grown up in North Korea, she was already familiar with the countryside. That part of her training was a refresher course, to allow her to get herself back into the mindset that she was once again living in North Korea.

The more important videos were those of the imperial palace, its grounds and interiors. These videos had not been easy to acquire, and the U Group had gone to extreme lengths to obtain videography of the inside of Kim Jong-un's living quarters. Learning her way around these places and acting as if she knew where everything was and what she was doing in the palace would be critical to the deception plan. If she opened the wrong closet door or turned down a hallway in the wrong direction, all might be lost. She doubted Kim Jong-un ever opened any of his own closet doors, but she wanted to have her role down perfectly, even if it was merely to give herself more confidence. By the end of her training, she expected to be more familiar with the Imperial Palace than KJU had ever been.

Drones had mapped the structure and layout of the Imperial Palace in Pyongyang where Kim Jong-un spent most of his time. He had dozens of homes around the country, but he spent most of his time in the main royal residence. With infrared and other new technologies, most of the interior of the palace with its hundreds of rooms was able to be plotted. The location of gates and security measures had also been revealed thanks to the information obtained by the drones.

Kim Jong-un's personal suite consisted of ten rooms, and he never went into any of the other rooms in the palace. He didn't go to other places in the residence because everybody and everything came to him. The drones were also able to identify where Kim Jong-un's bodyguards, servants, and closest advisors spent most of their time. How many people were around the man on a daily basis? Who were these people who talked to him and waited on him? Over time, the U Group was able to identify them and learn their names. Knowing the personalities of the people in this inner circle would be critical for Ji-su. She needed to know how to call each of the important players by name. She needed to be familiar with the face of each one and know what each one did for KJU. Charting the spaces and the people around the leader and their movements was complex, but Ji-su had to know it perfectly and be comfortable with every step she would take when she walked through the palace and the grounds.

In addition to the videos and the information the drones had produced, the U Group had finally been able to tap into KJU's life and monitor what went on in the North Korean royal palace in real time. Their hack wasn't as complete as Thomas's, and there were interruptions and glitches in their coverage. Ji-su watched Kim Jong-un as he went about his daily routine. She could understand everything that was said. Others from the U Group, who were also monitoring his life in real time but didn't speak Korean, had to use translators. Knowing what happened inside the palace would be especially valuable to Ji-su when she was there on site and impersonating KJU.

It would also be important to be able to see what happened inside the royal palace after KJU had been taken out of North Korea by the U Group's helicopter team. The U Group wanted to be able to see everything that was happening to Ji-su once she had taken on the role as KJU's impersonator. The U Group needed to be able to spot trouble, to be able to monitor those who were around the Supreme Leader, and to determine if or when anyone suspected that a substitution had been made.

She practiced with elaborate set ups of virtual reality. Every day she spent hours taking virtual walks through the palace so that she knew exactly where every hallway led and exactly where everything was in the little despot's immediate world. When the time came and she was finally inside the palace, she would be able to find her way around the royal suite without hesitation.

The mapping of the royal palace was important, not solely to train Ji-su, but also to help the extraction and insertion teams practice for their part of the mission. Early in the planning, it had been decided that the operatives who would take Ji-su into the palace and bring Kim Jong-un out would do their training in a secret facility located far away from command central on Whidbey Island. The helicopter team needed a remote and secret location where they could build a mock-up of the royal palace, or at least those parts of the palace they would need to access.

They would make dozens and dozens, even hundreds, of practice runs with the helicopter until their execution was flawless. These maneuvers required a lot of space and complete privacy. The location of their isolated and inaccessible secret base was not shared, even with those who were working on Whidbey Island. The two sites were in communication on a daily basis, but it made sense to physically separate the various aspects of the operation and to keep secret the locations of the various pieces of the mission. Potential leaks in one part of the organization would not necessarily lead to compromising any of the other parts.

Learning to speak and walk like the little guy was the easy part. Learning her way around his palatial environment was also easy. The difficult task for Ji-su was to bulk herself up to make her resemble a fat man, *the* fat man. There would be a lot of special clothes and perfectly contoured padding. There would be a make-up artist who would be able to do a great deal to transform her face into his. Kim Jong-un had an exceptionally feminine face to begin with, so that helped. But Ji-su was so terribly thin. Having grown up in the constantly famine-stricken world of North Korea, she was small and slight. Roly Poly was short, and Ji-su was short. But he was incredibly fat. It was going to take a lot of something to make Ji-su appear to be anything other than emaciated. Putty and temporary implants in her cheeks and jowls would help, but she needed to have a minimum amount of meat on her bones before the serious facial transformation could begin. She needed to have at least a little bit of fat on her face and body.

The U group had briefly considered doing reconstructive surgery on Ji-su's face, and she had agreed to that. She was willing to do whatever was necessary to make sure her mission was a success and that she was able to exact her revenge. But in the end, it was decided that temporary implants, wax applications, a perfect and perfectly ridiculous wig in the shape of an upside-down box, and artfully applied make-up would be sufficient.

Everyone who got to know Ji-su realized how committed and even obsessed she was with the campaign to remove Kim Jong-un from power and bring down the North Korean regime. All those who worked with the young woman hoped that if the mission failed, Ji-su would somehow be able to get on with her life. These same people, those who knew her best, also hoped that, if the mission was a success and after she had accomplished what she had set out to do, Ji-su would be able to move on and have a life after the mission.

Her entire life up to this point had been devoted to completing one goal. Once that goal was achieved, would Ji-su be able to find another reason for living? Decision makers inside the U Group decided not to alter Ji-su's appearance with plastic surgery. They would leave her with her own beautiful face underneath the implants and the wax and all the rest of the camouflage they would use to transform her into the puff-faced fellow who was Kim Jong-un.

Chapter 6

MACAU AND BOSNIA AND NORMANDY AND KUALA LUMPUR

H*e was a boy who* just wanted to be a boy. When he was young, he could pretend that he was only "just a boy," the boy he wanted to be. But as he grew older, the realities and circumstances of his life inevitably destroyed the fantasy that he was ordinary. He gradually had to accept that he was a child of privilege, that his family was wealthy and powerful, and that his ancestral lineage was both famous and infamous.

He eventually came to understand what it meant to live in exile and to realize that he could no longer reside in the country where he had been born. He knew his family lived a secretive and isolated existence. He didn't go to school like other children in Macau did. He didn't have playmates and friends as other children did. He and his sister were quite close. They only had each other, and until they were old enough to go to secondary school, they were educated at home by a tutor.

The boy had been brought to Macau by his parents when he was five years old. He'd had to leave the country of his birth because his father, who for many years had been regarded as the successor to their country's leader, had fallen out of favor with his own father, the leader of North Korea. Kim Jong-il was the boy's grandfather. The boy's father was no longer the anointed one, even though he was the oldest son and even though he carried the lineage of the Baekdu hyulton, the Baekdu bloodline. This bloodline supposedly legitimizes the Kim family as the divinely chosen leaders of North Korea. Deriving its name from Mt. Baekdu, the tallest mountain in North Korea, it is the symbol of Korean nationalism and confers special blessings that legitimized the Kim family. The boy's father had been disgraced and could no longer live in his own country. Their family was forced to leave North Korea, and they settled in Macau.

Macau had been a Portuguese territory until 1999. This formerly autonomous region is a city-state that occupies a small peninsula and two islands off the southern coast of China. Once a part of the Portuguese Empire, the small outpost in the Far East was one of Portugal's last surviving colonies. Portugal ceded Macau to China in 1999, much as Great Britain had ceded Hong Kong to China in 1997. The Chinese call the policy, "one country, two systems"—until the more powerful system decides it wants to crush the weaker system.

European empires were on the wane, and China was the new Imperialist power in Asia. China's fortunes were on the rise, and the greedy, omnivorous Asian colossus was devouring everything in its path. The neo-colonial power that China had become might allow both Macau and Hong

Kong a few years of watered-down autonomy and freedom, and then these once proud places would disappear forever into the maw of the Communist dragon.

Macau, for a few more years, would be allowed to have its own currency, passports, immigration controls, and legal system—all of which were supposedly completely separate from that of China. Macau has its own flag and theoretically operates independently, except for foreign affairs and defense. The terms of the 1999 agreement were that China promised not to interfere with Macau's way of life until 2049. In reality, this meant that China wouldn't force Communism on the capitalist city until that year.

The city of Macau is governed as a Special Administrative Region, an SAR. It has its own legislature, although Macau does not enjoy direct elections and has only a limited democracy. In recent elections, only the candidates chosen by Beijing had stood for election and had been elected unopposed. What would happen to Macau after 2049 remained an open question. Although Macau and Hong Kong were very close to each other geographically, so far there had been no large-scale demonstrations in favor of democratic reform in Macau, as there had been in Hong Kong. The majority of Macanese, however, support remaining an SAR even after 2049, rather than joining China proper.

Life in old Macau was quiet. It had resembled a rather sleepy colonial settlement, a mixture of Portuguese, Chinese, Malaysian, and other nationalities. Portuguese and Asian cultural influences characterized life in this low-key colonial city state, and the architecture and the food made it an exotic and delicious place to visit. At the end of the twentieth century, Macau began to undergo massive commercial and tourist development. The skyline is now dominated by high-rise buildings and hotels. Because gambling is legal in this small protectorate, Macau is overrun with casinos.

Growing up in an open and capitalistic environment like Macau was very different for the boy than it would have been if his father had been able to maintain his position as the anointed one, if his father had been willing to be the next leader of North Korea. But the boy's father had disdained the rigid, austere, militaristic environment of his country of origin. He had chosen instead to live a lifestyle that rejected Communism and the particularly odious values of North Korea. Because of his choices, he had been rejected and replaced as his country's next leader. Kim Jong-nam's half-brother who was 13 years younger was chosen as the person who would succeed their father in the dynastic leadership.

Kim Jong-il died in 2011, and the boy's uncle, the child-emperor, had assumed the presidency of North Korea. The boy and his family had been exiles in Macau, but they had felt relatively safe. The first-born son was not politically ambitious and in fact did not want to be the leader of North Korea. He had chosen quite a different life for himself and his family. He was no threat to Kim Jong-un.

Although the boy's family was living in exile and wanted nothing to do with the politics inside North Korea, the sense that they were safe completely changed when the boy's great uncle, Jang Song-thaek, was brutally murdered by KJU in December of 2013. Song-thaek's children and grandchildren were also killed. The leader of North Korea had imagined that his own uncle was plotting against him, so he had Jang Song-thaek and his entire family murdered.

Even though the boy's father had no wish or ambitions whatsoever to assume the throne in North Korea, the members of the Kim family who lived in Macau realized that the paranoid child-emperor felt threatened by any and all family members who were still alive, even if they didn't live in North Korea itself. Family members who lived in exile were also considered a threat by the erratic and fearful Emperor Roly Poly. The boy's family remained in Macau under the protection of the local police, but they no longer felt secure. They became much more cautious and careful about where they traveled, especially when they were outside of Macau. They traveled only under names other than their own.

When it was time for the boy to enter high school, he was sent away to a boarding school in Bosnia. He attended his secondary school, which was far away from Macau, using a false identity and a false passport. The boy's pretend name allowed him to travel safely to Europe from his home in Asia and to live incognito and securely while he attended school. He was unusually intelligent and an excellent student. He was well-prepared for his eventual entry into the wider world. In addition to his native Korean tongue, he'd learned to read and speak English, French, Portuguese, Dutch, and Chinese. He was especially gifted in science and math, and his years in high school were happy ones for the boy. He had friends his own age for the first time in his life. His friends, however, could never know his real name or anything about his real family.

By this time in his life, the boy was fully aware of who he was and why he had to live a secret life. He knew that he was from a very special family and that his branch of that family was essentially in hiding. The boy's father, Kim Jong-nam, never traveled outside of Macau except under a pseudonym. He had many different names and passports—covert identities which he used when he traveled. The boy's mother and sister didn't often leave their family compound in Macau, although his sister had been allowed to attend the Macau Anglican College in Taipa, Macau for high school.

After completing his secondary school education, the boy, who was now a young man, entered the Europe-Asia Programme at Sciences Po, a prestigious university in Le Havre, Normandy. Only two hours from Paris by train, Le Havre is France's biggest port and is historically linked to Asia as the entry point for Asian products arriving in France. Both the city and the curriculum at Sciences Po were uniquely appropriate for the young man's continuing education. Of course, the boy was able to live in France, only under a pseudonym and with fake papers.

Sciences Po's Le Havre campus was relatively small with only three hundred students, two-thirds of whom were from outside France. The classes were also small. This university made it possible for the boy to experience a culturally diverse student body and gave him exposure to an international community. He became comfortable with other young people from all over the world. Likewise, the academic rigor of the school offered a stimulating intellectual climate that challenged the young man. Campus activities and social life provided him with a full, varied, and relatively normal college experience.

His studies at Sciences Po included history and economics. He studied various kinds of societies, and his wide-ranging curriculum allowed him to compare and contrast Asian and European societies and cultures. Through the lens of the social sciences and the humanities, he learned about the different philosophical and artistic approaches of the countries of Asia and the Pacific—from India to Japan and from China to Australia. He loved his university days, but life was about to change for the young man who now realized that he had never been and never really could be "just a boy."

On February 13, 2017, the young man's father was viciously murdered by his father's own half-brother, Kim Jong-un, the boy's uncle. Traveling under the name of Kim Chol, his father was hideously and publicly attacked and killed in the Kuala Lumpur airport. The assassination had been carefully planned over many months by the wicked half-brother, who was an especially evil and terrible little man. After the assassination of his uncle Jang Song-thaek by KJU more than three years earlier, Kim Jong-nam had kept an especially low profile and lived an even more circumspect life than he had previously.

Kim Jong-nam's younger half-brother who now ruled North Korea was purging all family members, all progeny of Kim Jong-il, anyone who might be seen, however remotely, as a menace to his leadership, a threat to take over his throne as supreme leader.

Two unsuspecting women, thought to be prostitutes, were unwittingly recruited and extensively trained to be the assassins. An Indonesian woman and a Vietnamese woman were hired by an organization that was a front for the North Korean government's dirty tricks. The people who ran the North Korean company told the women that the business they were working for was an entertainment company that people hired to play pranks on their friends. The women were trained to pull pranks on men in airports, and they worked at this job for several months and were paid a reasonable wage to do it.

What these women later said they didn't know was that the pranks they had been playing on men in airports were in reality practice for the assassination they would unknowingly perform in 2017.

On February 13, 2017, each woman was given a solution that she was told to rub on a certain man's face when he arrived at the Kuala Lumpur airport. Having performed this same prank many times before, neither woman thought there was anything unusual about the prank they were asked to perform that day. They each wore clear latex gloves to protect their hands. One of the women took a cloth and rubbed one special solution all over the man's face. Immediately after the application of the first oily substance, the second woman applied the second liquid to the man's face. Both women escaped to the ladies' room and threw their latex gloves and the cloths that contained the noxious solutions in the trash can. They washed any remains of the pranking liquids off their hands and arms. Then they quickly left the airport as they had done many times before. Later they claimed they had no idea that this prank was any different than the others in which they had participated in the past. It was not until they were arrested that they realized they had killed a man.

The prank had been lethal. The man whose face they had rubbed with the two different solutions immediately became ill and called for help. Only a few drops of the poisonous pranking solutions that were used would have been necessary to cause sudden death. The pranking victim had been dosed with many times the amount that were required to kill him. At first, he complained of being unable to see. He exhibited severe sweating of his face and muscular twitching of his facial muscles and eyes. He complained of tightness in his chest and was unable to breathe. He complained of nausea and began vomiting. An ambulance was called immediately and arrived at the airport within minutes to take the victim of the prank to a medical clinic. He died in the ambulance, a casualty of VX poisoning. The assassination was a brazen and heinous way to die.

VX is short for "venomous agent X" and is an extremely toxic synthetic chemical. Now classified as a nerve agent and chemical WMD, it is the most potent of all nerve agents, even more toxic than sarin gas. VX was developed during World War II for military use in chemical warfare. Discovered as a result of experiments with pesticides research, in its pure form, VX is colorless and non-volatile. Because it is categorized as a weapon of mass destruction, it is banned from use by the Chemical Weapons Convention of 1993. Its danger is from direct application, the lethal method used by the two women in the Malaysian airport.

Neither one of the substances used in the applications to the victim's face would had been fatal on its own. Used alone, each solution was relatively harmless. It was the combination of the two solutions that caused a chemical reaction which resulted in the man's horrible death. This is why two women and two different applications of solutions were used. Applied together, one after the other, the chemical reaction that took place on the victim's skin resulted in the production of the complete VX formula. As the two liquids were mixed together on Kim Jong-nam's face, the combination produced the fatal substance that killed him.

Airport surveillance cameras and an investigation by Malaysian authorities identified the two perpetrators of the direct attack. Both were found and arrested within a short period of time, and both faced the death penalty if convicted of the crime of murder. The women claimed they had no knowledge that they were participating in an assassination. They said they had been led to believe that the solutions they were putting on the victim's face were entirely harmless. The women steadfastly claimed to know nothing about the toxicity of the substances they had used to "prank" their victim. Neither one of the women had been harmed in any way. Indeed, each solution was harmless until it was combined with the other solution. The women agreed to cooperate fully and told everything they knew to Malaysian law enforcement. Their stories implicated their North Korean employers in the murder plot.

Additional video footage from the Kuala Lumpur airport showed that a group of North Korean government agents left on flights immediately after Kim Jong-nam had been attacked with VX. Several of these North Korean agents on the videos were known to Malaysian authorities. Further investigation revealed that it was these agents of Kim Jong-un's rogue state who were responsible for recruiting and training the young women.

When Malaysian law enforcement realized that the North Koreans were behind the deadly VX poisoning and that the North Korean government had used at least one Malaysian national to assassinate one of KJU's political enemies on Malaysian soil, a diplomatic brouhaha and tit for tat expulsion of diplomats ensued between North Korea and Malaysia. Malaysia had maintained good relations with North Korea prior to the murder in Kuala Lumpur. The reckless poisoning, which could have harmed other innocent civilians, put Malaysia at odds with the very bad boys from North Korea.

It would be days before the autopsy results would confirm that the man who had been attacked in the Kuala Lumpur airport had died from a lethal dose of VX. Because he had been traveling under a passport that named him as Kim Chol, even more time would pass before the dead man was identified as Kim Jong-nam, first born son of the deceased former President of North Korea, Kim Jong-il, and half-brother of the current president of North Korea, Kim Jong-un.

When all the evidence was collected, the case was solved. Emperor Roly Poly had arranged for the successful assassination of this half-brother. Of course, the Hermit Kingdom denied everything, as they always did. They even denied that the dead man was the half-brother of the current leader of North Korea. North Korea's leadership maintained that the man in question had died of a heart attack and that the man who had died in the Malaysian airport had no connection whatsoever to the Kim family. This was the level of delusion that KJU, the little guy in charge, lived with on a day-to-day basis. No one came forward to claim Kim Jong-nam's body.

After his murder, Kim Jong-nam's family realized they were next on the list to be eliminated. They called on the Cheollima Civil Defense for help. The Cheollima is a mythological winged horse in East Asian folklore, and this fabled creature is capable of traveling long distances. In the Hermit Kingdom, it has been used as a North Korean symbol for rapid progress. The Cheollima group claims to have aided many high-level defectors escape from North Korea and says it is able to hide its web footprint to obscure its origins.

According to the story that was made public, the Cheollima Civil Defense extracted the Kim family from Macau. The branch of the family which was related to Kim Jong-nam had to flee their home in Macau where they had lived for more than fifteen years. Because they wanted to escape death, they had to leave behind their previous identities and most of their possessions. The maniacal leader of North Korea considered Kim Jong-nam's family too much of a challenge to his rule to allow them to live. It is said that the Cheollima Civil Defense, which is shrouded in mystery, continues to protect the members of the Kim family who are threatened with extermination by Kim Jong-un and his thugs. KJU had eliminated Jang Song-thaek's entire family. Kim Jong-nam's family believed they would suffer a similar fate if they did not voluntarily disappear from the face of the earth.

The Cheollima Civil Defense, the group that claims to have spirited the family out of Macau and into obscurity, thanked the governments of the Netherlands, China, the United States, and a fourth unnamed country for the emergency humanitarian assistance these countries had contributed to protect Nam's family. They particularly mentioned the Dutch Ambassador to North and South Korea, J.A. Von Kleeck, for his help. Canada was asked but refused to help because North Korea was holding a Canadian hostage. Canada did not want to participate in anything that might endanger their negotiations with the North Koreans. Kim Jong-nam's family was said to have flown from Macau to Taipei, and then they disappeared. They have been heard from only once since they fled Macau.

Chapter 7

NORMANDY AND THE NETHERLANDS AND MACAU

Kim Han-sol heard of his father's death on CNN. He knew his father had been scheduled to travel through the Kuala Lumpur airport on his way home to Macau in the middle of February. The young man assumed his father would be traveling under an assumed identity with a passport from another country. Most citizens of North Korea don't travel anywhere, and most people in North Korea don't have passports. Malaysia is one of the few places that people holding North Korean passports can travel relatively freely. Although Kim Han-sol knew his father would be traveling incognito, the men from North Korea who went to Maylasia to kill his father could freely travel there.

Even though his father was wearing a disguise, the son recognized his father when he saw his photo on the television set in his friend's apartment. When he understood from the news story that his father had been murdered, he left the gathering of young people who were drinking beer and playing video games.

Han-sol was overwhelmed with the shock and sorrow that anyone who has lost a parent experiences. His grief was intensified because his father had been murdered. He had been murdered publicly and in a horrible and theatrical way. Han-sol's father had been a distant parent who traveled frequently. Father and son had not been close. Perhaps Kim Han-sol was grieving as much for what had not been a part of their relationship as well as for what had been. Han-sol was shocked and frightened, but his immediate concern for what remained of his family overwhelmed his grief. Kim Han-sol lived in France and went to school there using a covert identity. He'd thought, because he had an Indonesian passport and an Indonesian name, that he was safe from the long arm of the North Korean death squads. When his father was murdered, he realized he had been a fool to think his family could escape the assassins. He realized he was no longer protected, and he was extremely worried about his sister and his mother who were still in Macau.

Han-sol tried to call his sister on her iPhone, but she didn't answer. He tried to call the landline at his home in Macau to reach his mother. No one answered at the house. He was panicked and hoped he wasn't too late to warn them. He left both his mother and his sister voicemail messages saying that he thought their husband and father had been murdered at the airport in Kuala Lumpur. Han-sol warned them that he was certain they were now all in danger of being assassinated.

Han-sol knew immediately who was behind his father's death. He didn't yet know his father's exact cause of death, but he knew that his own uncle, Kim Jong-un was behind the vicious murder. He feared that he and his mother and sister were next. He knew his mother and sister had to get out of Macau and go into hiding before KJU's assassins got to them. He was afraid that what was left of his family might have only a few hours before they were murdered as his father had been.

Kim Han-sol and his family had formed a close friendship with a diplomat from the Netherlands when the Dutchman had been posted to Macau in the early years of the new millennium. Nicolaas De Vriese lived in their neighborhood and had played soccer with Han-sol when he was a young boy. Nicolaas had been on the Olympic soccer team representing the Netherlands before he had joined the diplomatic service of his country. When he saw the young Han-sol kicking the soccer ball around in his yard, he couldn't resist inviting himself over to play with the boy. The boy's own father traveled constantly and was never at home. The boy's mother and sister stayed in the house most of the time, and they had no interest in soccer. The little boy was obviously lonely and loved having Nicolaas come over to play football with him. Nicolaas gave Han-sol many useful pointers about how to be a better soccer player, but most of all, Han-sol was grateful to have a friend.

Han-sol's father kept his distance from Nicolaas, as he kept his distance from everybody. But Han-sol eventually invited Nicolaas to have dinner with his family. Nicolaas was a bachelor and had no wife or children of his own. He was a charming dinner guest, and Han-sol's mother grew to trust the open and friendly Mr. De Vriese. She liked the man and was happy that her son had a male role model in his life. It didn't take Nicolaas long to figure out who Han-sol's family really was, but being a diplomat, he never broached the subject of their family lineage with them. Han-sol's family was clearly living in exile in Macau. Their quiet and circumscribed existence was designed to allow them to maintain low-profile lives in order to keep them safe. The children in the family had a tutor and didn't go to school with other children.

It was Nicolaas who made arrangements for Han-sol to attend boarding school at one of the United World Colleges. He discussed everything with Han-sol and with both of his parents. Han-sol's father reluctantly agreed to allow his son to leave home to attend the boarding school in Bosnia. Nicolaas did all of the paperwork and provided Han-sol with an Indonesian identity and papers so that he could travel to and study in Europe without fear that his real identity would be discovered. Indonesia was a melting pot of cultures and racial groups. There were many ethnic Koreans who lived in Indonesia, so Han-sol's birth certificate and passport which made him into an Indonesian young man was perfectly believable.

Nicolaas became Han-sol's mentor as well as his friend and soccer coach. Nicolaas even visited Han-sol in Bosnia when he was at school there. When Han-sol graduated from his secondary school and was thinking about colleges, Nicolaas arranged for him to attend Sciences Po in Normandy, France. Over the years, Nicolaas had advanced in the diplomatic corps of the Netherlands and was now stationed in Thailand. Even though he no longer lived in Macau, he continued to care about and pay attention to Han-sol and his family. Nicolaas was instrumental in convincing Han-sol's parents that his sister should be allowed to continue her education in a regular secondary school and attend high school at the Macau Anglican College.

It was not surprising that Han-sol would call on his friend and mentor when he needed help. He was able to get through to Nicolaas on his satellite phone. Nicolaas happened to be back home in Holland when he answered Han-sol's call. Han-sol told his friend what he knew. The world did not yet know with certainty that it was his father, Kim Jong-nam, who had been murdered in the Kuala Lumpur airport. But Nicolaas believed that Han-sol knew what he was talking about and had analyzed the situation perfectly. The older man agreed with Han-sol that he and his mother and sister were in grave danger. Nicolaas promised to do everything he could to help save their lives. The two men agreed that the women had to leave Macau immediately.

As much as they had tried to keep their lives in Macau low profile, everybody was aware that the half-brother of the current dictator of North Korea and his family had settled there. Han-sol knew his mother would resist any suggestion that she leave the home where she had lived for so many years. But it was imperative that Han-sol's mother and sister leave Macau. Nicolaas realized he did not have any time to convince them that they were in danger. He hoped he might be able to talk the mother into leaving Macau and go into hiding, if only to save her children's lives.

Han-sol knew that he would also have to disappear and leave his studies at Sciences Po. His friends in France had begun to put things together about his background, and he had probably not been as careful as he should have been about what he'd discussed with them. Although he trusted his friends and didn't really think any of them would betray him on purpose, he agreed that he too had to give up his current life. The stakes had completely changed with the assassination of his father. Han-sol was only twenty-one years old, but after his father's death, he was now the man of the family. He trusted that Nicolaas would help him save his mother and sister.

Nicolaas had many connections in diplomatic and intelligence circles. The Dutch diplomat knew he would have to call in some favors to make this happen, and he knew he had to move very fast. Because Han-sol was already in Western Europe, it would not be difficult to get him to a safe place. The two women were another story. They were half way around the world.

It would not be easy to convince them that they needed to leave Macau. They did not know with certainty yet that their husband and father had been murdered. Once that knowledge became public information, they should without a doubt be convinced of the danger they were facing. But by the time the world realized what had happened, it would already be too late to move them discreetly to a safe place. If the women could be convinced immediately that they had to leave Macau, before the news of Kim Jong-nam's death became public, they might be able to go into hiding before they, too, were sentenced to death.

Nicolaas decided that his best chance of convincing them was to tell them that they needed to go into hiding temporarily, for a few weeks or months, until the death of Kim Jong-nam and who was behind it could all be sorted out. If it was determined that his murder had been at the hands of someone other than the North Koreans, the women might be able to return to their home. If they became convinced that they were not in any danger from their insane relative KJU, they could make the decision on their own to return to Macau. But the women had to be persuaded that they needed to move without delay to a safe place. Once that hurdle was cleared, the next step would be to physically move them from Macau to someplace secret and secure.

Although Macau was still a city-state and theoretically retained a great deal of autonomy, in reality it was under China's thumb. All foreign policy decisions for Macau were made by China. China in fact made all decisions of any importance about what happened in the city-state. Getting Han-sol's family discreetly out of Macau might have to involve China. Nicolaas hoped the Chinese might be willing to let the family go if they were appealed to on humanitarian grounds. No one knew if there were North Korean agents already watching Han-sol's mother and sister in Macau. No one knew if there might already be a North Korean hit squad on its way to Macau to finish off the rest of Kim Jong-nam's family.

Nicolaas had to put his plan into action at once, and he would have to bring the Kim women out of Macau before he had finalized the arrangements about where to hide them permanently. It would be tricky and difficult to pull all the pieces together in time. Nicolaas was working on many angles simultaneously. He called his friend, the ambassador to North and South Korea from the Netherlands. The ambassador agreed to be the point man and the public face of the evacuation and resettlement of the family, if that story ever had to become public information. Everybody knew that eventually it would become public knowledge. But to give the family a chance to successfully disappear, the Dutchmen hoped to be able to keep their departure from Macau a secret for as long as possible. It would be helpful for many reasons if the responsibility for extracting and resettling Kim Jong-nam's family was shared among a number of countries and organizations.

The ambassador from the Netherlands to South Korea was assigned the task of speaking confidentially with the Chinese and ostensibly clearing the path for the family to leave Macau. China had traditionally been a close ally of North Korea, so this was an unusually delicate and difficult part of the negotiations. China might choose to reveal to the North Koreans that Nam's family was about to leave Macau. If the North Koreans were going to do something to harm the family, they would have to do it immediately, before Kim Han-sol's family left Macau and disappeared.

Nicolaas did not trust the Chinese, but he left it to the ambassador to try to work things out with them. Kim Jong-nam had died such a horrible public death, he could not imagine that the Chinese would fail to try to help protect the man's family. But Nicolaas did not want to share his plans with the Communists and asked the Dutch ambassador to delay speaking with the Chinese. Nicholaas urged the ambassador to slow down and draw out the negotiations as much as he could without raising their suspicions.

Nicolaas had a plan to save Kim Jong-nam's family that was designed to fool everyone, even the Chinese. Failing to obtain their permission for Han-sol's mother and sister to leave Macau might make the Chinese angry. But after Han-sol's family was out of Macau, Nicolaas didn't really care how angry the Chinese were.

Nicolaas would have liked to take the family to Canada. He felt they could be anonymous there, and although they might not care for the weather because it was so different from the weather in Macau, there were enough cities in Canada that Han-sol's mother and sister could get lost in that country. Both women spoke excellent French, and Han-sol's sister also spoke excellent English. Quebec and Ontario, cosmopolitan cities with large Asian populations, were both options. The West Coast and the Vancouver area would be the most comfortable for the family, but that would also be the most obvious place for the North Koreans to search for Kim Jong-nam's missing relatives.

That line of thinking and planning became moot when the Canadians refused to participate in any way with either evacuating or protecting Kim Jong-nam's family. The North

Koreans had arrested and were holding a minister who was a citizen of Canada. There was some kind of trumped-up charge against the man. The KJU regime was either demanding a ransom from the Canadians, or they believed that holding a religious person in jail had some kind of distorted public relations value. The Canadians were worried that if they helped KJU's enemies escape, they might compromise their chances of having the pastor returned to them.

Nicolaas knew he couldn't send the family to the United States, but he knew the United States would do whatever it was asked to do to aid in the escape and to help protect the family. He contacted a friend of his in the U.S. Department of State, a friend that he would trust with his own life. He knew she would be completely discreet about what had to happen to save the women. The U.S. diplomat had a position that was powerful enough to commandeer the necessary transportation resources and to keep absolutely secret from everyone what was being done to relocate the Kims. It was essential to keep the operation closely held and completely clandestine—even from those in her own state department and from her own government—until after it was a fait accompli.

Nicolaas would owe his American colleague an enormous debt if she was able to come through for him. He felt this mission was the most important of his diplomatic career. He didn't mind owing the U.S. diplomat, if she could save these people's lives. He knew she would be delighted to do it, for humanitarian reasons alone, not to mention the enormous pleasure it would give her to have a chance to stick it to the little fat face in North Korea. On a securely scrambled phone line, Nicolaas explained to her what his plan was. She liked what he proposed and agreed it would be an excellent way of covering their tracks.

Nicolaas got on the satellite phone again and placed the call to Han-sol's mother. This might be the most difficult sale he had ever made in his life. He would need all of his brains and all of his charm to convince this woman that she had to leave Macau and the home where she had spent the past fifteen years. As it turned out, it was not as difficult as he had thought it would be to convince Kim Jong-nam's widow that she and her daughter were in danger. Han-sol's mother had known Nicolaas a long time, and she trusted him. He was a good friend, and she knew he had the best interests of her children at heart. He had demonstrated this many, many times over the years, and he had always been right.

Han-sol's mother was relieved to know that he was already in a safe place, and she agreed to the plan that Nicolaas laid out for her. She and her daughter would have twelve hours to pack their personal possessions, their valuables, and some clothes. At this point, Nicolaas told them that they would be in hiding only temporarily, but he suspected that both mother and daughter knew differently. Nicolaas had arranged to transfer their financial assets so that neither the North Koreans nor the Chinese would be able to get their hands on any of it. The women would have to be ready to leave their home later that night. Nicolaas went over the plans twice more with both women to be sure they understood exactly what they had to do.

The first thing they had to do was to give their servants the day off. The Kims trusted their employees, but there was only one older woman they could count on for sure. She alone would be available to help them with their packing, and she was the only servant who would know that they were leaving Macau. In fact, she would be coming with them to their new home. Nicolaas knew their housekeeper Beatriz who had evolved into more of a companion for Han-sol's mother than she was a servant. Nicolaas acknowledged that she was considered to be a member of the family and that the family would not be able to function without her help, especially because of the moral support the Portuguese housekeeper gave to the two Korean women. Beatriz had been with the family since the children were infants. When the reality of the horror of the death of their husband and father began to sink in, they would need Beatriz more than ever. She would be accompanying them into obscurity.

Nicolaas was scrambling to put everything in place. He had it all arranged, except he still did not have a definite permanent location for the family. All of the extraction and transportation plans had been organized, and he knew he could find a temporary place for the family to stay. He preferred not to move them twice, as each transfer inevitably involved more people and would result in more chances that their whereabouts might be exposed. In spite of not having a final okay on a permanent destination, Nicolaas decided to go ahead with the operation and the current timetable. The three women would be leaving Macau that night.

Chapter 8

MACAU TO LONDON

A*t eleven o'clock that evening*, a white van arrived at the family compound. Except for Beatriz, all of the servants had been sent home or given the night off, so there was no one to witness the departure. There would be lots of rumors about when they had left and where they had gone, but no one who worked in the household would have seen them leave. There were only the three women who stood surrounded by their thirty-five pieces of luggage. It would be touch and go whether or not all of the trunks and suitcases would fit into the van. The van had entered the grounds through the service entrance. Delivery vans came and went through that gate all the time, so no one would give it a thought that a van had arrived and then later left the house on this particular night.

Nicolaas had explained to Han-sol's mother and sister how it all was going to happen, so they were ready with their belongings, waiting by the rear service door at the appointed time. Two men came to the door and, without knocking or asking if they could come in, entered the back hallway. They looked European but didn't say anything as they carried the luggage to the van. When the last of the suitcases and boxes had been loaded, the women followed the men outside. One of the men got into the driver's seat, and the other one helped the women up onto the van's bench seat behind the driver. Then he got into the front passenger seat. As instructed, two cell phones were left behind on the kitchen table inside the house. Han-sol's mother did not use a cell phone.

Twenty-five minutes after it had arrived, the white van left the grounds of the Kim's estate. Han-sol's mother cried as she left her home. In spite of wanting to believe that her absence was only temporary, she knew in her heart that she would never return. Macau now belonged to China, and the Chinese were in league with the North Koreans. She would not see her home again. As they drove towards Macau International Airport at the end of Taipa Island, Kim Sol-hui, Han-sol's sister, was silent, and Beatriz held the mother's hand to comfort her.

The van did not drive to the main passenger terminal of the airport but entered the airport grounds through a side entrance that wasn't used very often. The van drove onto the tarmac, and after a long and convoluted course around various runways and over some rough grassy areas, it came to rest beside a small private jet. The jet was parked far from the airport's main terminal. The women remained in the van until the driver and the man in the passenger seat had removed the luggage from the van and stowed it into the cargo hold of the jet. Then the passenger door of the plane opened and the stairway unfolded to the ground.

The man who had helped the women into the van, slid back the door on the side and helped the three climb down to the tarmac. They made their way to the stairs of the jet and up into the cabin of the plane. The white van was gone before the women reached the top of the stairway. There were seats for eight people in the small jet, and there was a male steward standing at the entrance to the aircraft. He nodded to the women as they came aboard. The steward spoke in French and indicated where he would be sitting and asked them to take seats on both sides of the plane. He explained that they would have more room that way, and the weight of the aircraft would be more evenly balanced if two people were seated on one side of the plane and two people were seated on the other side.

Less than a minute before the van carrying Han-sol's mother and sister and Beatriz had exited the rear entrance of their Macau compound, two white vans exactly the same as the one that held Han-sol's family, pulled out of the service entrance and also headed for the airport. Each of the three identical white vans took a different route. One route was not necessarily better than the other; the important thing was that each van made the trip via a different and complicated course. When one of the vans arrived at the airport, it left the highway via the exit that would take it to the airport's main arrival and departures terminal. Another one of the white vans approached the airport from the rear and drove directly onto the tarmac to a waiting private jet. The third van drove onto the airport grounds using a small gated side road and drove for a few minutes around the numerous runways set aside for private planes.

Three small private jets took off from the Macau International Airport at approximately midnight that night.

One plane flew to a small private airport near Manila in the Philippines. No one saw who had boarded that plane, and when it landed in the Philippines, no one was seen getting off. One of the three private jets flew to Camp Hansen, a U.S. Marine Corps Base near the town of Kim on the Island of Okinawa. That plane was never seen again at any commercial airport. The third plane flew to the Taoyuan International Airport in Taipei, Taiwan.

A group of three women disembarked from the plane in Taipei and made their way to the main departures terminal for Malaysian airlines. The three waited in the main terminal of the airport in Taipei for several hours. One of the women appeared to be European, and two of the women, probably mother and daughter, were Asian. They had the usual assortment of carry-on luggage stacked around where they were sitting. No one saw when they left the airport or knew what flight they'd taken. If anyone had been watching closely, they would have realized that the three had not boarded any flight to anywhere. One at a time, each woman got up to go to the restroom. When she got inside the stall, she took off the disguise and wig she wore, changed her clothes, and left the bathroom looking like a completely different person. Each woman left the airport alone in a taxi.

A U.S. Navy troop transport plane took off from Camp Hansen at five o-clock in the morning. The troop transport was much larger than the small private plane had been, and there were no luxurious leather seats for the three female passengers on the large plane. The seats had been reconfigured so that each of the women could lie down and go to sleep. Blankets and pillows were provided by a young United States Navy lieutenant. She pointed out where the women could find the head and asked if they would care for coffee or breakfast. All three women were hungry and asked for both.

The lieutenant busied herself in the galley and brought a tray to each of the women. They were pleasantly surprised to find a delicious hot cheese omelet, bacon, fried potatoes, fresh fruit, tomato juice, and warm bread rolls with butter and jam on their trays. The coffee was hot and strong. After they had eaten, all three of the women took advantage of the pillows and blankets and went to sleep. It would be a fourteen-hour flight across the North Pole from Camp Hansen to RAF Leuchars Station near Fife on the north east coast of Scotland.

It was dark again when the troop transport landed in Scotland. A car with a driver met the women at the bottom of the steps as they left the plane. The driver of the Bentley handed each woman a packet and reminded them that they each could bring two pieces of luggage plus their carry-ons with them in the car. The rest of their many pieces of luggage would follow. The women had all packed accordingly, so each one was able to point to exactly which ones of the many pieces of luggage were to go into the boot of the Bentley.

The women were exhausted and compliantly followed the directions they were given. They'd slept fitfully during the flight from Japan, and when they landed in Scotland, they were not fully awake. Inside the packet that each of the women had been handed was a Dutch passport. Each woman's passport had her picture on it, and each woman had a new name. There were birth certificates, credit cards, and other paperwork in the packets. The European woman's birth certificate said that she had been born in Amsterdam, although she couldn't speak a word of Dutch. The two Asian women's birth certificates said they had been born in Jakarta. All three passports had been issued by the Netherlands, and each was stamped with a permanent resident's visa that said the holder of the passport had been living in England for over a year. Scotland and England were always happy to welcome their friends from Holland.

The three would be staying at a hotel for a few days, and then there was a house waiting for them in the outskirts of London. The luggage that did not fit into the Bentley would be delivered to the house. On the floor of the back seat of the car, there were thermoses of tea and coffee and a picnic basket that held sandwiches and biscuits. It would be more than an eight-hour drive to their London hotel. It had already been a very long trip from Macau.

The women in the Bentley arrived in London at Brown's Hotel on Albemarle Street in Mayfair at six o'clock in the morning. The women were asleep in the car, and their driver checked them into their suite and arranged for their few pieces of luggage to be taken to their rooms. He filled out all the paperwork and presented their passports and credit cards in their new names at the hotel desk. He had taken care of everything, including the generous tips that employees who worked at Brown's Hotel had come to expect. He drove the Bentley to a side entrance of the hotel and gently woke the sleeping women. Quietly and unobtrusively, he escorted them up the elevator and down the hall to their five-room suite. No one, not even the concierge or the clerk at the reception desk, had seen them enter the hotel and go to their rooms.

Their driver handed each woman an electronic key to the suite and urged them to order their meals from room service. Because Kim Jong-nam had been murdered only a few days earlier, the man they had begun to think of as Mr. Bentley told them he wanted them to maintain an especially low profile while they were staying at the hotel and for several weeks and months in the future. After some time had passed, he pointed out that fewer people would be looking for them. KJU would never stop looking for them, but their faces and their names would not be constantly in the news. Their notoriety and fame would have diminished in a few weeks, or at least that was the hope. Mr. Bentley urged them to order a good English breakfast and then take a long rest. He pointed out that the jet lag and the travel schedule they had just endured would have been difficult for even the most seasoned travelers. They were to rest today. Tomorrow, he said, there would be a nice surprise. He left his mobile phone number with them, but he had never told them his name.

The women knew their driver was more than simply a driver. Although he was wearing a chauffeur's livery and cap, he had a military bearing and was obviously in command of much more than merely the silver-grey Bentley that he was driving that day. The Bentley was a beauty, but their driver looked as if he would be more comfortable at the helm of a battleship. They'd just met him, but they were all sorry to see Mr. Bentley leave. He was a reassuring presence in this new place.

Although they were in a foreign country and feeling somewhat lost, they knew they had not been abandoned in any way. Far from it. They knew that many people had been mobilized to organize the elaborate preparations which had been pulled together to extract them from Macau and bring them to England. They knew it had been a herculean effort to arrange and accomplish their escape in such a short period of time. Han-sol's mother realized they were not at all alone, but she could not help but feel lonely in this strange country where she had never been before.

The women ordered breakfast from room service as their driver and commander had suggested. They were used to the European petite dejeuner, and the enormous amount of food on the plate made the English breakfast seem more like dinner. Not one of the three could finish her servings of eggs, bacon, ham, broiled fish, potatoes, grilled tomatoes, fried bread, and baskets of toast and muffins with butter and jams of all kinds. As mixed up as their time zones were, they decided they would pretend the meal was dinner and go to bed right after they had eaten.

The suite had three bedrooms and three bathrooms plus a living room and a dining room. The travelers were happy to be able to take their first showers in two days and wash their hair. They were all road weary. The young Sol-hui had never traveled anywhere outside of Macau. Her mother had traveled many years ago when she was younger, but since the family's exile from North Korea, she had pretty much stayed close to home. Beatriz had never lived anyplace but Macau and had never traveled outside of its boundaries.

The long and complicated plane trip which had crossed multiple international borders and time zones had been an ordeal for all three women, none of whom had any real or recent experience with traveling or hotels or room service or any of it. Beatriz unpacked for both mother and daughter, and then they all went to bed. Except for Han-sol's mother, neither one of the other two women had ever slept in a bed other than her own, so sleeping in a strange country in a strange city in a strange hotel in a strange bed might have provoked a great deal of anxiety. But they were so worn out, any bed looked good to them, and they fell asleep with little thought about the strangeness of their situation.

They woke up in time for dinner, at the real dinner hour, and decided they would again take the advice of their driver and have their evening meal delivered to the suite. It was not only the breakfast that was different in England. They found most of the room service food offerings peculiar. They didn't know what many of the menu items were. Everything they had eaten had tasted good, but some of the time they hadn't been able to identify exactly what they were eating. For dinner they ordered soup and hamburgers and French fries from the room service menu. Everybody knew what soup and hamburgers were.

Fortunately, Sol-hui knew how to use the remote control to turn on the television set. Unfortunately, the news was full of her father's murder. They turned off the TV and decided they would read. Reading was the one comforting and familiar thing they could find to do. Sol-hui was ready for an adventure, and she was happy to be in England, even though she didn't know quite what she was supposed to do. She reminded herself that she'd graduated from an Anglican high school, after all. She ought to be able to do something right.

Her mother, however, was older and set in her ways. Because she had been in exile for so much of her life, she had become reclusive and fearful. She wasn't welcome in Korea anymore and hadn't been in Korea for almost twenty years. Macau was more home than any place else, but even there she had retreated into her compound and her garden. She'd been discouraged from leaving the grounds, and servants did the shopping and everything else that required stepping outside the safety of her secure but stifling environment. Thank goodness she had Beatriz here with her in London.

The next afternoon there was a knock at the door. Two waiters were standing there, each pushing a tea cart in front of him. They rolled the carts into the dining room of the suite and began to set up the elaborate tea. Although she was familiar with the ritual of afternoon tea and was delighted to see food she recognized and could put a name to, Han-sol's mother protested and said they hadn't ordered tea.

Just as the waiter began to explain what was happening, Kim Han-sol appeared in the doorway. He looked so handsome standing there and ran to hug his mother, his sister, and the beloved Beatriz who had helped to raise him. His mother began to cry as she held on to her son. She hadn't cried since she'd left her home in Macau, but seeing Han-sol for the first time in almost a year had triggered deep emotions within her.

Han-sol was taking charge now and explained. "I ordered the tea, Mother. It will be wonderful. Nicolaas has come across from Holland to join us, and he will be here any minute. Sit down and let these handsome fellows wait on you. Let's begin. I'm starving. We have smoked salmon tea sandwiches that are to die for, and we also have tuna salad which you will love. You must try one of each kind. The minced ham sandwiches with sweet pickle are quite tasty as well." People who lived in Macau eat a lot of fish, so Han-sol knew his family would be happy with the fish sandwich selections.

They were about to finish off the sandwiches when Nicolaas arrived. He hugged Sol-hui and paid his respects to Mrs. Kim and Beatriz. Everyone was glad to see him and knew that he had been the one who had arranged everything so quickly and so perfectly for their escape from Macau. Nicolaas expressed his condolences for the death of Kim Jong-nam and said he hoped the North Koreans would rot in hell for what they had done. He assured the women that KJU would not be able to find or harm the rest of the family. They finished the scones and the pastries and the pots of tea, and Nicolaas said he had to leave.

Before he left, he told Sol-hui he hoped she would be happy to know that she had been accepted at Cambridge. Sol-hui's eyes lit up and she smiled a big smile. Months earlier, Nicolaas had discussed with her the possibility of attending Cambridge, and he told her that he was willing to pull a few strings for her. She'd made her application but knew that her acceptance at the prestigious British university would depend on her academic records and recommendations from the Macau Anglican College. She had been a top student at the school in Macau, so she had her fingers crossed that she would make the grade. And she had! She could see that her mother was both pleased and sad to hear this news. Sol-hui would be living away from home for the first time. Han-sol would be completing his studies at Oxford. The older woman knew it was time for her children to leave the nest, and in fact her son had left the nest years earlier. The mother was sad as well as happy for her daughter. In the end it would be only the mother and Beatriz—except, of course, for holidays.

Han-sol has been called the Korean Prince, and he was an exceptionally handsome, intelligent, and well-spoken young man. His pleasant and engaging demeanor could even be said to be charismatic. He was certainly easier to look at and much more appealing to listen to than his uncle, the current leader of North Korea. It was no contest! It would not be any wonder if KJU wanted to remove his good-looking and likeable nephew from the future political scene of North Korea.

In 2012, Kim Han-sol had given an interview to a Finnish television station. Only seventeen at the time, he appeared to be eloquent, reasonable, and open-minded. In the interview, he called his uncle, Kim Jong-un a dictator. When a man claiming to be Kim-Han-sol appeared in a short, forty-second video clip on U-Tube in February 2017, just a few days after the assassination of his father, facial recognition software confirmed that the man in the video was indeed the son of the man who had called himself Kim Chol and had been murdered in the Kuala Lumpur airport. Han-sol quickly flashed his passport at the camera and claimed in the video that he and his mother and sister were safe and in hiding. He said he "hoped things would be better soon." It was not clear from his statement whether he meant "better" specifically for his own family members or more generally for the entire country of North Korea. Perhaps his words were intended to have a double meaning. North Korea has always been a nation cloaked in mystery and obfuscation.

Chapter 9

ENGLAND

A *few days after their arrival* at Brown's Hotel, the military man who had driven them to London in the Bentley arrived in a van to drive them to their new home in the British countryside. His chauffeur's livery and cap were gone, and today Mr. B wore a dark blue, nondescript uniform. They had been expecting him this morning, and they were packed and ready to move on to the next phase of their adventure.

When the women answered the door of their suite, their mysterious driver was delighted to tell them they looked rested and as if they had recovered from their travels. He was upbeat and cheerful, but he still didn't tell them his name. He'd brought a cart on wheels from the lobby to hold their luggage. Within a couple of minutes, he'd loaded the cart with the luggage and the women onto the elevator. He told them their hotel bill had been taken care of and that it would be better if they didn't show themselves in the lobby. They left the way they had arrived, through the side door of the hotel. The van that would take them to their new home, Brierley

House, was parked there. To the three women the nameless Mr. Bentley had now become Mr. B.

The women didn't tell him that they'd snuck out of their rooms the previous afternoon and gone down to the hotel's lounge for tea. They'd been cooped up for several days and were anxious to see the rest of the hotel. They had read in a guidebook that Brown's Hotel had a wonderful afternoon tea, and they wanted to try it in the lounge. They put on their outdoor coats, went down to the first floor on the elevator, and left the hotel through the side door. They had called ahead for a reservation for tea, which is what their guidebook had told them they should do to guarantee a table at the time they wanted. They'd made their reservation in a fictitious name. The three women were dressed appropriately for tea at one of London's most prestigious hotels. They walked around the corner of the hotel to the main entrance.

Entering the front door as if they had no connection to the hotel other than the fact that they were arriving for a wonderful tea, they made their way to the lounge and took their time enjoying Brown's fabulous scones with lemon curd and clotted cream, pastries of all kinds, many cups of tea, and an extra order of smoked salmon tea sandwiches. They paid the bill for their teatime treat in cash and left a substantial tip. They left the lounge and exited the hotel, exactly as they had arrived, through the main entrance. Then they walked around the corner of the hotel again to the side entrance, went back into the hotel, and took the elevator up to their suite. They'd had fun dressing up for tea and being sneaky and pretending they weren't really staying at the hotel. No one had seen them leave or come back in through the side door. No one who had seen them in the tea lounge had suspected that they were actually staying at Brown's. They were feeling ever so clever that they'd had an outing of sorts and had fooled everyone.

When they'd arrived in London, it had been very early in the morning and still dark outside. They'd not been able to really see anything of the city. Now they were having a wonderful sightseeing trip. Mr. B was regaling them with stories, speaking as if he was a tour guide, as they drove past Buckingham Palace, Trafalgar Square, and Westminster Abbey. They had the impression that he was taking them via the scenic route, not the shortest way to their new home. Their driver and caretaker wanted them to have some fun and experience the sights of London. He'd been all business and quite taciturn in the past, but today he was obviously enjoying being able to show off his magnificent city. Mr. B's British accent had let them know this was home for him. They asked questions and practiced their English. Sol-hui's English was excellent because she'd studied at an Anglican school, but the other two women needed the practice. They were in England now, and they were going to have to learn how to communicate.

After the tour and an hours-long drive out of town, the van pulled off the main highway and drove for some time on smaller side roads. Then they stopped in front of a pair of iron gates. Mr. B punched in a code on a keypad that stood on a post beside the entrance. The gates slid open, and they drove through as the gates automatically closed behind them. They continued down a gravel driveway through a grove of trees that finally ended in front of a substantial and attractive stone house surrounded by a garden. It would be quite a magnificent garden when spring arrived.

Brierley House was in the middle of nowhere and there was no one else around. It was quiet and green, and the sun was shining. It was the first of March, so it was cold outside. More often than not, March days in England are cold and rainy, but today was glorious. It was a perfect day to welcome the women to their new home. Mr. B helped them exit the van. He opened the front door of the house with an old-fashioned key on a large brass ring and stepped aside so they could enter.

In the entrance hall they found their pile of luggage that had arrived with them on the plane to Scotland. There was a drawing room to the right of the hall, and a warm and welcoming fire blazed in the fireplace. The house was furnished in the English country house style. The three women made a quick tour of the upstairs, and each one found her bedroom. There was an extra bedroom for Han-sol when he came to stay. It wasn't home in Macau, but it was home for now, in England. It was a welcoming and happy place, and they would be safe and comfortable here. Sol-hui knew she would be leaving soon for Cambridge and would be living here only during holidays and weekends. She was young and ready to spread her wings and leave home, wherever that home was.

Someone had prepared lunch and set the table for the women in the dining room. There was a pot of vegetable soup on the kitchen stove. On the antique mahogany table in the dining room, there was an assortment of sandwiches arranged on a blue and white platter and covered with a linen napkin. There was a beautiful fruit salad in a crystal bowl. The table was set with a white linen tablecloth and napkins and what was probably real silver. Mr. B explained that there was a cook who came with the house. She lived in the nearby village and came to the house every day except Sunday.

Mrs. Gunther cleaned the house and was, also and most importantly, their bodyguard. She would be their liaison with their protectors in the British Secret Service. She'd prepared the lunch for them and would be back later in the afternoon to clean up the dishes and to ask them what they wanted her to fix for dinner. She was out doing errands now. When she got back to the house, she would help them sort out their trunks and suitcases that were stacked in a heap in the front hall. Mrs. Gunther would take care of them.

As he was about to leave and go out the front door, Mr. B turned around and asked if they had enjoyed their tea in the lounge at Brown's Hotel the day before. Then he winked, and leaving them speechless and a little chagrinned, he was out the door and off in the van. All along, someone had been watching them at the hotel. They hadn't been as clever as they thought they'd been.

Beatriz was a companion, personal assistant, and lady's maid for Han-sol's mother, Shin Jong-hui. Beatriz packed and unpacked for her lady and took care of her clothes. She helped her in and out of the bath and helped her dress. She brought her coffee and breakfast in bed. She brought her tea and did anything else her lady wanted her to do. Beatriz received a salary but was not regarded as a servant. Beatriz was relieved that there would be a cook and someone to clean. It had been a long time since she'd done that kind of work, and her age was such that she had her hands full taking care of Han-sol's and Sol-hui's mother.

When Mrs. Gunther returned to the house, everyone knew it. She was a large, loud, and cheerful soul, and she greeted the new residents of Brierley House with hearty hellos and the bustle of one who is confident in her position. She had brought two young men in military uniforms with her and ordered them around as if she was a drill sergeant. They brought in bags of groceries from Mrs. Gunther's truck. Beatriz told the soldiers where each of the trunks and boxes and suitcases in the front hallway was to go, and Mrs. Gunther made sure the men carried everything up the stairs carefully and delivered everything exactly where it belonged. As soon as they'd finished their tasks, she gave them each a bag of biscuits and sent them away in their jeep.

Mrs. Gunther bustled around the kitchen for a while and in a few minutes carried an enormous tea tray into the drawing room. She announced that it was four o'clock, and tea would be served at four o'clock every day. Mrs. Gunther would not always be joining them for tea, but she had things to explain to them today. It was their first day at Brierley House, and she was going to tell them how things were going to be. Mrs. Gunther was tall and sturdy and looked as if she were very strong. She was a person who inspired confidence. Everyone gathered in the drawing room in front of the fire, and Mrs. Gunther served the tea, passed the cucumber sandwiches, and cut the cake. She began to lay out the rules of the house.

"My real name isn't Mrs. Gunther, but that's what you'll call me. Mostly everyone calls me Mrs. Gunther because I carry a gun." Mrs. Gunther laughed at her joke, reached into the pocket of her apron, and brought her gun out for everyone to see. Shin Jong-hui gasped, and everyone's eyes got wide. The three women from Macau stared at the gun that looked so large and menacing here in the middle of this chintz and slipcovered drawing room. "If you were Americans, you wouldn't bat an eye. Not everyone in England is allowed to carry a gun, but I have a permit and a whole room full of trophies that would give you some idea about how good I am at shooting this gun." She laughed again. "Lighten up, I'm not planning on using it. I'm just showing it to you to let you know I can protect you."

The women tried to smile, but the business with the gun was quite outside their usual realm of things to think about. Mrs. Gunther shrugged her shoulders and continued, "Blimey, such a serious bunch of you! Now, let's talk about food. Everybody likes to talk about food, and I am an even better cook than I am a marksman. Ha Ha! I can make any cuisine you want to eat, and I am adventurous and love to try new things in the kitchen. I know you are from Macau, and I am excellent with both Portuguese and Chinese food. I'm not so on top of Japanese and Korean cooking, but I am willing to learn."

Beatriz wanted to break the ice and establish some kind of bond with this woman, so she offered an olive branch, "I've brought a cookbook of Portuguese and Chinese fusion dishes that we liked to eat in Macau. I'd love to share it with you. If you want to learn new things, the cookbook might be a good place to start."

Mrs. Gunther was more than enthusiastic, and Beatriz could tell the woman really did love to cook. This woman might be big and brusque and more than a little bit bossy, but she had a good heart and wanted to please them. "Go and bring me that cookbook, and let's find something delicious to make for your first dinner at Brierley House." Everything would never be all right again for these displaced persons, but at least for now, everything at Brierley House was going to be all right.

Chapter 10

CHINA

The story was all over the news that North Korean agents sent by Kim Jong-un had tried to assassinate his nephew Kim Han-sol who had been hiding in Beijing. Allegedly, the Chinese had foiled a plot to kill the son of Kim Jong-nam. Kim Jong-nam had been assassinated by his half-brother's agents in the Kuala Lumpur airport in February. Security had been increased around China's 19th National Congress of the Communist Party, and the Chinese government claimed this was the reason that two of the seven individuals involved in the plot against Kim Han-sol had been arrested.

Details of the story were difficult to obtain, but it was reported that the North Korean dictator KJU had sent a team of assassins to Beijing to kill his nephew. The twenty-two-year-old young man was an intelligent and attractive alternative to Emperor Roly Poly and was therefore a potential threat to KJU's repressive and failed regime in North Korea. Han-sol and his family had gone into hiding after his father was murdered in Malaysia.

Those who wanted to protect the possible heir to the North Korean dynasty had made extraordinary efforts to keep secret the whereabouts of Han-sol and his mother and sister. Because North Korean hit squads were routinely sent against KJU's enemies, the location of the family's hiding place was unknown to all but a handful of people. The details of the family's escape had been closely guarded information known only to those few who had participated in their departure from Macau.

The Chinese, among a few other nations, claimed they had helped with an emergency evacuation of the family from their home in the Chinese protectorate after the assassination of Kim Jong-nam in Kuala Lumpur. A few rumors circulated which hinted that Kim Han-sol and his family were hiding somewhere in China. The attempted assassination plot uncovered in Beijing was yet another indication that the family was indeed living in the land of the lucky bat.

Nicolaas De Vriese read this news that came over the wires with disappointment. He found it disgusting that the Chinese were claiming to have assisted in the disappearance of KJU's nephew. From the outset, De Vriese had not believed the Chinese when they'd promised that the whereabouts of Kim Han-sol and his mother and sister would remain top secret, known to only a few trusted individuals in the country. Nicolaas had never believed the Chinese would be able to keep Han-sol's location a secret, whether because of a desire of some within the Chinese government to get rid of the young man and protect the despicable KJU or because the Chinese found it impossible to keep a secret, any secret.

Addicted to bribes, members of the Chinese intelligence services were as full of leaks as an antique sieve. Based on these legendary and well-known characteristics of China's secret-keeping abilities, Nicolaas had taken extra special precautions to protect the family that he had cared about for many years. He had arranged their escape and safe house far away without a word to the Chinese.

He had told no one in either the Dutch or Chinese governments or embassies abroad where Han-sol and his family were going into hiding. Only a dozen completely trustworthy individuals in the U.S. intelligence community and a similar few inside Great Britain knew where the family was living. Because Nicolaas did not believe that the Chinese were really ready to give up North Korea as a close ally, no matter what they said in public, the Dutchman had arranged several ruses which were designed to fool both the Chinese and the North Koreans.

One of these ruses was his effort to install, in a secret hiding place in China, a family that closely resembled that of Kim Han-sol. The people were the same ages and the same size. A close look at their faces would reveal that they were not members of the royal family, but their appearances were close enough. Some would be fooled. In fact, there was not only one counterfeit family in place that resembled that of the young challenger to the North Korean throne. There were several of these "families" in place in China, around the Far East, and throughout the world that, from a distance, could be said to look like Kim Han-sol, Kim Sol-hui, and Shin Jong-hui.

One of these imposter families had been set up with a residence in Beijing, and within a few weeks, this family had been murdered by the North Korean agents of KJU. Surveillance cameras outside and inside the residence of the faux family had recorded the attack and the murders of the three at the hands of the North Koreans. The problem was that these agents from the Hermit Kingdom had murdered the wrong family.

Nicolaas had led the Chinese to believe that indeed the real family was living in Beijing, although he always refused to tell the Chinese exactly where in Beijing he had stashed them. The murder of the pretenders confirmed his belief that the family would not be safe in China. Whether the information had been leaked intentionally, accidentally, or because of a bribe, three innocent people were dead by mistake.

The Chinese were unwilling to reveal that the North Koreans had killed anybody. They pretended that it had been merely an assassination attempt, not a murder of three innocent people. The Chinese loudly denounced the North Koreans and were publicly angry with them because there had been an assassination on their soil. But this public and official outrage was all for show. Behind the scenes, the Chinese were furious that the wrong people had been killed. As long as Kim Han-sol was alive, the North Koreans would keep sending hit squad after hit squad after him. The Chinese would have to continue to pretend they were protecting the young man.

When Nicolaas and his team had made arrangements to evacuate Kim Han-sol's family from Macau, the Chinese had insisted that the family must end up going into hiding someplace in China and only China. They wanted Han-sol to spend his exile in a socialist or communist country. They wanted the North Korean, Kim Han-sol, to be indoctrinated into and convinced of the advantages of the collective and state ownership of the means of production.

The Chinese Communists felt living in Macau had been seductive and counterproductive to the values of the socialist totalitarian countries. The Chinese didn't want the possible successor to Kim Jong-un to spend any more time in a country with a capitalist economy.

Nicolaas had solemnly promised the Chinese that the family would end up in China, but he had absolutely no intentions of keeping that promise. Nicolaas told the Chinese that he intended to send the family on a circuitous route through Asia before settling them in one place permanently. He said he wanted to move them around randomly to obscure their trail so that the North Koreans would be confused.

In order to deceive anyone who was watching where the Kim family was going to stay permanently, the Chinese agreed that it was a good idea for Nicolaas to move the family around to different countries. But Nicolaas had to promise that he would never take them to Hawaii or to Japan. The family would be allowed to move through Indonesia, Russia, the Philippines, Thailand, Vietnam, Malaysia, and even Australia, but the Chinese were adamant that they never be allowed to travel to Hawaii or Japan.

Citizens of China were banned from being allowed to visit these two locations. Nicolaas was amused because the Chinese were worried that if Kim Han-sol and his family were allowed to travel to either one of these two places, they might find them to be so wonderful, the family might want to stay. The Chinese didn't want Kim Han-sol and his mother and sister to ever experience the beauty of Hawaii in the United States or the freedom and energy of a thriving Asian economy such as Japan. Canada might have been acceptable as a temporary home for the family because it had some elements of a socialist state in place. But Canada had refused to participate because of their ongoing negotiations with the North Koreans about the release of the Canadian pastor.

Nicolaas had a team of people who moved the pretend royal families, the lookalikes, around with the sole purpose of spreading disinformation about where the Kim family really was. He'd even had the audacity to propose to the Chinese that he move the family through Taipei, Taiwan. The Chinese initially balked at this but finally agreed it would be a good way to throw off any pursuers.

The government of the People's Republic of China were sworn enemies of the government in Taiwan. It would certainly be throwing the North Koreans a curve ball, if they believed the people they were pursuing were living in Taiwan. It was an elaborate game of chess with feints and fakes and lots of slight-of-hand. Nicolaas promoted the complex manipulations as a distraction, a way of masking what he really had done for Kim Han-sol and his family.

Nicolaas trusted all of the people he had asked to help protect the real North Korean family. He had purposely split up the members of the family and had located them in different places. Most of the time the adult children would be living in quarters at their universities. Everyone in the family was living under a new identity with a new name. No one would connect them or think they were members of one family, let alone the Korean royal family. Occasionally the family would be in one place, staying at one house, but that would not happen often. Nicolaas planned to be there himself when the family was together. He felt they were safe temporarily, but he worried a great deal about the long term. Kim Jong-un was never going to give up on hunting down his nephew. He would send out however many assassination squads it took to find and kill him.

Because most of the world would assume the family was living in Asia someplace, Nicolaas felt they were well-hidden in England. More than anything else, Nicolaas wanted to keep the family safe, but he also was hoping that living in a democracy and attending the great universities of Oxford and Cambridge would further open the minds of the younger generation to free speech and the market economy. He scorned the socialist and communist propaganda the Chinese wanted to foist on a possible future leader of North Korea.

Many pieces were moving on the chess board. What the Chinese didn't know was that the real game was being played on an entirely different board, in an entirely different room, in an entirely different building, in an entirely different country, and in an entirely different part of the world. The Chinese were out of the loop. They could chase their tails and leak as many locations as they wanted to about where Kim Han-sol and his family were living in China. Nicolaas hoped that all of his machinations and subterfuge would work until Kim Han-sol was ready to take on the heavy mantle of leadership and return to the country of his birth.

Chapter 11

PYONGYANG, NORTH KOREA

O*f all the things he* liked to do, more than anything else in the world, the Supreme Leader Kim Jong-un enjoyed threatening the United States with nuclear weapons. No one was ever exactly sure what was going on inside his head, but there was no question that whatever was going on in there, it was chaotic and confused. Some days, it seemed as if he were absolutely determined to deliver a nuclear weapon to the shores of the United States. His advisors, mostly those in the military, tried in vain to caution him against attempting to realize this goal. They knew, as everybody in the world knew, that if the North Korean dictator ever launched a nuclear weapon against the United States, the entire country north of the 38th parallel would be obliterated in the blink of an eye. There would be nothing left of North Korea. There would not be a person left alive, and the former Hermit Kingdom would be radioactive into infinity. But Kim Jong-un was not a rational man. He was a petulant little boy, an indulgent petty tyrant who fantasized about his greatness and was not always in touch with reality. He was an incredibly dangerous fellow.

The other thing that competed for Kim Jong-un's attention, in addition to an obsession with his weapons of mass destruction, was his love of exotic and rich food. He flew caviar to Pyongyang from Iran, Kobe beef from Japan, and champagne from France. His people were starving and eating sawdust and millet, but he indulged his excesses with the best that his foreign exchange dollars could buy. He liked to eat shrimp that were still alive. He said he liked the way the shrimp felt when they were wiggling down his throat and swimming around in his alimentary track. He did not know how much was too much, especially with food. He binged and gorged himself on some occasions to the extent that he had to be carried from the table to his bed because he was too stuffed to move away from the table or walk on his own. He was a true hedonist and a glutton.

His doctors had tried to put him on a diet, but he became furious when he was not allowed to eat everything he wanted. All of those around the supreme leader had come to the conclusion that it wasn't worth it to try to monitor or restrict his food and drink intake. He was spoiled, and when he didn't get his way, he flew into a rage. His doctors told him that if he didn't change his terrible diet, he would face an early death. But instant gratification always seemed to win out with KJU. He wanted what he wanted when he wanted it. He was incapable of looking to the future or recognizing that his bad decisions had consequences. Those around him had stopped years ago trying to control his behavior or get him to be reasonable. He knew he was powerful, and part of his fun was to taunt and threaten others with his nuclear toys.

The United Nations had repeatedly levied sanctions on North Korea's exports, imports, and international financial institutions and transactions. The sanctions were designed to pressure KJU to stop making nuclear weapons and to stop trying to develop his ICBM capacity to deliver these weapons to the United States and others. Increasingly stringent measures designed to cripple the economy of the already devastatingly poor country had not, to date, had any impact at all on the rhetoric or actions of the authoritarian ruler. He spent his foreign exchange dollars on imports that did nothing to improve the conditions of his people but had everything to do with indulging and enhancing his own fantasies of glory and power.

His people starved, and he stuffed himself with live shrimp and imported delicacies. The sanctions did not mean anything to this man who was concerned only with his own power and extravagant excesses. If he had been a democratically elected leader, he would have been voted out of office for his bad behavior and because of the things he was doing to bring economic disaster to his country. But this man had no restraints on his nepotistic power. He would continue to ignore the world's disapproval and feed his own selfish and insane desires. It was often difficult to determine at what point the supreme leader's speech and thinking ceased to be framed within the ever-shifting confines of his fragile grasp on reality and became the full-blown hallucinations of a deranged megalomaniac.

None of the sanctions imposed by the world community seemed to have any impact, and somehow Kim Jong-un found the money, even if it was out of the healthcare budget of his people, to buy the yellowcake he needed. He could always manage to bargain for the nuclear triggers, the technical experts from Iran, and the ICBMs from Russia.

He gloated over the fact that some of the yellowcake he used in developing his weapons came from the United States. It was illegal for him to have any of the American yellowcake. He loved the fact that a former U.S. Secretary of State had sold off parts of U.S. uranium reserves to the Russians, and that, after it passed through Canada to undergo an enrichment process, North Korea was receiving some of its yellowcake from Wyoming. He appreciated the irony of the fact that the yellowcake from Wyoming might one day end up as part of an atomic weapon aimed at the United States.

Other rogue states were complicit with North Korea's nuclear ambitions, even as they developed their own weapons. Iran and Russia sent technical assistance to North Korea, and it was feared and rumored that in return for their help, North Korea was supplying Iran with the nuclear capabilities they so desperately wanted. Two reprobate and irrational nations who shared their knowledge and materials, two irresponsible and unpredictable regimes who were in possession of nuclear weapons and were without any constraints on their power, made the world a much more dangerous place.

Iran now had all the money it needed since the United States had made a deal with that country regarding its nuclear weapons. The agreement with Iran was designed to delay Iran's acquisition of a nuclear weapon. There were mixed reviews among the experts and among the public as to whether or not this deal with Iran had been worth the cost. Could this rogue state be trusted? To provide himself with some kind of a foreign policy legacy, the U.S. president had relaxed economic and other sanctions on Iran.

Iran would now be able to buy nuclear weapons technology from North Korea with hard currency. This currency possession would give Kim Jong-un all the international buying power he could possibly want. No wonder KJU ignored and thumbed his nose at the U.N. sanctions. Even the Russians were getting in on the act. Iran was flush with U.S.

cash and was now able to pay Russia for its ICBM technology. Iran in turn could pass on this Russian ICBM technology in exchange for the North Korean nuclear weapons assistance. It was a great deal for all the bad boys in town, all the way around, any way you looked at it.

U.N. sanctions were unable to do anything to bring KJU into compliance or force him to show any restraint, either in his behavior or in his rhetoric. The international community was impotent to influence anything he chose to do. Even China, North Korea's one-time and long-time ally, often lost patience with the naughty little boy in Pyongyang. China was North Korea's most affluent and powerful ally and did not want a collapse of the Kim Jong-un regime. Fearing that the fall of the North Korean dictator would result in South Korean and United States troops occupying the country, China sought to prop up the Pyongyang government. China supported KJU, no matter how dangerous his behavior, to prevent possible reunification of the Korean Peninsula. China did not want Western troops on its border, just across the Yalu river.

KJU almost seemed to thrive on shame and the poor opinions of other nations. He did not give a rip what the rest of the world thought of him. He was drunk on his own power and his own fantasies of destroying the United States. There could be one and only one way to solve the problem and that was to end Kim Jong-un's reign. No diplomatic efforts and no international sanctions were ever going to make any difference. KJU would continue to rant and rave and be a miscreant until he was gone. Removing KJU from power was the only way to solve the problem once and for all.

Some past presidents of the United States had pretended North Korea didn't exist. Others had tried to negotiate with the leader of North Korea. Food and other commodities were given to North Korea in exchange for promises that North Korea would reign in its atomic weapons programs. These past deals had ended up with the USA in the role of major chump because North Korea never lived up to any of the promises it made.

In exchange for what they'd been given, the North Koreans laughed at the gullibility of the Americans and couldn't wait to rope them into another bad deal. After the agreements had been negotiated and North Korea got everything it wanted, they completely ignored their end of the bargains. They could never be trusted, never. A new president might think he could come to terms with these people, and every time he failed. The North Koreans were the crooks of the world. They had no intentions of living up to any compacts they had signed or any promises they had made. They were only about getting what they wanted, and then they betrayed everybody's trust.

Thomas was especially intrigued when he saw the Iranians appear, particularly where he really was not expecting to find them, at the palace of Kim Jong-un. As he sat in front of his computer screen in upstate New York, Thomas found this a fascinating and frightening show to watch, the coming together of two of the oddest and most despicable bedfellows of the decade.

Here were the crazed and fanatical Shia theocrats, who were determined to destroy the state of Israel, hobnobbing with the insane Emperor Roly Poly, who was determined to destroy the United States. It was a mutual admiration society, an association based solely on the desire to inflict horrific destruction in the world. The only things these two outlaw nations really had in common were their quest for power and their desire to annihilate the countries they despised.

It was a curious crowd. The languages of Farsi and Korean are worlds apart, and none of the Iranian potentates spoke Korean. Likewise, none of the important Koreans spoke Farsi. But of course, there were translators who accompanied each retinue wherever they went. Some of these translators were trustworthy, and some were not. Language misunderstandings as well as many other kinds of confusion slowed down the negotiations. The cultures of these two nations were like night and day. The clothing of each group on its own was exceptionally odd by world standards, and the styles were so different from each other. The customs and manners, the demeanor of the two groups of desperadoes were worlds apart. Were these people even from the same planet?

Watching these performers move around in the rooms together was similar to watching a movie in which the actors were partly from a century in the distant past and partly from a cartoon. It was the twilight zone of ancient times meets tin pot funny papers. Their tastes in food were polar opposites, except for the Iranian caviar that everybody loved. Their religious cults were completely at odds. The Iranian cult of Shia Islam was all about Allah, and the North Korean cult was all about Kim Jong-un.

KJU in fact murdered those who refused to accept and worship him as a god. His god-like status had been conferred on him by his father. North Koreans who wanted to practice religions other than the religion that required them to worship the Supreme Leader were killed. Kim Jong-un would accept nothing but adoration as a god. Would these two exceedingly bizarre countries ever be able to reach a consensus about anything?

What they did have in common was their desire to be bullies. Each country wanted to be able to intimidate others with their own nuclear weapons and ICBM technology. That was the driving force that motivated them to try to breach their many differences and come to some kind of an agreement. Iran called constantly for the destruction of Israel. North Korea threatened the United States daily—whether it was Hawaii, Alaska, California, Oregon, or Guam. Iran and North Korea were engaged in an awkward and difficult negotiation, but each party had something the other one wanted. They wanted to make a deal. Both countries eschewed and disdained private enterprise as a contemptible system which was beneath the purity of their socialist fantasies. Now they were in fact brokering for big stakes, bigger than anyone had ever bargained for.

Chapter 12

SKANEATELES, NEW YORK

T*homas was worried. He had* inadvertently stepped into a hornet's nest of a negotiation. He'd been watching terrible trouble in real time, in a virtual and electronic capacity, as the Iranians and the North Koreans got together to share their perilous knowledge with each other. Each regime on its own was a threat, but if they were able to share their nuclear and missile technologies, they would both become much more dangerous players on the world stage.

Thomas was desperate that responsible countries learn of these conversations that were taking place between the Iranians and the North Koreans. He felt he needed to share what he'd observed with trusted intelligence services. Thomas sent videos to all the agencies he thought needed to know about what was happening. In the past, Thomas had sent, anonymously of course, important information to the U.S. and British governments. He immediately sent them copies of the videos he had made of the negotiations that were currently taking place inside the North Korean royal palace. Thomas never left a fingerprint behind, so the agencies who received the videos would never know who had sent them. Thomas had to trust that someone in a position of authority would pay attention to his gift of information and treat it with the credibility it deserved.

One never knew, however, what policymakers in gatekeeper positions would decide was important and what wasn't. In the past, Thomas had sent information he'd acquired, through his hacking, to British and American intelligence agencies, about ISIS and other Middle Eastern terrorists and about possible upcoming attacks in Europe and the United States. The British seemed to pay more attention. But for whatever reason, some of the administrations in Washington hadn't wanted to know about anything that was detrimental or defamatory to Muslims, even the ones who were known to be quite dangerous.

Everybody knows that not all Muslims are terrorists, but everybody also knows that there are some Muslims who are terrorists and want to kill Americans and other nonbelievers all over the world. Unfortunately, Thomas's priceless information about upcoming attacks had often been ignored and shut down. People had died.

Thomas didn't know how the information he hoped to share about North Korea would be handled by the new administration in Washington. The new people in town seemed to be more into chaos than they were into ideology. It was frustrating. Thomas wanted to do his small part to keep his adopted country and other free nations of the world safe, but he felt his often-invaluable information was disregarded. He was being snubbed.

After discovering that there was another group eavesdropping on Kim Jong-un, Thomas was eager to find out more about them. They were trying to keep an exceedingly low profile, and they were doing an excellent job of hiding themselves. Thomas was impressed with their electronic discretion, but he felt he had to find out who they were and what they were doing. In spite of his extraordinary abilities on the Internet, he was having a hard time figuring out who they were and what their agenda was.

Because they were speaking in English, Thomas hoped they were working in conjunction with the United States and/or Great Britain. If this group was on Thomas's side, he wondered if he should share his information and his technology with them, whoever they were. He wanted to help them if they were the good guys. He would not disclose any information he had until he could confirm who the group was and who they were working for.

Thomas shared his concerns with Sergei, and they discussed what Thomas had discovered while monitoring the meetings between the Iranians and the North Koreans. Sergei wasn't surprised that Vladimir Putin had sold his country's ICBM technology to Iran. Everybody knew that was going to happen, once Iran could afford to pay for it. Iran now had cash to finance all kinds of terrorism and trouble-making in the world.

It was disturbing to both Thomas and Sergei that the Iranians were sharing and dealing with the North Koreans. Everybody feared Kim Jong-un's irrational and irresponsible behavior. The fact that KJU was meeting with the Iranians at his palace was very bad news indeed. Sergei told Thomas he would concentrate on trying to find out about the group who was also hacking into Kim Jong-un's palace in real time. If Sergei could find out who was doing that and discover what they were up to, Thomas would be able to decide whether or not to share his information with them.

Although neither one could put a finger on exactly why they felt time was growing short, Thomas and Sergei both felt a sense of urgency about the collusion between the North Koreans and the Iranians. Was it the saber rattling in North Korea? Was it the U.N. finally acting in concert with more stringent sanctions to increase the pressure on the little North Korean despot? Was it the current disorganized administration in Washington which had decided that the North Koreans, after years of U.S. presidential pretending the DPRK didn't exist, could no longer be ignored? There was saber rattling going on in Washington, D.C., too. Was it too little too late?

Even though Thomas had sent the incriminating videos of the Iranians and the North Koreans making a deal, physically together and conspiring in Kim Jong-un's palace, he didn't feel he could leave it to the intelligence agencies of the free world to do anything about it. Thomas did not trust his own government to act on the recent information he had discovered. One past administration had ignored much of the pertinent intelligence that had to do with the buildup of ISIS. One former president had dismissed ISIS as "the JV team" and wouldn't even utter the words "Islamic terrorism." He pretended there was no such thing and wanted to talk about the Crusades.

Terrorists had stormed Charlie Hebdo and a Jewish grocery store. People had been murdered in Paris. Then there was Belgium and Nice and all the rest of the places where Muslim terrorists had killed for the sake of Jihad. The administration in Washington had been determined not to acknowledge those events. Now everybody only seemed to want to talk about climate change. Even when the United States was pretending North Korea didn't exist, the Hermit Kingdom had been steadily and relentlessly building its nuclear arsenal and improving its long-range missile technology.

The pro-Muslim president was gone now, but Thomas didn't have any faith that the new guy would pay any more attention than the previous administration had. He did not trust the government or the intelligence services to take any of it seriously, let alone take action based on the disturbing events he had uncovered.

Thomas was an enormously intelligent man and cared deeply about his adopted country. His success as an inventor was driven by his creativity, not by any need to earn a living or a desire to become richer than he was. He was already quite a wealthy man. He could choose to sail his sailboat or do anything else he wanted to do for the rest of his life. Instead he chose to try to monitor some of the bad guys in the world and do what little he could to expose them and their evil deeds.

Chapter 13

WHIDBEY ISLAND, WASHINGTON, USA

T*he U Group's operational plan* was elaborate and complicated. There were multiple and distinctly separate pieces of the plan. Each part was being prepared in isolation from the other parts. This strategy of separation had been a cornerstone of the secrecy and security precautions that were vital to the U group's mission. If one piece of the puzzle was exposed or compromised, the people involved in one part of the plan would know almost nothing about what was happening with the other parts. It was an insulated cell strategy. You couldn't reveal, if caught and questioned, what you didn't know.

The U Group's central command at Whidbey Island would, when the time came, pull the various pieces together and direct the coordination of the overall operation. The extraction and insertion teams knew what they were supposed to do, and they were ready. The South Korean para-military piece knew what it had to do. The group in charge of diversions, who would set things in motion with overwhelming confusion and multiple distractions, had their plans in place.

The military neutralization faction hoped they would be successful in their role. False trails had been carefully laid. If everything went as anticipated, the multiple parts of the plan would come together as they were intended to. Timing was everything, and the operation would take place over a period of several days.

The extraction and insertion people had studied in detail how the United States' Navy's Seal Team 6 had been able to successfully fly its helicopters undetected across international borders into Pakistan and into the Osama Bin Laden compound. It wasn't easy to breach another country's sovereign airspace, even if that country is an ally. Seal Team 6 had not asked the government of Pakistan's permission to go after Bin Laden, and the Seals had not notified them that they were going into their country to assassinate the Saudi who had helped to mastermind 9/11.

Because the Pakistani intelligence service was believed to be in bed with Islamic terrorists and because many believed that the Pakistani government had been harboring and protecting Bin Laden and his entourage inside their country for years, the Seals could not take the chance that the Pakistanis would leak information about the operation or warn Bin Laden ahead of time. The Seals could not take the chance that Bin Laden would be warned that they were coming. If information about the operation was leaked, they feared that Bin Laden would be moved to a different location. The campaign to take out Bin Laden was well underway before the Pakistanis realized anything was happening. Unlike the operation to assassinate Bin Laden, the U Group's mission was not to kill Kim Jong-un but to capture him and hide him away from the world for the rest of his natural life.

The U Group's insertion and extraction team would go into North Korea using helicopters identical to those used by the North Korean Air Force. The U Group would use MD 500C helicopters in their operation. These McDonnell Douglas aircraft would be painted dark green, the identical color of the helicopters in this class which are used by the military in North Korea. The MD 500C was a general utility helicopter, and several of these aircraft had been procured for use by the U Group. Several years previously, the North Korean Air Force, by circumventing U.S. export restrictions, had illegally obtained eighty McDonnell Douglas MD 500 helicopters. The markings shown on these North Korean Air Force helicopters were copied precisely onto the U Group's five MD 500Cs. The most distinctive marking was, of course, the red star in a white circle, the definitive logo that indicated these aircraft belonged to North Korea.

It was imperative that the U Group's helicopters be indistinguishable from those of North Korea. Having several of these identical helicopters in the air at the same time over the North Korean presidential palace was critical to creating the confusion and mayhem that would surround the U Group's incursion into North Korean air space. The fleet of bogus helicopters would allow the U group to enter the grounds of the Presidential Palace for the purpose of kidnapping KJU and replacing him with a look-alike.

The E-I teams had practiced until they thought they could flawlessly perform the many intricate steps of their maneuvers. Of course, in the real world, even when one thinks one has considered and planned for every possible contingency, the unexpected always rears its ugly and unwelcome head. The E-I teams continued to perfect their skills while they waited on the readiness of the other pieces of the complex operational puzzle. Hopefully, everything would come together when the plan was activated.

Ji-su felt she was ready. She had gained a few pounds, although not as many as her tutors would have liked. Two make-up artists and her costumers had done a remarkable job of transforming her into the Devil Twin. It truly frightened Ji-su when she was in full costume and make-up and looked in the mirror and saw what had become of herself. She shuddered as she tried to find Ji-su inside the plastic contouring of her face and body, the military style uniform, the black square flattop wig that resembled an extremely badly made toupee, and the rest of it. All traces of the young woman she'd once been had disappeared. She hated her enormous double chins. She had become her nemesis. The implants in her face and cheeks and the extra weight of the padding she had to wear were very uncomfortable, but Ji-su never complained.

Ji-su was so committed to her mission that she scarcely felt any pain or discomfort. She knew she would have to wear her disguise for at least twenty-four hours or even longer. She could scarcely contain her impatience until the raid began. She was fanatical about her desire to get on with her part in the drama. She honestly didn't care if she died in the process. It was that important to her. Her tutors worried about her mental health, as well as about her weight.

Part of Ji-su's role as KJU, if her impersonation was able to hold up for any length of time, was to convince

KJU's closest palace guards to assassinate some of North Korea's highest ranking military personnel. Ji-su hoped she would be able to give orders for the executions of key leaders.

Five helicopters, painted to exactly resemble DPNK military helicopters, would invade North Korean airspace. Four helicopters would land in the gardens of Kim Jong-un's palace. One helicopter of the five would be intentionally crashed into a park next to the grounds of the royal palace. Of the four remaining helicopters, two contained the extraction and insertion teams. The other two helicopters belonging to the U Group that would land inside the perimeter of the royal palace were there to cause confusion and to distract from the helicopters that contained the E-I teams.

In addition to the helicopter crash in the park next to the royal palace, a number of other accidents, threats, and confusing and confounding incidents would take place throughout the country. Clever diversions and deceptions at every turn were designed to spread disinformation and delay among the North Korean military. These were intended to create situations which required helicopters. Helicopters would be demanded at the home of the Supreme Leader. Arriving at the royal palace among the helicopters that had been requested and actually belonged to the North Korean military, the phony helicopters would contribute to the pandemonium necessary to allow the U group's critical helicopters with the extraction and insertion teams on board to land and accomplish their mission to abduct KJU and replace him with a member of the U group.

Once the North Korean leader had been taken from North Korea and arrived in South Korea, the South Korean arm of the U Group would take over. The South Korean government knew nothing about the U Group's operation and would of course vociferously and publicly disavow it. Because the operation was not sanctioned by the South Korean government, or in fact by any other government, it was essential that all the planning and activities of the U Group be kept secret. It would be critical to keep a tight lid on all information, especially when KJU was finally on South Korean soil.

The military neutralization force, the MNF, another distinct and separate piece of the U group's organization, had the most difficult job of all. It had the extremely difficult task of trying to prevent a disaster in North Korea, once those in power realized that Kim Jong-un was gone. The whole elaborate substitution and impersonation by Ji-su was an effort to delay the knowledge and realization that Kim Jong-un had been kidnapped. But at some point the truth would inevitably become known.

The U Group needed the substitute KJU to remain in place until the real KJU was successfully apprehended, was spirited out of the Hermit Kingdom, and was secured at his new home in South Korea. Having Ji-su in place for even twenty-four hours would give the military neutralization force a chance to secure the country's atomic, chemical, and biological weapons. And it would give them a little bit of time to exert some control over North Korea's military commanders.

No one in the U Group knew whether or not Kim Jong-un had designed a "dead man's switch" of any kind in case he was ever killed or kidnapped. Suicide vests worn by Muslim terrorists could detonate, even after the person wearing one had died. The U Group worried that Kim Jong-un might have devised a similar kind of nuclear dead man's switch. Would nuclear warheads automatically fly from North Korean airspace if something happened to the leader of the DPNK? No one knew the answer to that critical question, and it was the most urgent concern of the military neutralization force.

The MNF not only had to contend with the nuclear option; they also had to worry about an insurgency within the ranks of the military when the generals and the colonels realized their leader was no longer in the country or in command. A plan to seize control of the military was in place, but that was another unpredictable aspect of the U Group's plan. By necessity, the U Group was operating outside of any legitimate sanctioning by a nation state. The group's ability to manage an entire country's military establishment was limited.

Even if the action were being led by a powerful nation state, that country would be faced with the enormous uncertainty of how loyal the army was to its former leader. Would an unhinged North Korean military leader decide to go down swinging and take out the whole world as he unleashed North Korea's nuclear arsenal without restraint? Would those missiles even fly?

The MNF group had sleeper agents inside the military of the DPNK, but the country was so generally disorganized and unpredictable, there were no guarantees that the military establishment was not also disorganized and unpredictable. The reaction of the military to the loss of their leader was the biggest unknown, the "sticky wicket," in the U Group's plan.

The U Group had worked for years to secretly recruit members of the North Korean armed forces. The U Group wanted and needed first-hand information about what was going on inside the North Korean military. Knowing they would be presented with a volatile situation when their plans for toppling Kim Jong-un came to fruition, the U group wanted their people, their sleeper agents, to be ready on the inside in positions of power. The hierarchy of the Korean People's Army (KPA) was so shrouded in secrecy that one never knew what was rumor and speculation and what was the truth. Did anybody inside the North Korean military really know for sure what was going on?

The military officers who might disagree with Kim Jong-un's policies or his rhetoric, had to keep their opinions to themselves or be executed outright. KJU was infamous for his periodic and murderous purges of the North Korean military's high command as well as for the brutal killings of his own family members. Given these massive violent and fatal rampages the little man engaged in from time to time, it was a miracle that there were any people left to lead the troops. Anyone who strayed even the slightest bit from KJU's posturing and marketing of the national grandiosity was in danger, not only of losing their position in the government and their freedom, but also of losing their lives. The prisons and the mines, as well as the cemeteries, were full of those who had expressed even the slightest disagreement with the Supreme Leader's policies.

Without their dictator, there might be a revolution among the people, and chaos could engulf the entire country. What happened when the United States invaded Iraq was an example to be reckoned with. People who have lived under a brutal and repressive authoritarian regime for decades, those who have never experienced freedom, may be inclined to lose all control when the feared despot is finally gone.

In Iraq, they'd pulled down statues of the old leaders. They'd looted and burned buildings. They'd danced in the streets and shot off guns in a kind of frenzied festivity. When a revolution is in progress, it may not take long for the celebration to get out of control and to become violent. The full consequences of removing Kim Jong-un could not possibly be predicted ahead of time. These outcomes were unknown and of great concern to the U Group. They were doing everything they could to plan for all contingencies, all the possible results that might flow from regime change. But they did not have a crystal ball and could not foretell the future. They could not possibly predict and plan for everything that might happen.

Chapter 14

DNIPRO, UKRAINE AND ODESSA, UKRAINE

P*etro Pavlychko had once been* a proud young Ukrainian design engineer for the Soviet Union's Yuzhmash factory in Dnipro. Petro was a rocket scientist, a real one and an unusually smart one. He worked for Yuzhnoye which was the bureau that designed the rocket engines that were made at Yuzhmash. Yuzhnoye and Yuzhmash produced the country's finest and most powerful rocket engines that propelled the ICBM fleet of the Union of Soviet Socialist Republics.

Petro himself had contributed to building the deadliest missile in the Soviet arsenal, the giant SS-18. He had worked all of his career to improve and perfect the engine which made the SS-18 such a success, the engine that made the Soviet ICBM able to fly halfway around the world. Petro considered the RD-250 engine his baby, his creation. The engine in the SS-18 missile was so powerful it could hold ten nuclear warheads and hurl them thousands of miles across several continents. Petro was proud of what he did for his communist country.

On December 26, 1991, the USSR, Petro's beloved Soviet Union, crumbled and was no more. The end had been a long time coming, but at last the world power, which had pretended for decades to be the equal of its military adversary in the West, broke apart. The old Soviet Union became the much smaller Russian Federation under a non-communist ruler, Boris Yeltsin. Petro's own country, Ukraine, at last established its independence and was now a separate nation state that was no longer a part of Russia.

Petro had never imagined that this could happen. He thought the Soviet Union was invincible and would be a vital force in the world forever. He had spent his entire life working to guarantee that the USSR had hegemony with, and Petro believed superiority over, the West in the area of ICBM engine technology. Petro wondered what would happen to the once powerful nuclear arsenal that had made the USSR and its ICMB rockets such an influence to be reckoned with.

At first, Petro's life in Ukraine changed very little when the new government took control in Russia. At first the leaders of the new Russia continued to want the powerful ICBMs. The factory at Dnipro continued to be one of Russia's main suppliers of the SS-18, even after Ukraine gained its independence. But, as the years went by, it seemed as if the United States and the other countries of the Western alliance were going to be friends with their former nemesis, which had been downsized and transformed into the new Russian Federation.

Petro noticed that priorities had changed. Not as many orders were coming into the factory. There was not as much emphasis on research and development. Not as many resources were being devoted to missile technology or to the technology of improving the engines which powered those missiles. The new Russian Federation had taken over the seat of the old USSR in the United Nations, along with its veto power on the UN Security Council. The Russian Federation, at least initially, seemed to be more interested in making peace with the West and becoming prosperous than it was in building more and more powerful ICBMs and developing more nuclear weapons.

Then Vladimir Putin came to power. He brought with him his ambitions to rebuild the territory and the power of the former Soviet Union. He wanted to put Humpty Dumpty back together again. Fortunately, this goal would prove to be unattainable, but Bad Vlad was determined to seize as much of the world's real estate as he could.

In 2014, Russia annexed Crimea with little trouble. In the aftermath of the 2014 Ukrainian revolution and the ousting of pro-Russian Ukrainian President, Viktor Yanukovych, Putin sent soldiers into Crimea on February 27, 2014. After a very questionable referendum in Crimea, Russia annexed the country into the Russian Federation. It was the most brazen and blatant land grab of the new millennium. Weak and negligent leadership in the United States during those years allowed Russia to get away with marching into another country and, with Nazi-like arrogance, declaring it to be theirs. The United States and the countries of NATO had rolled over and played dead while Russia stole Crimea. The United States and other countries of the West allowed Putin to take Crimea without much of a peep.

The United States and other nations of the world had stood up to Sadam Hussein in 1990 when he had made a similar land grab in Kuwait. In 1939, the countries of Europe had finally come together to take a stand against Adolph Hitler, and they went to war when the little Austrian tyrant had marched into Poland and declared that country was his own. The administration in power in the United States at the time of the Crimean annexation had failed to react and had allowed Vladimir Putin's Russia to get away with aggression of the worst kind.

Petro lived in Eastern Ukraine, and the divisions in his country, both geographical and political, became even more strained and obvious. Ukraine had always been the "Bread Basket of the USSR," and Russia wanted its bread basket back. After the pro-Russian President, Viktor Yanukovych, was ousted and the Russians annexed Crimea, relations between the Russian Federation and Ukraine were in turmoil.

Vladimir Putin wanted to take back Eastern Ukraine. His ultimate goal was to get all of Ukraine back under Russian control. Putin did not believe Ukraine was a separate country. He believed Ukraine was part of Russia. As one facet of his crusade to rebuild the Soviet Union, Putin would be willing to risk everything to bring Ukraine back under Russian domination. Petro hoped, when Russia began to reassert itself in Ukraine that the Russians would ramp up their orders for more ICBMs. But it turned out that the Russians did not want to order any ICBMs and powerful missile engines from the Dnipro factory. The Russian Federation cancelled all upgrades to the missiles carried by their nuclear surface ships and submarine fleets.

Petro suspected that the Russians were afraid to have such a strategically important factory inside a country which regarded itself as an independent entity. Consequently, Petro and the other employees at the Yuzhmash factory were underemployed, and the factory was awash in unpaid bills and low morale. Employees were being laid off, and many Ukrainian missile engineers and atomic experts were out of work. Those who did not lose their jobs might as well have been fired because they were not being paid on a regular basis. The entire town of Dnipro fell on hard times.

Petro Pavlychko was an angry man. He was well-educated, and for much of his career, he had held a position of power and responsibility. His job had paid well by Soviet and Ukrainian standards, and he had been a respected member of the community. All that was gone. His factory now made trolley cars, buses, and tractors. There was no longer any demand for Petro's powerful ICBM engines. There was not enough work at the factory to keep Petro employed full time. He was no longer needed. In fact he did not want a job at a factory that manufactured farm equipment and vehicles for public transportation. It was a slap in the face. Gone was the economic security. Gone was the prestige. Gone was the glory.

In 2010, a group of North Koreans had attempted to steal missile secrets from the Yuzhmash factory. These representatives from the Hermit Kingdom had focused on stealing advanced missile systems, liquid-propellant engines, spacecraft, and missile fuel supply systems. North Korea had already developed its own atomic weapons technology. Now it was attempting to steal the means to launch its nuclear weapons outside the Korean peninsula, primarily at the United States and at North Korea's other enemies around the world. The North Koreans, who'd tried to steal missile technology from the factory at Dnipro, were caught. As far as anyone knew, no hardware or plans of any value were transferred to North Korea at that time.

Petro had not known anything about the attempted theft of missile technology from his factory until the North Koreans were arrested. The embarrassing incident was swept under the rug by those who ran the factory and by the Ukrainian government. However, when his own chance to betray his country came, he did not hesitate. Part of his betrayal was because he did not know what country was really his own.

For most of his early life, he had lived in the USSR. Then he had lived in an independent Ukraine, in a region which had strong ties to the new Russian Federation. Then the 2014 Revolution had changed a great many things in Ukraine. Petro sometimes felt that, living in Eastern Ukraine, he lived in an outlaw part of his own country. Some people in Dnipro were ethnic Russians and felt a loyalty to that country. Some who lived in Eastern Ukraine were from Crimea. Still others were ardent Ukrainian nationalists. Petro didn't really know where he fit in or if he was now a man without a country.

Part of the reason Petro embraced betrayal was because he felt he'd been betrayed by both the Russians and by his own country Ukraine. He no longer had the job he had been trained to do. His betrayal was in part to express his anger as well as a desire to punish those who had taken from him, not only his job, but also his identity. He had lost the prestige of working on ICBMs and was now working on building engines for tractors! It was a terrible blow to his pride and his ego. Most of all, he needed and wanted the money. He was not being paid regularly, and he had bills of his own to pay. His economic situation had deteriorated, along with everything else. When the chance came for him to remedy his economic woes, he jumped at the chance.

The North Koreans did not approach him directly. They had learned from their failed attempt to steal Russian technology in 2010 that they had to be more discreet. Petro was approached by a Ukrainian, a fellow-countryman who was now in the employ and on the payroll of the DPRK. This agent of the North Koreans asked Petro if he would be willing to sell his knowledge and the designs of the mighty RD-250 engine which powered the giant SS-18 ICBM missile.

The amount of money Petro was offered was so large, he never for a minute considered turning it down. He bargained with the North Koreans. He told them that for even more money, he would sell them prototypes, several of the actual engines they wanted to copy and produce in North Korea. Petro knew that these engines were unused surplus, leftover RD-250s forgotten in Russian warehouses. He knew where the engines were stored, and he thought he could gain access to them. He imagined that he had struck it rich.

The deal was made, and details were worked out. Petro would turn over his designs and his knowledge of how to build the RD-250. He would bring five of the already manufactured engines to the port of Odessa on the Black Sea. The North Koreans would deposit the agreed-on sum in a Swiss bank account for Petro. Petro was a savvy scientist and engineer, but he was not a good negotiator. He was even worse at watching his back or anticipating the unexpected. Petro trusted the Ukrainian who was in the employ of the North Koreans, but the North Koreans were the ones in charge. History had shown that they could not be trusted to live up to any agreement of any kind whatsoever.

Petro was still in a position of some authority at Yuzhmash, but asking for five RD-250s to be transferred to Dnipro was taking a big chance. He decided it was worth it, and he made the request. He'd made up a complicated-sounding reason having to do with safety, quality control, fail safes, and whatnot, to explain why he needed to examine five of the high-powered engines. Most of the people who had once known about the engines had forgotten they still existed, that they were sitting virtually in mothballs in a warehouse in the former Soviet Union. But Petro had not forgotten. He finally got permission to have the engines transferred from Russia, and they were sent to him at the factory in Dnipro.

He had promised the North Koreans that he would deliver the engines to a warehouse in Odessa, Ukraine's seaport on the Black Sea. Once he had revealed to them the location of the warehouse where the engines were stored, his part of the deal would be fifty percent completed. Half of his money would be deposited in Switzerland.

The second half of the deal would be concluded when he turned over the designs and drawings accompanied by his written explanations of how to build the RD-250 and install the engine into a rocket. After he had given this critical information to the North Koreans, he would check to see if the remaining half of the promised payment was in his Swiss bank account. When he had confirmed that all of his money had been deposited, the engines and all of the plans would belong to the North Koreans. Petro would be a rich man.

The North Koreans were on their own to figure out how to move their engines out of the warehouse in Odessa and get them to North Korea. Petro would never go back to his job at the Yuzhmash factory. He had plans to move to the French Riviera. He would no longer be bothered by Ukrainian-Russian politics or by Dnipro's harsh winters. He would enjoy his golden years basking in the sunshine and eating French food.

Petro decided he would personally drive the engines from Dnipro to the warehouse in Odessa. He'd never done anything like this before, but he didn't trust anybody else to transfer the engines for him. It wasn't only that he didn't trust anyone else to do it, he didn't really know anybody, trustworthy or not, that he could call on to do it for him.

Petro couldn't move the engines by himself. At a weight of about 1,600 pounds each, just for the engine, one engine was obviously much too heavy for a man to lift. The engines were awkward and large with dimensions of thirty-nine inches in diameter and more than one hundred inches in length. With all of the necessary crating and protective packaging, when ready for shipment, each of the containers which held an engine would weigh considerably more than a ton, more than two thousand pounds.

Petro was an engineer, and he thought he could figure out a way to get the engines to Odessa. He was going to have to hire people to help him. He was going to have to find a heavy-duty flatbed truck to transport the engines. Each crate would have to be secured on the flatbed for the more than eight-hour drive from Dnipro to Odessa. It was a complicated operation. There were many stages to the transport plans, and it was up to Petro to put it all together.

The shape and the weight of the containers would attract attention. Petro personally stenciled each container with large letters, designed to mislead anyone who was curious about the cargo. Each crate that contained a missile engine was labeled as containing "spare aircraft parts." In a way this was true, as the engines inside the crates were intended to be used for something that flew. Petro rented a truck and hired a company that knew how to load and secure the large containers onto the flatbed for transport. If the man who was loading the truck believed his cargo was spare aircraft parts, there was no reason for him to be suspicious and no reason for Petro to be nervous.

Petro had exhausted his savings to rent a warehouse in Odessa. The warehouse had to be large enough to hold the flatbed truck carrying the containers. Petro wanted to be able to drive the truck directly into the warehouse and leave it there. He did not want to have to unload the heavy cargo. The truck was rented, but Petro intended to be long gone before anyone realized that the rented vehicle was never going to be returned. Once he had driven his valuable truckload of freight into the warehouse, Petro didn't intend to unload the flatbed or move the containers. He intended to leave immediately for Switzerland and then for France.

Petro met with the North Korean agent and turned over the keys to the flatbed truck and the information about the location of the warehouse. After the North Korean agent had checked the warehouse and confirmed that the engines were there, he authorized the transfer of half of Petro's funds to Switzerland. Petro used his computer to check his Swiss bank account to be sure that half the money he'd been promised had indeed arrived. It had, so Petro turned over the plans and other paperwork essential to building the RD-250 engine and making it operational.

At his hotel in Odessa, Petro checked his Swiss bank again to see if the second half of his money had been deposited. As he was using his laptop to access his account, there was a knock on the door of his room. A man's voice said, "room service." It was the oldest trick in the book. Even though Petro knew he had not ordered from room service, he answered the door anyway. A man with a gun and a silencer shot him twice in the heart and once in the face. Petro died before he'd even opened the door all the way. The man took Petro's computer from the desk in his hotel room, hung the "Do Not Disturb" sign on the outside of the door, and left Petro lying dead on the carpet in a pool of blood.

Petro's Swiss bank account that had been intended to finance his future, a future filled with warm weather and pâte de foie gras, was emptied before Petro's body began to cool. It would be two days before Petro was found. It would not be the first time a hotel maid had found a man dead from an assassin's bullets in one of the rooms in the Odessa hotel.

Chapter 15

ODESSA TO PYONGYANG

Within an hour of Petro's death, the flatbed truck loaded with ICBM missile engines was sitting on a remote pier at the Port of Odessa. Each of the crates on the truck had been stamped with several additional words that indicated it was being shipped to an import-export company in Singapore. Within two hours of Petro's death, the engines had been loaded into the deepest cargo hold of a Greek cargo ship sailing under the Panamanian flag. No one aboard the freighter suspected there was anything special about the five crates of spare airline parts which had been taken on as cargo in Odessa.

The freighter had also taken on one passenger at the last minute, but he hadn't shown any particular interest in the crates of spare airline parts. The bill of lading said that the five crates were headed to Singapore with a transfer in Goa. Most of the other cargo on this particular freighter was also going to Goa on the west coast of India. Within three hours of Petro's death, the Greek freighter had departed the Port of Odessa and was headed on its long and circuitous journey out of the Black Sea through the Bosphorus Strait to the Aegean Sea and into the Mediterranean. The Greek ship would proceed through the Suez Canal, into the Red Sea, through the Strait of Bab-el-Mandeb, and into the Indian Ocean. It would be days before the cargo reached its first transit point, the city of Mormugao, Goa's main port.

The five large and heavy crates containing the ICBM engines never left the pier in Mormugao. Each crate was loaded onto a special vehicle the size of a heavy-duty John Deere Gator. The five carts were attached one behind the other and driven in tandem resembling a train. The train of carts drove to a place on the pier where a smaller Indonesian ship, the *Sahanaya Star*, was docked. The Sahanaya Star was flying the Liberian flag. The carts drove directly up the gangway onto the deck of the ship and were secured in a special garage-type cargo area. No one seemed to give the train of five carts a second glance. Once again, a passenger booked a cabin aboard the Sahanaya Star at the last minute. He seemed unconnected to any of the ship's cargo.

The Sahanaya Star left Goa and headed for the Port of Singapore. It was a long and complicated route. Once in Singapore, which is the world's second busiest international port, the five carts rolled off the Sahanaya Star and onto the pier. The carts were driven to a remote area of the port where they sat for more than twenty-four hours. The driver and a couple of men with guns stood guard over the little train to be sure nothing was stolen. The next night, a somewhat derelict North Korean fishing boat docked at the out-of-the-way berth, a distant pier at the Port of Singapore.

The fishing boat probably had a name, but it didn't have the name painted on its stern for all the world to see. The anonymous fishing boat had just unloaded a shipment of shark fins and shrimp. Its cargo areas that usually carried seafood were now empty. The fishing boat had been especially prepared to receive the carts carrying the crates that were marked as spare airline parts. A wide, sturdy plank was put in place to connect the pier with the boat, and the carts easily rolled up the gangway and onto the vessel. Once on the deck of the fishing boat, each cart proceeded to its own individual compartment. The five compartments, each of which had been specially built to conceal a cart, would appear to anyone who came aboard the fishing boat to be part of the ship's bulkheading. The fishing vessel didn't expect to be stopped on its return trip to North Korea, but if it were searched, no one would find anything.

The passenger who had traveled inconspicuously with the ICBM engines since they had left the port of Odessa was greeted warmly by the captain of the North Korean fishing vessel. The two watched the loading of the carts into their individual compartments and went to the captain's quarters for a celebratory drink. Within forty minutes of its arrival at the remote pier in Singapore, the North Korean fishing boat was loaded and headed out on its return trip. It had been a precision operation. The five Russian ICBM engines were now on their way to North Korea and into the arms of Kim Jong-un.

The engines were a few of the final pieces in the Supreme Leader's quest to become a full-fledged nuclear power. The engines that would be modeled on these Russian prototypes would power the intercontinental ballistic missile systems the North Koreans so desperately wanted to be able to build and launch at their enemies. The North Koreans already had their atomic warheads, and now they would be able to weaponize their nuclear technology.

The Iranians, flush with cash after sanctions had been lifted as part of the Iranian nuclear deal with the United States, made another of many deals with the North Koreans. They'd bought the knowledge about how to make a nuclear weapon from the North Koreans with the money they had received from their deal with the USA. The North Koreans used the money they'd been paid by the Iranians to finance the research and development of their own ICBM technology. Both rogue states had been able to get what they wanted. It was win, win, all the way around for two of the world's worst troublemakers.

On July 4, 2017, North Korea fired an ICBM that stunned the world. The North Korean missile carried its payroll farther than any of the nations of the civilized world had thought was possible. The Hermit Kingdom, later in the month of July 2017, fired a second long range ballistic missile that proved once and for all that North Korea did have advanced ICBM technology and was not just a one-trick pony. KJU was ready to take on the United States, and the world was plunged into another dangerous round of threatening bellicose words and saber rattling.

Chapter 16

SKANEATELES, NEW YORK AND SERGIYEV POSAD, RUSSIA

Acutely aware that dangerous events were transpiring in North Korea, Thomas had listened in on the deals that had been made and were being made between Kim Jong-un and the Iranians. He continued to monitor the activities of the North Korean nuclear program. But it was Sergei who finally figured out what the mysterious U Group on Whidbey Island was up to. Sergei had uncovered the plans of the secretive unit of English speakers who were also monitoring in real time, the comings and goings in North Korea's royal palace. Sergei did not grasp the full complexity or know all the details of the U group's plans, but he thought he had figured out that they were attempting the incredibly daring move of kidnapping the Supreme Leader of the DPNK, Emperor Roly Poly, the infamous KJU. Sergei also suspected that the group hoped to substitute a look-alike for the little despot, to insert their own ringer in his place.

Sergei didn't know if the plan was to try to leave the substitute in the royal palace for a few hours or days or whether the plan was to leave a fake Kim Jong-un in place for the long term. It was an impossibly ambitious plan. Sergei wondered if the people who were organizing this mission had any idea how unlikely their chances were for success. He hoped and wished they would succeed. He would love to see Kim Jong-un gone forever from the news and from the world stage where he strutted around like a stuffed pepper and threatened other countries on a daily basis. Sergei wondered how any group could hope to accomplish this audacious plot. If somehow they were able to achieve the impossible, what would the consequences be for North Korea and for the world?

Sergei's discovery of the U Group's plans to kidnap KJU and leave a look-alike in his place definitely got Thomas's attention and brought him on board the North Korean project full time. Thomas worried that what this group was planning to do was something too extreme. He worried that they were foolish to think they had the ability to achieve it. The group was not connected, at least that either Sergei or Thomas could determine, to a particular country. They were not discernibly linked to any official intelligence agency in the world or to any military organization. How could they possibly hope to have a prayer of accomplishing their mission?

Thomas and Sergei both continued to be intrigued and puzzled by the origins and identity of this anonymous group that was attempting to do the unimaginable. Everyone in the U Group spoke English, but its members apparently were from several different countries. Because the organization did not appear to be sponsored by a particular nation state or group of nations, the source of their funding was difficult to trace. Thomas had always believed in following the money, but whoever was funding and directing this group was so secret that Thomas couldn't find out who it was. His inability to discover more about the group was a challenge.

He and Sergei decided that a top priority for their time and attention was to discover who this group was and to monitor every step they took towards achieving their difficult if not impossible task.

There were at least two venues that needed to be monitored in real time. Thomas and Sergei began to actively watch the U Group on Whidbey Island at the same time they were watching the North Korean royal palace. Sergei was the first to find Ji-su, and when he saw her on his computer screen, he began to understand what this mysterious U Group had in mind.

Somewhere they had found a person who resembled KJU, a female who spoke Korean with a North Korean accent. Sergei saw her both when she was dressed in her disguise as the Supreme Leader and when she was dressed as herself. He was amazed at the uncanny and extraordinary facial resemblance between the slim, unknown young woman and the fat and infamous North Korean leader. Sergei was likewise stunned at the skill of the makeup and costume people who had been able to transform a skinny woman into a very fat man. The alterations had been so complete, Sergei thought she might actually be able to fool everybody into thinking she really was KJU. He realized, however, that she would be able to pull off the ruse only for a short period of time.

Clearly, the young woman had a costume that was convincing as long as the stuffing and the plastic stomach and all the rest of it remained in place. Sergei could not imagine what would happen once it was time for KJU to bathe or undress to go to bed. The substitution would be totally exposed when one of those moments arrived. Whoever was preparing the young woman for the impersonation did not intend for her to fool anybody for very long. Thomas and Sergei agreed they needed to devote more time to watching the mysterious woman who could be made to look like the North Korean leader.

It was decided they would divide their time between the two critical sites. Sergei would spend his time electronically monitoring the young woman on Whidbey Island who so closely resembled KJU. She was clearly the key to the entire enterprise this group was attempting to undertake. If Sergei watched her activities, he would know when her organization's plan went operational. Sergei would know, when the woman was moved from her training base on Whidbey Island, that something was going down.

Sergei named her in his own mind, The Thin One, because of the contrast between her body build and that of Kim Jong-un. He would watch her and try to think of a way that he and Thomas could protect her. He was concerned that she had already resigned herself to not being able to return from her mission. How could anyone hope to get out of the spot into which she was willingly putting herself?

As they observed and got to know the various players, Thomas and Sergei learned more about the mysterious U Group that was undertaking this preposterous scheme. However ridiculous the plan seemed to be and however hopeless they believed it would be to achieve a successful outcome, the two men developed great sympathy and respect for these courageous few who had taken it upon themselves to do something so outrageous.

Although both Thomas and Sergei wanted to do what they could to help, they decided they would only watch and wait for the time being. They didn't want to upset the plans of the group by announcing that they were watching what was going on. Because the group was clearly obsessed with secrecy, Thomas and Sergei guessed that any sign from an outsider that the group's operation had been discovered might cause an immediate shutdown and perhaps a cancellation. They didn't want to frighten these people who were working so hard to remove the Evil Emperor.

Thomas knew his real time hacking and translation software were superior to what the unknown group had. He had observed that their spying on the royal palace in real time was spotty and often had gaps. He wanted to find a way to transfer his superior monitoring technology to them. He wanted them to have more consistent coverage so they wouldn't run into blind spots. Even if the U group failed in its efforts to substitute the young woman for KJU and even if the entire operation turned out to be a disaster, Thomas and Sergei wanted to assist these people, this brave and secret organization. To Thomas and Sergei, it looked like a suicide mission all the way around, but they wanted to do all they could to help.

There were so many things Thomas and Sergei wanted to know. What was the group's activation timetable for their project? How long did they dare to leave their impersonator in place and expect her to continue to fool those closest to KJU? What would be the reaction of the North Korean generals once they realized their Supreme Leader was gone? Would they unleash their nuclear weapons on the world in anger and retaliation? What were other elements, if any, that the mysterious group had put in place as part of the kidnapping scheme? How would they gain access to the presidential palace to extract KJU and insert his clone? Were they planning to kill KJU? It wouldn't be a loss to the world if that's what they hoped to do. If they didn't intend to kill him, what were they going to do with him? Where would they take him?

Had the woman who would take the place of KJU already

resigned herself that she would be a martyr? Did she plan to die as part of her mission? What about those who would be taking KJU out of the royal palace and inserting the young woman in his place? Did they think they could possibly survive this high-risk undertaking?

Thomas and Sergei watched and waited. They collected information and tried to figure out exactly what the U Group's plans were. Thomas sent videos to various intelligence agencies about what was going on inside the palace of the Supreme Leader, but he decided to keep the U Group's existence a secret from everyone. Sergei watched Ji-su and saw what everyone saw who watched this young woman. She was obsessed with her mission. She never relaxed. She pushed and punished herself with the preparations for her part in the upcoming drama. Sergei worried about her as everyone who got to know her worried about her. Both Thomas and Sergei sensed that the "go" signal for the operation was coming soon. Whoever was pulling everything together seemed to be waiting for something—a date, a time, an event that would be the signal that it was the moment for their plan to unfold.

The rhetoric between the United States and North Korea escalated. The United Nations' Security Council added additional sanctions against the Hermit Kingdom, designed to severely restrict and hurt the economic activity of this already poor country. North Korea shot medium-range missiles over the non-nuclear nation of Japan—twice! During the last week of August 2017, North Korea fired a missile that flew over the northern Japanese Island of Hokkaido. Pyongyang was increasing the nuclear stakes and putting the entire world at risk for nuclear holocaust. Emperor Roly Poly was wallowing in his own hubris.

The United States and South Korea participated in their most intense and flamboyant joint war games in decades. North Korea threatened to attack the American military outpost of Guam. The United States rolled out a new airplane and flew it over and around the Korean Peninsula. The world was getting way too hot and way too volatile for comfort.

North Korea announced that on Sunday, September 3rd, it had successfully conducted a test on a hydrogen bomb. This was the sixth nuclear test conducted by the Pyongyang regime. North Korea had conducted its first atomic test in 2006. The September 2017 underground explosion created a 6.5 magnitude earth tremor that was felt in South Korea and China, making this bomb the most powerful weapon North Korea had ever tested.

Experts said the blast was four to sixteen times more powerful than any the North Koreans had set off before and was an explosion in the hundreds of kiloton range, roughly equivalent to 100,000 tons of TNT. This weapon was said to be potentially far more destructive than the bombs dropped on Hiroshima and Nagasaki during World War II. Pyongyang stated that their hydrogen bomb could be fitted into the nose cone of its ICBMs which it had tested in July. This may have been the final straw for the United States and for the world.

Chapter 17

NORTH KOREA

What no one was expecting, or at least what no one would ever admit they were expecting, was the surprise United States bombing attack on North Korea. A few minutes after midnight on the morning of September 11, 2017, B-1B Lancer bombers and other planes took off from Naval Base Guam and Andersen Airforce Base, also known as Joint Region Marianas on the island of Guam. Why that particular date was selected was never explained. Had September 11th been chosen because of its symbolic value; because the weather was just right; because all of the pieces for the operation were finally in place; because the situation with North Korea had become untenable as it existed; because North Korea had quite recently set off its most powerful nuclear weapon to date and claimed it was a hydrogen bomb; or because the United States had finally become sufficiently angry that it decided to put the North Koreans in their place on that day? September 11th was the day the sky finally fell for Kim Jong-un.

The B-1Bs reached their objectives in North Korea in the early morning hours. Daylight was no longer necessary to identify and decimate a target. No nuclear weapons were loaded into the bomb bays of the U.S. bombers. But the weapons that would rain their destruction down on the nuclear facilities, hidden deep inside the caves and hundreds of feet below the surface of the ground, and other targets in North Korea, were anything but harmless. The predecessors of these weapons had been known as "bunker busters" during the first Gulf War in the early 1990s. During the ensuing nearly thirty years, these bombs had been made even more powerful and even more precise. The U.S. military thought it knew the locations of every nuclear weapons production and storage facility in North Korea, every location where ICBMs were being manufactured and stored, and everywhere that biological and chemical weapons were hidden.

Part of the bombing mission in North Korea had to include destruction of the conventional artillery the North Koreans had positioned near the DMZ ready to attack South Korea. Every possible way for Kim Jong-un to retaliate had to be taken out simultaneously. It was a total onslaught. Everything had to be destroyed at the same time, for fear that Kim Jong-un would retaliate, when he realized that the pipe dream he'd had for his country to become a nuclear power, an atomic player on the world stage, was gone. Would he send an undiscovered or unaccounted for weapon to destroy South Korea or Alaska?

There was one and only one chance to destroy North Korea's nuclear and other dangerous weapons' capabilities. Everything had to be wiped out in a first strike. The bombing was precise and directed in such a way that the North Korean civilian population was minimally impacted. The goal was not to destroy the entire country or to kill any of the poor souls who were living under the thumb of the North Korean madman. The goal was to castrate his ability to wage war against others, especially with his weapons of mass destruction. Military planners in the U.S. had for years been keeping track of the locations of North Korea's weapons and missiles. The U.S. planes that had attacked North Korea were gone by the time the sun rose that morning. The September 11th assault was the first and last opportunity to destroy Kim Jong-un's ability to harass or harm the world.

The U Group's own operation had begun only a few hours before the massive attack on the major military facilities in North Korea. Someone in the U Group had to have known what the American super power had planned. The U Group had sent their players into the game ahead of time. The timing could not have been coincidental. Likewise, someone in the United States military had to have known about the U group's plan to kidnap the North Korean leader and leave a substitute in his place. Someone had to have coordinated the timetables for both operations in such a way that the U Group's mission would take place almost simultaneously with the major assault on the North Korean weapons installations.

No one who was involved on the ground with the U group's plans would ever admit that they knew what was coming from the United States military. It was true that most of them didn't know, but the congruence of the timing said it all. The U Group's helicopters had taken off from their staging island in the Pacific, and the U Group's operation was launched, a few hours before the major bombing assault by the United States began.

The U Group's operation started with multiple well-planned distractions and the creation of chaos in various parts of the North Korean kingdom. The U Group wanted as many of North Korea's own helicopters buzzing around in the air as possible. Diversions had been planned such that North Korean helicopters and military personnel would be required to deal with various disturbances and rescue efforts throughout the country. Resources would be strained in this country which was disorganized to begin with and not even competent in many respects, especially when it came to taking care of its citizens' needs. Civilians and their well-being had never been a high priority in North Korea.

The U Group wanted North Korea's resources responding to trouble. They wanted multiple helicopters in the air outside of Pyongyang as well as in the immediate area around the royal palace. It would be under the cover of these real North Korean military helicopters, hovering in chaotic confusion, that the U Group's own helicopters would enter North Korean air space and make their way to the palace in Pyongyang. The perfectly painted bogus U Group helicopters would meld seamlessly with the real North Korean helicopter fleet that was responding to the confusion that was occurring throughout the country, especially in the area around the royal palace.

One of the favorite ways that ethnic North Koreans, who were lucky enough to have escaped the Hermit Kingdom and live in China, celebrated their weddings was to have the ceremony and the reception aboard a hired boat that traveled on the Yalu River. The wedding party and guests boarded the watercraft which was decorated and decked out to celebrate the nuptials. There was such a demand for this kind of wedding that an entire industry had grown up to accommodate the custom. There were wedding boats which did nothing but provide exclusive settings for these celebrations. The boats were equipped with catering services, and in fact provided the entire matrimonial package. It wasn't an inexpensive way to get married, and only those with sufficient funds could afford the Yalu River wedding excursions.

A lucky ethnic North Korean couple who lived in China was celebrating their wedding and reception on board one of these special wedding boats in the late afternoon of September 10th. The happy pair and their guests were enjoying the traditional dish of noodles cooked in beef broth and the other special food associated with Korean weddings. Many of the guests were quite drunk by the evening. The Yalu was a busy river, and it was not unheard of that boats ran into each other while navigating their way up and down the waterway.

At the moment when the wedding festivities were in full swing, a Chinese freighter out of Hong Kong plowed into the side of the wedding boat. Guests who were dancing and frolicking on the deck of the party ship were tossed around, and quite a few were thrown into the waters of the Yalu. The collision had occurred exactly at the point where the wedding party boat was passing closest to the North Korean shore. Getting as close as possible to North Korea was part of the risk, the excitement, and the fun of having one's wedding on the boat that skirted the boundaries of the Hermit Kingdom, taunting the Kim government and the poor people who still lived in that sad place. At the moment when the wedding boat drew closest to the North Korean shore, it was struck a fatal blow and began to sink.

More than one hundred wedding guests had to be recovered from the water. Those who had been thrown into the water and couldn't swim had to be rescued when the freighter crashed the wedding boat. Both North Korean and Chinese responders rushed to the river to try to save lives. Those wedding guests who could swim, made their way to the North Korean shore which was the land refuge closest to where the wedding boat was sinking. Those who were in the water and couldn't swim clung to those who could and tried to survive in the cold waters of the Yalu until they could be rescued and taken to safety. It was complete chaos, a major tragedy resulting in a number of casualties.

The collision of the two vessels put a severe strain on the emergency response resources of the North Koreans and on Chinese responders out of Dandong. Assets available to respond to an emergency in North Korea were scarce to begin with, and they were unprepared to deal with the boat accident on the Yalu River. It was necessary to call for help from all over the country to try to handle the situation.

During the chaos of the not-so accidental accident and the subsequent rescue, several operatives of the U group team who had been "guests" at the wedding on the boat were able to slip into North Korea. They swam to shore, changed into the North Korean military uniforms they carried, wrapped in plastic in their handbags, and made their way toward their rendezvous in Pyongyang. A group of three of these "guests" found the vehicle that had been left for them. They had their fingers crossed that the old Russian car would make it to the North Korean capital.

Various accidents and explosions, fires, traffic incidents, and a plethora of other distractions and disruptions, were planned to occur simultaneously to put a strain on civilian and military rescue resources in North Korea. All of this chaos occurred throughout the country within a small window of time. The objective was to create so many crises, large and small, that deployment of resources would be in turmoil and strained beyond their capabilities.

At almost the precise moment the Chinese freighter collided with the wedding boat, a helicopter that appeared to be a North Korean military helicopter crashed into a park next to the grounds of the royal palace in Pyongyang. The helicopter was immediately engulfed in flames. Emergency responders rushed to the scene of the crash, and additional military helicopters flew to the scene. The helicopter which crashed into the park had all the same markings as the helicopters of the North Korean Air Force, but the North Korean Air Force reported that it did not think it had any helicopters missing. Military officials went to the park to investigate. Because the crash had occurred so close to the presidential palace, additional helicopters from throughout the region were called in. Confusion reigned.

As all of this bedlam was unfolding, three of the U Group's helicopters, disguised as belonging to the North Koreans, landed on the grounds of the royal palace. One additional U group helicopter hovered in the air awaiting its signal to land in the garden, close to the area of the palace where the North Korean dictator had his suite of rooms. This helicopter that waited in the air carried Ji-su who was more than ready to step into her role of impersonating Kim Jong-un.

Satellites, drones, and human intelligence had been tracking the exact whereabouts of Kim Jong-un minute by minute up until and including the exact moment the helicopters landed in his garden. When the three U Group helicopters landed, South Korean nationals dressed in North Korean military fatigues and armed with machine guns rushed into the royal palace. Body guards and servants fell as the barrage of bullets from the weapons of the U Group cleared the way for the extraction team to proceed.

Two members of the U Group team were wounded in the assault, one critically, as they made their way into the inner sanctum of the North Korean leader. KJU had a safe room, and it was essential that he be grabbed and secured before he made it into this hideout.

The extraction team had to kill his closest body guards to get to Kim Jong-un, but they finally were able to put their hands on him. He was immediately sedated with an injection from a hypodermic needle and put inside a specially prepared steel box on wheels. The steel box was spirited out of the royal palace. All the hours spent practicing in a mock-up of the palace had paid off. The extraction team moved quickly and confidently to secure their prisoner and move him to the waiting helicopter. The extraction team had done its job, and within several minutes of landing on the grounds of the presidential palace, three U Group helicopters, one carrying two wounded members and one carrying their roly poly prize, were in the air and on their way back to their secret staging island in the Pacific.

As soon as Kim Jong-un was in the hands of the extraction team, the insertion team's helicopter landed in the North Korean leader's personal garden. It was chaotic inside the palace, and the insertion team, with automatic weapons drawn and firing, carried Ji-su, who was wrapped in a cloak that hid her completely, into the inner sanctum of the North Korean dictator. Kim Jong-un was at that moment unconscious and being lifted out of North Korea by another U Group helicopter.

As soon as the insertion team reached Kim Jong-un's safe room, they opened the door, shoved Ji-su into the safe-room hidey-hole, and dragged two of the more seriously wounded body guards into the room with her. The room was locked with the faux Kim Jong-un and two dying body guards secured inside. While Ji-su was being secured in the safe-room, one member of the U group had hidden her escape motorcycle in a garden shed. The insertion team had done its job, and within minutes of landing, this helicopter was also on its way back to the staging island in the Pacific.

Kim Jong-un, who was still unconscious, was safely and securely in the hands of the U Group's South Korean resettlement team, hours before the United States' B-1B bombers took off from Guam. And Ji-su who looked exactly like the man she had been created to impersonate was safely locked in the North Korean president's safe-room before the U.S. attack on North Korea began.

Chapter 18

SKANEATELES, NEW YORK AND SERGIYEV POSAD, RUSSIA, NORTH KOREA

What the U Group did not know was that Thomas and Sergei had been monitoring every move they'd made from the moment the U Group's first helicopters landed on the grounds of the North Korean leader's palace. The two men had watched as KJU was drugged, put into the container with wheels, and loaded aboard the U group helicopter. They'd watched as the helicopter carrying Ji-su landed. They saw her covered with a cloak, being hustled into the presidential palace.

Thomas and Sergei had not only observed, they had also helped the U Group operatives as they made their way through the palace. Members of the U Group had no idea the Thomas and Sergei were watching them from thousands of miles away. Thomas was watching from Skaneateles, New York, and Sergei was watching from Sergiyev Posad in Russia. These two cyber helpers had been their all-seeing guides for the operation. Both Thomas and Sergei had been able to see what the operatives on the ground could not always see.

They tapped into the communications systems the U Group operatives were using. Each member of the U group on the ground was wearing an earpiece.

Thomas and Sergei had been able to warn the men and women who were rushing into the palace to look left or right for threats they might not have seen. They told them when trouble was coming unexpectedly around the corner or through a doorway. They were able to assist the operation in other ways that greatly reduced the U Group's casualties. These warnings and instructions were given to the U Group as a disembodied voice speaking English through the earpieces to members of the extraction and insertion teams.

It was not until the debriefing after the operation that the U Group teams began to ask each other who had been giving them instructions and warnings through the earpieces. Because the U Group had no idea anyone else was in on their operation, it was as if an omniscient being or aliens from outer space had been able to see what they were doing. They knew the help had not really been aliens from outer space. They knew an unknown entity had compromised their security, but in a good way. The mysterious voice that had spoken to them through their earpieces had guided them and warned them of dangers inside the palace. Lives had been saved because of this unknown but all-knowing and all-seeing benefactor.

Thomas and Sergei had been watching and waiting for weeks. They'd known an operation was imminent and had figured out how to break into the U Group's communication systems. The two former Russian spies wanted to help, although they did not have much confidence that the U Group had a snowball's chance in hell of succeeding in their mission. Sergei had been watching and listening to everything that happened to Ji-su, and when she disappeared from the Whidbey Island compound in the middle of the night, he knew the U Group's operation was a go. Ji-su was the key, and when she was put on board an airplane and moved to the staging area in the Pacific, Sergei knew the action had begun.

Thomas always listened in on U.S. military operations, and he knew something extraordinarily big was in the works for North Korea. Neither Sergei nor Thomas had been able to figure out what the relationship was between the U Group and the U.S. military, if indeed there was any relationship. The U Group's members who were headquartered at Whidbey Island seemed to be made up of people from many countries, not only from the United States. Thomas had not been able to find any definite link between the U Group's upcoming operation and whatever the U.S. was planning for North Korea. It seemed to Thomas that the U Group was operating completely independently of any nation state's authority.

Thomas watched troop movements and movements of ships and planes of many countries throughout the world. He had rigged a map on a television screen in his library. Whenever a ship or a significant number of aircraft from a major developed country moved from one place to another, a computer program automatically moved a symbol of that ship or plane on Thomas's map. Each ship and plane carried the flag of its nation. Thomas could see at a moment's glance where most of the world's military ships and planes were positioned at any given time. He had observed during the latter part of August that the U.S. Navy and Airforce were moving significant numbers of planes and personnel to Guam. Kim Jong-un had specifically threatened to attack Guam, so increasing the U.S. military presence on this small island was not a surprise.

It was the magnitude of the movements of resources that tipped Thomas off that something big was about to happen. Weeks earlier, several aircraft carriers began their slow maneuvering through the waters of the Indian Ocean and the Sea of Japan towards South Korea. War games and exercises with South Korea were given publicly as the excuse for the carrier movements, but Thomas knew this was more than a joint military exercise or a practice run for the United States. He wasn't able to put an exact time or date on when the military operation would begin, but he was certain that there would soon be a decisive military move against North Korea.

Thomas would never presume to interfere with U.S. military operations, but he felt he could contribute something to the U Group's attempts to kidnap North Korea's dictator. Thomas was skeptical that the U Group could succeed in such a daring and foolhardy attempt, but he and Sergei were going to do everything they could, in a virtual sense, to assist. Both men were amazed when the U Group had succeeded in seizing Kim Jong-un and spiriting him away from his presidential palace. Even as they were actively giving instructions to aid the insertion team on the ground as it carried Ji-su into the palace and then into the safe room, the two former spies were shocked that the U Group had so far accomplished an almost unbelievable feat.

Sergei had become concerned and even convinced that Ji-su had decided she was participating in a suicide mission. There didn't seem to be any provision for extricating her when it was ultimately revealed that she was not really Kim Jong-un. And the substitution would eventually and inevitably be revealed. The only question was how long it would take before she was exposed as an imposter. She looked the part and had practiced long and hard to be convincing in her role, but the ruse could not continue for many hours or days going forward. She was doomed.

Sergei was worried sick that there was no plan to save her life once she had been found out. He realized that, during the months he had watched her train and prepare for her role as a stand-in for the North Korean president, he had grown to respect and admire this young woman. She was willing to risk everything to take out an evil dictator and to try to save the world from a nuclear holocaust that could be brought on by an egomaniacal madman.

Sergei also found himself fighting a little something, nagging at his brain and maybe at his heart, that suggested he might have developed a fondness for the beautiful North Korean orphan who was so single-minded in her dedication. Sergei knew he didn't want her to die. He wanted to save her life, if possible. But what does one do if the person whose life one is trying to save doesn't want to be saved? Sergei was worried that Ji-su had decided there was no escaping from the North Korean palace, that her death was inevitable. She acted as if she wanted to die or at least was indifferent to whether she lived or died. Sergei was determined that she would live.

Both Sergei and Thomas had recorded everything they'd observed during their weeks and months of keeping watch over the North Korean presidential palace. Thomas had sent many videos to various U.S. and British intelligence agencies of the Iranians meeting and making deals with the North Koreans. Thomas and Sergei had documented everything, for themselves and for posterity. Sergei went back over the tapes of Ji-su's insertion into the palace. There was something he had seen that had sparked his curiosity but which he'd not had the chance to follow up on with everything else that was happening during those chaotic and drama-filled minutes when KJU had been taken from the palace and Ji-su had been inserted.

Someone had brought something from Ji-su's helicopter and hidden it in a garden shed near KJU's private patio. Sergei thought he'd seen a small motorcycle being hoisted out of the helicopter and pushed into the shed. He reran the footage of Ji-su's arrival at the palace and sure enough, he saw a motorcycle being secured behind lawn mowing equipment in the garden shed. He was amused that for all the man's hatred of America and everything made in America, KJU had chosen a John Deere riding lawnmower that somebody used to mow the grass in his private garden sanctuary. What a hypocrite he was, but of course there were no factories that produced tractors in North Korea. He would have had to buy a lawn mower from someplace else, and he had bought the best for his own garden.

Sergei had to think about the implications of the presence of the motorcycle. It had been brought by Ji-su's insertion team and was secured inside the supreme leader's private quarters and gardens. Sergei guessed that the motorcycle was for Ji-su to ride when she was ready to make her escape. But where would she ride, and what or who would be waiting for her when she got there? Was she planning to ride a motorcycle all the way to South Korea? Sergei knew from monitoring Ji-su's cottage on Whidbey Island that, as a child, Ji-su had successfully walked to freedom across the DMZ to South Korea. Sergei didn't think she had a prayer of escaping from the palace in Pyongyang, but he was going to confer immediately with Thomas about developing a plan to save Ji-su, motorcycle or no motorcycle.

Chapter 19

PYONGYANG, NORTH KOREA

As *Ji-su was being lifted* off the helicopter and hustled into the royal palace wrapped in a blanket, one of the women on the U group's insertion team had whispered in her ear that after midnight the United States would attack and destroy all of North Korea's weapons of mass destruction as well as their missile capabilities. There would be no need to worry about North Korea retaliating against South Korea or any other country. Ji-su was stunned to hear this news. Her face was covered, so she couldn't see who had given her the message. If only it would turn out to be true!

The woman who had delivered the message about the bombing also stressed to Ji-su that, In spite of the surprising news about the upcoming attack on North Korea, Ji-su was not to alter in any way, her carefully prepared plan with regard to what she was to do and say. Ji-su was to stick to every word of her carefully constructed script and perform her part exactly as she had practiced it for so many months. Ji-su couldn't help but now wonder if the U Group and her personal role in their mission had in fact always been part of a larger plot to attack North Korea.

There was a two-fold purpose for all of the elaborate planning built around her impersonation of KJU. One objective of the masquerade was to prevent, for as long as possible, those close to the supreme leader from sounding the alarm that he had been kidnapped. KJU had a close cadre of personal body guards who were with him constantly, even when he was in the bathroom. Known informally as The Chosen, these men served a function similar to what the Secret Service did for the president of the United States. But KJU's Chosen agents had duties that went far beyond protecting their charge. This group of loyal and ardent followers were highly trained, and in addition to being his body guards, they were KJU's own squad of assassins, enforcers, and gofers. This tight group of hand-selected and devoted warriors were tasked with making sure that KJU's enemies, the real ones as well as those who were perceived or imagined, were taken care of immediately and effectively.

This team of men who lived with and served KJU on a daily basis, this unit of deadly sycophants who hovered around KJU and knew him best, would be the most difficult to fool with an impersonation. If Ji-su could deceive this crew, even briefly, she would have been successful in her mission. Her goal was to convince, even for just a few hours, The Chosen, the palace security guards, and the military personnel she knew would appear on the scene when they heard that there had been an attack on the royal palace, that KJU was still alive and well inside the safe room of the palace. If she could keep those in command from learning that the real KJU had been kidnapped, they would be reassured that the supreme leader was still in power and in control. The well-planned trickery would give the U Group the little bit of precious time they required to spirit the real KJU away into captivity, to his own special secret prison, where he would live out the rest of his natural life. The longer Ji-su could deceive those who were always in attendance around KJU that he was fine, the more time the U Group would have to make their escape with Emperor Roly Poly.

Ji-su was to remain in the safe room for as long as possible and follow through with her script, shouting orders over the intercom and calling for retaliation against North Korea's enemies. If the United States was successful in destroying the missile silos, the centrifuges, the atomic weapons storage, and all the rest of it, there would not be anything left with which to retaliate. Ji-su would not have to worry that any retaliation would occur. From the outset, Ji-su had been resigned to the fact that once she was discovered to be an imposter, she would probably die. Now, given the changed circumstances that had to do with the operation by the United States military, she might have a chance to escape from the royal palace.

In addition to convincing those outside the safe room that KJU was inside and was continuing to function as their leader, Ji-su would also, in her role as KJU, give orders to The Chosen to execute specifically selected powerful and effective members of the North Korean military. Ji-su, acting as KJU, would announce that these generals and colonels had been part of a coup against him in his position as the supreme leader. The faux KJU would denounce these military leaders and declare that the men on the list had tried to depose him as president of North Korea and take over leadership of the country. He would demand their executions; in fact he would demand their beheadings. Eliminating top members of the North Korean military would hinder the ability of the KJU faithful to muster a retaliatory response and would keep the chaos evolving in North Korea.

The longer she could stay in the safe room and out of sight, the longer she could be certain the ruse of her impersonation would not be discovered. She would stay inside the safe room as long as she could and speak to those outside through the old-fashioned intercom system. She'd practiced for weeks to learn how to operate the outdated microphone. It was time for Ji-su to embrace the role she had rehearsed for so long and to become Kim Jong-un. She gathered her resolve and stepped into her role as KJU.

The story the imposter KJU told those outside the safe room was that there had been an attempted kidnapping by unknown perpetrators. These enemies had stormed his inner sanctum and tried to kidnap and kill him. As the attackers had rushed into his private rooms, KJU reported that two of his bravest body guards had swept him off his feet and made a mad dash for the safe room. Ji-su, now speaking as KJU, reported that the two loyal men, who sadly lay dead inside that safe room with KJU, had held off the kidnappers and made it possible for him to reach the safe room. KJU announced that he had almost been murdered, but the loyal body guards had saved his life. Two of The Chosen who had died inside the safe room would receive North Korea's highest award for bravery, etc. etc.

Ji-su spoke as KJU to those who had gathered outside the safe room of the royal palace. She let them know, no thanks to any of them, that KJU was uninjured and in good health. KJU screamed about how poorly he had been protected. He shouted that heads would roll because security had been lax. He displayed without restraint his furious, extremely unreasonable, and frightened side, as he ranted from inside the safe room. He announced that he was going to stay where he was until he could be assured by his security team and by his trusted military personnel assigned to the royal palace that all the attackers and potential kidnappers had been apprehended or killed. Before he would emerge from his sheltered space, his safe room, he wanted a guarantee that he was absolutely secure.

This behavior was perfectly consistent with KJU's narcissism and his cowardly personality. Ji-su, as the imposter, was playing exactly to the prescribed role. No one suspected that it was anyone but the real KJU who was shouting orders from the safe room and demanding reassurance that everything was under control. It was predictable that, under the circumstances, the supreme leader would want to know with absolute certainty that there was no longer any threat whatsoever to his exalted personage.

At first KJU demanded an immediate investigation to uncover every detail about who had attacked him in his home. He stressed that he wanted to know that every person who had been in on the plot to kidnap him would be hunted down, found, and punished. Before he would come out of his hiding place, he wanted to be certain that every one of them was either in jail or dead.

Then, he suddenly switched gears and announced with great conviction that he knew who his attackers had been. He believed the attempted coup had been the plot of a military junta, a betrayal from within his own military. He said he knew who his betrayers were and could identify which of his generals were members of the rogue faction. This abrupt change of focus, tactics, and orders was not surprising. The erratic Roly Poly often jumped chaotically from one ordered command to another.

The person who was shouting orders from the safe room was certain that these conspirators, who he knew were jealous of him and wanted to steal his power, were behind the assault on the palace. Even though he could not imagine how the assailants had made it into his inner sanctum, KJU demanded that the traitors be found and punished. KJU's arbitrary and capricious leap from demanding an investigation to being absolutely certain who was behind the attack, was entirely consistent with the man's disorganized thinking and unpredictable behavior. Those around him were used to his contradictory and ever-shifting ultimatums.

KJU became specific and named the names of those he believed were behind the attack on his palace and his person. He declared that he knew without any doubt exactly which military leaders had betrayed him. The generals and others who had turned against him had defied his leadership. They had tried and failed to seize power from the supreme leader. The list of those KJU said he was convinced were behind the attack had, in fact, been carefully prepared by the U Group. The names included the strongest and most effective leaders in the North Korean military. If these specific generals were removed and killed, the military would be in a decidedly weaker position. The list of "traitors" that KJU would blame for the plot against him was a list of the country's finest and most loyal warriors.

KJU's voice was wild with anger as he demanded the heads of these conspirators. He screamed through the intercom that, at the moment he emerged from his safe room, he wanted to see these men lying dead in a row without their heads. He ordered that The Chosen were to take charge of the retaliation and threatened further reprisals if his orders were not obeyed immediately. He shouted that it was a top priority, in order to maintain the sovereignty of the country of North Korea as well as to maintain the integrity of the country's military, that these generals be executed wherever they were at this moment. He wanted them all tracked down and killed, and then he wanted all the bodies brought to the palace, their heads cut off, and the corpses lined up for him to see as soon as he came out of hiding. KJU made these demands within the first hour of his isolation inside the safe room.

All of the screaming and angry behavior from KJU had been previously scripted for Ji-su and was in keeping with the tyrant's personality. Investigators would be heading in confusing and contradictory directions and sent to follow completely false trails. Those on missions of retaliation and revenge ordered by the fake KJU, would be sent against their own military leaders. From his safe room, KJU had pointed to a revolutionary faction within the North Korean military, so that was where investigators and assassins would look for the guilty ones who had tried to kill their leader. The names on the list, those that KJU had specifically identified as the people he wanted exterminated, had been chosen in order to inflict a huge blow to North Korea's military hierarchy. With the elimination of these top-ranking military personnel, there would be even more disorder.

The call for mass executions had happened before. KJU had ordered vast purges of his military leaders a number of times in the past. When he believed they were plotting against him, whether they really were or not, he had ordered brutal and pitiless assassinations of his own close relatives. No one was at all shocked when he again called for mass executions of his best generals. When Kim Jong-un felt threatened, he killed people, even if they were his best people. In addition to having the effect of decimating the North Korean military's top brass, the tantrums KJU's displayed inside his safe room gave the U Group more time to get away with their prize prisoner.

What those outside the safe room did not know was that an attack on their country was coming from the air. Because of the whispered message in her ear, Ji-su knew what was coming. The pretend KJU would remain in his safe room in the royal palace until the U.S. air assault on his nation began. Once he received word that the bombing had started, he would tell his body guards and the others that he intended to remain inside his safe room until someone could tell him that the attack had ended and that the aggressors had been driven from the skies and shores of North Korea. Of course, that word would never come, because the foreign aggressors would destroy every weapon that KJU valued. The assailants would demolish all of his dreams of being a nuclear power in the world.

Meanwhile, KJU continued to shout orders to his minions over the intercom system. Those who did his bidding were used to having orders shouted at them, so KJU's tirades from inside the safe room were not that different from what usually happened. If KJU's voice sounded different to anyone, they blamed the antiquated intercom system for the discrepancies. Their leader had made it clear that he wanted the bodies of the traitors lined up with their heads cut off. Now, as a result of the attacks by the United States, KJU was staying inside the safe room until the bombing had stopped.

After the attack on their country had begun, none of those outside the safe room were surprised that KJU was afraid to come out. He was a coward and would remain in hiding until he was certain the coast was clear. What Ji-su had not counted on ahead of time was that she would have an additional excuse for remaining in the safe room for an even longer period of time.

Chapter 20

PYONGYANG, NORTH KOREA

N*orth Korea was in chaos* after the bombing of its weapons installations by the Americans. Fortunately, there was nothing left in the arsenal with which to retaliate against either the United States or South Korea. Even the conventional artillery the North Koreans had positioned near the DMZ aimed at South Korea had been completely destroyed. Western intelligence agencies had seized control of the North Korean media, and they were running carefully pre-prepared videotapes of the supreme leader railing against the United States and threatening to retaliate.

These videos ran partly to keep alive the myth that KJU was still in control of North Korea. The videos had been photoshopped, using actual footage of the real KJU speaking and shouting, to make the puffy-faced little man look even sillier and more impotent than he already was. On the surface, the message was to demand revenge for the attacks against North Korea. At a more subliminal level, the North Korean people were made to see how ridiculous and ineffective their little dictator was in a crisis. The videos had been made with two goals. One goal was to convince the North Koreans that KJU was still in the country. The other goal was to undermine the North Korean population's faith in their leadership.

The military was floundering. All branches of the Army, Navy, and Air Force of North Korea were mobilized for retaliation, only to find they had nothing left with which to retaliate. Soldiers were defecting by the thousands. North Korea was not the most organized or well-run country under the best of circumstances. Food and oil shortages made simply feeding its people almost impossible. With its weaponry destroyed, North Korea's reason for being had disappeared.

KJU had made becoming a nuclear power the centerpiece, the sine qua non of his reign, and now he had nothing. High ranking military leaders did not know where to turn. They, too, saw the silly ranting and raving of their Emperor Roly Poly on television. The videos spoke about the attacks on North Korea's important military infrastructure, so the public knew these videos were not old ones that were being rerun. The videos could not have been made before the September 11th attacks by the United States on North Korea.

Rumors were flying everywhere throughout the country. One military source was absolutely certain that KJU had been murdered and that his dead body had been taken away by American marines in a Black Hawk helicopter. Another rumor that had a lot of credibility was that KJU had been kidnapped during the B-1B bomber attacks. The rumor was that KJU was being held for ransom by a rogue group of unknown conspirators, probably South Koreans. South Korea supposedly had threatened "decapitation," and high ranking North Korean Army officers believed this rumor to be absolutely true. No one had seen the supreme leader in person since the U.S. attack had begun, so everyone was trying to figure out what had happened to him. Another rumor was that the palace had been attacked by a revolutionary faction of the North Korean Air Force flying a fleet of rogue helicopters. Another speculation was that KJU had escaped with his life and was in hiding. There was a small grain of truth in each of these rumors, but no one knew anything with any confidence. Uncertainty ruled the day.

After a catastrophic event, even in the most organized societies and those countries where the media has the freedom to discover and report anything and everything to a public hungry for information, at first it is almost impossible to sort out truthful intelligence from speculation and hyperbole. In the United States after the terrorist attacks of September 11, 2001, the U.S. government and the media had, for the most part, been able to figure out what had happened in a matter of hours. But in a severely deprived and backward North Korea, it was impossible to know what is really going on under normal circumstances. After a massive bombing attack by the United States, reliable information about what was happening was in extremely short supply.

The country of North Korea was built on a fabric of lies and had always conducted its day-to-day business in a fantasy world. The propaganda machine that spewed falsehoods, sugary praise, and ridiculousness about KJU was an intrinsic mainstay of North Korean culture and daily life. When asked if they believed what they heard on their government-run television and radio channels, the North Korean people always said out loud that of course they believed what their government was telling them—one hundred percent. However, the reality was that the people knew not to believe anything they heard from their state-controlled media. In the wake of the attacks on North Korea, there was no information available to the public. Even if there had been any, most of the people of the country would not have believed it.

Ji-su had stayed in the safe room at the presidential palace during the period of time when she knew that the B-1B attacks by the United States were continuing. After sitting for hours in the safe room with two dead body guards, she adjusted her stuffing and her makeup and decided it was time to make an appearance in the palace outside the safe room. This would be the test to see if anyone was going to buy her act as the supreme leader.

She grabbed her kit bag that had her life-saving gear in it. In the bag were two satellite phones, the keys to her motorcycle which was supposed to be hidden close by in the garden shed, two changes of clothes, a make-up repair kit, a very thin and lightweight but incredibly strong rappelling line, a bundle of currency from different countries, and a few other things Ji-su thought she might need to survive a run for her life. She was certain her tenure as Kim Jong-un would not last long. It might be only a matter of minutes until she was exposed as an imposter. She was already trying to determine if there was going to be any possibility of escape.

Ji-su as KJU burst from the safe room to find, not the crowd of body guards and military people he had been expecting to see. He found just a few of KJU's Chosen crew. As promised, ten corpses were laid out on the floor, immediately outside the door of the safe room, with their heads sitting beside the bodies.

KJU walked down the row of dead generals and kicked each one of them a few times with his steel-toed boots. The smell of blood and death was overwhelming. The U Group knew from studying KJU's behavior over the years that the little tyrant liked to kick the dead bodies of the people he'd ordered killed. They assumed it must give this cowardly mini-man some kind of perverse satisfaction to abuse the bodies of his enemies, even when they were no longer any threat to him.

The impersonator KJU kicked and stomped and stormed around the room, shouting and screaming, exactly as Ji-su had watched the real little guy behave on the hundreds of videos she had watched during her months of preparation for this role. She was convincing, and she didn't allow anyone to get too close to her.

KJU demanded to know where everyone was. Considering that the supreme leader had been attacked and almost kidnapped, he wanted to know why there weren't more people gathered in the royal palace. KJU had been informed, while he was in seclusion, that there had been an attack on North Korea by the United States. But everyone was afraid to tell KJU the truth about the severity of the strike against North Korea.

No one had yet dared tell him how much of his precious weapons program had been destroyed by the bombing raids. Who wanted to be the first to tell the supreme leader that his dreams of making North Korea into a full-fledged nuclear power in the world had been decimated? He would have to go back to square one with his atomic weapons development and his ICBM program. Nobody wanted to be the one to give this terrible news to KJU.

KJU screamed his usual tirade against the United States and their cowardly allies. He ranted and raved about the American terrorists, his standard diatribe. KJU commanded that someone remove the stinking corpses of the bodyguards who had been locked with him in the safe room. Those two brave men were to be given medals and heroes' funerals.

No one was willing to tell the leader the extent to which his country's dreams had been destroyed, so the dictator continued to act as if he expected his latest orders to be obeyed at once and without hesitation. Ji-su had to know that, if the Americans had succeeded in their bombing campaign, the military and the entire country would be in complete chaos at this moment. Planning military honors and elaborate funerals for two dead body guards would not be high on the list of priorities in the aftermath of the destruction that had been reigned on the country by the U.S. bunker buster bombs.

Ji-su felt her impersonation had held together and been convincing. She'd stayed in the safe room for much longer than she'd originally thought she would be able to hide there. Much had happened while she was in seclusion. The country was in disarray and was indeed without leadership at this point. The North Koreans knew exactly what had hit them, but they were unwilling to fully acknowledge the consequences. The military command that remained and was not lying on the floor of the Pyongyang royal palace without their heads, did not know what to do or where to turn. They had no weapons of mass destruction left in their arsenal. Retaliation against any country was out of the question now. Regrouping had never been considered as an important strategy for North Korea. They had never considered that their power might be destroyed in only a few hours. Their answer to everything that happened was always to tell the people and the military to look to the supreme leader to tell them what to do.

KJU announced that he was hungry after his long stay in the safe room, and he ordered food brought to his private dining room at once. He gave instructions about what he wanted to eat and seated himself, in solitary splendor as he often did, at the table awaiting his feast. When it arrived, he gorged himself on a few of the delicacies and then threw the rest of the food on the floor. Ji-su knew this had happened many times before when KJU got into a snit and began behaving badly. In full-blown tantrum mode, the impersonator KJU shouted that the hot food was cold and the cold food was lukewarm. He wasn't eating any of it.

Ji-su knew she had already pushed the envelope past what was believable. The Chosen who knew KJU well would undoubtedly be questioning why he looked so different. Ji-su knew the time had come when she had to end the charade and either die or try to put her escape plan into action. Enough time had passed that she felt quite certain that the kidnapping of the real KJU had been successful and that he was now nowhere near North Korea. Her mission had been accomplished.

KJU said he was going to bed, that the attacks on his person and the news of the bombings by the United States had drained all of his energy. He didn't want to be disturbed. He ordered the few Chosen that were in the dining room with him not to accompany him to his bedroom. This was unusual for KJU, because The Chosen were always at his side. They even slept in his bedroom. When they protested about being excluded from his presence, he shouted at them and told them he didn't know which of them he could trust any more. He told them he was going to lock his door and keep them all out.

KJU was acting especially paranoid, which was not really a surprise to any of the people around him because he was always paranoid. It had been an especially bad twenty-four hours for Emperor Roly Poly, and The Chosen decided to honor his wishes and stay away as he stormed into his bedroom and locked the door behind him. Important military leaders had been beheaded. Ji-su had given the U Group more than enough time to get away. Now it was time to save herself.

Ji-su had stayed inside the safe room for an extended period, and after she emerged, she had purposely wasted time making a fuss over the dead bodies. Then she had ordered food and thrown it on the floor. She'd been able to delay so that it would be dark again outside when she attempted to make her escape.

The chin and cheek implants were killing Ji-su. It had been almost impossible for her to eat any of the food that was served to KJU. She'd had to throw it on the floor. She stripped off her dark North Korean zoot suit, the military-style uniform garb that KJU always wore. She unhooked and peeled off the layers of plastic forms and stuffing she'd worn to make her body resemble that of KJU. She got rid of all the implants in her face and mouth. She thankfully pulled from her sweat-soaked head the horrible box-like toupee wig that had made her such a convincing impersonator of the supreme leader.

She bundled up every last bit of her costume and put it all into the large plastic trash bag she'd brought folded up inside her kit bag. The bag of trash was a lot of material to carry away with her, but it was essential that no one find any parts of the disguise she had worn when she'd pretended to be KJU. The more confusion and mystery that surrounded KJU's disappearance, the better.

Ji-su put on the brown North Korean Army uniform she had brought with her in her kit bag. She had a different wig to wear as she escaped from the palace grounds disguised as a young male North Korean Army officer of lower rank. After she had escaped the environs of the palace, she would throw away the second wig and allow the wind to blow through her own short, dark hair. With her closely cropped haircut, she still looked like a boy and could ride her motorcycle without fear. It was illegal for women to drive motorcycles in the wonderfully enlightened DPRK.

While on Whidbey Island, Ji-su had practiced how to disengage the security measures around KJU's bedroom windows and doors, both electronic and mechanical. She opened the bedroom window and took the lightweight but incredibly strong rappelling wire from her kit bag. She attached the line securely to the window sill and threw both her kit bag and the trash bag filled with the remains of the outfit she'd worn for her stint as KJU to the ground below.

As she had practiced many times, Ji-su climbed out the window. As she held herself at the top of the rappelling line, she lowered the window as much as she could. Holding on to the rappelling line, she made her way down the side of the palace wall to the garden. It was a difficult climb, and just before she made it to the ground, she scraped the palm of her hand on the wall of the building. Some blood began to flow, and she wiped her hand on her uniform. Ji-su didn't think anybody would ever notice a little bit of blood on the wall. She unhooked the rappelling wire from the window ledge above, gathered it up, and returned it to her bag. All the evidence of both KJU's presence and his escape had now been removed.

Ji-su's adrenalin pumped wildly as she inwardly rejoiced that her mission had been a success. She allowed herself to hope as she realized she was indeed in the process of trying to escape. She was certain that for the rest of her life, she would be going over and over what had happened in the past few hours. But for now she told herself she had to concentrate on her getaway. For the second time in her life, she might be able to escape from North Korea.

She ran to the closest shed in the garden where she expected to find a motorcycle waiting for her. When she opened the door and looked for the motorcycle, she didn't see it. Her heart sank when she realized her means of escaping was not where it was supposed to be. She was finished. She was exhausted, and she couldn't even think about making her way out of this horrible country on foot. She sat down on the floor of the garden shed, defeated.

Just then, one of the satellite phones in her kit bag vibrated. No one had the number to either one of her phones, and they were both turned off. So how was it possible that someone was calling her? She dug into her bag and found the vibrating phone. On the screen was the face of a Slavic-looking man who wore the vestments of what Ji-su guessed had to be those of the Russian Orthodox Church. He was not any member of the U Group that Ji-su had ever encountered, but she knew she'd been completely isolated from most of the rest of the team. This man night be a member of the U Group that she'd not met. She could not imagine who this person or this priest might be, but her situation couldn't be worse. She answered the phone, and the man immediately asked if she spoke English. His English was perfect, and he sounded as if he was an American. Again, she was completely confused. This man had to be a Russian, so why was he asking her if she spoke English?

"Yes, I speak English but not fluently."

"I can't speak any Korean, but I have a translation device that can change my words into Korean, if you prefer."

"English is fine. What do you want?"

"I want to help you. I want to help you escape and get back to your home in South Korea."

"Who are you, and how do you have this phone number?"

"It's not important who I am, and I will explain later how I happen to have the phone number. Right now, you need to know that your motorcycle was put into the wrong shed. It's in the shed that is farther away from the palace, close to the exterior perimeter of the palace grounds. Start moving there. I will tell you if you need to take cover. I can see what is happening around you. You are safe if you move right now and quickly. No one is close to the other garden shed."

"What in the world? How do you know any of this ... ?"

"Please! I will tell you everything later, but now you must get to the motorcycle and get away from Pyongyang. I want to save your life, so I will be watching you as you make your way home."

"How can you possibly know ...?"

"Later. Now it is essential that you move towards that garden shed. Now go!"

Ji-su picked up her two bags and ran towards the other shed. She opened the door, and sure enough, right there in front of her, hiding behind a large John Deere tractor, was her small motorcycle. She grabbed the key out of her bag. She tied the bag of trash and the kit bag onto the back of the motorcycle which was the same one she had practiced riding so often on Whidbey Island. She dragged the cycle from the shed.

The motorcycle started immediately, and she was completely at home riding it. There were remarkably few guards standing around, and she waved to them as she gunned the engine. The guards waved back at the young North Korean Army officer who was leaving the presidential palace. She rode away from Pyongyang on the military-issue motorcycle, made in Japan.

Chapter 21

THE PACIFIC OCEAN

Everything the U Group had planned and prepared for had been done with great care and consideration. Likewise, the training and staging locations for the U Group's attack on the North Korean royal palace had been thoughtfully chosen. There are many uncharted atolls, coral reefs, and islands in the Pacific Ocean, even in the Yellow Sea and in the Sea of Japan. Some of these patches of land surrounded by water are uninhabited and uninhabitable. Many are so small and are located so far away from anything else that it was not deemed to be useful to name them or to include them on a map. Many are arid and inhospitable and have no fresh water source. A few of the desolate places had once been known. Some of these now-abandoned islands had been used during World War II to refuel planes for wartime missions. After the war was over, they no longer had a purpose, and many were forgotten.

One member of the U Group team was an expert on the location and topographical characteristics of these lost places. He constantly studied and monitored the isolated bits of land that stuck up out of the Pacific, and he knew which ones had the necessary space and flat land for runways. He knew which of these sites had once contained the primitive landing strips leftover from World War II. He chose one atoll that was ideal for the U Group's insertion and extraction teams to build their mock-up of Pyongyang's North Korean royal palace to use to practice for their mission. It was determined that this practice facility be located in the Pacific Ocean, but not too close to North Korea.

The selected atoll was remote. It was designated and referred to as S-1. The teams that would practice for the operation in North Korea ate and slept on a yacht anchored off shore. If any curious ship happened to come by, the cover story was that the owner of the yacht was a rich eccentric who liked to travel to places that were completely off the map. A member of one of the teams even had an old-fashioned Commodore's uniform complete with a billed cap to put on if he were required to impersonate the eccentric yacht owner. But no other ships came by to inquire about anything.

The yacht was well-equipped with an excellent kitchen and comfortable quarters for the U Group's team members. A seaplane arrived weekly with supplies and mail. The men and women lived on the yacht and practiced on the island for months. The yacht was equipped with the latest in satellite communications which enabled the U Group command center on Whidbey Island to stay in touch with them. The excellent satellite communications also allowed the members of the teams, who were mostly South Koreans and ethnic North Koreans who had escaped the Hermit Kingdom and were now living in other countries, to watch their favorite television shows and movies.

When it was time for the operation to begin and before the insertion and extraction teams had left the S-1 location, they'd completely dismantled the mock-up of the royal palace and everything else they had brought with them to the island. They were not going to need the faux royal palace any more. They were heading for the real thing. All evidence that there had been any human activity on the island of S-1 was scrupulously removed to the yacht anchored in the off-shore cove. The yacht then delivered the personnel to the staging island, S-2, and the yacht sailed away.

The expert on uncharted Pacific Ocean land masses had located another island, closer to the Korean Peninsula that was the ideal spot to use as a staging area for the helicopter assault on North Korea. This location was designated as S-2. This island which was chosen as a staging area was also not found on any map. It was located fairly close to North Korea. Fishermen undoubtedly knew of its existence, but it held no real interest for them. It was barren and empty of any kind of wildlife, Because there was no fresh water available on the island, most thought it was uninhabitable.

A rough and temporary airstrip for small planes and an adequate helicopter landing pad were constructed on S-2. During the few days just before the North Korean operation began, the helicopters arrived on S-2. The teams who would ride in the helicopters and storm the royal palace were delivered from S-1 and stayed in tents on the island. Most were ex-military and used to living in difficult circumstances. Their commitment to what they hoped to accomplish was more than sufficient motivation for them to be able to endure the primitive conditions on the island. The teams lived on the staging island, S-2, for only a few days.

After the operation had been completed, the plan was that four out of the original five helicopters, which had been painted to look exactly like those of the North Korean Air

Force, would hopefully make it back successfully to the anonymous staging island S-2. One of the U Group's helicopters would have been intentionally crashed into the park next to the North Korean royal palace.

As soon as the other four helicopters landed back on the staging island, S-2, after their mission, the injured members of the teams, if any, would be transferred to fixed wing aircraft. Small planes equipped with medical personnel would immediately take off from the primitive runways to airlift any wounded U Group members to medical centers in Japan. Once the helicopters had safely delivered the insertion and extraction teams back to the staging island, the counterfeit North Korean fleet of MD 500C look-alike helicopters were to be flown into the sea to disappear forever.

The transportation of their trophy, Kim Jong-un, was an obvious priority for the U group. As soon as he arrived on the Pacific staging island, the still unconscious dictator was immediately transferred to a special helicopter marked with the logo of a South Korean commercial enterprise. A replica of this helicopter, which was exactly like the one that now carried the former North Korean president, flew in and out of South Korea daily. There would be no suspicion when this particular helicopter requested entry into South Korean airspace. The helicopter would deliver this man, who had formerly terrorized his own country and the rest of the world, to a temporary safe house before he was moved to his own special place of residence, his final home for life in South Korea.

Once their part in the plan had been completed and their prize, KJU, had been transferred to his special prison, the U group would remove all traces of the operation's preparations from the staging island S-2. Uninjured personnel were to be airlifted to an undisclosed location for medical checkups and two weeks of debriefing and R and R. Within several hours of the conclusion of the mission, which had kidnapped KJU and inserted Ji-su into the royal palace, all evidence of the operation would be obliterated. There would be nothing left that could point to the fact that any Pacific islands had once been used to train anyone for participation in the audacious events that had occurred in North Korea.

After both S-1 and S-2 had been scrubbed and the personnel were gone, the support marine craft that had been anchored off-shore sailed away from the locations that had been the staging area for the most brazen kidnapping operation of the decade, perhaps the century. Within a little more than twenty-four hours, no one would be able to find any evidence that the U Group or its helicopters or its planes had ever been on either one of the deserted islands. The U Group had prepared with tremendous diligence, and they erased their presence with equal care. The North Koreans and anybody else who was looking could investigate ad nauseum. They would find no evidence of anything, anywhere.

Chapter 22

SKANEATELES, NEW YORK AND SERGIYEV POSAD, RUSSIA

T*homas knew he badly needed* a break. He was going to have to force himself to take some time off from monitoring his computer screens and the unbelievable events that had unfolded in North Korea. He'd stayed up late too many nights and missed a great deal of sleep because of the time zone differences between Pyongyang, North Korea and Skaneateles, New York.

Kim Jong-un, against all odds, had been successfully kidnapped from his palace in North Korea. Ji-su was now hiding inside the safe room at the palace, shouting orders to the minions outside to take care of the traitors in their midst. Listening to the diatribe made Thomas smile. And then there was the completely unexpected but not entirely surprising bombing attack by the U.S. and their B-1B Lancers, their F-35Bs, and their bunker buster bombs.

This show was really too good to leave, but Thomas realized he'd overdone it. He had to allow his mind and body to rest. Sergei, who was in Russia and whose circadian rhythms were more in sync with the days and nights in North Korea, was keeping a careful eye on Ji-su as she skillfully played her part from inside the palace safe room.

Even though Thomas hated to miss a minute of the drama that was playing out half-way around the world, he was recording all of it and would watch it later. Thomas knew he had to eat a decent meal and get a good night's sleep. His trips to the grocery store, his food intake, and his sleep patterns had suffered severely in the past several weeks. But he wasn't sorry. His innovative computer programs had worked better than he'd ever imagined they would. He was quite certain that his and Sergei's intervention into the operation to kidnap KJU had helped to make it a success. At the very least, their surveillance had reduced the U Group's casualties. Using his real-time computer apps, there were no more secrets.

Thomas parked his Range Rover at the triplex and drove his motor scooter to the Sherwood Inn. It was seven o'clock, and it was almost dark. Thomas loved Skaneateles in the weeks of the early fall. The weather in the middle of September was warm during the day and cool, even a little bit cold, at night. He needed his leather jacket tonight and looked forward to sitting by the fire at the Sherwood after dinner. He arrived at the inn and said a quick hello to the bartender, Sam O'Connor. Sam knew Thomas well and asked, as Thomas walked past the bar directly to the dining room, where he'd been keeping himself. Sam liked Thomas, and Thomas liked Sam. Thomas told him that he'd come by after dinner for a drink.

Thomas ordered the lobster bisque which was deliciously rich and full of large chunks of lobster meat. It was such a wonderful bowl of soup, it almost brought Thomas to tears. Nothing should taste as wonderful and be as satisfying as the lobster bisque at the Sherwood Inn. Because he was hungry and was celebrating a victory of sorts, a victory over evil, Thomas ordered the sixteen-ounce New York strip steak rare, a baked potato with everything, and the steamed asparagus. He added an additional side order of onion straws that were a new item on the Sherwood menu. They were sweet and salty and crunchy.

At Camp 27, Peter Gregory had been forced to eat French fried onion rings because they were thought to be popular in the United States at that time. Peter Gregory hated the hard-as-a-rock circles that consisted of lots of heavy fried cornmeal surrounding the tiny sliver of a tasteless onion. Once he'd arrived in the USA, he'd never ordered French fried onion rings because of the Camp 27 memory. But these onion straws at the Sherwood Inn were almost as sweet as candy. The batter on the outside of the sweet onions was light and crispy. There was no cornmeal anywhere near the tasty morsels.

Thomas had a delicious meal and knew that he would be taking part of it home for lunch the next day. He had a glass of Pinot noir with his dinner and ordered two slices of custard pie boxed up to take home with his other leftovers. Custard pie made a great breakfast. Thomas had missed the wonderful food at the Sherwood Inn. He'd stayed away because he didn't want to be around the crowds of tourists who filled the restaurant during the summer. And this summer he'd been too busy watching events in North Korea via his virtual real time hack to think about going to town frequently.

Making his way to the bar, he sat on one of the tall stools and ordered a cup of coffee with cream and sugar. Sam wrinkled his forehead and wondered why Thomas was on the wagon tonight. Thomas never drank more than one glass of red wine anyway, but tonight he was ordering coffee.

Anticipating Sam's question, Thomas told him, "I had a glass of Pinot with my dinner. I'm having coffee now, and then I'm going to get wild and crazy and order a brandy to sip in front of the fire." Sam laughed and delivered the coffee with a small silver pitcher of heavy cream, a silver sugar bowl full of sugar cubes, and a set of tiny silver tongs. The two chatted and Sam wanted to know what Thomas had been doing all summer. Sam knew Thomas didn't like to come to the Sherwood's bar or restaurant when all the summer people were swarming around, but Sam knew he loved the Sherwood Inn. Thomas told Sam he'd had a lot of work that had a time limit. He hadn't been able to postpone the deadlines, so he'd been scarcer than usual.

Thomas almost always turned up for dinner at the Sherwood Inn on the Tuesday after Labor Day. That hadn't happened this year. He'd had other things to do. Thomas asked to have a snifter of brandy brought to him in his chair as he sat in front of the bar's fireplace. He was feeling philosophical tonight, and somehow a brandy seemed as if it was the perfect drink to have when one was feeling philosophical.

"This is the first time I have ever known you to order brandy. Are you celebrating something?" Sam knew Thomas's habits well and was curious about the brandy.

"I guess I always feel as if I should be celebrating something. There is always something to celebrate in life, don't you think?"

"I think I should be celebrating your positive attitude. So many people come in here whining... with their sad stories and their complaints. It sometimes gets me down. You are always upbeat and have something uplifting to say. So yes, whenever you are in here, I am thankful for you and will celebrate having you as a customer."

Thomas laughed and took his seat in front of the fire. He would love to have told Sam that he had, the night before, helped to remove one of the world's most dangerous forces of evil from one of the world's most downtrodden countries. He would love to have been able to share with Sam what he, Thomas, knew about what had just happened in North Korea. Sam and the rest of the world would learn soon enough that Kim Jong-un was no more, that he had disappeared, never to be seen again. But Thomas realized he could never reveal what he knew or anything about his part in the spectacular events that had occurred today in the Hermit Kingdom.

Most people in the bar were talking about North Korea and the U.S. B-1B's and other forces which had attacked North Korea's nuclear and ICBM capabilities earlier that morning. Everyone was surprised that the American president had really had the nerve, many said the balls, to go through with the attack. Kim Jong-un had been getting away with way too much for way too long. Previous U.S. administrations had pretended to use diplomacy to deal with the man. Or they had ignored him completely and acted as if KJU and North Korea didn't exist.

Finally, an American president had decided that enough was enough and had summoned the courage to do what needed to be done. Everyone was surprised that there had not been more collateral damage. Of course, the word coming out of North Korea was that millions had been murdered by the American aggression, but actual satellite footage showed the bomb sites and made liars out of the North Korean news reports. To be sure, some people had died, but few buildings other than those specifically targeted had been destroyed. Precision-guided bombs and powerful bunker buster, non-nuclear weapons technology, had saved the day with a minimal loss of life.

China and Russia were vociferously criticizing the United States for the bombing, and they were calling for an official condemnation in the United Nations Security Council. A reporter for the *Wall Street Journal*, however, leaked the information that the Chinese and the Russians, as well as the South Koreans, of course, had been fully informed in advance about what was going to happen in North Korea. Both long-time allies of the DPRK were secretly and tremendously relieved that the U.S. had finally stepped up to the plate and taken out the weapons that the mad little fat fellow had been using to threaten everybody in the world during the past months and years. The entire world heaved a huge sigh of relief, even as it simultaneously condemned the American president for his audacity.

Thomas listened to the conversations that were going on around him at the bar, and he felt a tremendous sense of satisfaction that he had been able to participate in a small way with the success of the mission. Of course, nobody yet knew that KJU had disappeared. Videos of him ranting and raving and promising retaliation, videos which had been prepared for this specific occasion by the U.S. intelligence services, were being played and replayed on North Korea's television station.

KJU urged his fellow workers to stay calm and loyal. Their national honor would be avenged, and their pride in their country would become greater than ever in the future. It was all baloney, but all of it was necessary to prove at least temporarily that KJU was still in power and still in charge. He did look incredibly silly as he pranced around. Thomas had to shake his head and laugh as he thought of Ji-su, who had done a heck of a good job imitating the North Korean leader.

North Korea would find out soon enough that their leader had disappeared. The rumors about what had happened to him would run the gamut. He was dead. He was in prison in South Korea. He was being charged with war crimes in the United States. He had been kidnapped. He had been deposed by a group of his own military. After the United States had destroyed his prized nuclear weapons, he had escaped to his estate in the south of France. He was being held at Guantanamo Bay. He was being held in the U.S. prison at Fort Leavenworth. He had finally revealed that he was a spy, a secret agent for South Korea. He had finally come out of the closet as a homosexual. He was undergoing a sex change operation that would transform him into a fat little girl. In the absence of any accurate information, the rumors became sillier and sillier.

Thomas dozed off in front of the fire. He was behind on his sleep, and he wasn't used to drinking brandy after dinner. His phone vibrated at 11:15 and woke him from his nap. It was Sergei, who said he urgently needed to talk to Thomas. Putting money on the bar, he waved goodnight to Sam. Thomas stood beside his Lambretta motor scooter in the parking lot of the Sherwood Inn and returned Sergei's call. Sergei answered and quickly brought Thomas up to speed about what was happening with Ji-su. Thomas had never heard Sergei sound frantic before, but Sergei was definitely worried about Ji-su. Thomas wondered if she'd been able to make her escape from Pyongyang.

"I took the night off from watching the computer screens, Sergei. I'd driven my good humor into the ground watching Emperor Roly Poly day in and day out. I'd not been eating regularly, and whenever I wanted to watch what was going on in North Korea in real time, I had to stay up all night. I went to the Sherwood Inn tonight for a really nice dinner. I even had a half a glass of brandy while I was sitting in front of the fireplace in the bar. It would have been a whole glass of brandy if I hadn't fallen asleep before I'd finished it. I wish you'd been with me. Sorry, I had to take a break. I thought Ji-su was locked in the safe room."

"She's escaped from the royal palace on a motorcycle and is riding it north from Pyongyang. Her getaway plan was to meet up with some guys dressed in North Korean Army uniforms who were driving an old car. They were supposed to be the ones to get her out of North Korea through Sinuiju and Dandong." In the past few weeks, both men had become quite familiar with the locations of the cities in North Korea and Chinese cities close to the North Korean border.

"That sounds like a pretty reasonable plan as long as she can get into China from there and get from China back to South Korea. I'm sure she's well acquainted with how that part of her escape plan is supposed to work." Thomas knew that Sinuiju was on the Yalu River directly across from the Chinese city of Dandong.

"I honestly don't think anybody believed for one minute that she would ever make it out of the palace alive. Her people planned meticulously for how they would get her inside, and they had a script for what she was to do and say once she was there, pretending to be KJU. I'm afraid they assumed that once she was discovered, she would be instantly executed and would never have the chance to try to get away. The escape plan has not been thought through as meticulously as all the rest of it was. The idiots even put her motorcycle, the one she was supposed to use to get out of Pyongyang and rendezvous with her escape team, inside the wrong shed in the palace garden. If I hadn't noticed where they'd put the motorcycle and looked back at the video to check on where it was, she would be dead by now." Sergei had not calmed down during their phone conversation and was still unusually upset about Ji-su.

"So you located her motorcycle and told her where to find it. And she found it! That's all you can do. Yesterday, you were so concerned and believed she was on a suicide mission. You didn't think she even wanted to get out of North Korea with her life. At least now she's trying to escape."

"I'm afraid that she and everybody else thought she would die, and nobody really paid much attention to how to get her out of there. The problem is that the team with the car that she was supposed to meet up with has met with disaster. They will not be at the rendezvous point outside Pyongyang. She will wait and wait for them, and they will never show up."

"So call her and tell her they aren't coming. Tell her she's going to have to come up with another plan to get out of the country. We might be able to do something to help with that, although at this point I can't imagine what that would be." Thomas was surprised at the intensity of Sergei's concern. His friend was usually calm, cool, and collected.

"She's speeding away from Pyongyang and won't pick up her phone while she's riding the motorcycle. I've left her three messages that she's to call me back. I've sent her two texts, telling her the contacts she was to meet are either dead or in jail." Sergei was obviously very closely involved on a moment-by-moment basis with Ji-su's escape.

"Give me a couple of minutes to think about this. Where can we tell her to go? She'd heading towards China now, away from South Korea. If she hadn't been told to head north, she could be almost to the south by now." Thomas was a little groggy from the brandy, and it was past his usual bedtime. He was trying to think things through and come up with a plan for Ji-su.

Sergei continued to fill in Thomas about what was going on. "The country is in chaos, as you might imagine. Members of the army are deserting, and people are trying to escape across the DMZ into South Korea which doesn't want all those refugees coming into their country. Likewise, others are trying to escape over North Korea's northern border, across the Yalu River into China. China doesn't want them pouring into their country either. The Chinese long ago set up strict border controls, a wall if you will, to keep the North Koreans out. The Chinese have been trying to keep the Koreans out of China for the past thousand years, and they've never really figured out how to plug all the holes in their border. Sound familiar? Now people in North Korea are really desperate and will do anything to escape the chaos. Ji-su could never make it across the border into China going north without the proper paperwork, which she doesn't have. Likewise, she would be blocked from going across the DMZ into South Korea if she headed south. There's no route to freedom for her, none!" Sergei was becoming frantic again as he tried to figure out what options were available to Ji-su for her escape. He couldn't come up with anything.

"Don't be so discouraged, Sergei. I know you must have given this some thought as you watched her in her cottage preparing for this mission. What can we do?"

"I could fly to Vladivostok and try to get her out from there. Vladivostok is only a few hundred miles from Pyongyang. Most people in the West don't realize that Russia's far eastern territory has a border with North Korea. It's a small border in the middle of nowhere, but it is a border."

"If you went to Vladivostok, how would you get to her from there? You'd have to go … " suddenly Sergei interrupted Thomas and told him Ji-su was calling. Sergei had to go.

When Thomas left the Sherwood Inn's parking lot, he drove to the triplex on the motor scooter. He picked up the Range Rover and drove to his home on Skaneateles Lake. He rolled down the windows as he made his way out of town on Route 41A and breathed in the wonderful night air. He felt so lucky to live in a place as beautiful as Skaneateles. It was true there were too many rich people living in the town during the summer months. Thomas himself was very rich, but he was a year-round resident, so he counted himself as a native, not merely a summer visitor.

The next day was supposed to be sunny and warm, and Thomas had hoped to take his GP-14 sailboat out on the lake for a long sail. But having had this latest news from Sergei, it looked as if Thomas would be back inside his library looking at computer screens as he tried to find a way for Ji-su to escape. He would look at his maps when he got home and try to figure out how Sergei could get to Ji-su and bring her out of North Korea.

Chapter 23

NORTH KOREA AND SERGIYEV POSAD
AND VLADIVOSTOK, RUSSIA

Sergei quickly told Ji-su that the people with the car, the people with whom she was to rendezvous, would not be at the meeting place when Ji-su arrived. Their car had broken down for the last time between Sinuiju and Pyongyang. The men in the car had been dressed as North Korean Army personnel, and when other army personnel stopped to help with the old car, the real North Koreans had realized the ones in the dilapidated car were phonies. There had been a brief shootout, and two of Ji-su's rescuers had been killed. The other one had been taken to jail. The car was kaput. That rescue plan was in the ditch, and Sergei wanted to know from Ji-su if she knew of any secondary plan to save her, a back-up, in case the first scheme fell apart. There was no back-up plan.

Ji-su knew the geography of North Korea quite well. Sergei told her to try to make it on her motorcycle to the town of Wonsan, a fishing town on the eastern coast of North Korea. Both Ji-su and Sergei knew that Wonsan, the fifth largest city in North Korea, was not a town known only for its seafood. It had been an important center for missile technology. Many of North Korea's ICBMs had been developed there and had been fired from near that location on the North Korean coast. Firing missiles over the Sea of Japan was not a sensible thing to do, especially when you didn't know whether or not your missiles would really be able to fly. All of that was now unimportant as a result of the bombing raid by the U.S. which had destroyed the missile silos and factories near Wonsan. Sergei hesitated to suggest that Ji-su travel to Wonsan because that city might be a complete mess as a result of the bombings. On the other hand, the confusion might help Ji-su disappear into the crowd.

At this point, nobody in North Korea or anywhere else in the world knew that someone had tried to impersonate KJU or that he had been taken out of the country. Only the few who had planned and executed the operation had any idea that there had been a kidnapping and a substitution. Likewise, no one outside this group had any idea what Ji-su looked like. Nobody could possibly be looking for her, and this gave Sergei a small glimmer of hope that he might be able to save the beautiful Ji-su.

Although Ji-su did not understand exactly who Sergei was, how he was able to see what was happening around her, or why this Russian priest wanted to help her, she trusted him. He had found her motorcycle, and so far, he had given her good advice. She was still alive, and she told him she would head for Wonsan. Ji-su had already dumped the bag of trash that held her KJU disguise. She'd thrown the bag that contained her costume, her KJU wig, and her stuffing over the side of a bridge into a rushing river. She had watched for a few seconds as the garbage bag was tossed and turned by the swirling water and finally burst apart. The remnants of her impersonation were scattered in a hundred different directions and finally pulled under to sink to the depths. Ji-su felt a small moment of joy when she saw the pieces of her disguise disappear below the surface of the water. Bye, bye, KJU!!

Ji-su told Sergei she thought she could make it to Wonsan. She had two containers of extra gasoline in the saddle baskets on the back of her motorcycle. The drive was more than five hours, and the road was poor. But Ji-su thought she could make the trip, if she were lucky and there were not too many road blocks. She had no papers that identified her as a North Korean citizen, so if she were stopped and asked to present her papers, it might be all over for her. Sergei knew that Ji-su was smart and told her he thought she would be able to take care of the problem with the papers when the time came. Sergei crossed his fingers and hoped he was right about that.

Sergei and Ji-su agreed that, to save the battery on her cell phone and because she would be concentrating on driving over rough terrain, Ji-su would turn off her phone while she was on her motorcycle. Few people in North Korea had personal cell phones, and cell phone towers were few and far between in the backward DPRK. Every hour on the hour, Ji-su would turn her phone back on briefly and send Sergei a text to let him know she was all right. They would speak again when Ji-su arrived in Wonsan.

Sergei told Ji-su he was coming to get her, and to that end, that he would be taking a long plane flight from Moscow to Vladivostok in Russia. He promised to let her know when his flight was about to take off as he would be incommunicado while he was in the air. Sergei planned to leave Moscow as soon as Ji-su had found a place of refuge and rest in Wonsan. He prayed that she would be able to find such a place.

Sergei made his plane reservations and spoke to his superior at Sergiyev Posad. His superior and mentor, with whom Sergei was quite close, knew all about Sergei's personal history and a little bit about some of Sergei's exploits with Thomas. Sergei's mentor knew that sometimes he took trips to unknown destinations, and the older man was accommodating when Sergei asked for time off from his priestly duties. He knew that Sergei had killed people because Sergei had come to him to talk about the guilt and remorse he felt for having taken the lives of other human beings.

They had talked for many hours about forgiveness, about right and wrong, and about the difficulties of making hard choices in the real world. Sergei's mentor at the Sergiyev Posad monastery believed in Sergei and knew that he was an exceptionally good man at his core. He allowed Sergei to leave the monastery when he asked permission to do so because he knew that if Sergei had to leave, it was always for a purpose that served the greater good.

Sergei was packed and ready to leave for Vladivostok in a couple of hours. He had contacted the St. Seraphim monastery on Russky Island outside of Vladivostok to let them know that he would be arriving from Moscow to stay with the brothers. The monks at St. Seraphim knew Sergei from his efforts to try to educate them about computers. Sergei had never visited the Diocese of Vladivostok, and the clerics at St. Seraphim were anxious to welcome the brilliant and accomplished computer whiz priest, Father Sergei Ivanov.

In addition to being the home of St. Seraphim, Russky Island is the location of the southern span of the Russky Bridge, the world's longest cable-stayed bridge. The Russky Bridge crossed the Eastern Bosporus and connected the island to the mainland portion of Vladivostok. Once he arrived in Vladivostok, Sergei had a comfortable and hospitable place to stay. But once he had reached that destination at the far eastern border of Russia, so far away from Sergiyev Posad, he didn't have the slightest idea what he would do to try to reach Ji-su and bring her to safety. He had turned that part of the planning over to Thomas.

During his flight to Vladivostok, Sergei would be in the air for almost nine hours and completely out of touch. He would be incommunicado with Thomas and Ji-su by cell phone and by computer. He was rarely out of control over anything in his life, but he had made the decision to take this trip and take this risk to try to save a brave and lovely woman.

Sergei, a man who had always been so certain of his calling and his direction in life, especially since he had become a priest in the Russian Orthodox Church, was struggling with the feelings of urgency and distress he was experiencing about Ji-su's safety and ultimate rescue. This was something new for Sergei, and it was both pleasant and unpleasant. Ambivalence is difficult for everyone, but it is especially difficult for clerics who tend to see things as absolutes, in black and white. Sergei was not comfortable with ambivalence, but he was driven and determined to save Ji-su. There was no ambivalence about that.

Sergei sent Ji-su a text to let her know that he was boarding his plane in Moscow. He told her he would be out of touch for more than nine hours. Sergei had hoped to delay his departure until Ji-su had reached Wonsan, but there were not that many flights from Moscow to Vladivostok. Sergei took the next flight that had a seat available for him. He told Ji-su to find refuge in Wonsan with a kind family. She could make up a convincing story about why she needed their help. Ji-su had told Sergei that she had money, so she could make it worthwhile for a poor family to take her in. She would need to stay with them for several days until Sergei and Thomas could organize her rescue. Sergei also sent a text to Thomas that he was leaving Moscow for Vladivostok.

Thomas had spent many years of his life despising the Soviet Union and everything it represented. He still loathed Vladimir Putin and everything he stood for, but since Thomas had reconnected with Sergei and they had become close, Thomas no longer hated the Russian people. He felt sorry for them. They had suffered terribly under the Soviet system. They had finally gained their freedom. They had experienced a few years learning to enjoy a taste of democracy along with a taste of the market economy. Things had been looking up for the Russian people.

Then a former KGB thug came to power and threw all of that progress toward embracing freedom out the window as he began to reassemble the old Soviet Empire. That was never going to happen, but Putin's aggression in Crimea and Ukraine and his threats against the Baltic States were a constant cause of concern for the West. Putin's aggression was especially frightening for those newly free nations who had recently escaped from Communist tyranny.

Thomas did not want to have to do business in Russia, and he did not want to buy anything he didn't have to buy from that country. He didn't want Vladimir Putin, reputedly the richest man in the world, to have one more cent of hard Western currency than he already had. Thomas realized he was allowing his emotions and his disgust with Russia's current leader to cloud his judgment. He tried to clear his head.

Thomas finally got on the Internet, bit the bullet, and bought a boat. After looking at the map and considering all the options, Thomas had decided the fastest and safest way for Sergei to bring Ji-su out of North Korea was by water.

Russia shared a border with North Korea, and there was some limited land transportation available between North Korean cities and Russian cities. Given the circumstances and considering that Ji-su had no papers or passport, Thomas felt that travel by boat through the Sea of Japan was preferable to travel by land. A water rescue would not expose Ji-su to official borders and require her to present paperwork she didn't have. Travel in North Korea would be at a standstill now after the bombing raids a few days earlier. Travel in Russia always required a lot of papers and travel permits. Ji-su had none of that.

Ji-su had a South Korean passport somewhere on Whidbey Island in the United States, but that didn't do her any good right now. Ji-su could not have, under any circumstances, taken her South Korean passport with her into North Korea. If she'd been discovered carrying such a document, it would have instantly signed her death warrant. When she'd left Pyongyang, she'd driven her motorcycle north, not south, and she now had no safe way to get to South Korea.

Time restraints also weighed heavily on Thomas's decision. If Sergei could get Ji-su to St. Seraphim on Russky Island, she would be safe there. Then Thomas could figure out a way to get new identification and travel documents to her that would allow her to travel back to South Korea. All things considered, Thomas opted to buy the boat and plan Ji-su's escape by water. He hoped he had made the right decision.

Thomas bought the old-fashioned Chris-Craft Commodore cabin cruiser rather than rent it because it was easier to obscure a purchase than it was to obscure a rental. Thomas had become savvy over the past few years about the advantages of doing certain kinds of business and making certain kinds of purchases through anonymous LLC corporations.

He'd set up one LLC through which he handled everything he absolutely did not want traced back to himself. He'd set up the obscure LLC in the Cayman Islands, and the maze of holding companies that held the LLC insured that there were many layers that removed Thomas from any possible connection with the entity. It was through this LLC that he purchased the vintage fiberglass boat that Thomas hoped would be able to provide Sergei with a way to save Ji-su.

The boat was old, but it had been first-rate quality when it was originally manufactured. The boat's first owner, who had lived in Depoe Bay, Oregon, had taken excellent care of his beloved Chris-Craft, and the owner's son had in turn taken good care of it when he'd inherited it from his father. It had a beautiful mahogany interior, and the galley and the head had been completely redone not too many years earlier. When the son of the original owner had celebrated his 80th birthday, he'd decided his yachting days had come to an end. He sold the cabin cruiser to a Russian company that gave tours of the water and the sights on the Peter the Great Gulf around Vladivostok.

The Russian company had renamed the Chris-Craft the *Anastasiya* and had the name painted in Cyrillic letters on the stern of the cabin cruiser. The company owned several boats, and an agent, acting on behalf of Thomas's LLC, offered to buy the sixty-foot-long Commodore for considerably more than it was worth. Thomas acquired the boat he thought made the most sense for the job it was going to be asked to carry out.

Thomas had not wanted a new or flashy boat. He'd wanted a low-profile, uninteresting boat that looked kind of boring but would perform reliably. The boat had to have been well-maintained, and the engine had to be in prime working order. Thomas had checked out the company which had bought the cabin cruiser from the Oregon family, and he was assured that the current owners had also taken good care of the engine. Thomas arranged for a Russian company to install extra fuel tanks in the Chris-Craft. As an engineer and inventor, he was used to doing this kind of work himself. It was difficult to trust someone else with such an important job. He didn't trust the company to do the work, but he was half a world away. What were his options? It was a rush job, and that made Thomas even more doubtful that it would be done right.

Thomas hired an independent company to go over the Chris-Craft, check out the installation of the additional fuel tanks, give the boat a tune up, and make sure everything was as good as it could be for such an ancient cabin cruiser. To further obscure the origins of the boat, Thomas had the name *Anastasiya* painted over and the name *Marina* painted in Cyrillic letters in its place on the stern. Thomas also rented a boat slip on the water in Vladivostok where the *Marina* would stay until Sergei was ready for it.

Thomas had arranged for all of this in less than a day, and now he had the problem of finding someone who could captain the boat for Sergei. Thomas knew a lot about sailboats, but he knew almost nothing about inboard powerboats. Sergei knew nothing about boats of any kind, so he was at the mercy of whoever Thomas hired to take him where he wanted to go. Because Thomas was working under such a tight timetable, he was unusually nervous about the background of the Russian boat captain he was about to hire. Thomas didn't trust anything about Russia to begin with, and he didn't have time to properly vet the person he'd hired to pilot the *Marina*. Thomas was more than a little uneasy about the man, and Thomas hated to feel uneasy about anything.

Thomas wanted the *Marina* and its hired captain, Vasily Bulgakov, to be available for Sergei when he stepped off the plane from Moscow. He knew it would be a couple of days before Sergei and the boat would set out on their journey through the Sea of Japan. Thomas wanted to give Sergei a chance to get used to the *Marina* and try to get a read on the person who'd been hired to captain the powerboat. Little was known about that person, and Thomas would continue his investigation into Vasily's background. If he turned up something bad, there might still be time to hire someone else.

Thomas arranged for a company to stock the Chris-Craft with food and water and supplies so the Chris-Craft would be ready as soon as Sergei determined it was time to leave on his rescue mission. Thomas had done everything he could think of to provide Sergei with what he needed. Sergei had probably also figured out that the easiest and safest way to reach Ji-su was by water, and he was probably not too thrilled about that. It was the best that could be done given the circumstances and the amount of time they had.

Chapter 24

WONSAN, NORTH KOREA

J*i-su made her way over* the more than 125 difficult miles between Pyongyang and Wonsan. She'd occasionally had to drive off-road through impossibly rough terrain to circumvent the checkpoints that were posted along the main highway. Because of the bombing the day before and because Wonsan had been one of North Korea's main missile production sites, Ji-su had expected there would be checkpoints and delays along the route. She was counting on the chaos in the coastal town, known for its fishing and seafood, to provide her an opportunity to remain off everybody's radar screen for as long as possible.

Ji-su had worn the army uniform during the entire motorcycle ride, but she decided, when she reached the outskirts of Wonsan, to put on the civilian clothes she'd brought with her. She ruffled her own closely cropped hair. She was wearing pants and hoped she could still pass for male as she completed her journey from Pyongyang. Because women were not permitted to drive motorcycles in North Korea, she could be arrested if someone thought she was a female driving a motorcycle.

As she drove along the dusty roads towards Wonsan, Ji-su had given a great deal of thought about where in the area she would have the best chance of finding a family that would take her in and hide her for a few days. She decided she would fare best by approaching a fisherman's family. Fishermen traveled to other parts of the world and, because they were able to make comparisons with the lifestyles in other countries, they were more likely to be aware of the short comings of North Korean ways. Fishermen frequently defected from the Hermit Kingdom.

Ji-su headed her motorcycle towards the water and the huts where fishermen's families lived. She'd never been to Wonsan, but she'd lived in North Korea when she was a child. Soon she found herself in a fishing village a few miles outside of the city. She hid her motorcycle under some bushes and hoped nobody would steal it. If anyone did take it, the cycle had more than served its purpose.

Ji-su sat down on the ground near one of the fishing huts and took a book out of her kit bag. She began to read, not so much because she was interested in what she was reading but because she saw some children playing nearby and wanted to pique their curiosity. The book with the colorful cover had been published in South Korea, and all children in that free and open land to the south had access to many books like this one. But the book with the colorful cover was obviously not something that was often seen in North Korea. Sure enough, within a few minutes, one of the children came over and stood by Ji-su, staring at her and eyeing the book. Ji-su looked up and smiled at the child. She thought the child was a boy, but it was impossible to tell from his or her clothing whether she was speaking to a little boy or a little girl.

"Do you want to look at this book with me?" Ji-su invited him to sit with her. He nodded and sat down beside Ji-su. "What's your name?" Ji-su asked the child.

"I'm Ri Song-gi. I'm five years old. Who are you?"

"I'm Ji-su. Do you live nearby, Song-gi?" Ji-su asked the little boy. The boy nodded and pointed to a primitive fisherman's hut nearby.

Ji-su read aloud from her book, and the little boy was enthralled. They were fast friends within minutes. Eventually, the boy's mother came looking for him and found him with Ji-su. The boy's mother told him it was time for him to come to the house for supper. The mother had little choice but to invite her son's new friend to eat with them.

"We don't have much to offer you to eat, but we invite you to join us. I am Mrs. Ri."

This was what Ji-su had been hoping would happen, and she accepted with grace and gratitude. The Ri family gathered in the hut for their meal, and they were cordial to Ji-su. The fisherman husband was there, but there were no other children except for Song-gi, the boy who had made friends with Ji-su. The food was meager, and Ji-su didn't eat much, although she was starving after the exhausting day on the motorcycle without anything to eat. In North Korea, animal protein such as pork, chicken, and beef are an unaffordable luxury for almost the entire population of the country. The fisherman's family meal consisted of kimchi, a Korean dish made with cabbage, a little rice, and some tiny bits of fish.

"My husband is a fisherman so we are lucky to sometimes have fish to eat with our rice and cabbage. Most people do not even have fish to eat. Things are not as bad as they were years ago when there was a terrible drought. Some of our fellow countrymen ate sawdust and tree bark to fill their stomachs. There is not much, if any, food value in these things, but filling one's stomach with anything at all helps reduce the pain of hunger. That is why they ate the sawdust and the tree bark. We always had a small garden, and my husband usually was able to save back a few fish for us to eat. We did not suffer as so many others suffered." The fisherman's wife was talkative, but the fisherman himself, Mr. Ri, was silent throughout the meal.

Song-gi's family seemed to be pleased to have a guest and proceeded to tell Ji-su all about the city of Wonsan and about the bombings which had just occurred. Wonsan had its own hydroelectric plant which made it one of the few places in the country that did not experience regular blackouts. The family did not have electricity in their hut, but the government had promised that electric lines would be brought to their village within five years. One day, they would have electricity, and everyone was relieved that the electric plant had not been destroyed by the Americans.

Finally the family asked Ji-su what she was doing in the fishing village outside Wonsan. She wore city clothes and seemed to have city manners, and they were curious. She said she was from Chongjin, a medium-sized industrial town to the north and the country's third largest city. She told her hosts she had been visiting her aunt in Wonsan when the bombing had begun two nights earlier. She told them that her aunt had been killed and her aunt's house had been destroyed. Ji-su had been left with only her kit bag and no other clothes or possessions. All of her things had been lost when her aunt's house had been bombed.

Ji-su tried to look sad, although she couldn't quite make herself cry. She said she was not able to get back to Chongjin because of all the confusion in the country. She told the family she had money and wanted to pay them for the meal they had so graciously fed her. She asked if the Ris would allow her to rent a spot on the floor of their hut where she could sleep for a few days, until she was able to make arrangements to get back home.

The family told her she could stay, even though they had little room in the hut and little food to share with her. At first, they protested when she offered them money to buy more food, but after she said she hoped to stay with them for several days, they seemed more willing to accept her contribution. Ji-su was so tired the first few nights she stayed with the fisherman's family, she had no problem going to sleep on the dirt floor. After three days, she desperately wanted a shower and a chance to wash her hair.

Most importantly, she needed to find a place to recharge her satellite phones. There was no electricity in this fishing village. Ji-su told the fisherman's wife that she was going to try to make it to Wonsan to see if she could buy a bus ticket or find a way to get back to her home in Chongjin. She asked the family if she could return to the fishing village to stay with them if she could not find a way back to Chongjin.

Ji-su was hoping her motorcycle hadn't been stolen and was pleasantly surprised to find it still hidden under the bushes where she'd left it. She had a little bit of gas left and drove the cycle into Wonsan. The city was in chaos as she had expected it would be, but she had money and was able to buy gasoline. She had a harder time finding a place to charge her phones. She had a charging cord, but finding someplace that had electricity where she could plug in the cord was a challenge. Finally, she decided to try one of the expensive hotels where foreign tourists stayed when they visited the city. She found a place where she could leave her motorcycle and paid a somewhat suspicious-looking boy to watch it for her for two days.

Because Ji-su had cash, she was able to get a room at the hotel. She couldn't wait to feel hot water on her skin and hair. She'd not had a shower or a real bath since days before when she'd stripped her body of the Kim Jong-un disguise. The fisherman's family didn't have any indoor plumbing or running water, so she'd only been able to bathe with water from a basin. She knew she wouldn't feel completely free of the disgusting KJU mess until she had scrubbed and scrubbed away the last traces of her impersonation.

Imagine her disappointment when the manager of the hotel told her there would be hot water only between eight and nine every other night. There would be electricity, if they were lucky, from four to six each morning. There was no room service, and two meals a day were being served in the dining room. Ji-su had forgotten, during the years she had lived in South Korean and on Whidbey Island, how primitive and deprived life was in North Korea. She was staying in one of the best hotels in one of the country's largest cities, and she still couldn't get a hot bath when she wanted one or charge her phone when she needed to. She could work around the rationing schedules the hotel had presented to her, but she couldn't help but despise what the Communists and the Kim family had done to impoverish the country of her birth.

Ji-su needed clean clothes. She had worn her clothes for three days and had washed them out in cold water each night before she went to bed on the floor of the fisherman's hut. The clothes never dried completely, and every morning she had shivered as she put on her cold, damp underwear and long pants. She hoped there would be at least one store still open in Wonsan. Or, she might be able to find an open-air market where she could buy something that would fit her. Consumer goods had always been in short supply in North Korea, so Ji-su knew there would not be a good selection. She would consider herself lucky if she could find anything at all. She did not give any thought to fashion. She only wanted something that was clean and wouldn't fall off her painfully thin body.

When she found some new boys' long pants and underwear and a used sweater for sale, she was happy to pay the outrageous price the woman with the kiosk was asking. Ji-su found a black windbreaker jacket with a hood at another stall in the marketplace. The windbreaker was dirty and had a rip in the side, but it would help to keep out the cold air.

Ji-su finally did get hot water and was able to wash her hair. The food served in the dining room was terrible by South Korean and Whidbey Island standards, but at least the sheets on the bed were clean. Ji-su plugged in her phones, and after two days, they were fully charged. Even with money, life in North Korea was more than grim, and she couldn't wait to get out of the place.

She finally heard from Sergei who had arrived in Vladivostok. He was staying at a monastery on Russky Island and was making preparations to rescue her by boat. Ji-su thought this sounded like a terrible idea, but she was so anxious to leave the country, she didn't raise any objections. She trusted Sergei the priest, this man she had never met in person, and he had not let her down yet.

Sergei wanted to know if she could possibly make it to Chongjin. That city was closer to Vladivostok, and it would be easier and quicker for Sergei to get her out of North Korea from there. Ji-su could think of only one way she could possibly meet up with Sergei in his cabin cruiser near Chongjin.

She was almost discouraged and ready to give up, but she decided to try her luck with Mr. Ri, the fisherman whose family had taken her in. She checked out of the hotel and was relieved that the boy with whom she had entrusted her motorcycle had not run off with it or sold it. Ji-su knew he'd been riding it around, but she filled it up with gasoline again and made her way back to the fishing village.

Ji-su was torn between wanting to be straightforward with the fisherman about why she needed to get to Chongjin or making up another lie about herself. She knew she would be taking a terrible risk by speaking the truth, and she had no idea how the Ri family would react to her candor. She decided to take the chance and be honest with them. She carefully planned how she was going to ask Song-gi and his parents if they were willing to leave behind their country and defect from North Korea to Russia. Ji-su told Sergei what she was going to do, and he didn't try to talk her out of bringing the Ri family with her. If it was the only way she could get out of North Korea, that was fine with him. Sergei told her he would bring more provisions on board the boat for their journey across the Sea of Japan. He would tell the monks at St. Seraphim that there would be additional arrivals in a couple of days.

Chapter 25

WONSAN, NORTH KOREA

When Ji-su returned from her trip to the city of Wonsan, she brought pork and other special food to the fisherman's hut for their evening meal. When Song-gi's mother saw what Ji-su had brought, Mrs. Ri eyed her with suspicion. How had this woman been able to procure these delicacies which no fisherman's family was ever able to afford? Where had she even found meat to buy? It was never available in the village market at any price. Song-gi's mother had been wary of Ji-su from the beginning and had guessed that she was not exactly what she said she was. Ji-su tried to reassure the family that she'd only meant for the precious food to be a gift as a thank you for their kindness to her. In spite of the fact that they were a simple fisherman's family, they were smart and realized that something else was really going on.

As the family enjoyed the lavish meal Ji-su had provided, she began to question them about how they honestly felt about their lives in North Korea. When Song-gi had fallen asleep in his mother's lap and long after the sun had gone down, the three talked by the light of the oil lantern that made but a tiny inroad into the darkness of the hut. Ji-su asked if they had ever imagined leaving their homeland for another country. Song-gi's mother had a guarded expression as she looked at her fisherman husband. Could they possibly trust this woman who had appeared out of nowhere? She had money and city clothes. Her accent wasn't quite right for Chongjin, where she said she'd come from.

Finally, the husband nodded, and the mother began to cry. When she finally found her voice, she told Ji-su that almost everyone in North Korea was poor and that fishermen's families, although not the poorest in the desperately poor country, all lived at a subsistence level. She said, of course, they had dreamed of a better life, for themselves and for their child. Of course, they had wondered how it would be to have enough to eat and to live in freedom. But they dared not speak of it, even to each other. It was only a dream. It was something they could only wonder about, not something they could ever allow themselves to hope for.

Ji-su felt her own tears as she listened to the woman's desperation and heard her express her long-unspoken wish for a life that Ji-su had the luxury of taking for granted. Ji-su explained what she was offering them and how it would happen. She told them they would leave North Korea and go to Vladivostok where they would live with the Russian Orthodox monks at St. Seraphim until they could decide, with the help of the clergy, where they wanted to go and what they wanted to do. Ji-su told them it would be risky, and they might be caught and killed as they made their escape in the fishing boat and then in the cabin cruiser as they crossed the Sea of Japan. She told them that if they were lucky, once they had made it to St. Seraphim on Russky Island, they would be safe and with people who would take care of them.

Song-gi's mother rocked her son back and forth in her lap as she sat on the dirt floor of their hut. The tears once again streamed down her face. She looked at her husband with pleading eyes, and he nodded in agreement. They would leave with Ji-su in two days' time. Now that they had made such a momentous decision, all three were exhausted. It was time to rest. There were preparations to be made, and the next two days would be busy. There would be no more time for tears and little time for sleep.

Ji-su had almost nothing to pack to take on the trip. She had a few clothes and the things she had brought with her in her kit bag. She knew that the Ri family had almost nothing in the way of material possessions. Little Song-gi had one toy and one change of clothing. He had a pair of homemade sandals but no sturdy winter shoes. Ji-su helped Song-gi's mother pack up their clothes and the paltry assortment of household goods the family owned. They packed at night, after Song-gi had gone to sleep. Ji-su was sad to see the few forlorn bundles of belongings that were assembled and ready to be transferred to the fishing boat. The Ri family had hardly anything to take with them to their new life.

The night of their departure in the fishing boat, they waited until after midnight to leave the hut. The fisherman had loaded his family's bundles onto the boat little by little, off and on during the day and evening. He didn't want to attract attention by carrying their things from the hut to the boat all at once. Unusual activity of any kind was noticed in the small village.

Finally, it was time to leave. Song-gi's mother carried him down to the water and boarded the fishing boat that would take them away from their lives in North Korea. Ji-su brought up the rear. The fisherman was already on board. Their departure from the fishing village near Wonsan was silent and unnoticed. Song-gi's mother did not even look back at the hut that had been her home for so many years. She was looking forward now. They were on their way.

The fisherman was in command. He knew where their meeting place was to be, and he was confident that they would find the Chris-Craft. This was his world, his world on the water, and he was confident here. Song-gi slept in his mother's arms, and his mother slept, too. She would need all of her strength to guide her small family through the next days and weeks of uncertainty. She knew her husband would have been content to stay in North Korea and that he had taken this risk because he knew she wanted it so much. She would have to carry the burden of their decision once her husband was no longer in control, once he was no longer a confident fisherman operating his boat on the water.

Ji-su couldn't sleep. She was so tired, but there was too much for her to think about. Her whole life had been spent working towards the destruction of the North Korean regime, and she was proud of the small part she had contributed to accomplish that. No one knew what would happen to North Korea now. No one could predict what would transition out of the current chaos.

Ji-su realized she had never given any thought to the fact that she might have a life to live after her goal had been achieved. She had never thought or planned beyond the day when she would be the stand-in for the hated Kim Jong-un. Her identity and her entire reason for being had been tied up with his, with bringing him down. Now that he no longer ruled, now that her mission had been accomplished, she had nowhere to go with her life. She had a family that cared about her in South Korea, but she had taken them for granted and used them to facilitate her revenge. She had not even seen them or communicated with them for almost two years. She was still a member of the South Korean military. Was that where her future lay?

She had never thought she would have a future, and now she had no idea what in the world she wanted that future to look like. The journey she'd been on for most of her life had come to its conclusion. She wondered where her next journey, the next journey that had already begun, would lead her. Finally, Ji-su also drifted off to sleep.

Chapter 26

NORTH KOREA AND THE SEA OF JAPAN

Ji-su had been in regular contact with Sergei about their plans. She'd tried to be careful and use up as little as possible of the battery charge on her satellite phones. If she lost her ability to communicate with Sergei, their escape would never happen. Ji-su knew that Sergei was coming with a boat to meet them a few miles off-shore from a small uninhabited island in the Sea of Japan, an island near Chongjin. Although the island would be within sight of the meeting place, the longitude and latitude exactly marked the spot at sea were they would rendezvous. Mr. Ri, the fisherman, knew the island and agreed that it was a good place for the two boats to meet.

Ji-su knew that Sergei was not entirely comfortable with Vasily, the man who'd been hired to pilot the Chris-Craft. Because Sergei had no boating skills, he felt he was at the ship captain's mercy. Sergei had been trained at Camp 27 to live in Minot, North Dakota, far away from any ocean. He'd never learned to operate a watercraft of any kind. Having spent most of his last fifteen years in a Russian Orthodox monastery, he'd never even had the chance to go for a ride aboard a powerboat. He wondered if he would be seasick. He knew he had no idea how to navigate or how to operate the Chris-Craft. He hated to be without complete control over his life. Getting onto an unknown boat with an unknown sea captain in a port city where he had never been before was certainly taking a risk. It seemed entirely foolhardy to Sergei to put his life in the hands of someone he didn't know, didn't like, and didn't trust, and take off across a huge body of water to an unknown destination.

While Sergei was onboard the boat, he would be out of sight of land for nearly the entire trip. It was almost more than he could stand to think about. He hated to take a weapon with him because he despised violence and hated guns. But, his gut told him there might be trouble on the horizon, and he needed to be prepared. He decided to pack his handgun and sufficient ammunition. He'd been trained to use the gun many years ago, and he'd used it only a few times since he was a teenager. At one time, he had been an excellent shot. The last time he had been forced to use his gun, he had promised himself he would never use it again.

The Chris-Craft was provisioned with food and water, and all gasoline tanks were full. Sergei didn't get a good vibe from the captain of his boat but felt he had no choice except to deal with Vasily. It was too late now to find a replacement. Vasily seemed to know a lot about boats, and he assured Sergei that he had operated a cabin cruiser exactly like the Chris-Craft many times before. Vasily had a smug attitude, and he knew very well he had the upper hand in this situation. The only thing that Sergei had to hold over Vasily's head were the two remaining payments he owed the man.

If Vasily failed to meet up with the fishing boat that carried Ji-su and the fisherman's family, he would not receive his second payment. If he did not return everyone safely to the pier on Russky Island, he would not receive his final payment. Sergei hoped the financial inducement would motivate Vasily to do what he had promised. Sergei could tell Vasily was sneaky, and he was worried that the captain of their boat had some other agenda in mind. Sergei was a priest and not a suspicious person by nature. His instincts told him not to trust Vasily, but he could not put his finger on any specific reason for his misgivings about the sea captain from Vladivostok.

The meeting between the *Marina* and Mr. Ri's fishing boat was set for five in the morning. The island near where the rendezvous would take place was within the off-shore maritime limits claimed by North Korea. Officially, by law, the island was in international waters, but no one was going to take the North Koreans to the Hague to try to dispute their claims. The island was at the outer limits of where the North Koreans guarded their shore with their patrol boats, and while it was still dark, the fisherman felt it would be a safe place to meet.

The fishing boat arrived early and waited. Ji-su and the fisherman's wife and son were hiding below deck. When the Chris-Craft didn't show up, the fisherman began to grow nervous. He considered putting his nets over the side of the fishing vessel in case a patrol boat came by to check on what he was doing, just sitting there, not bothering to fish. At the moment he was preparing to cast his nets into the sea, the cabin cruiser came in sight. It had turned off its engines and its lights and was coasting the last few hundred yards towards the off-island rendezvous. It would be up to the fisherman to maneuver his smaller boat close to the Chris-Craft so that his passengers could climb aboard the larger boat.

After Ji-su and the Ri family and their belongings were aboard the powerboat, the fisherman would abandon his own boat. He would leave behind forever his only asset in the world, his way of earning enough to support his family, his entire way of life. Someone, perhaps a North Korean patrol boat, would find the abandoned fishing boat floating free in the Sea of Japan and briefly make a note that another North Korean fisherman had been lost. His extended family might be notified, and nobody would care very much. Such was life in the Hermit Kingdom.

The transfer of passengers was made, and Song-gi briefly woke up and asked his mother where he was. She hushed him and told him to go back to sleep, that he was safe. Sergei was standing on the deck of the *Marina* at the top of the aluminum boat ladder to help Ji-su climb aboard. She smiled at Sergei as he extended his hand to her and pulled her on board the cabin cruiser. Even with her hair cut short and even with her ragged clothing, Sergei thought Ji-su was the most beautiful woman he had ever seen.

Sergei held onto her hand a little longer than he needed to and almost failed to help the poor fisherman who was behind Ji-su on the ladder. Sergei eventually let go of her hand and reached out to assist Mr. Ri as he climbed onto the deck of the power boat. Ji-su asked Sergei to be sure that Song-gi and his family had water and something to eat. Sergei offered to show them to their quarters. They were frightened and emotionally depleted and were grateful to have a place to sleep and be left alone.

Ji-su went to the bridge to introduce herself to the captain. She didn't care for Vasily any more than Sergei did. He had an excited and threatening glint in his eye when he met Ji-su, and she suspected that he was up to something. When she'd been doing her service in the South Korean military and even though she'd been in the Army of the Republic of Korea, Ji-su had learned to navigate at sea and knew how to operate several different kinds of watercraft.

South Korea is a peninsula that might as well be an island. The country is surrounded by water on three sides, and its fourth side was a no man's land, a no-go zone that blocked all access to what was north of the DMZ. Anyone serving in the military in South Korea had to learn about the water, about navigation, and about boats. It had been a few years since Ji-su had received her military training, but she remembered most of what she'd been taught.

Ji-su's excellent sense of direction gave her the first hint that something was not right with the course the boat was taking. She was worried because the Chris-Craft seemed to be heading closer to North Korea rather than away from the land. It was essential that they avoid the North Korean patrol boats at all costs. They were already too close to, if not actually inside, North Korean waters. Ji-su suspected that the captain had pointed the boat to approach rather than avoid the mainland. She was sure of it when she saw the lights of Chongjin ahead.

She tried to confront Vasily, but he spoke only Russian and hardly any English. Ji-su spoke no Russian. She yelled for Sergei to come to the bridge to translate for her while she questioned the captain about what he was doing, where he was taking the boat. Vasily, of course, had no idea that Ji-su knew anything about navigational charts or how to operate the Chris-Craft. To Vasily, she was just a girl.

Sergei heard the alarm in Ji-su's voice and checked to be sure the gun in his pocket was loaded. He had been afraid there would be some kind of trouble with the captain, and now it seemed as if his fears had been realized. He climbed to the bridge to find Ji-su and Vasily shouting at each other. Neither could understand what the other was saying. Ji-su quickly told Sergei in English that the Chris-Craft was headed towards North Korea rather than away from it. Vasily was taking them all in the direction of terrible danger.

Sergei began to question Vasily. They were both speaking Russian, so Vasily couldn't pretend he didn't understand what Sergei was saying to him. The captain became belligerent. He said he had additional business to conduct off the shores of Chongjin. He was meeting another boat at sea, he said. He thought he had the others in the Chris-Craft at a disadvantage, and he intended to follow through with his plans, even if it put them all at risk. Sergei demanded to know what this additional business was that might get them killed.

Vasily didn't think it mattered at this point if he told Sergei the truth. He told Sergei he had brought a valuable shipment of drugs on board the Chris-Craft and had made arrangements to sell them for a large amount of money. Vasily let Sergei know that he didn't care about collecting on the final payments that Sergei still owed him. The money Vasily would make from the sale of his drugs would be ten times more than the money Sergei owed him.

The only reason Vasily had taken the job as the captain of the *Marina* was to have a way to get to the place where he'd set up his drug deal. He was not going to back down. The Chris-Craft was headed back to North Korea. Sergei could not allow that to happen. He drew his gun and pointed it at Vasily. Vasily drew a large knife. He'd never expected the priest to be carrying a gun, and he'd brought a knife to a gun fight!

Vasily immediately grabbed Ji-su and held the large knife to her throat. His defiant look, which he directed at Sergei, dared him to do anything with the gun. What Vasily could have no way of knowing was that Ji-su, the woman he thought he was holding hostage with a knife, was an expert in the martial arts. She reacted instantly and threw Vasily to the ground. Before Vasily could even begin to wonder what had happened to him, Ji-su had him pinned and immobilized on the mahogany floor of the bridge. Ji-su shouted for Sergei to grab the loop of nylon anchor line that was hanging on the wall. Sergei tossed the line to Ji-su, and she expertly trussed Vasily up as if he was an American Thanksgiving turkey. Vasily wasn't going anywhere, and Sergei hadn't had to use his gun. Ji-su told Sergei to keep the gun trained on Vasily while she turned the boat around.

Ji-su was quite comfortable using the navigation charts, and she figured out the course they had to take the moment she saw where their boat was located. She knew what she had to do, and although she was not that familiar with the Chris-Craft, she was smart and a quick study. She knew she could learn how to operate the *Marina*. She also knew she had to figure it out without a second's delay. Sergei watched in amazement as Ji-su immediately took control of the boat and turned it around. Finally, they were heading back out into the Sea of Japan, away from Chongjin, and towards the safety that international waters would provide.

The sun was coming up. As Sergei and Ji-su were each about to heave a sigh of relief, thinking they were speeding away from North Korea and on their way to freedom, Sergei spotted a North Korean patrol boat following in their wake. Ji-su pushed the Chris-Craft to go faster. She knew the North

Koreans would follow them into international waters to try to catch them. The North Koreans did not respect any international laws or any international boundaries. Their arrogance gave them permission to do whatever they wanted to do. Ji-su realized the Chris-Craft could not outrun the patrol boat. At some point, they would have to stand and fight. Sergei had a gun, and she had the knife she'd taken from Vasily. She was afraid the men in the North Korean patrol boat would have automatic weapons. One knife and one handgun were no match for an AK-47 or two.

Ji-su thought the North Korean patrol boat was a small one and probably only had two people aboard. Ji-su had an idea. She told Sergei what they would have to do and asked if there was any extra fuel on board. How hard would it be for him to get two or more buckets of gasoline up on deck? She told Sergei to wake the fisherman and bring him to the bridge so that Ji-su could give him his instructions.

In less than a minute, the sleepy fisherman appeared. Ji-su explained about the North Korean patrol boat and that the Chris-Craft couldn't outrun it. The fisherman's eyes filled with fear as he was obviously contemplating what would happen if he and his family were returned to North Korea. He began to explain to Ji-su that they would all rather be dead than go back to torture and imprisonment in North Korea. Ji-su hushed him and told him that nobody was going back to that terrible place. They were going to fight for their lives, and she explained to him how she hoped they were going to do that.

Sergei brought two bailing buckets full of gasoline to the rear deck. He'd also found several cans of Sterno in the galley. Ji-su was especially thrilled to see the Sterno. Ji-su sent the fisherman and Sergei to search the boat for some light-weight containers to hold the gasoline. She shouted her directions from the bridge as she struggled to keep the boat on a straight course at full speed. She yelled her orders to Sergei in English and to Mr. Ri in Korean. She told them they had two minutes to find something and be back on deck. The fisherman returned with an old-fashioned rubber inner tube. Sergei found a waterproof duffel bag that had probably once belonged to someone who'd spent the night on the boat. Both of these receptacles seemed suitable for what Ji-su wanted to do, and she gave the men their instructions.

The patrol boat was gradually gaining on the Chris-Craft, and Ji-su knew that it would only be a few minutes until it overtook them. Both boats were well into international waters by now, but of course, as Ji-su had predicted, the North Korean boat was proceeding at full speed to attack the cabin cruiser, completely ignoring the illegality of doing so.

Sergei and the fisherman quickly prepared their make-shift bombs. They filled the old inner tube with gasoline, and after lining the duffel bag with several plastic garbage bags, they filled it with gasoline. They made wicks out of strips of cloth. Sergei had his gun ready. The fisherman, who had years of experience handling fishing nets and throwing them where he wanted them to go over the side of his boat, would be the one to toss the homemade bombs. It all had to happen with split-second timing, and there was no time for any practice.

The patrol boat had to be close enough to the Chris-Craft for the fisherman to lob the containers of burning gasoline into it. If the boats were too far apart, the gasoline and Sterno bombs would be lost in the sea. If he waited too long to throw the gasoline-filled receptacles, the fisherman might be severely burned. If he held on to the burning balls of death for too long, waiting for exactly the right moment and the right trajectory, he could be in trouble. If he waited too long to toss the incendiary devices, they could all be dead from the AK-47s.

Ji-su slowed the Chris-Craft to allow the patrol boat to pull closer. She gave the signal to Sergei to light the Sterno cans and put them inside the containers holding the gasoline. Sergei lit the wicks that hung like burning tails from the inner tube and from the duffel bag. Sure enough, there were two men in the North Korean patrol boat. One man was steering the boat and the other was standing at the bow ready to fire his machine gun. Sergei turned the gasoline bombs over to the fisherman and aimed his gun at the head of the man who held the AK-47. Everything happened so quickly in the next few seconds, it was difficult to say afterwards what had happened first.

Sergei hit the man holding the machine gun with two quick shots to the head, but not before the North Korean with the AK-47 had fired several rounds. At least one round went into the fisherman's leg. But before he went down, the fisherman had been able to hoist the duffle bag and throw it into the patrol boat. The fisherman's arms were burned as he'd held onto the fiery bomb and waited to throw it into the patrol boat at just the right moment. The fisherman fell backwards on the deck, his left leg bleeding badly.

Sergei picked up the gasoline-filled inner tube and hurled it with all of his might into the patrol boat that was about to crash into the rear of the Chris-Craft. Both of the bombs had hit their target. Both had landed on the deck of the patrol boat, and the patrol boat was on fire. The pilot of the patrol boat left his post on the bridge and ran to the bow of the boat with his machine gun. He was about to fire at the two people on the open rear deck of the cabin cruiser. Sergei again raised his gun and fired two shots into the face of the second North Korean.

Sergei was either a naturally excellent shot or he had been extremely lucky. He hadn't practiced his marksmanship in years, but he had been bull's eye twice in only a few seconds that day. Both men in the patrol boat were down, and there was no one steering on the bridge of the North Korean boat. It veered off to the side, now fully ablaze from the homemade gasoline bombs. Ji-su, who had watched all this action from her position on the bridge, put the cabin cruiser on full speed ahead and pulled away from the burning hulk that had been the North Korean patrol boat.

The *Marina* headed farther out into the Sea of Japan. Sergei threw his gun down on the deck and dropped to his knees to see what he could do for the injured fisherman. A huge explosion caused both Ji-su and Sergei to look behind them. The patrol boat had blown up, and now it was simply a fireball in their wake. The debris from the explosion would float on top of the water for a while, and then it would sink below the surface forever. A few pieces of flotsam and jetsam might eventually turn up on the shores of North Korea or some other country. Those bits of debris would be the only clues as to what might have happened to one of North Korea's patrol boats and two of the Hermit Kingdom's sailors.

Everyone aboard the *Marina* had done their jobs perfectly, but the fisherman had paid the highest price for his excellent work. Sergei wanted to do everything he could to save the man's life and his leg. Years earlier, Sergei had received some first aid training, and he immediately began applying pressure to stop the bleeding. In addition to the terrible damage to his leg, Mr. Ri had burns on his hands and arms. He was trying not to cry out in pain, but Sergei knew that between the gunshot wound and the burns, the man was suffering terribly.

Chapter 27

SEA OF JAPAN AND RUSSKY ISLAND

The sun was climbing higher in the sky, and Ji-su planned to take the *Marina* into the Sea of Japan to hide it. The logistics and the timing of the rendezvous between Mr. Ri's fishing boat and the Chris-Craft had made it necessary for most of the *Marina*'s return trip to Russky Island to occur during daylight. This was not ideal under the best of circumstances. Ji-su did not think the North Koreans would send another boat after them, but she didn't want to take any chances.

The *Marina* had on board an incredibly bad Russian sea captain named Vasily who had illegal drugs in his possession. The cabin cruiser also had on board several Korean nationals who had no papers or passports, no visas, and no permission to enter Vladimir Putin's police state. One of these illegal North Koreans was badly wounded. Song-gi's family had never had any papers of any kind, and as poor North Koreans, they would all be persona non grata anywhere in Russia. Ji-su was a citizen of South Korea, but her passport was in a suitcase somewhere on Whidbey Island in the United States. Because it was half way around the world, that South Korean passport was not going to be of any use to her in Vladivostok.

The Chinese and the Russians and everybody else had been trying for years to prevent the North Koreans, who were constantly trying to defect from their failed nation, from entering more prosperous countries. Nobody wanted to take in the North Korean fishermen's illiterate families who had no useful skills and no assets and would become a drain on the benefits of the socialist welfare states.

One of Ji-su's options was to head straight for Russian territory, to Kraskino or even Slavjanka or one of the islands off the coast of Russia in the Zaliv Pos'yeta, the Bay of Posyeta . Russia had a small border with North Korea, and that border was close to Chongjin. But what would she do if she made it to Kraskino or Slavjanka or some island nearby? Neither she nor the North Koreans had any documents to allow them to enter Russia. If Ji-su made land anywhere in Russia, the Koreans would be illegal. They could be arrested, and Mr. Ri was in desperate need of medical attention.

If she decided to land the *Marina* any place but Russky Island, she would have nobody. If she headed for Russky Island, they had the brothers of St. Seraphim to help them and lead them to a safe place. Russky Island was the only possibility that offered any chance of saving the fisherman's life. It was the only hope for Ji-su and the Ri family.

For a multitude of reasons, she knew she couldn't approach Russky Island until after dark. But Ji-su was also fully aware that every minute she waited to deliver her precious cargo put the fisherman's life increasingly at risk. He needed immediate care, and any delay decreased his chances of staying alive, let alone saving his leg. It was a difficult dilemma, but she decided that it was most important to save Song-gi and his mother at all costs. She would wait until after dark to sneak onto Russky Island.

Sergei had assured Ji-su that the good brothers at the monastery of St. Seraphim would be able to handle all of these problems, once their boat reached Russia. Ji-su trusted Sergei, but she worried that he might be placing an undeserved amount of trust in the Russian Orthodox Church. She had no choices other than the plan laid out by Sergei. She concentrated on becoming familiar with the Chris-Craft and charting a surreptitious course to approach Russky Island. She wanted to make a landing there after the sun went down. She hoped Mr. Ri would last that long.

Sergei was tending to the fisherman's wounds and had finally been able to stop the bleeding. But there was nothing he could do to ease the man's pain. The man's leg was so severely wounded, even if the fisherman's life could be saved, Sergei doubted that his leg could be. Ri had lost a lot of blood and was slipping in and out of consciousness as he lay on the open deck in the stern of the Chris-Craft. Sergei had decided not to move the injured man for fear of doing further damage and had brought some pillows and blankets from the cabin below. He carefully elevated the fisherman's damaged leg and did everything he could to try to make him more comfortable. Sergei hoped that keeping the man warm and hydrated might help to mitigate the effects of the trauma. Sergei knew the fisherman needed fluids. Ri seemed able to swallow small sips of water, but when Sergei tried to give the man a drink of vodka to take the edge off his pain, Ri had refused to swallow it and had allowed the vodka to dribble out the side of his mouth.

Song-gi and his mother had been awakened by the sounds of gunfire during the melee with the North Korean patrol boat. Sergei had shouted at Mrs. Ri to keep her son below decks and find the most secure hiding place the two of them could fit into. In spite of the fact that Mrs. Ri had probably not been able to understand a word he'd shouted at her in Russian and in English, she went back below decks and had stayed out of the way. Finally, when there had been no more sounds of automatic weapons coming from above where they were hiding, Mrs. Ri decided it was safe to come out. She came on deck to help Sergei take care of her husband. She didn't want Song-gi to see how badly his father was hurt, so Sergei took the little boy up to the bridge to be with Ji-su. Of course, Ji-su was busy and had little time to pay attention to the boy, and then there was Vasily lying in a lump on the floor.

To keep the drug dealer from screaming, Sergei had stuffed some rags in Vasily's mouth and secured the gag with duct tape wound around his face and head. From time to time, Ji-su had used her martial arts skills to make Vasily unconscious. Ji-su knew how to paralyze and put Vasily to sleep for a while without hurting him. As she was trying to steer their course through the Sea of Japan, it was less distracting if Vasily were lying still and not squirming and fighting his restraints and trying to shout and get rid of the gag in his mouth.

When Song-gi saw Vasily tied up and lying in a heap, he asked what had happened. Ji-su explained that the man in the corner was a criminal who had put them all in danger. She told Song-gi that the evil Vasily had wanted to sell drugs for money and that he was going to be arrested and put in jail because of his illegal behavior. Song-gi seemed to accept this story, and he looked at Vasily, shook his head, and said to the unconscious Russian, "You are a bad, bad man." Even if Vasily had been conscious, he wouldn't have understood the boy's remarks to him which had been made in Korean, but Ji-su understood. She had to smile and told the little boy she agreed with him completely.

Song-gi asked her why they were on this boat and where they were going. The boy asked Ji-su if his father was going to be all right. Nothing had escaped the notice of the five-year-old. He had a million questions for Ji-su. She answered them all as best she could, and then she put Song-gi on a stool beside her where he could watch what she did as she steered the boat toward what she hoped would be a better life for the little boy and his family.

Sergei had been in touch with the brothers at St. Seraphim. They'd known before he left Russky Island on his trip to North Korea that he would be bringing undocumented foreign nationals with him when he returned from his mission. They were prepared to deal with all of that. What they were not prepared to deal with was that one of these people would be in critical condition and close to death from loss of blood as the result of a machine gun fight with the North Koreans. They also had not planned to have to deal with the bad man Vasily and his stash of drugs. They assured Sergei that Vasily was an easy fix, that they could take care of the Vasily problem with hardly any effort. But finding the necessary doctors and the necessary blood transfusions to save the life of the Korean fisherman presented a much more difficult challenge. It would take some time to put all of that together, and time was something they did not have.

Because of the complicated human cargo the *Marina* carried and because of her own undocumented status, Ji-su did not think it was wise to dock the boat at the rented slip in Vladivostok. The Chris-Craft had been berthed there before it had set out on its rescue mission. But there were too many other boats close by and too many people milling around the pier, day and night, to unload the *Marin*a there. Ji-su had to find another way to land the *Marina* and reach Russky Island. She left it to Sergei to arrange the unofficial and unobserved nighttime landing. She kept the Chris-Craft out of sight of land until Sergei could finalize their landing location, the timetable they would follow, and their rendezvous on the beach with the brothers from St. Seraphim.

At last, Sergei told her he had a plan. At least he thought he knew how to get the *Marina* to shore on Russky Island. He still did not have any confirmation that there were arrangements in place to try to save Mr. Ri's life. Ji-su found the spot on the map where she was supposed to attempt to land the Chris-Craft. It was on the beach, not a place where a boat of any size would normally be able to go ashore.

It had begun to rain as the cabin cruiser waited off shore for darkness to arrive. By the time the sun went down, the rain had turned into a serious storm and was coming down in torrents. Lightning and thunder filled the sky around the port of Vladivostok and around the Russky Island beach. The cold October wind howled, and the surf was much too rough. As she approached the landing spot on the beach, Ji-su told her passengers, who were standing below her on the deck beside the unconscious Mr. Ri, that she didn't think she could land the *Marina* on the shore. The beach was rocky. It was even more dangerous than she'd thought it would be to attempt a landing in the surf.

Ji-su could almost not see the faint outline of four men standing in the blowing rain at the edge of the water, waiting for the *Marina* to come ashore. Sergei was in communication with the rescue party, and when they heard that the boat was not going to be able to make it to the beach, Ji-su saw the four monks begin moving out into the surf. They were going to swim to the Chris-Craft. Ji-su asked Song-gi and his mother if they could swim. When they nodded that they could, she asked if they thought they could swim to land from where the *Marina* was positioned off shore. She shouted to them that they that should go over the side of the boat and try to swim together through the surf to safety.

The water was quite cold in October around Vladivostok. The lightning streaked and lit up the sky. The wind and the rumble of the thunder were so loud that no one could hear what anyone was shouting at them. Song-gi looked terrified as he and his mother disappeared over the side of the *Marina* and began to struggle in the strong current to make their way toward land. One of the four rescuers who was swimming toward the boat broke off from the group and made his way through the rip current to pull Song-gi and his mother to safety. Ji-su nearly collapsed with relief when she realized that the little boy and his mother were going to make it to shore and to freedom—if one could claim that Vladimir Putin's Russia was in fact freedom. At least it wasn't North Korea.

The three remaining rescuers continued to make slow progress towards the *Marina*. It was rough going in the storm. They were swimming against the tide. Ji-su wasn't sure they would make it. Finally, the three pulled themselves up onto the deck of the Chris-Craft. One of them hoisted the now unconscious fisherman onto his back in the classic lifesaving fireman's carry and, with the help of the other two rescuers, eased himself gently back into the stormy sea and roiling surf.

Ji-su was still on the bridge, trying to hold the *Marina* steady in the terrible weather conditions. The two remaining rescuers hurried to meet with Ji-su. They both spoke a little bit of English. Ji-su told them she could swim to shore on her own. She pointed to Vasily, and the men nodded, letting her know that they knew what the story was. She gladly gave up the wheel of command and climbed down to the deck where Sergei was waiting for her. He took her hand, and the two went over the side of the boat together and began to swim to shore. They clung to each other. Both were strong swimmers, but they were sorely challenged by the storm's rough seas.

Finally, they made their way, cold and exhausted, onto the beach. Sergei lifted Ji-su from the rocky ground and carried her in the direction that the Russian monks had taken Song-gi and his mother and father. A van from the monastery was waiting on the road just beyond the beach. Ji-su had her arms around Sergei's neck. In spite of being soaked through to the skin and frozen to the bone, she felt completely safe and taken care of, perhaps for the first time in her life. She buried her face in Sergei's neck, and he held her in his arms until they made it to the monastery van which would transport them to a place that was warm and dry and secure.

The two rescuers still aboard the *Marina* were both accomplished watermen. They were monks, but they had grown up with the sea and were comfortable around all kinds of boats, even American-made powerboats. In spite of the terrible weather conditions, they brought the *Marina* into the slip at the pier in Vladivostok, the exact spot from where the boat had begun its journey less than thirty-six hours earlier. A truck from the monastery was waiting for them near the pier. The two unloaded the belongings of the Chris-Craft's passengers into the truck.

The monks turned their attention to Vasily. He was awake now. It wasn't long before these two strong men were able to convince the drug dealer and former sea captain to tell them where on board the *Marina* he had hidden his drugs.

These were the goods he had hoped to exchange for cash in a drug deal at sea off the shores of Chongjin. They loaded Vasily, who was still securely tied up with the nylon anchor line, into the cab of the truck with his drugs and his duffel bag of clothes.

The clerics had plans for Vasily. They did not intend to harm him. They intended to leave punishment, not to God this time, but to the authorities whom they knew would love to get their hands on a drug dealer. Vasily would be awfully sorry he had ever signed on for this last seagoing venture. He would be even sorrier that he'd tried to combine his cruise with a business deal... selling drugs. Vasily would never see the light of day again.

Chapter 28

ST. SERAPHIM

As soon as they arrived at the monastery, a team with a stretcher rushed to the van and carefully transferred Mr. Ri into the back of an ambulance. The fisherman's wife tried to follow, but she was restrained from accompanying her husband. She needed to stay with her son to comfort and reassure him in this strange, new place where they all found themselves. A kind and portly priest guided the mother and son to the kitchen of the monastery. Wet and bedraggled, Ji-su and Sergei followed along behind.

Most of the water-soaked passengers from the *Marina* were too exhausted to eat any of the food that was laid out on the table for them—except for little Song-gi. He was hungry, and his eyes grew wide as he saw the feast of sliced meats and cheeses and the loaves of white bread. He looked up at the priest who had led them to the kitchen, and the priest smiled and nodded his head. The priest spoke no Korean, and Song-gi did not understand or speak a word of Russian. But Song-gi understood that he was being given permission to eat the food that was in front of him. He had never used a knife and fork, so he filled his plate and ate with his fingers.

At one end of the table, there was a plate of cupcakes slathered with pink buttercream icing. Again, Song-gi's eyes grew wide as he silently asked if he could help himself to a cupcake. He closed his eyes with pleasure when he took the first bite. He'd never tasted anything similar to the cupcake or the buttery, sweet vanilla-flavored icing on top of the cupcake. He ate two cupcakes. His mother was worried that he would eat too much and make himself sick. Finally, after he'd finished a glass of milk, Song-gi climbed up onto his mother's lap and went to sleep. The priest led the mother and son to their sleeping quarters. Tonight, for the first time in their lives, they would sleep on clean, white sheets in real beds.

Ji-su didn't want to leave Sergei, but she knew she had to sleep. Another sympathetic priest, recognizing that these people had been through a terrible ordeal and needed to rest, led Ji-su to her room, a spare cell-like space with a bed, a chest of drawers, a desk, and a chair. Attached to the bedroom, there was a tiny bathroom with a bathtub. Ji-su wanted to take off her wet clothes and wash the salty seawater off her skin and out of her hair, but she didn't have the strength to do any of that. She fell asleep on top of her bed, still dressed in her damp clothes. Sometime during the night, someone came into her room and covered her with a soft, warm blanket.

Sergei had a similar simple bedroom next to Ji-su's. He wanted to check on how Ri the fisherman was doing and what was being done about Vasily. But he finally was able to put his questions, and his need to be in control, in the hands of God and in the hands of the good brothers who were taking care of things for God that night.

While the exhausted travelers were sleeping at the monastery, Mr. Ri was receiving life-saving surgery at a private medical clinic on Russky Island. The island across the Bosporus from the mainland part of the city of Vladivostok was the home of Far Eastern Federal University. An excellent hospital, Far Eastern District Medical Center, was associated with the university and provided inhabitants of the island with first rate medical care. For so many reasons, of course, it was impossible to take the North Korean fisherman to the university hospital. The poor man was in the country illegally to begin with and was not covered by Russia's universal health plan. To make matters worse, he had been wounded by an automatic weapon, and technically, all gunshot wounds had to be reported to the government and would be investigated.

But the monks at St. Seraphim had connections in the medical community. One of their own had been a well-known orthopedic surgeon before he'd retired from his medical career and decided to attend the seminary to become a priest in the Russian Orthodox Church. Dr. Gregor Volkov had not practiced medicine for more than six years, and he would not presume to think that his skills as a surgeon were current or up to standards. He did however have younger friends who were excellent surgeons, and Dr. Volkov knew he could trust some of them with this confidential task.

Russia had always been a land of secrets, a land of intrigue and mystery. Things were not always what they seemed to be in this country of the czars, this country of Stalin, this country of Putin. Sometimes survival depended on subterfuge and duplicity. When Brother Gregor heard what was required, he had known exactly the person to call and exactly where the emergency surgery could take place. He had a friend who ran a private clinic which was primarily a place for wealthy people to go to convalesce after undergoing an operation or after a serious illness. Those who chose not to go to one of the rather grim state-run convalescent homes and could afford to recover in a better place, had private options. One of those options was the Matryoshka Clinic on Russky Island. There were treatment rooms at the clinic, but there was no fully outfitted operating suite. They would have to make do, and they would have to do whatever they were going to do in a hurry.

Dr. Gregor Volkov mobilized the surgeons he trusted and arranged for everything that was necessary to be quickly and quietly transported to one of the treatment rooms at the Matryoshka Clinic. O negative blood for transfusions, IV fluids, and everything that could possibly be required to save Mr. Ri's life would be on hand. If he made it through the surgery, there was a secluded and private recovery room, usually reserved for the rich and famous, where Mr. Ri could stay for a couple of days until he was out of immediate danger. Then he would be transported back to the monastery where he would be watched over by Brother Gregor until he was fully recovered. The brothers spent most of their days in prayer, but when called upon to do good works, they were always delighted to have a little action in their lives.

The surgery that the fisherman was facing was a difficult one. He had gone for many hours without much-needed blood and IV fluids. His blood volume was dangerously low. The man had been malnourished for years before he'd been shot. There was a possibility that he could lose his leg. There was a possibility that he would die before, during, or after the surgery. Infection might have already set in.

The good news was that the machine gun bullets which had destroyed his leg had been through and through shots. A portable X-ray machine, which had been brought into the make-shift surgical suite, indicated that Mr. Ri had no bullets lodged in either the bone or the muscle of his leg. That was the good news. The not-so-good news was that his tibia and fibula were fractured and a piece of his left femur had been blown away from the rest of his thigh bone. He had also suffered significant damage to the soft tissues and the skin on his leg. Repairing all of this destruction would be a long, involved, and tedious operation and would require attaching many screws to put the bones of the man's leg back together. Furthermore, reconstruction of muscles, tendons, arteries, and nerves would also be necessary if the fisherman were to have any hope of being able to use his leg again. The men who would perform this ghost surgery on a man who wasn't really in their country would do their best for him.

They worked all night and into the next day, and the fisherman was still alive at the end of it all. The doctors had hoped to be able to finish the surgery before dawn, but it was four o'clock in the afternoon before they left the operating room. The surgeons were way past being exhausted, but they thought they had saved the man's life. They thought they also had a chance of saving his leg. It didn't matter to these physicians that the man was from North Korea or that he was in Russia illegally. He needed their care, and that was all they had to know about him. To a doctor who lived by the Hippocratic Oath and was a true healer, Ri the fisherman was everyman and everywoman.

After the surgery, Dr. Gregor Volkov returned to the monastery and spoke with Song-gi and his mother. Volkov was happy to report that their father and husband had come through the surgery without any unexpected complications. He would have a long recovery, and he might never walk again. Mrs. Ri gasped when she heard the news that her husband might never walk again.

Brother Gregor hastened to tell her that he thought they had been able to save her husband's leg, but there were no guarantees about whether or not his terribly damaged appendage would be able to function in the future. Only time and the healing process, and a great deal of physical therapy, would determine the extent to which the fisherman would be able to live a normal life in the years ahead. Volkov assured Mrs. Ri and Song-gi that everything possible would be done for their loved one.

The fisherman's wife grabbed the surgeon's hand and thanked him. She began to cry. In North Korea, her husband would have been left to die or shot like a lame horse. No one in the Ri's former country would have gone to the trouble to try to save his life. He was a humble man, a poor man. He could not pay for any of the care that he had received. Mrs. Ri was overwhelmed with gratitude for everything that had been done for her husband. She loved him and valued his life. She knew nothing of the Russian Orthodox religion and nothing of the Christian faith. Therefore, it was somewhat shocking to her that here in a foreign country, in this unfamiliar and confusing place, others also valued Ri.

Chapter 29

ST. SERAPHIM

They both knew something was happening between them, but neither one knew what to do about it. Sergei was almost fifty years old. Ji-su was in her thirties. Because of the lives they'd lived up to this point, neither one of them had ever had a romantic or serious intimate relationship with anyone. Sergei's years of training at Camp 27 had programmed him to avoid emotional attachments of all kinds. He'd literally been brainwashed not to fall in love or care about another human being, only to care about the USSR.

After Camp 27 and his years with an unloving family in Minot, North Dakota, Sergei had become a member of the priesthood in the Russian Orthodox Church. Although there is no vow of chastity and Russian Orthodox priests are allowed to marry, Sergei had gone into the monastery at Sergiyev Posad where most of the priests are single.

Ji-su had been so full of anger and so focused on revenge for most of her life, she had programed herself to focus on retribution and on her mission. She had lived her whole life around working towards bringing down the evil regime in

North Korea. She'd hardly noticed that she had a family in South Korea that loved her and took care of her. During all the years of her education and her years in the South Korean military, she had been so eager to punish, so full of hate, that she'd had no room in her heart or in her life for love or even for real friendship.

She had spent her time and her energy working towards one goal for all of her adult life. She had believed she would die during the very risky attack on the North Korean royal palace. When she found herself on the other side of accomplishing her life's single ambition and found she was still alive, she didn't know what to do with herself, let alone how to handle the feelings she had begun to have for Sergei.

He had saved her life. At the moment when she'd believed everything was all over, as she sat in the garden shed of the North Korean royal palace and realized that her motorcycle was not where it was supposed to be, the small hope that had begun to grow inside her that she might survive her mission began slipping away. When one of her phones had vibrated, Sergei had been on the line to tell her what to do, to tell her where her motorcycle was. Then Sergei had told her that her escape plan had evaporated, but he had come up with a new one. He was in constant communication with her from that time on, ready to tell her where to go… to find a way to survive and to live. He had been with her every step of the way as she made her escape from Pyongyang to Wonsan.

And then Sergei had flown from Moscow to Vladivostok to rescue her in a boat, a boat he had no idea how to operate. He had gone to extraordinary means to save her life. He had helped her through the rough and dangerous water to the beach on Russky Island, and then he had literally carried her to safety and freedom.

They had an extraordinary history together. She'd never had anybody watching out for her the way Sergei had. She somehow knew that he shared her feelings, but neither one of them had ever had a relationship. Neither one of them had ever fallen in love before. Neither one of them had ever had a lover. They were as inexperienced as two children when it came to love and any kind of physical expression of that love. What they were experiencing was so new and so odd to both of them, they had no words for what they felt. They had no way to speak of it, and they had no way to express in any nonverbal way, or in any way at all, what they were feeling. They were both terribly naïve, both terribly innocent, both terribly shy—unknowing and awkward in the ways of love.

The day after they found themselves at the monastery of St. Seraphim on Russky Island, they were both so exhausted from their ordeal, they slept most of the next day. When they finally woke up and went outside their small cell-like bedrooms, they realized their bedrooms were next to each other. This made everything even more awkward. Everything that had happened between them up until this moment had been conducted in crisis mode. It had been a rescue operation, a matter of life or death, and the great escape.

Nothing about their interactions had ever been at all ordinary or normal in any way. They had never had a casual conversation, a routine day or even an uneventful few minutes that was not filled with fear and urgency. Although they both spoke English, they did not know how to talk to each other about anything other than their violent objectives and trying to save their lives and the lives of others. They didn't know how to relate to each other. They did not really know each other yet at all. How could they possibly love each other, if they could not even talk to each other?

The first thing they both wanted to know was how Mr. Ri was doing. Had he survived his surgery? Had his leg been saved? The brothers told them that no one really knew the answers to those questions yet. Ri was still in surgery. They'd had no word yet from the clinic where Ri had been taken. Ji-su asked about Song-gi and his mother and was told that they were still asleep. There was no news, so the two did not even have the North Korean family to talk about.

Then Sergei asked what had been done about the Vasily problem. The monks who were in the room made eye contact with each other as glances shot from one to another, but they said nothing. Sergei knew something was going on, but no one was talking. The brothers knew something, and that something had to do with Vasily. One of the brothers told Sergei the situation with Vasily was ongoing and still in progress. When there was a resolution, they would give Sergei the news.

Sergei and Ji-su were hungry and went to the kitchen of the monastery. They'd missed lunch but the cook took pity on them and made them a Russian breakfast. They sat at the rectory table across from each other and eyed each other shyly. The crisis of the night before had past, and now they were just two people sitting across the table from one and other and eating breakfast together. Did they have anything at all in common? Did they have anything to say to each other in the light of day?

Sergei knew a little bit more about Ji-su, but Ji-su knew nothing about Sergei. They ate their meal in silence, and Sergei said to Ji-su, "Let's take a walk outside." They needed to get beyond the awful and intensely awkward place that they were in. It was October, and Vladivostok was feeling the first chill of winter. Ji-su had only the thin clothes she'd worn in Wonsan and in the boat in the Sea of Japan. Sergei had a coat, and he took it off and put it around Ji-su's shoulders. She looked up at this man who had saved her life and only the night before had carried her out of the cold ocean waters.

Ji-su asked him if he had a family. She would look back at this moment and wonder why this was the first question she had asked him. It was the first question that had come into her mind, and she always wondered why this was the first thing that had occurred to her. Her question said more about what was important to her than it did about what she wanted to know about Sergei.

Sergei began to tell her about his life, his extraordinary and unusual life that had been anything but normal. He began by telling her about Camp 27 and his childhood, in fact his lack of a childhood, there. He told her everything about himself. He told her about Minot, North Dakota and the cold Communists who had pretended to be his parents. He told her about how he had found his way back to Russia after the fall of the Soviet Union, and then about how he had found his way to God. He told her how Putin's thugs from the old KGB had taken him from the monastery and sent him back to the United States to search for Peter Bradford Gregory. He told her about finding George Alexander Thomas, his fellow orphan from Camp 27, who was now his only family.

He cried with sorrow because he had never had a real mother or father. He cried with happiness when he told her how he had finally found his comfort and solace, his joy in the Russian Orthodox Church. His becoming a priest had provided him with the love and acceptance that he'd never found anywhere else in his life. Sergei could not remember when he had ever cried before. Ji-su held Sergei's hand as he cried. Then she began to tell him her own story. She told him everything. He held her hand as she cried and told Sergei her story.

Chapter 30

NORTH KOREA

"*I'm not your real mother.* You may have wondered why we don't look alike and why I am really too young to have given birth to you. You must have suspected something over the years, suspected that you were adopted. You must have wondered if my husband and I were your real parents. I should have told you all of this a long time ago. The reason I waited is because I always told myself that you were too much of a child to know and understand the truth. But, the real reason I've never told you where you really came from is because I was a coward. I love you so much. I hate to admit this to you or to anyone, but I love you more than I love my own children, the children I gave birth to, the little ones who live here with us, the ones you have always believed were your younger brothers and sisters. I love you more than I love them. I will never tell them this, and they will never know that I do not love all of my children equally. Perhaps the reason I love you more is because I saved your life, because I had to risk my own life to nourish you and keep you alive.

"I was only twelve when I was taken from my family and brought to Pyongyang. My parents and brothers and sisters were farmers and lived in a poor village near Sukchon north of Pyongyang. I was very beautiful and well-developed as a young girl, and I was strong and healthy. Someone from the government saw me working in the fields of the commune that was near my parents' house, and they brought me, against my parents' will, to live in Pyongyang. I was kidnapped from my family and taken to live in the presidential palace of North Korea with the idea that I would become a wet nurse.

"I was obliged to have sex with a high official in Kim Jong-Il's government. This man forced himself on me every night until I became pregnant. As soon as it was determined that I was carrying his child, the man who had impregnated me was no longer allowed to visit me. It was important that I carry my child to full term, and I was protected. I was given special food and special treatment. I was never hungry, and I even had a small room of my own. I was so young and so naïve at the time that I didn't really understand what was happening. In fact, I had no idea what was going on or what was expected of me. I just did as I was told. I was thirteen when I gave birth to a little boy. They let the little boy stay with me only for a brief period of time. I was allowed to nurse him for a few days until my milk came in. I continued to be well fed and treated kindly.

"I had a minder, a woman who took care of my clothes and watched everything that I ate and drank. She was bossy, and I didn't care for her. But she made sure I stayed healthy. When my little boy was only two weeks old, he was taken away from me, and I was moved to another part of the royal palace. I was one of several wet nurses who had been brought to the royal palace to become pregnant so that we could nurse a set of newborn twins, a boy and a girl. I didn't know who the parents of these twins were, and I didn't know the names of the twins. I simply nursed them when they were hungry and it was my turn to feed them.

"After a few weeks, I was told that I was to take the newborn girl twin and move out of the palace. Again, I didn't understand what was going on. The newborn baby girl and I were sent to an apartment in Pyongyang, away from the palace grounds. I didn't know where we were. My minder was with me at all times, and she continued to see to my food and my well-being. I kept asking about my son, but I was told that my breast milk was serving a higher purpose than nursing my own child. I was a healthy young woman, and I produced great volumes of milk. The little baby girl that I nursed in that apartment was you.

"One day, my minder came to me and told me that the powerful decision makers in the North Korean government and the royal family had decided I was to go back to the royal palace and nurse your brother, the newborn boy twin. I was told that you would be taken care of by someone else. My minder told me I would not see you again and was never to ask about you. In fact, I was threatened that I would be killed if I ever mentioned to anyone that you had ever been born or ever existed. No one was to know that the newborn boy had been a twin. No one was to know that there had been a baby girl born to the same woman on the same day as the baby boy was born. My minder let slip that you had been born first, that the baby girl twin had been born before the baby boy twin was born. I didn't believe my minder when she told me you would be taken care of by someone else. I suspected that they planned to kill you, and one night, just before they were to take you away and send me back to the royal palace to nurse the infant boy twin who was your brother, my worst fears were realized.

"When my minder thought I was asleep, I listened at my bedroom door and overheard a conversation between my minder and a government official who had come to the apartment. He said he would be coming back the next day to pick you up and that you would be 'taken care of' with a humane and civilized death. You would feel no pain. They discussed whether or not my minder thought it was necessary to also 'take care of' me. My minder said she didn't think it was necessary, that I was young enough and compliant enough that she felt they could count on me to keep my mouth shut and not to reveal that you had ever been born. I had an abundance of breast milk. Apparently, a couple of the other wet nurses had not worked out. Their milk had dried up, and they needed me at the royal palace to nurse your twin brother.

"I was only thirteen, and I had already lost my little son when he was only two weeks old. I have no idea what happened to him, but I suspect they 'took care of him,' too. All they wanted was my milk. They didn't need another baby of a poor, teenage mother. There were already thousands more mouths to feed in the DPRK than there was food. I knew in my heart that they had killed my son, and I was determined that they were not going to kill you, too.

"I bundled you up against the cold night and escaped from the apartment. You and I made our way back to my family's village near Sukchon. I told them what had happened, and when they heard my story, of course they were frightened. They sent us away to live with my grandmother in the mountains because they were afraid the neighbors would become suspicious when I suddenly reappeared with a new baby. My parents were also afraid that my younger brothers and sisters would inadvertently allow something to slip about my return and about the baby I had brought with me.

"You and I lived with my grandmother until you were five years old. My grandmother and I were able to hide you, feed you, and pretend that you did not exist. We played with you and loved you, and no one ever knew you lived with us. Then I met my husband and fell in love. I told him everything, and he agreed that we would raise you as our own child. We moved to Kaesong Province, far away from my grandmother's house and far away from where my parents and my brothers and sisters lived. We decided that to keep you safe and to keep myself safe, we would never have any further contact with my family. In a few months, I was pregnant with your oldest sister.

"Now you know the story of where you came from. I don't know who your biological parents are, and I don't know the name of your twin brother. But I have strong suspicions about who your parents are and who your twin brother is. I do know that you are someone who may have royal blood. Maybe I should not have kept this story from you for all these years, and then again, maybe I should never have told you about any of it. But I decided you deserved to know the truth. Keeping you in the dark has been bothering me for a long time. I'm sorry that I've not told you the truth until now. I wanted you to know your story, and most importantly, I wanted you to know that even though I am not your birth mother, I have cared for you and nursed you and loved you from almost the moment you were born. Please forgive me if I have wronged you in any way. You will always be my first daughter."

Ji-su recounted her adopted mother's story to Sergei, almost word for word the way her mother had told it to her more than twenty years earlier. Ji-su had never shared the story with anyone before she told it to Sergei. Only a few weeks after her mother had told Ji-su her story, soldiers had come to the family's home and murdered the entire family, except for Ji-su. She had climbed up and hidden in the branches of the one tree that still remained on the land near her parents' hut.

Ji-su had been completely traumatized by watching her entire family have their throats cut, and then she had almost died making her way across the DMZ to South Korea. She didn't often think about the story her mother had told her about her birth, and for years she had tried pushing it out of her consciousness. She thought of it once in a while, but it didn't seem as immediate or as important to her as the death of her siblings and the death of the only parents she had ever known. Dealing with that tragedy had consumed her, and she had begun to focus on revenge and train herself for the retaliation she hoped to bring to the perpetrators, the evil North Korean regime.

Whoever her twin brother had been and whoever her birth parents had been were of little or no importance to her, as she worked hard to get her education and to train herself in the martial arts. It did not occur to Ji-su that the reason her North Korean family had been murdered might have had something to do with the fact that Ji-su's adoptive mother had once been a wet nurse for the North Korean royal family. The wet nurse had disappeared with a royal baby and kept herself and that baby hidden from the authorities for more than a decade.

Ji-su told Sergei everything she knew about the U Group. Their work was finished, as far as Ji-su knew, but she had been in on only a limited part of their activities. She wanted Sergei to know all about how she had been recruited and trained and everything about the operation that had been designed to substitute her for KJU. Sergei told Ji-su about how he and Thomas had stumbled on to the U Group's activities when the two of them had been hacking into the electronics in the North Korean royal palace in real time. Sergei told her everything, and Ji-su told him everything. Their previous lives had been characterized by deceptions and lies, and full disclosure was the most important thing. They held nothing back. There would be no more secrets between the two of them.

Perhaps it had been Sergei's own life story of having been an orphan that motivated Ji-su to tell him the story that she too was an orphan. In fact, she had been made an orphan twice. They were two orphans, and that might have been one of the things that had drawn them to each other. Ji-su wondered if there was a unique kind of loneliness reserved for orphans. Was there a special kind of need that was shared only by others who had also experienced that special kind of need? Who else could possibly recognize or understand it?

Whatever might become of these two in the future, whether it was each one of them alone or the two of them together in some way, they had shared everything about themselves. They'd shared what they thought was important. They'd shared the little things that came out of their mouths by accident. It was vital to both of them that they know every possible thing about the other one and that they share every detail about themselves. Perhaps all the talking was a way of avoiding for as long as possible any inevitable physical contact. Their hours of telling each other about their lives had built a kind of trust and intimacy that neither one had ever experienced before. They might at some time in the future become lovers, but they knew they would always be friends.

Chapter 31

SKANEATELES, NEW YORK

All of a sudden, Thomas felt uncomfortably out of things, sitting in front of his computer screens in Skaneateles and watching events unfold in Vladivostok and in Pyongyang. He didn't really want to be in either location in person, but now that most of the action appeared to have ended, he wondered if he had any role left to play in these continuing dramas. His electronic surveillance capabilities had not extended to Wonsan, to the sea near an island off Chongjin, or to the monastery of St. Seraphim on Russky Island.

Thomas had grown used to being able to see what was happening in real time from half a world away, and he had been spoiled by being able to know about everything as it was happening. Now all of a sudden, he had lost his eyes and ears. Of course, his eyes and ears could not be everywhere he wanted them to be. Now that there were many places where the most recent action and events were unfolding, Thomas began to feel as if he were an irrelevant player. He hated that; he was used to being in charge and being all-knowing.

Sergei had let him know, via satellite phone, everything that had happened on the mission to rescue Ji-su, so Thomas knew that both Sergei and Ji-su were safe now at St. Seraphim. Thomas knew that the North Korean fisherman had been severely wounded in the gunfight aboard the Chris-Craft cabin cruiser, recently rechristened the *Marina*, and had undergone life-saving surgery. Thomas had his suspicions confirmed when Sergei told him about the criminal Vasily and his drug deal.

Thomas was relieved and delighted that Sergei and Ji-su and the fisherman had been able to defeat the men in the North Korean patrol boat. He wished he'd been able to see that action in real time, but Sergei had somehow managed to make a video and would be sending it. Thomas would have to wait for the recording in order to see the attack and the ultimate success of the brave and ingenious people on board the cabin cruiser. He knew how much Sergei hated guns, in spite of being an excellent shot. He was anxious to see how Sergei's expertise had saved the day and dispensed with the North Korean coast guard boat and its crew of two.

Thomas was anxious to see exactly how the homemade bombs had been constructed. His admiration and respect for Ji-su had increased exponentially after he'd heard Sergei's glowing reports of her single-handed take down of Vasily, her ability to commandeer the *Marina*, and the way she had coped in a crisis to fend off the North Korean patrol boat. He couldn't wait to see her in action on the video.

Thomas knew the fisherman was fighting for his life somewhere on Russky Island. Things were out of his hands, and Thomas knew that Sergei and Ji-su had also fought for their own lives, not only aboard the *Marina* but also as they'd struggled to swim to shore during the storm. Until they had abandoned the Marina, Sergei had done a great job of keeping Thomas up to date about what was going on through their satellite phones. Sergei had left his phone on the Marina when he'd jumped into the water, and who knew when he would be able to retrieve it. Thomas knew Sergei was exhausted and had to sleep. He accepted that Sergei would be incommunicado while he caught up on his rest.

Thomas would have to wait to be brought up to speed on everything that was happening at St. Seraphim. Now that the major crises were in the process of being resolved, Thomas was somewhat annoyed with himself that his program to hack into other people's lives in real time had been as successful as it had been. He was even more annoyed with himself that he'd enjoyed spying on the enemy as much as he'd enjoyed it. He'd never before felt really obsessed about anything or as if he might be addicted to something. Now he realized, when he'd been cut off from the action, that he might have become addicted to the adrenalin rush of participating in and having real time information.

Something else was puzzling him and making him somewhat uncomfortable. He had noticed weeks earlier, when Sergei had volunteered to watch Ji-su prepare for her mission against KJU, that Sergei's voice softened a little bit whenever he talked about the brave young woman who was putting her life on the line for what she believed. Sergei had openly shared with Thomas that he thought the woman was a fanatic and that he was concerned about her mental health. Sergei had specifically been worried that Ji-su was convinced she was participating in a suicide mission, with no hope of escape.

Sergei had gone to extraordinary lengths to help save this woman and rescue her from North Korea. Thomas also was a novice in the world of love and romance and relationships.

The only woman he'd ever loved had been murdered years ago, and he had never wanted to experience the pain of that kind of loss again as long as he lived. But drawing on the little bit that he did know about relationships, he was beginning to suspect that Sergei was falling in love with Ji-su. He didn't know if Sergei himself was aware of what was happening or of the extent to which his feelings for Ji-su had begun to drive his decisions and his behavior.

The experience of falling in love was a world that had been discouraged, prohibited, and purposefully brainwashed out of both Thomas and Sergei at Camp 27. How would they possibly be able to recognize the feelings that were so foreign to them and had been forbidden to them during their formative years? The rest of the world has a difficult time recognizing love and then dealing with it. Even if one has not been expressly conditioned to eliminate these feelings from one's life, love is always a risky business. It was completely unknown and frightening territory to Thomas and to Sergei. Thomas felt a stab of jealousy and then a stab of joy, for this new predicament that Sergei was now experiencing.

Thomas took refuge in watching the presidential palace in Pyongyang. He was quite curious to see what would happen when the Chosen realized that Kim Jong-un had disappeared and was nowhere to be found. Even the chaos that had inevitably ensued in that dark place and even the disorder and anarchy that was occurring everywhere in the country of North Korea was more understandable and less confusing to Thomas than was Sergei's love life.

Thomas had stopped watching everything in real time now that Ji-su was no longer in danger. But he had continued to record what was happening inside the royal palace. Now that he had some time on his hands, he decided to catch up on what had happened there after Ji-su had made her getaway. He was curious about what had happened when KJU's sycophants finally realized he had vanished.

After many hours of knocking on KJU's bedroom door and trying to get him to come out or at least to answer their inquiries, The Chosen had finally decided to disobey KJU's orders that he be left alone. KJU had often exhibited bizarre behavior in the past and had disappeared before, sometimes for days at a time. What tipped off his closest bodyguards that something serious might be going on was that KJU had not requested any food. Everyone knew he had a voracious appetite and that he could not go for any period of time without eating. The Chosen and the other military guards inside the palace were concerned that KJU had become ill inside his bedroom and needed help. They finally made the decision to break down the door to see if everything was all right. They knew that their choice to disobey KJU's orders was to invite the possibility of death, but they decided they needed to risk it.

They broke into the leader's quarters. No one was inside. They searched the bedroom, the bathroom, the dressing room, KJU's private movie viewing room, and everywhere else. The bed had not been slept in at all. There was nothing out of place inside the bedroom, no signs of a struggle or a kidnapping. There were no signs of a disturbance of any kind. There was not a trace that KJU or that anyone had recently been in the private quarters. It was mysterious and quite puzzling. After they had looked everywhere, The Chosen issued an alarm. There would be a palace-wide search for their leader. They would investigate the grounds and gardens. No one could begin to imagine how KJU had left his bedroom suite. Several guards had kept watch outside the only door to his rooms, a door which KJU himself had locked. No one had entered or left KJU's suite through that door for many hours.

Finally, one of The Chosen realized that a window in the bedroom had been opened. For security reasons, this was thought to be impossible. Opening the window from the outside was out of the question. And the man was so paranoid about somebody being able to get to him that no one had ever imagined KJU would want to open the window from the inside.

The Chosen examined the window carefully and found the slightest scratch on the window sill. A rope or some other device could have left the mark. That might have been how someone had gained access to KJU's private quarters. Or it might be how KJU had escaped from his bedroom—through the window. But why would he have done that? And how could he have done that? He was so fat, he could never have climbed out of his bedroom window and climbed down the exterior wall of the palace. Perhaps he had finally gone completely mad? Had the U.S. attack on North Korea's weapons capabilities pushed him over the edge? Had his well-known paranoia completely taken over his personality and his behavior? But, even if all of that were true, where could he have gone? Was he wandering around in the garden? No one could find a trace of him anywhere.

Investigators examined the ground at the foot of KJU's window. They found some bushes and other garden plantings that had been slightly trampled, but only a little bit. They could only speculate that someone, somehow had escaped through the window and made their way down the side of the palace wall. Everyone knew that, physically, KJU could not have possibly accomplished such a feat. What had happened to KJU was a complete mystery to everyone connected with the royal palace.

One extremely sharp-eyed official who was assisting in the search saw what he thought might be streaks of blood on the wall of the palace. The very faint brown smear had been left on the outside wall, just under KJU's window where the garden shrubs had been slightly disturbed. The investigator called for a forensics team to come and take a sample of the dried brown substance. North Korea did not have many competent crime scene investigators. They had few competent professionals of any kind. But someone was finally found who could determine if the stain on the wall was blood. To everyone's great surprise, a luminal test confirmed that the brown splotch on the wall was indeed blood.

Investigators scraped pieces of the brown substance from the wall and took several samples of the blood to a DNA lab. Years earlier, DNA analysis had sometimes taken weeks for the results to be known, but with improvements in DNA technology, even in North Korea, the time required to get a DNA test result back was only a few days. This DNA test was a priority, even in a country that had recently been attacked by the world's greatest superpower, in a country that no longer had a leader.

Thomas knew exactly what had happened to Kim Jong-un, and he also knew exactly who had opened the window of KJU's bedroom and escaped down the outside wall of the palace. Thomas had not seen Ji-su scrape the palm of her hand as she'd rappelled to the ground, so he didn't pay much attention to all of the excitement about the blood and the proposed DNA test. The blood might be from a gardener who had cut himself with the hedge trimmers. It might be animal blood. Thomas could think of a dozen different explanations for the blood that had been found on the wall, but he knew with absolute certainty that it was not KJU's blood.

The U Group had made some plans for the chaos they knew would ensue after KJU's disappearance was discovered. The United States and their allies, who had been in on the planning of the bombing of North Korea's nuclear weapons and ICBM facilities, had likewise planned for the chaos they knew would result from the attack. Sleeper agents in the North Korean military came forward to take command. Several key generals, those who had been especially loyal to KJU, had been eliminated on Ji-su's orders.

The members of the military and others in government, who had kept their opposition to the Kim family's rule a secret until now, struggled to bring some kind of order to the disarray in which the military and the country as a whole now found itself. Thousands of military personnel had defected and gone home to their families. Members of the military as well as civilian citizens of North Korea had tried to cross the Yalu River and escape into China. Still others were trying to cross the DMZ to get into South Korea.

In addition to trying to plan for how to keep the North Korean military from exploding into some kind of counter-revolutionary coup, a North Korean government in exile had been set up, operating out of South Korea. This government in exile was made up of former elites from North Korea who, having become disillusioned with Emperor Roly Poly and his brutal and insane tactics throughout the years, had defected. They'd regrouped to try to save their country from disintegrating in the aftermath of the air attacks. They wanted to build a strong and free North Korea and eventually reunite the former Hermit Kingdom with its other half, with their much more prosperous and successful fellow countrymen in South Korea.

Germany had been able to reunite its two long-divided parts, its capitalist and its communist divisions, into one united and whole country. It had been chaotic at first, and it had taken time to join the two disparate systems and put the country back together again. If Germany could do it, the members of the government in exile believed that Korea could also do it. It would be a massive effort. The East Germans had not treated their people well, but the communist ideologues who had ruled East Germany were not even close to being in the same league with the way the Kim family had treated the poor people of North Korea. It would be a long and difficult road, but at least some people had hope and were working on it.

Thomas wasn't constantly watching in real time, as he previously had observed, everything that was happening in the royal palace in North Korea. The horse had left the barn, and it was only a matter of time until The Chosen were arrested and tried for their crimes, only a matter of time until the light of truth and freedom would illuminate and destroy the darkness of the former regime of KJU.

Thomas was eating well and sleeping again. There was no more middle-of-the-night, real-time spying on North Korea. Thomas was mostly paying attention to what was happening on Russky Island when he was lucky enough to have an email from Sergei. Imagine Thomas's surprise when he played a video from the day before ... from Pyongyang. He was able to listen in on a discussion about the DNA results from the blood samples taken from the exterior wall of the palace a few days earlier. He almost fast forwarded through the conversation because he knew the DNA results would not yield anything of interest to anybody. Thomas was hardly ever wrong, but he would be entirely wrong this time.

Chapter 32

SKANEATELES, NEW YORK

T*homas recorded everything he observed* when he was hacking in real time. When he'd discovered something that warned of serious trouble or a future attack and when he believed it was important enough, he sent anonymous videos to national intelligence services all over the world. Sometimes he wanted to use his videos to double check on what he thought he'd seen or heard. He was happy to have a video of this particular conversation, the meeting during which the investigators were discussing the results of the DNA tests that had been done on the blood found on the exterior wall of the North Korean royal palace. He'd not really been paying attention to his computer screen when he'd watched this video the first time.

Thomas didn't have a great deal of faith in anything that happened in North Korea, especially anything scientific. His skepticism was partly due to the fact that he doubted the competence of just about everyone and everything in that extremely backward country—especially because everyone was inclined to lie about everything, Even if there was no reason to lie other than merely for the sake of lying, people lied. Especially now that there was so much disruption throughout the country and because their little dictator was missing, Thomas doubted everything.

The men seated at the table in a conference room at the royal palace passed around the papers they'd received from the laboratory. Their foreheads wrinkled, and they shook their heads. They read and reread the laboratory report. Although they were reasonably intelligent men, none of them who were reading the results of the DNA testing understood everything that was written on the report from the lab. The technical terms were confusing, and the results were even more confounding.

No one at the table wanted to begin the conversation, but finally, one police technician who understood the report better than the others said there had to have been some kind of a mistake. He was certain the lab had mixed up the specimens or messed up the tests. That was an explanation everyone at the table could concur with, and they nodded their heads in agreement. There were plenty of examples of Kim Jong-un's DNA in the royal palace, and several of these had been submitted with the unknown blood sample from the wall outside of KJU's bedroom.

The men at the table had been hoping for a match with KJU's blood or they had been hoping for a complete exclusion of KJU as the possible source of the blood on the wall. They got neither a perfect match nor an absolute exclusion. What they got was disturbing and even frightening to them. Most of the people at the table had a difficult time deciphering the lab report, and finally the person with the most expertise in DNA matters gathered his courage and spoke to the group about what the lab results implied.

The unknown blood sample was a close match with KJU's DNA profile. But the results were not an exact match. The results that had been received were accurate only if the samples were from two people who were closely related. These would be the results if the two samples had been taken from siblings. What was an impossible fact was that the DNA tests indicated the blood on the wall had come from a female! Mouths dropped open. No one wanted to ask the difficult questions. Finally, one of them said, "He's never been able to conceive any children. The child that was born to his wife and the child that was born to his mistress, neither one of these are his biological children. We know this to be a fact."

"What about his doctor? We know he won't let anyone, even his closest bodyguards, into the shower room when he is bathing. But his doctor has to have examined him. His doctor must know if he has ... well, male anatomical parts."

"No matter how secretive and paranoid he is, he could not have fooled everyone for all these years. He has to be a man. He went to a boys' school in Switzerland. Don't you think they would have checked him out? There has to be a mistake in the lab tests. We'll have to start all over again."

"Of course, the man himself, or the woman herself, is nowhere to be found at the moment, so we can't check this out for ourselves. I don't know anything about transgender people or anything about that. All of that is completely against the law here, and nobody is even allowed to talk about it. Is it possible that he has a male anatomy but has female DNA? Do we have anybody who knows about these things? This is the only thing I can imagine that might explain all of this, other than a mistake by the lab or a mix-up in blood samples. And, are we absolutely certain that the examples of DNA we took from the royal palace for comparison were those of Kim Jong-un? Really, though, I have to tell you that the test results we have right now are too close a match for the blood on the wall to have been from anyone except KJU or a female sibling. ”

“He does have a female sibling, but she has a different mother. The female sibling is in boarding school in Europe and would never have been anywhere close to that wall where the blood was found. KJU’s half-sister’s DNA profile would not be anything like this one which is such a close match to his ... except for the double X chromosome.”

“The first thing on our agenda is to redo the blood tests. Take new samples and run all new tests. That will at least rule out laboratory error.”

Thomas was stunned to be privy to this conversation about the DNA results. He thought he knew the real explanation about why the blood tests had come back as being so similar to those of KJU, but with the X chromosomes. He could hardly believe what he had heard and seen. What he knew had to be true. He couldn’t even begin to imagine how this had happened. He knew Ji-su had been born in North Korea, and he knew she had an uncanny resemblance to Kim Jong-un. She weighed about a quarter of what KJU weighed, and her face was quite beautiful. The former leader of North Korea had an ugly and repellent, bloated face. But there was a definite resemblance. One reason Ji-su had been selected to participate in the incredibly brazen mission to kidnap KJU and substitute Ji-su in his place was because, in spite of the differences in their bodies and the discrepancies in body fat, she had looked so much like him.

Thomas was going to have to think about this information and what he was going to do with it. He did not want any of it to be true. KJU’s cronies and followers didn’t want the lab results to be accurate because they did not want to believe that KJU was a woman or some kind of transgender person with male anatomical parts and female DNA. Thomas knew the lab results were accurate. There had been no mistakes. Thomas didn't want Ji-su to be KJU's sister because he did not want this lovely young woman to carry the burden of being linked in any way biologically with the disgusting little man who had ruled his country with such cruelty and narcissism. How could the two possibly be related?

Thomas even wondered if Ji-su could have been some kind of test tube baby. He decided he would also wait for the results of the second set of lab tests on the blood sample, before he jumped to any final conclusions. But he knew in his heart, without any question, what had happened. Because Thomas knew that KJU had never climbed out of his bedroom window and down the wall of the royal palace, the blood on the wall could not possibly be his. Only Ji-su had accomplished that athletic feat. It was Ji-su who had left her blood on the wall.

Thomas had hardly ever discovered anything in all his years of hacking that he hadn't known what to do with, but he had no idea what to do about this. He and Sergei kept no secrets from each other, but considering the way things were evolving between Sergei and Ji-su, Thomas wondered if he had the right to tell them what he knew to be true. On the other hand, did he have the right to keep this information from them?

Thomas had never faced such a crucial moral dilemma before. Ji-su might never recover mentally from being told that she was the sister of KJU. She had dedicated her entire adult life to destroying the Kim dynasty and its latest ruler on the throne, KJU. And now she might have to be told that she was in fact a member of that family. Thomas was more than lost. He was devastated. He needed to take his sailboat out on the water and forget his computers. He knew it would be impossible to forget, but he was at least going to try to block from his mind everything he had learned from his hacking today.

Thomas was in a fog, but he was able to rig his sailboat and get it out onto Skaneateles Lake. His GP-14 sailboat was his refuge, his escape, his relaxation, his way to commune with nature, his way to transform himself, the only thing he remembered from his years spent at Camp 27 that had given him the slightest moments of happiness. He would sail all the rest of the day until he wore himself out. Because he was an albino, he had to stay out of the sun in the middle of the day. This fall afternoon was overcast, and in upstate New York, the weak October sun would not give him a sunburn.

He wished he had somebody with whom he could talk over this latest problematic development, but in similar situations in the past, he'd always talked things over with Sergei. The predicament he faced at this moment was all about Sergei, so he couldn't talk anything over with Sergei until he had sorted it out in his own mind. He would go to the Sherwood for dinner tonight. He needed to get away from his computers for a while. He'd spent all summer consumed with Ji-su and the U Group. He'd lost sleep and missed lots of meals. Could he possibly be suffering from PTSD as a result of the situation he'd participated in electronically in North Korea. All the real-time hacking he'd been doing might be catching up with him. He had witnessed some really horrendous things as he'd watched the Iranians and the North Koreans plot world destruction.

He wondered if this recent revelation had hit him so hard because he felt for Ji-su and for Sergei. All three of them shared the unhappy personal history that they'd been lied to about where they'd really come from. None of them really knew anything about their origins or their birth families. Sergei knew he was Russian, but he knew nothing of his biological family. Thomas had always believed that he was Russian until Sergei had read his KGB file and found out that in fact Thomas's birth family was from Hungary. But that was all that Thomas knew for sure—that he was Hungarian. As far as Thomas knew, Ji-su had also been lied to and knew nothing about her true biological origins.

It began to rain on Skaneateles Lake while Thomas was sailing. He had failed to check the weather report before he'd gone out on the lake. He'd lost track of time and didn't realize how long he'd been on the water. A bad storm was coming, and the sky was very quickly growing dark. Thomas was such an accomplished sailor that following the wind and controlling his sailboat came automatically to him. He didn't have to think about what he was doing when he was sailing. It was second nature, and he never really gave it much conscious thought.

Today his mind was a million miles away. Thomas was completely distracted. He knew at some level that he was getting cold, but he was completely oblivious to the fact that the rain was coming down in torrents and soaking him to the skin through his flimsy windbreaker. A dark funnel cloud was forming in the north, and the wind was picking up. There were whitecaps on the lake. But Thomas was inside his own head and not paying attention. He almost always paid attention to everything around him, but today he'd found himself thrown back into his own past, back into Sergei's past, and back into the past of the woman that he was certain Sergei had begun to love.

He wasn't paying as close attention as he should have been to the wind and the weather. If he had noticed the funnel cloud, he would have immediately headed for land and the shelter of his boathouse. But he was in another world, living in another time. A wild and unexpectedly robust gust of wind caught the sail of his GP-14 and jerked the tiller out of his hands. The uncontrolled boom began banging wildly back and forth. As Thomas struggled to control his boat, the boom swung across hard and slammed him in the head. Another gust of wind from the funnel cloud pushed the mast down into the water. The boat capsized in the lake, and Thomas was caught unconscious underneath his overturned sailboat.

Chapter 33

SKANEATELES, NEW YORK

T*homas's sailboat overturned close to* town, and only that fact saved his life. If he'd capsized farther out on the lake, it's doubtful anyone would have seen his boat in the water in time, let alone imagined that there might be someone floating unconscious underneath the upturned hull. As it was, two motorists driving by Shotwell Park in the storm saw him aboard the GP-14 struggling to keep the boat upright one minute. The next minute they saw the boat's mast go under the water. One of those who'd watched him disappear grabbed his cell phone and called 911.

The two men in the car stopped and tried to watch the water through the storm. They hoped and expected to see the man from the boat come out from under his overturned craft and swim towards shore. But no one knew he'd been hit in the head and rendered unconscious by the sailboat's boom. Thomas was an excellent swimmer, but not even excellent swimmers can swim when they are knocked out cold. Thomas was not going to be able to swim to shore on his own today.

The storm was raging, and no one in their right mind would venture outside in this weather, let alone take a boat out on the water. But the Skaneateles water rescue team had a job to do. There were tornado warnings in the area. A tornado had been sighted in Melrose Park. Conditions for rescuing someone from the lake could not have been worse, but there could not be any delays today, no matter what the weather report said. The Skaneateles Fire Department mobilized their water rescue efforts and launched a rescue boat.

Because of the exceptionally wealthy tax base and the outrageously high property taxes, the town of Skaneateles had well-funded municipal services, including the schools, police department, and fire department. Skaneateles Fire and Rescue had top of the line equipment and well-trained personnel, In spite of the terrible storm, they were in the water beside Thomas's boat within minutes of receiving the emergency call. They'd seen boats overturned this way before. Because they had an eyewitness account that a person had been seen sailing the boat, they knew there could be someone underneath the overturned sailboat who desperately needed help. A diver in scuba gear was ready to go into the lake, and as soon as the rescue boat was in position, he let himself down into the choppy water and swam underneath the capsized sailboat.

The diver had a nearly impossible time getting Thomas out from under the boat. When the diver reached him, Thomas still had a pulse. But it was so weak, it was almost non-existent. Thomas's body had become tangled in the mainsail sheet, the rope attached to the boom that he would have held onto to let the sail in and out. The sheet was wrapped around and around Thomas's body and around the tiller. Fortunately, part of the scuba diver's gear was a dive knife, but the ropes were nylon and weren't easy to cut away. Precious minutes were wasted as the diver struggled to cut Thomas out of his rope bindings. Finally, Thomas was freed, and the diver brought him out from underneath the GP-14.

The two of them were lifted onto the rescue boat, but by the time Thomas was finally in the life saving craft, he had stopped breathing and no longer had a heartbeat. CPR was administered immediately. After several nerve-wracking minutes of pounding on his chest and using the defibrillator, Thomas coughed up what seemed like gallons of water and began to breathe again. His heart was working, but nobody knew for sure how long that would last.

By this time, the boat had arrived at the dock, and an emergency evacuation helicopter from the New York State Police had landed in Shotwell Park. Thomas was loaded on board, and thanks to a skilled rescue team and excellent emergency treatment, he was still breathing and his heart was still beating when the helicopter lifted off for the hospital. The blow to his head was of great concern to the EMTs aboard the air ambulance.

Sam, the bartender, had just arrived for work at the Sherwood Inn. He parked his car in the parking lot and ran to the Sherwood's front yard. When he saw the police cars, the rescue vehicles, and the commotion across the street, he wondered what all the excitement was about. Then he saw the capsized sailboat in the water. He had watched Thomas sailing his boat enough times that, even though the boat was now upside down in the lake and even though there was barely any visibility because of the rain, Sam knew the upside-down boat belonged to Thomas. Sam raced to the helicopter to confirm that the man who had been rescued from the water was who he thought it was.

Sam O'Connor knew that Thomas was a loner and didn't have any family. Once or twice a year, Thomas's one friend visited him. The two of them came to the Sherwood Inn often for lunch and dinner. Thomas's friend's name was Sergei, and he had a Slavic face. Sergei did not resemble Thomas in the slightest, so he couldn't possibly be a family member. Sam didn't know Sergei's last name, but the man spoke perfect American English. It was always a surprise to Sam because Sergei wore foreign clothes and had a strange haircut. He looked like someone from a movie, either *The Third Man* or *Gorky Park*. In spite of knowing it wasn't going to happen, Sam always expected that when the man opened his mouth, he would speak with a foreign accent. But when the Russian-looking guy ordered a drink or began to talk, he sounded as if he had grown up in Ohio or Wisconsin. His flat middle-western speech didn't fit with his appearance. His obvious close friendship with Thomas had always made Sam curious.

Sam had never seen Thomas sit with or talk with anybody else in the bar or in the dining room. Thomas had once told Sam that the only woman he had ever loved had been murdered. When Thomas had shared this with Sam, he'd immediately regretted disclosing the personal information. People told bartenders things all the time, so Sam recognized that Thomas was sorry he'd revealed too much about himself.

That night, almost immediately after his admission about the woman he'd once loved, Thomas had left the Sherwood Inn bar. He hadn't come back in for almost two weeks. There was a great deal more to that story than Sam was ever going to know. But he did know that Thomas had no wife and no children and really nobody else in the world except his unusual but close friend Sergei.

Sam worried that Thomas might not have health insurance. He knew Thomas was a wealthy man, and Thomas tipped him accordingly. Most people in the population need to have insurance to pay their medical bills. But sometimes the very rich were self-insured and didn't bother to get health insurance. Sam knew that Dr. Solomon Dollimer was Thomas's personal physician, his internist. Dollimer was probably the best doctor in the Skaneateles area, and he didn't take insurance. He was a concierge doctor. He was expensive, and patients had to pay a yearly fee to be able to schedule an appointment with or have a phone call with Dollimer. Only the well-to-do could afford to consult Dr. Dollimer.

The doctor had been on the staff at Cornell University Medical College in New York City and been a professor in the medical school. He'd finally become fed up with government interference in the practice of medicine and with all the paperwork that took up his valuable time, time he could be spending with his patients. One day several years ago, Solomon Dollimer had decided to leave his position at the medical school in New York City, sell his Upper East Side co-op, and move away from the crowds and the traffic.

He'd retired to Skaneateles where he lived in a small, somewhat run-down house built in the 1940s. He saw patients in his house in a no-frills examining room, which was in fact one of the guest bedrooms of the doctor's cottage. Dollimer had no nurse and no receptionist. He didn't send out any bills. He was a one-man band, and he practiced medicine because he loved it. He had a long waiting list of people who wanted to become his patients and pay a boatload of cash to have Dollimer take their blood pressure. Only the death of an existing patient could move you up a notch on the waiting list. Dollimer was such a good doctor that his patients lived a long time, so it would be a significant wait for most on the list.

Sam knew that Thomas saw Dr. Dollimer, and this was another reason he worried that Thomas didn't have any health insurance. Thomas had talked to Sam about how he admired Solomon Dollimer for escaping the rat race and the nightmare of government meddling and the morass of paperwork. Thomas liked the fact that Dollimer didn't have a fancy office or any support staff. He liked the doctor's independence. Thomas was himself the completely independent man, so it was no wonder the two had found each other and liked each other.

Sam realized he probably knew more about Thomas than anybody else in town knew about him, except possibly for Dr. Solomon Dollimer. Sam hadn't thought about it before, but now he was thinking about it. Bartenders knew everything about everybody else's business, whether they wanted to or not. So Sam also knew that Dr. Dollimer was on a month-long cruise somewhere off the Dalmatian Coast near the former Yugoslavia. He wouldn't be available to vouch for Thomas's medical status or his ability to pay for medical care.

Sam decided he would find out where the helicopter was taking Thomas. Sam planned to call the hospital and tell them he would personally guarantee the hospital bill for Thomas. Sam knew Thomas would appreciate this and would make good for all the expenses which were incurred. Sam would also be sure that Thomas's sailboat was hauled out of the water and taken to The Best Boatworks, which was, of course, the best boat works in town. He knew how much Thomas loved his little boat, and Sam was hoping Thomas would one day be healthy and back out on Skaneateles Lake sailing again.

Sam was late for work but made his phone calls. He was able to find out that Thomas had been taken by helicopter to Upstate University Medical Center, the hospital associated with Syracuse University. Everyone who came into the Sherwood Inn bar that night was talking about the water rescue and the overturned sailboat. Sam knew Thomas liked to keep a low profile, almost as if the man were in hiding from something. Thomas was so solitary and made such a point of keeping to himself, it had occurred to Sam that he might be in witness protection or a similar program. Thomas was the nicest, mildest, and kindest of men, so Sam could not imagine that he had ever been in trouble with the law, or what in the world he might be hiding from.

If someone approached Thomas or sat beside him in the bar, Thomas was always polite, but it was like pulling teeth for the poor soul who might be trying to start a conversation or get to know Thomas. Thomas would talk to the curious, but he would not really say anything. He had a way of turning the questions others asked him about himself back onto the person who had asked the question. Most people enjoy talking about themselves, really more than they enjoy hearing about the lives of others. Thomas used this human trait to his advantage and always ended up listening to the people who sat beside him and wanted to be his friend.

Tonight, everyone wanted to know everything about the man who had been out sailing in the storm and who had capsized and then been rescued. Would he be all right? Had he been injured? Thomas would have absolutely hated the attention he had brought on himself by his unfortunate accident. Sam himself wondered why Thomas had been out on the lake in the storm this evening. He knew Thomas was a sensible, cautious, and careful person. Sam knew that Thomas would hate the notoriety his accident was causing, even more than he would hate the injuries he had sustained or more than the damage his beloved GP-14 had suffered.

After he finished his shift, Sam called the hospital in Syracuse and asked about Thomas's condition. Of course, with all the government regulations regarding confidentiality, no one was willing to tell him anything. Sam decided he would go to the hospital in person the next day and ask to see Thomas. That would be the only way he would ever be able to find out anything. Sam wanted to find out how to contact Sergei so he could tell him about Thomas's accident. He wanted to let Sergei know where Thomas was hospitalized, but he had no idea what Sergei's last name was or how to get in touch with the man, Thomas's only friend.

The next afternoon before he had to go to work at the Sherwood Inn, Sam drove to the hospital in Syracuse. He was able to find out that Thomas was in the ICU. Only family members were allowed to visit patients who were in the ICU, and then only a limited amount of time was allowed for each visit. Because Sam guessed correctly that there would not be any family members waiting to see Thomas, he hoped he might be able to convince one of the nurses who controlled access to ICU patients that he was a relative of some kind. When he got to the ICU, he signed in and stated with confidence that he was Thomas's cousin. He had to show his ID, which was not a problem. He was surprised when the nurse greeted him with delight and was thrilled with the news that he was Thomas's cousin.

"We don't even know this man's full name. We're so glad to have someone from his family come in to give us some information."

Sam was thinking to himself—be careful what you wish for. He was not only going to be allowed to see Thomas, but he realized he had also become the main source of medical information and every other kind of information for Thomas's hospital care. Because he had called the day before and assumed responsibility for Thomas's hospital expenses, his name was already on the paperwork. He was everybody's new best friend—from the woman who manned the nursing station at the ICU to the people in the billing office at Upstate University Medical Center.

In reality, Sam was the man's bartender, not his cousin. He wondered how many of the hundreds of questions he'd be asked would either go unanswered or be answered incorrectly. He decided he would make up the answers to the questions that didn't really matter and say he didn't know to the ones that really did matter. Basically, he was flying blind. He rationalized not turning and running out the door of the hospital by telling himself that it was better for everyone if the hospital knew a little something about Thomas, even if some of it was wrong, than not to know anything at all. At least he knew that Thomas's real name was George Alexander Thomas. Everybody called him by his last name, Thomas, but he really did have a full name.

Sam explained to the ICU nurse who was filling out the paperwork that his cousin was wealthy, but also exceptionally reclusive and eccentric. He'd never been married and didn't have any children. His parents were deceased. Sam said that his mother and Thomas's mother were sisters. For Sam, that explained the discrepancy between their last names, but the nurse didn't care anything about that.

Sam could only guess at Thomas's age, although he remembered that a few years earlier, Thomas had said something about celebrating his 50th birthday. Sam made up a birthdate for Thomas and said that Thomas had been born in Cazenovia, New York, a nearby town where Sam himself had been born. He made up a vague, general, uninformative, and completely false medical history but said that Dr. Solomon Dollimer was Thomas's regular physician.

The nurse visibly relaxed about the financial questions and the hospital bill when she heard that Thomas's internist was Dr. Solomon Dollimer. Everybody in the local medical community knew Dr. Dollimer, and all were aware that he treated well-heeled patients exclusively. Sam added that he may not have all the details of the medical history exactly right, but the hospital could get all of it from Dr. Dollimer when he came back to town. The ICU nurse reassured him that they could get access to Thomas's medical records if they needed them. Everything was electronic and computerized these days. Everything was totally confidential and secure, but everything was also completely accessible —whatever that meant.

The ICU nurse was mainly concerned about any allergies that Thomas might have. Sam knew that Thomas was allergic to hazelnuts and oak trees. They had discussed allergies one time when a man in the bar had ordered a glass of the after-dinner drink, Fra Angelica. Thomas had never heard of it, and Sam explained that it was a liqueur made from hazelnuts. Thomas told the bartender that he was allergic to hazelnuts and to be sure he never served him any Fra Angelica. Thomas added that he was happy to say that the only other thing he knew he was allergic to was oak trees. He said he had a bad time in the spring when the oak trees were blooming. Thomas had added that he was quite happy he wasn't allergic to something good like lamb chops or spaghetti. Sam told the nurse about the allergies and added that he didn't think Thomas was allergic to any medications. At least Thomas had never mentioned that he was.

When all of the questions were answered, Sam was allowed to see Thomas for ten minutes. The nurse explained that Thomas had suffered a serious head injury. Surgery had not yet been required, but the neurosurgeon was keeping an eye on the brain swelling and on Thomas's EEG as well as his EKG. Thomas had been unconscious since he'd been rescued from the water the previous afternoon. The doctors were watching Thomas especially closely because his heart had stopped after he'd been taken out of the water. He'd been given vigorous CPR, and then a defibrillator had been used to get his heart started again.

The paramedics on the scene didn't think his heart had stopped for more than a minute or two, so no one was really worried about serious brain damage because of his heart. But they were worried because no one knew how long Thomas had been in the water without being able to breathe. And then there was the blow to the skull and the concussion. One never knew exactly what injuries might have occurred. There was always the chance that a subdural hematoma might develop, but the medical staff was observing everything constantly and carefully. The nurse said all of Thomas's brain scans showed normal activity, as did his heart monitor. His lab work was all normal. He just hadn't been able to wake up yet. She assured Sam that Thomas's neurosurgeon was excellent, the best at the hospital, and that everything possible was being done for Thomas.

Sam suspected they always said these things to family members who were worried, but he was glad to hear it anyway. Now that he'd suddenly acquired a new cousin, Sam knew he was going to have to visit every day—or at least until Thomas regained consciousness. Not that Sam minded visiting. He liked Thomas and genuinely cared about his recovery from the accident. But mostly Sam wanted to be able to get in touch with Sergei and let him know that Thomas had been hurt. Now he realized it might be several days before he could find out that contact information for Sergei.

Chapter 34

ST. SERAPHIM

The fisherman returned to the monastery at St. Seraphim. His doctors thought they'd been able to save his leg, but they weren't certain how functional it would be in the long run. Months of healing and rehabilitation were ahead. Song-gi and his mother were thrilled to have their father and husband back with them. The brothers were warm and welcoming when Mr. Ri arrived. Everyone at St. Seraphim had grown very fond of Song-gi and his mother.

The boy was a ray of sunshine, and he was learning Russian. He was even teaching the monks a few words of Korean, as he learned his Russian. The monks had decided they needed to begin Song-gi's education while he was living under their roof. He was only five years old, but every morning for three hours and every afternoon for two hours, one of the brothers in the monastery sat with him and taught him arithmetic, reading, writing, history, geography, languages, or science. The monks took turns, depending on their area of expertise, to teach Song-gi. He was an unusually bright child and learned quickly. He soaked up every word that he was taught, and teaching the little boy was a delight to the brothers.

Song-gi's mother had kept herself busy helping in the kitchen. She was a hard worker and a superlative cook. The inhabitants of the monastery had noticed a tremendous improvement in the quality of the food since Mrs. Ri had arrived. She'd had her own vegetable and herb garden in North Korea and knew how to use spices. The monks said she made the best pierogi and borscht, the traditional Russian dishes the old cook thought were his specialties.

Mrs. Ri also prepared Korean and Chinese dishes which widened the culinary repertoire at the monastery. She prepared vegetables in delicious ways so that the brothers actually wanted to eat them. Other than onions, beets, and cabbage, few vegetables had put in an appearance at the monastery table in the past. The cook, who had been making meals for the brothers for decades, might have been jealous of the Korean woman, but he was old and was delighted to have help in his kitchen. It would only be a matter of time until he turned everything over to Mrs. Ri.

Sergei and Ji-su were in a world of their own. Sometimes they were so engaged in their discussions of everything under the sun that they forgot to show up for meals. It was no secret to anyone at the monastery what was happening between the two of them. They had begun to hold hands when they walked around the gardens and the courtyard of the monastery. There was one stone bench in the courtyard that was their favorite, and they always seemed to end up sitting there. No one had ever seen them kissing, but that was what everyone expected would happen soon. Priests in the Russian Orthodox Church do not take a vow of celibacy, but Sergei's commitment to the religious life at Sergiyev Posad and his commitment to God were well-known, even as far from Western Russia as Vladivostok and Russky Island. The brothers held their collective breath and wondered how in the world this would end. Would there be a romance? Would Sergei ever return to Sergiyev Posad?

Sergei and Ji-su loved each other. They had grown extraordinarily close in the few days they had spent recovering at St. Seraphim. Neither one had any experience in relationships with the opposite sex. They knew they wanted to be together and wanted to be close to each other, but they didn't know how to talk to each other about the way they felt. They were more akin to children or clumsy teenagers. One day they began to talk about their awkwardness and their mutual lack of experience. Ji-su took the lead.

"I have never been with a man, Sergei. I have never made love to anyone. My life has always been so focused and so consumed with my mission that I never had time for any kinds of relationships, either friendships or romances. I have strong feelings for you and want to be close to you, but I don't know what to say or do about it."

Sergei was delighted that Ji-su had brought up the subject, and he had information of his own. "I am ashamed to say that I have never been with a woman. At Camp 27, we were forbidden to have relationships, and we were trained not to become emotionally involved with anyone when we were sent to our assignments in the United States. My friends in high school and college were always talking about girls and scoring and how far they were going with their girlfriends and their sexual prowess and all of that. But I had been conditioned, even brainwashed, not to feel anything for anybody. I love you, Ji-su, and I think I want to make love to you. But I don't know how either."

That afternoon, Ji-su took Sergei by the hand and led him to her tiny bedroom. She closed the door and locked it. She led Sergei to her bed. "We are both virgins. We don't know anything, so we will figure out this making love thing together. I love you, Sergei, and I know I want you."

They did not come out of the room for two days. When Sergei and Ji-su finally made an appearance in the kitchen, they were both glowing and blushing furiously. Everyone knew what had finally happened, and everyone at the monastery was happy for the two lovers. No one said a word until one of the brothers finally said, "You must be hungry." Everybody laughed.

The hypnotic veil of romance enveloped Sergei and Ji-su, and neither one wanted to think ahead in time. Neither one wanted to worry about the future, even about what was going to happen the next day. They were living completely in the moment. They both knew that the realities of their lives would have to be confronted at some point, but for now, they were absorbed in each other. Nothing else existed or really mattered.

The spell was broken when Sergei received a telegram from overseas. It was from a man named Sam O'Connor who was a bartender at the Sherwood Inn in Skaneateles, New York. The telegram did not contain good news. Sergei knew that Thomas had been out of touch, and he'd been vaguely concerned that he hadn't heard from his friend in several days. But his preoccupation with Ji-su had kept him from becoming as worried as he should have been.

The telegram told Sergei that his friend George Alexander Thomas had been seriously hurt and had almost died in a boating accident on Skaneateles Lake several days earlier. Sam, the bartender, urged Sergei to come to the hospital in Syracuse, New York where Thomas had only recently awakened from a coma. Sam told Sergei that he had sent the telegram as soon as he had been able to find out from Thomas where Sergei was. Sergei was devastated. He had been so involved in his own happiness that he had neglected his friend. He told Ji-su he would have to leave her and go to the United States to be with Thomas.

Because she understood the special relationship between Thomas and Sergei, Ji-su understood Sergei's need to be with his brother of the soul. She encouraged and supported his decision to go to New York. She was heartsick that Sergei was leaving her, and she would miss him terribly. She knew that he would miss her, too, but he had to go. He didn't want to leave Ji-su, but he wanted to be with Thomas. He made his travel arrangements, and the two spent one last night together, making love, clinging to each other, and crying because they could not bear to be apart.

Ji-su almost asked if she could go with Sergei, but she knew that, for many reasons, he had to make this journey alone. She didn't have any papers or any passport. She would not be allowed to travel to the United States with Sergei, even if he had wanted her to go with him. Using one of his several false identities, Sergei flew from Vladivostok to Seattle and from Seattle to New York City. He rented a car and drove to the hospital in Syracuse.

Chapter 35

SYRACUSE, NEW YORK

As soon as Thomas awakened from his coma and the doctors determined that his condition was stable, he'd been moved out of the ICU and into a private room. Sam had requested the private room because Thomas was such a reserved and quiet person. Sam knew that when Sergei finally came, the two friends would want to be alone to talk. Thomas would not want to share a hospital room with another patient who might have a large, noisy family that came to visit him at all hours of the day and night.

Sam O'Connor had arranged to meet Sergei at the hospital and introduce him to the staff. Thomas was recovering slowly. By the time Sergei arrived, he was able to speak out loud. Thomas had only been able to write notes to communicate when Sam had asked him how to contact Sergei. At least Thomas's mental functioning had been working well enough for him to remember how to find Sergei and communicate that information to Sam. Thomas had told Sam to contact the monastery at Sergiyev Posad, and Sam had called them. Fortunately, enough people spoke English at the monastery that they were able to let him know that Sergei Ivanov was still at the monastery of St. Seraphim on Russky Island near Vladivostok. Sam had decided the best way to reach Sergei in Vladivostok was with a telegram. A telegram was so old school, but Sam wanted to be in touch as soon as possible and wanted to get Sergei's immediate attention. A telegram in English would avoid telephone language difficulties.

The doctors had told Sam they thought Thomas would make a complete recovery. The part of his brain that allowed him to speak had been injured, but they were sure his speech would return. The neurologist told Sam that the damage to Thomas's brain was similar to what a mild stroke might have caused. The doctor expected Thomas to be able to recover his ability to speak on his own, but if he didn't recover quickly enough or completely, a speech therapist would be helpful. Sam hoped that Thomas would be able to speak to Sergei when he arrived.

One reason the doctors knew that Thomas would be able to speak again was because of something that had happened when Thomas had first awakened from the coma. Everybody who had observed Thomas's behavior that day had found it quite odd and difficult to understand. The first thing he had done when he woke up was to start singing. He'd opened his eyes and then burst out with an old Burl Ives ballad from the 1940's, a song that was popular long before Thomas was ever born. He'd started to sing: "Yo, ho, ho, the wind blows free; oh, for the life on the rolling sea." He'd sung this line over and over several times, and then he was silent.

The nurses and the aides had all come running to see who was singing in the ICU and making such a commotion. No one knew why he'd burst out in song or why he'd picked that particular song, but the doctors were thrilled to see that he was finally awake and to hear him verbalizing. What no one knew was that Thomas sang this song to himself when he was sailing his GP-14. After his unexpected outburst of song, Thomas had clammed up completely and hadn't said anything more for days. Finally, he began to speak again.

Sergei was introduced to the staff as Thomas's cousin, and the nurse seemed to buy that in spite of Sergei's looks and foreign clothes. It seemed Thomas had acquired quite a few cousins. Sergei didn't look as if he could be related to Thomas in any way. Sergei was small, and he had swarthy skin and dark curly hair. Thomas was a tall albino. Since Thomas had been moved out of the ICU, the staff was not nearly as strict about who came to visit.

Sam told Sergei everything the doctors had told him about Thomas's condition and everything about the care he had received since the accident. He told Sergei the story about the Burl Ives ballad Thomas had been singing when he woke up from his coma. Sergei knew exactly why Thomas had been singing that song. He couldn't explain it to anybody because nobody could ever know about Camp 27, but Sergei smiled when he heard the story. When Thomas sailed his catboat on the Russian lake, he had liked to pretend he was at sea. Thomas had always liked the Burl Ives song that the musical director at Camp 27 had thought was a popular American folk song. Thomas had always loved the water. Sergei hoped and prayed that after his accident, Thomas would still love the water and would one day be back out on it again, sailing his sailboat.

Thomas was asleep when the two men entered his room. Sam excused himself and said he would leave the two of them alone. The Russian sat down beside the bed and took Thomas's hand in his. When Thomas woke up, the first thing he saw was Sergei sitting in the chair beside him. He squeezed Sergei's hand, and tears rolled down his cheeks. Sergei leaned over and gave Thomas a big bear hug, or at least as big a hug as he could manage, given all the tubes and wires that protruded from almost every inch of Thomas's body.

Thomas was still quite weak from his ordeal, and he tired easily. Sergei could see right away that his friend had a long way to go to recover the strength and stamina he had enjoyed before the accident. Sergei decided to keep things as light as possible for the time being. There were weighty issues to be discussed, but Sergei didn't want to force these on Thomas until he was stronger. Sergei asked Thomas how he was feeling. You can't ask a more banal question than that.

Thomas was so glad to see Sergei. He needed to talk to somebody he could trust. He trusted Sam O'Connor, but Sergei was his closest and dearest friend. Thomas didn't want to tell anybody else that he couldn't remember anything about his accident on Skaneateles Lake. He couldn't remember anything about getting into his boat or going sailing that day. In fact, the entire day of the accident was a blank for Thomas. He knew this wasn't unusual. He knew that people who were in car accidents or suffered other kinds of trauma sometimes had temporary amnesia about what had happened just prior to the accident or traumatic event. You didn't necessarily have to hit your head to experience this kind of memory lapse.

Thomas knew there was something very important that he had to tell Sergei, but no matter how hard he tried to remember what it was, he couldn't. Thomas almost felt it in his bones. It was almost an alarm of some kind. He was terribly frustrated because he couldn't remember anything about that day, the details of his near-drowning, or the matter of life and death he had to talk to Sergei about. He even said to Sergei that he had something vital to tell him but couldn't remember what it was. Thomas wore himself out talking to Sergei and wracking his brains to remember the important message. He fell asleep while Sergei was talking to him.

Sergei slipped out the door of the hospital room. He knew that Thomas had a long journey back to good health. Sergei was sad to see his friend so weak. Thomas definitely wasn't the same man he'd been before the accident. Sergei wanted to be at the hospital the next day when the doctor made his rounds. He needed to have a serious talk with the doctor. Thomas hadn't wanted to tell his neurologist about the amnesia, but Sergei felt it was important for the doctor to know.

Sergei had the keys to the triplex. In fact, he had the keys to everything that belonged to Thomas. Thomas had made certain that Sergei knew everything about his properties and about his finances. Sergei was Thomas's heir, and Thomas's will left all of his sizeable fortune to Sergei. Sergei and Thomas had two joint credit cards that were paid every month by one of Thomas's LLCs. Sergei always let Thomas know when he was putting something on one of their joint cards, but he didn't think it really mattered to Thomas. Sergei had charged the airline tickets from Vladivostok to New York on one of the cards. It was an expensive ticket because he'd bought it at the last minute and because he'd had to fly first class for the Seattle to New York leg of the journey. The only seat left on that flight had been in first class, so Sergei had taken the seat and paid full price. Although he knew that Thomas was worth a tremendous amount of money, he never wanted to take advantage of his friend's generosity and wealth. Thomas had once said to Sergei that he had more money than he could possibly spend in a hundred lifetimes.

Sergei would stay at the triplex while he was in New York.

He had been to Thomas's house and barn on the Skaneateles Lake, and he loved staying there. But without Thomas there as his host, it wouldn't be the same, and Sergei didn't want to stay overnight at the house. There was a comfortable guest condo in the triplex. Thomas made sure the beds were always made up with clean sheets and that all three condos were neat as a pin. Sergei had stayed there in the past. He would be close to downtown and attract less attention by staying at the triplex than if he were coming and going from Thomas's place on the water.

Sergei drove from Syracuse to Skaneateles and parked in one of the garages at the triplex. He knew that Thomas's mail would have accumulated while he was in the hospital, and he would take care of that for Thomas. Thomas had an old-fashioned mail slot in the front door of his condo where he received his mail. The mailman always dropped the mail through the slot. At least there wasn't an overstuffed mailbox on the street to draw attention to the fact that Thomas hadn't been at home for weeks.

Sergei made a mental list of all the things he needed to do. In addition to dealing with the mail, he had to do something about Thomas's hospital bill. Thomas could afford to pay the bill, but he wouldn't be paying with insurance. Sergei knew the bartender Sam had paid for the ambulance and had covered other costs of Thomas's care. Sergei would have to reimburse Sam for all the expenses he had incurred.

Sergei also had to do something about Thomas's sailboat. Sam had started the process by having the boat towed out of the water and taken to be repaired. Sergei would have to make arrangements to pay the Best Boatworks and to store the boat for the winter. Sergei would need to make at least one trip to Thomas's house on the lake to throw away the spoiled food in the refrigerator. He would go one night after dark. There were probably other things at the house that needed attention. Thomas had always taken care of everything for Sergei when he'd needed something. Now it was Sergei's turn to take care of Thomas.

Sergei ached for Ji-su. He sometimes thought he would go mad with missing her. He knew they had to be apart for a while, but his loneliness and longing sometimes resembled actual physical pain. He wanted to talk to Thomas about Ji-su, but he knew it would be a long time before Thomas was able to talk about anything complicated. Sergei's relationship with Ji-su was indeed very complicated.

Sergei had hoped that Thomas would be able to work his magic and get some kind of passport or new identity for Ji-su so that she could travel, but it was unlikely that Thomas would be able to do anything like that for some time. Sergei realized how he had depended on Thomas for so many things. He missed his dear friend and his brother of the soul. Even though the man was lying in a hospital bed a few miles away, Sergei didn't feel as if the man Thomas used to be was really there. Thomas was not himself at all. Sergei hoped that one day, he would be able to get his old friend back.

Sergei let himself into the guest condo at the triplex, and sure enough the place was spotless as always. He gathered up the mail. He put down his duffel bag and backpack in what he had begun to think of as his bedroom. He was too tired to sort through the mail tonight, but he would start on it first thing in the morning. He decided he would go to the Sherwood Inn for dinner tonight, and he knew that would cheer him up. Thomas loved the place, and so did Sergei. Over the years, they'd had many fun dinners and talks sitting in front of the fire in the bar. Tonight Sergei would order lamb chops, Thomas's favorite. He would talk to Sam the bartender and try to get more details about Thomas's accident. There hadn't been time for Sam to tell him everything at the hospital. Sergei knew that Sam would be happy to know he was off the hook for Thomas's hospital bills.

It was Saturday night, and the Sherwood Inn bar was booming. Years ago, Skaneateles had been a sleepy little resort town whose population swelled during the summer months. In the old days, things began to wind down after Labor Day. By October, the summer people had gone back to their work lives and their cities. In recent years more and more people were staying on in Skaneateles into the fall. There was a huge seafood festival in September that brought thousands to the small town. It was now well into October, and Sergei was almost not able to get a seat at the bar.

Sam came over immediately and took Sergei's order for a vodka on the rocks. Because he was Russian, Sergei thought he ought to like vodka, but he really didn't. He always ordered it in a bar, and then the drink just sat there mostly untouched as Sergei tried to make himself drink it.

"Why do you always order vodka on the rocks, Sergei, when you clearly don't like it? Tell me what you'd really like to drink." Sam was asking.

Sergei laughed, "I love Coca Cola, always have. Bring me a Coke with lots of ice—tall glass."

There were so many people at the bar, Sergei knew he wouldn't be able to have much of Sam's time, at least before dinner. He drank his Coke and went into the dining room for lamb chops. After dinner, he returned to the bar, and this late at night there were some empty seats. Sergei started to question Sam about the boating accident that had almost killed Thomas. Sam had arrived at the scene as Thomas was being unloaded from the rescue boat, and he hadn't seen the accident with his own eyes. But he'd heard lots of discussion from the customers at the bar about what had happened. He told Sergei everything he knew.

Sam wanted to let Sergei know he continued to be puzzled by Thomas's reckless behavior on the day of the accident. "What I don't understand is why Thomas was out in such a terrible storm. There was a tornado warning, and the rain was coming down in sheets. On my way to work that afternoon, I had to pull off the road several times because I couldn't see a thing, even with my windshield wipers going at top speed. Thomas wouldn't have been able to see his hand in front of his face out on the water. Why would he have gone out in the first place, and when it got so bad, why didn't he head for home? He's always so careful and so cautious. He always checks the weather before he goes sailing. This behavior, to ignore a bad storm that was coming our way, was quite out of character for the Thomas I've known for so many years."

"He doesn't remember anything at all about the day of the accident. He not only doesn't remember the accident itself; he doesn't remember anything about what he did for that entire day." Sergei wanted Sam to know that either the head injuries or the trauma of the accident had caused Thomas to have amnesia.

"So I can't ask him what the heck he was thinking when he was out in a horrible thunder storm. He doesn't remember what he was thinking." Sam summed it up.

"I agree with you that taking his sailboat out that day was not the way Thomas usually runs his life, and I also wonder what he was thinking ... or why he wasn't thinking. We may never have the answer to that question. It depends on how much of his memory comes back and how much he wants to tell us. I hope he will look back on what he did and realize how reckless he was. This is not the time for scolding, however. The poor man doesn't remember why he made a foolish decision. At least he hasn't forgotten his entire former life. He still knows who he is and who we are. I guess we should be thankful for that." Sergei was thankful Thomas had pulled through the ordeal without worse consequences.

Eventually, Sergei slipped away from the bar and went home to the triplex. He wanted to call Ji-su and knew that there was a fourteen or fifteen hour difference between the time zones. It was eleven o'clock on Saturday night in New York, so it would be one o'clock in the afternoon on Sunday in Vladivostok. It was already tomorrow for Ji-su. Sergei wondered if talking with Ji-su would make him feel better or worse.

Chapter 36

ST. SERAPHIM

J*i-su had lost all of* her phones during the wild and crazy past few weeks of her life. What devices she had managed to take with her on the *Marina* were probably now all at the bottom of the sea. Sergei had bought them both new satellite phones before he'd left for the United States. They would have a way to communicate with each other while they were apart. Ji-su had been completely out of touch with the U Group since September 10th, the day she was inserted into the North Korean royal palace to impersonate Kim Jong-un. So much had happened since that day.

After climbing out of the royal palace, she'd thought only of her survival and escape from North Korea. After arriving at the monastery, she'd only been able to think about Sergei. Time had slipped away from her, and it was already October. She felt she was now in a safe place, even though she didn't have any papers or legal permission to be in Russia. With Sergei gone, she now had time to think about her situation and what she was going to do.

She could not help but question whether or not she should be in touch with the U Group. She wondered if any of the people who had lived and worked in the safety of the beautiful stone and wood house on Whidbey Island ever expected to see or hear from her again. Ji-su herself had expected to die during her mission, and she was sure everyone else connected with the operation had expected the same. Who would have imagined that someone like Sergei was watching out for her and would save her life when he'd seen her sitting on the dirt in a garden shed in Pyongyang? But he had been there. And he had saved her more than once. She had survived.

The original plan for her escape had been for her to be taken to a safe house in South Korea. The alternative plan had been for her to go to another safe house—in Dandong, China. All of those plans had fallen apart. Ji-su had not contacted anyone to let them know she was alive. She had left all of her clothes and all of her papers, including her South Korean passport, at the cottage on Whidbey Island. She had assumed that once she'd made it to one of their safe houses, the U Group would have taken her back either to the United States or to South Korea.

Ji-su was still on active duty with the South Korean Army. She had been on loan to the U Group through a top-secret special operations program. Her commanding officers knew she was on a special ops assignment that might take years, so they would not be expecting to see her again—until they saw her again. Before she had joined the U Group, she'd intended to make the military her life's career.

Ji-su had been completely incommunicado, and no one associated with the U Group or in South Korea even knew she was still alive. She was entirely absent from everybody's radar screen. She realized that she now had a unique opportunity. Because everyone from the U Group and from her former life probably assumed that she had died on the risky mission in North Korea, she had the chance to disappear forever and have a different life. She could choose her life, her own future.

She could choose to reestablish contact with the U Group, and she could choose whether or not to go back to the Army. She was free at this time in a way she had never been free before. She was mentally free as well. For almost all of her adult life, she had been obsessed with and committed to bringing down the North Korean dynasty. She'd finally had the chance to play a role in achieving that goal. She was no longer weighted down by her desire for revenge and retribution. She had accomplished it.

Then there was the situation with Sergei. She loved him so much and wanted him so much. She could not imagine her life without him. But guilt had begun to creep into the edges of her conscience. Before she had met Sergei, Ji-su basically had no life other than her wish to destroy. Now she was working with a blank canvas going forward. She had no ties that kept her from loving Sergei unconditionally and making her future life with him. The difficult realization for Ji-su was that this was not true for Sergei. He had loved the life he'd been living before he'd ever heard of Ji-su.

Unknown to her or to anybody except Thomas, he'd watched her on Whidbey Island as she prepared for her mission. He'd met Ji-su for the first time when they'd spoken to each other on their cell phones. Then he'd first seen her in person before dawn one morning. She had stepped out of a North Korean fishing boat, climbed an aluminum ladder, and taken Sergei's hand as he helped her up on to the deck of the *Marina*. Ji-su knew Sergei loved her, but she also knew that Sergei loved God, loved being a priest in the Russian Orthodox Church, and loved the monastery at Sergiyev Posad. Sergei had a life apart from her that was ongoing. It was a life he had lived with joy and a life he still cherished.

Neither Ji-su nor Sergei would ever trade what they had found together, the time they had spent getting to know each other and loving each other. But in the light of day, Ji-su was struck by the realization of her own selfishness. She had made assumptions about her relationship with Sergei and about the future they could have as individuals and as a couple. She began to doubt her right to have Sergei in her life. She did not want to deny him his life's work as a priest. She did not want to take him away from the commitment he had made to God and to the church. She would never forgive herself if she expected or allowed him to give up the things that made him who he was. She was beginning to see that there were some unusually difficult choices on the horizon for both of them, but especially for her. She would have to be the one to bite the bullet and take the high road, or more accurately the hard road.

Ji-su cried herself to sleep that night. She loved him so much and wanted to have a life with him. But the more she faced the truth, the more she realized that such a life could never be. She knew that she would have to be the one to make the extremely painful but necessary choice for them to go back to their lives without each other. She had only the military to go back to. It was painful for Ji-su to realize she had to figure out her own future, a future without Sergei.

As far as Ji-su knew, the U Group's work was done. She didn't know if it had been disbanded in the weeks after KJU's abduction. Each sector in the overall operation had been purposely kept in the dark about the activities and personnel who were working in other sectors. Ji-su didn't know where the extraction and insertion teams had practiced their drills. She didn't know what had happened to KJU after he'd been put aboard the helicopter in the garden of the North Korean royal palace. She had no idea where he was now.

She didn't know if there was anybody still in residence at Whidbey Island. She did wonder what had happened to her clothes and her passport. She realized that she was not able to completely walk away from the U Group. She needed some closure with regard to the operation she had worked so hard to make successful. She did have an emergency number she could call, and she decided she would call it in the morning.

The next morning she called the U Group's emergency number and left a message. She said she had made her escape from North Korea and asked that somebody call her back. She wanted to know how she could retrieve her clothes and passport from Whidbey Island. She gave the number of her new satellite phone and hoped somebody would respond. She was still wrestling with her guilt and what to do about Sergei, but sadly, in her heart she knew what she was going to have to do.

Sergei called her from Skaneateles before the U Group contacted her. Hearing his voice made her wonder if she were crazy for even considering her plan to convince Sergei he had to go back to Sergiyev Posad and his life as a priest. Talking to Sergei, let alone being with him, weakened her resolve to do what she knew she had to do. She was going to have to break off her contact with Sergei, but she couldn't do any of it over the phone. She would have to see Sergei again and tell him in person what she had decided. It would be the most difficult thing she'd ever done in her life, but she knew it was for the best. No matter what she decided to do going forward, she would have to stay at St. Seraphim at least until Sergei returned. She would have to look into his eyes and tell him she didn't want to have a life with him. She wondered if she could ever possibly convince him she was telling him the truth.

Her phone rang, and Ji-su knew it had to be the U Group calling back. Only the U Group and Sergei had her number. Her controller from the mission was on the phone, and she sounded overjoyed to hear that Ji-su had survived and was alive and well. Ji-su only half listened to what her controller had to say. She was still thinking about the conversation she was going to have to have with Sergei. She answered the women's questions but was distracted. Ji-su was careful not to mention Russia or anything about where she was.

Ji-su brought up several times that her passport and clothes were still on Whidbey Island. Finally her controller addressed that issue. Her things had been sent to her home in South Korea, back to her family there. The facility at Whidbey Island was still open and still had work to do. Because no one had heard anything at all from Ji-su, they assumed she had died or was in a North Korean prison somewhere. They'd sent her things to her family. They had not told her South Korean family that she was dead, but the message was clear when her belongings had arrived at their house without her.

Ji-su was angry that her things had been sent so quickly to her family in South Korea. She insisted that her controller retrieve her clothes and her passport and send them to her. The controller said they would do what Ji-su wanted them to do. Ji-su said she would send a text with the address where her things were to be sent. She reluctantly agreed to go to South Korea for a debriefing once she had received her passport. She hoped that might motivate the U Group to send her belongings more quickly.

Ji-su didn't want anybody to know exactly where she was right now. She considered asking one of the monks to open an anonymous post office box for her in the city of Vladivostok. Sergei was now in the United States. Ji-su decided it would provide her with more anonymity if the U Group sent her things to a post office box in New York City. She began to wonder if the people in the U Group were really happy that she had lived through her mission. Could she trust them?

Although Ji-su didn't really think anyone would be coming after her, she wondered if, technically, she was now a deserter from the South Korean Army. Once she had her passport in hand, if the U Group followed through and sent the passport back to her, she would be able to travel wherever she wanted to travel. She could go back to South Korea, or she could join Sergei in Skaneateles, New York. The thought that she could join Sergei in the United States was tempting, and she scolded herself for allowing her mind to go in that direction.

She would have to decide where she wanted to go. She had to admit to herself that, right now, she didn't really want to go anywhere. She realized she loved living at St. Seraphim, and she wanted to stay right where she was. She was not ready yet to move on from this safe place. But she was going to have to work on a way to earn her keep at the monastery. Song-gi's mother was certainly paying her way by cooking for everyone. Ji-su would have to find something to give the monks in return for allowing her to live with them. She wondered if they would even consider allowing her to stay at the monastery forever. Ji-su realized she still needed time to figure out exactly what she wanted to do with the rest of her life.

Chapter 37

SYRACUSE AND SKANEATELES, NEW YORK

Sergei couldn't sleep after his phone conversation with Ji-su. She hadn't sounded like herself. He'd only been away from her for three or four days, and she already sounded distant. Something wasn't adding up. He tossed and turned and finally got up at two o'clock in the morning. He started working on Thomas's mail. It was mostly junk, but there were a few bills that needed to be paid. Most of Thomas's mail and bills went to one of his LLCs and were taken care of by an anonymous administrative assistant. Only the few bills that were necessary to maintain the illusion that Thomas actually lived in the triplex were mailed to the condos in Skaneateles. Sergei was authorized to pay Thomas's bills, and he took care of them. Finally he was tired, and he went back to bed at four o'clock. He slept until ten.

Sergei loved to go to Johnny Angel's for breakfast, and when he was dressed, he drove his rental car to the center of town. If he had time, he would have lunch at Doug's Fish Fry which was another favorite. If not Doug's today, then the next day for sure. Sergei loved fried fish. He planned to drive to Thomas's house and barn on the lake this morning to check on the place. He would clean out the refrigerator and take care of anything else that looked or smelled as if it was suffering from lack of attention due to Thomas's absence.

Sergei would have preferred to go to Thomas's lake property after dark. Since he'd decided to go in the daytime, he would have to be extra careful that nobody saw him on the road. As it turned out, there were too many people driving up and down on Route 41A on this Sunday morning. Sergei decided to park his car a good distance away and walk back to Thomas's invisible gate. It had been some time since he'd been to the lake house, and he hoped he remembered everything he needed to do to get into the compound.

Thomas was a neat freak and always left everything ship shape. When Sergei got to the house, he was shocked to find computers that had not been shut down, TV screens still turned on, and videos that had obviously been left running for weeks. Leaving things in this kind of disarray was not at all how Thomas usually kept his house. Thomas was obsessive and paranoid about never leaving the house unless he had every last thing zipped up perfectly. Something had to have been wrong with Thomas, for him not to have cleaned up his mess before he'd left to take his boat out on the lake.

Sergei checked the refrigerator, and sure enough there was spoiled food inside. He grabbed a garbage bag and filled it with the offending items. He put the bag outside so it wouldn't smell up the house. He would take the garbage with him when he left.

Sergei seated himself at Thomas's library table and began to shut down the computers, the TV screens, and the videos. There was one video paused on a screen. Sergei looked at the time stamps on the video and realized that Thomas had rerun this particular clip four times. Sergei wondered what in the world Thomas had found that was so interesting about this particular video. He punched the keys to rewind and play it again. What he witnessed shook him to his core. It was the video Thomas had recorded of the meeting in the North Korean royal palace where the men sitting around the table had been baffled by the DNA results that had come back from the lab, the analysis of the blood that had been discovered on the outside wall of KJU's residence.

Sergei knew, as Thomas had known, exactly what the results of the DNA tests implied. He didn't waste his time wondering if KJU had male anatomy and female DNA, and he knew there had not been any mix up on the part of the lab. He realized that the laboratory results confirmed what he had never wanted to think about, what he dreaded almost more than anything else in the world. This video told him the terrible truth, the indisputable fact that his beloved Ji-su was the sister of Kim Jong-un. Sergei knew Ji-su was KJU's twin sister.

Sergei had additional information that Thomas didn't have. Ji-su herself had shared with Sergei what her adoptive mother had told her about the story of her birth and her true biological parentage. Ever since Ji-su had told her story to Sergei, he had tried to push it from his mind. But of course he wasn't able to ignore what he'd heard. There was the uncanny resemblance between Ji-su and Emperor Roly Poly that everyone could see. In spite of the extreme differences in their weights, Sergei had suspected the two might be related. He hated that it was true, but the evidence was overwhelming. It was true. Ji-su and Kim Jong-un were twins, sister and brother.

Sergei knew that Ji-su had left her DNA on the side of the royal palace when she'd made her escape. He had seen the scrape on her hand where she had injured it when she'd gone out the window and rappelled down the wall. Sergei was afraid that this news about the DNA tests, this fact, might destroy the woman he loved. How could he ever tell her this terrible truth? They had promised that no matter what, they would never keep any secrets from each other. If he was to be honest and if he was to deserve her trust, he would have to tell her. She had to know. He wondered if she had ever suspected the truth. She had to have wondered when she looked at herself in the mirror. When she'd heard the story the woman who raised her had told her, Ji-su must have imagined what the rest of the story might be.

Sergei replayed the video two more times to be sure he hadn't missed anything. He sent a copy to his phone and to his computer which he'd left in Vladivostok. Then he went into all the rooms of Thomas's beautiful house to check the windows, the thermostats, and everything else he could think of. He secured all of the electronics in exactly the way that Thomas would have done it—if he'd been thinking clearly. Sergei locked the house, and taking the bag of garbage away with him, he made his way back to where his car was parked. He would have to skip lunch today. There was no time to go back to Skaneateles for that fish sandwich. He headed for the hospital in Syracuse and left the garbage bag in a dumpster along the way. He hoped he hadn't missed Thomas's doctor's rounds.

Thomas was again delighted to see Sergei and seemed in better spirits than he'd been the day before. He also seemed less confused, and Sergei was thrilled to find his friend more talkative and making more sense. He asked Thomas if he remembered anything more about the day of his accident. Thomas shook his head. Sergei felt he needed to let Thomas know he'd been to his house and what he'd found there. "I went to your house to check on things. I cleaned the spoiled food out of the refrigerator." The look on Thomas's face let Sergei know that practical problem hadn't ever crossed Thomas's mind. "I also saw that you'd left the house in a hurry. All of your computers were still on and left out on the library table. I shut everything down the way I know you want it to be done, and I checked all the windows. Everything is fine there now, closed up tight as a drum."

Sergei watched Thomas's face to see if there was any hint that Thomas might remember the video about KJU's DNA. There was not a flicker of recognition of any kind. Obviously, Thomas still remembered nothing about the video or what he had done that day. He'd looked somewhat puzzled and chagrined when he heard that he hadn't closed down his electronics as he usually did. Sergei said to him, "I'm not scolding you, Thomas. I only wanted you to know that everything is taken care of. I shut down all the computers and put your library back the way I know you want it to be. You must have been upset or in a hurry to have left things as you did. Nobody is as neat and compulsive as you are. It's okay."

Thomas was obviously trying to figure something out. He was quiet and worried. Sergei didn't want to get into the DNA thing with Thomas until he was stronger and thinking more clearly. Eventually he would have to talk to Thomas about what he had seen on the video, but he was hoping that Thomas might remember it on his own.

The doctor finally arrived, and Sergei introduced himself as Thomas's cousin. He said they had grown up together and were very close. They were brothers. This was all true, except for the part about Sergei being Thomas's cousin. He left the doctor with Thomas and walked down the hall, but he was back at the door of the room when the doctor left. He asked the doctor if he could talk to him at the nurse's station. Sergei brought up the issue of Thomas's memory loss. The doctor told Sergei what he already knew—that this kind of amnesia was not unusual and could be expected to resolve on its own. Sergei asked the doctor some specific questions about Thomas's injuries. They discussed possible physical, occupational, and speech therapies and when Thomas might be expected to be released from the hospital.

Sergei was willing to stay as long as Thomas needed him. He was of course more than anxious to get back to Ji-su, but right now, Thomas came first. Ji-su understood and supported Sergei's wish to stay with Thomas as long as he needed help. When Thomas left the hospital, he would go to the triplex. Sergei would have to arrange for Thomas to have appointments with the various therapists. He would need some kind of assistance to help him take care of things around the house. Sergei knew Thomas would hate having strange people at the triplex, but it might come to that. Thomas might have to accept, at least temporarily and in order to get well, a life that he wouldn't be happy with. It might be a long time before Sergei could return to Russky Island.

Ji-su had sent Sergei a text, asking him to rent a post office box for her in New York City. She told him she had contacted the U Group and wanted them to send her passport and her clothes to the post office box. Sergei was disappointed that Ji-su had contacted the U Group. He had hoped she would take the opportunity that she'd been presented with to end that phase of her life once and for all. Sergei had hoped the U Group would believe that Ji-su had died during her mission to North Korea. He wanted Ji-su to begin a new chapter of her life with him, unencumbered by anything from the past.

But Ji-su had requested the post office box. She wanted her passport. She wanted her clothes. Sergei drove to the city and rented the post office box for her. He returned the next week to pick up her passport. Either the U Group had not sent the clothes or someone had absconded with them. No clothes had been sent, but the passport was in the post office box. Sergei reluctantly and sadly sent the passport to Ji-su. She had asked him to send it express mail, and he respected her wishes and sent the passport as requested.

Chapter 38

SOUTH KOREA

J*i-su contacted the U Group* and told them she would return to South Korea for a debriefing. Because the U Group had not wanted many people to see her before her mission, she had been isolated from most of the other members of the U Group on Whidbey Island. With a great deal of help from Sergei, she had saved herself and escaped from North Korea. She couldn't really blame the U Group for abandoning her and assuming she was dead or in prison. She knew she would have to make up a different story about her escape when she told it to the U Group debriefing team.

She couldn't tell them anything about Sergei and Thomas and the fact that they had been able to hack into the North Korean royal palace and watch what was going on there in real time. It was essential, according to Sergei, that the availability of Thomas' technology be kept a closely guarded secret. No one could know about it. Ji-su would have to make up a story about her successful rescue to get around the fact that Thomas and Sergei had been watching her, had helped in the U Group's operation, and in the end had saved her life.

Ji-su hadn't been back to South Korea for almost two years, and she was worried about how she would feel returning there, even briefly. She had lived on Whidbey Island in isolation and thrown herself into her role as Kim Jong-un so completely, she didn't really know where she belonged any more. Ji-su had begun to doubt the U Group. After she had successfully fulfilled her mission, the members of the group had probably been relieved that their impersonator had died. Ji-su realized her death would have tied up a number of loose ends for the operation. She began to worry about her safety ... if she were to reveal where she was living now or if she returned to South Korea. In spite of the fact that she no longer completely trusted the people of the U Group, Ji-su felt she owed them the debriefing she had promised. She decided she would travel to South Korea, even though she was afraid that her life might be in danger there.

Ji-su decided that Sergei had enough to worry about right now, and she didn't want to involve him with her trip to South Korea and her meeting with the U Group. She decided that she would tell him all about it when the trip was finished and she was with him in person. She was able to get a round-trip flight from Vladivostok to Seoul, and she would only have to be in South Korea for two days.

She met with her U Group controller at a high-rise hotel in Seoul. She found she dreaded spending time in a big city. The traffic, all the tall buildings, so many people rushing everywhere, the hundreds of stores, and the pace of life in Seoul had not bothered her when she had lived there in the past. After spending almost two years on rural Whidbey

Island, a few days in a fishing village in North Korea, and then several weeks at the monastery of St. Seraphim, she felt as if she was no longer cut out for urban living. The hustle and bustle, that so many city dwellers thrive on in Seoul and other metropolitan areas, now made Ji-su nervous. All she could think about, while she was staying at the luxurious hotel in South Korea's capital city, was getting back to her cell-like room and narrow bed at the monastery.

Ji-su passed her debriefing with flying colors. She scolded the U Group insertion team for putting her motorcycle in the wrong garden shed. She told them that she'd been angry when she hadn't found it where it was supposed to be, but then she'd found it in another shed. She told of her escape on the motorcycle to Wonsan. She left out all references to Sergei; the Chris-Craft cabin cruiser, the *Marina*; the confrontation with the North Korean patrol boat; Vasily the crooked sea captain; and everything else that had been arranged and orchestrated by Thomas and Sergei.

Ji-su decided she also would leave the identity of the Ri family and their role in her escape completely out of her report to the U Group. There was no need for the U Group to know anything about Russky Island or St. Seraphim. She told them that she had made her way across the border into China. She said the chaos of the previous few days and the bombing by the Americans had aided in her being able to slip out of North Korea. The U Group knew she'd escaped with currency from various countries and a phony passport. She told the members of the debriefing group that she had taken a flight from China to New York City where she had been resting and recovering ever since.

Everyone who was in on the debriefing praised Ji-su's ingenuity and courage. They said they admired her ability to save herself and to make it from North Korea to China and then to New York. Ji-su thought to herself… no thanks to the U Group. Ji-su was informed that the U Group had extensive plans in place to try to rehabilitate North Korea after the old regime had fallen. The U Group offered her a number of positions going forward, but she told them she did not want to stay in South Korea or ever live in North Korea. She said she hoped they understood that she had devoted so much of her life to preparing for this mission. She now intended to put all of that behind her and move on to a new life in a new place. Ji-su was still uncertain what direction she wanted her future life to take.

Things were completely in flux in the former Hermit Kingdom. The ad hoc, temporary ruling body was a group of generals, some of whom had been sleeper agents laying low and waiting for something to change the status quo in North Korea. When that had finally happened, they had come forward. Others who had secretly despised the Kim family, especially KJU, came out of the shadows and declared their desire to work towards a new North Korea.

North Korea was still so disorganized that no one knew exactly what direction the country would take or what the new system would look like. Some favored reunification with South Korea. Some favored an independent North Korea, based on democracy and freedom. Some favored a modified Socialist system. Others couldn't wait for the people of North Korea to have the material goods those in the south enjoyed. It would take months and years for the country to sort itself out.

There was something else Ji-su knew she had to do while she was in South Korea. She was going to ask the U Group for something most people would imagine was impossible. She wanted to see the man she had devoted her life to bringing down. She wanted to see him in person, and she was going to try to make it happen. Nobody wanted her to see him, but she told the U Group they owed her this one request. She had not been compensated in any way for the risks she had taken. She told them that she was unable to move on with her life until her demand was granted.

The reason she gave for wanting to meet with Kim Jong-un, wherever in the world he was now, had to do with her own mental health. She said she was having nightmares and was unable to sleep. She blamed her anxiety attacks on PTSD resulting from the mission. She told the U Group she needed closure. She said she'd had recurring dreams that KJU was not really in custody. She dreamed that he had escaped from the place where he'd been held and was coming after her to kill her. She asked repeatedly if the U Group was certain that he was being kept at a secure facility. Ji-su told them she thought she could resolve her fears and her discontent if she could see him in his prison, if she could be assured that he would never be able to escape. She kept up her barrage in spite of being told no, over and over again.

At first they told her they didn't know where KJU was and that, for security reasons, they had turned him over to others. The U Group did not operate prison facilities. Ji-su argued that they had to know who they had turned him over to, even if they didn't know exactly where he was being held at the moment.

Apparently, KJU had been tried in absentia, in a secret South Korean court, for murdering hundreds of people, including several members of his own family. All due process legal requirements had been followed, and Kim Jong-un had been convicted of multiple counts of murder by a secretly empowered jury. He had been sentenced to death, but his death sentence had been reduced to a life sentence in an institution because he had been deemed to be insane. He was a criminal, and he was insane. Everybody knew that. The U Group told Ji-su that KJU had been sent to a maximum-security facility for the criminally insane. No one was allowed to visit there.

Ji-su thought she would never be allowed to see him and have the closure she was seeking, but the U Group surprised her. They told her that the next morning a car would pick her up at the hotel. Ji-su doubted that the car would ever arrive, but in fact it did. Before she got into the official-looking limousine, the driver placed a hood over Ji-su's head. When she protested, he said one of the conditions of the trip they were about to take was that the hood had to remain in place. She would not be allowed to see where they were going.

It seemed to Ji-su that they drove for a long time. When they finally stopped, the limousine driver removed the hood from Ji-su's head. The limousine was parked inside a warehouse-like structure without any windows. The walls and the floors were concrete, and there was nothing in the building that gave Ji-su the slightest hint about where she might be. It was a bunker.

A woman in a military uniform, a uniform that Ji-su was not able to identify, helped her from the car and asked if she needed to use the bathroom. Ji-su said she did, and the woman escorted her to a primitive facility. The woman waited outside the door for Ji-su and then escorted her to an elevator. The woman apologized but insisted that Ji-su had to wear the hood again. She said the hood was not only to keep her from knowing where she was going but was also for Ji-su's protection. The woman explained that all visitors to the secure facility were required to wear the hood. There were security cameras everywhere, and it was important that Ji-su's face did not turn up on one of them. It was important that no one know she was visiting this facility for the criminally insane. Likewise, it was important that none of the inmates ever see Ji-su's face.

The woman accompanied Ji-su on the elevator. Either the elevator was old, or they were going down into the center of the earth. It seemed as if it took forever to reach their destination. At times, Ji-su had the feeling the elevator was going sideways. Was that even possible? Finally, the elevator came to a stop. Ji-su's escort led her to a small windowless room where the hood was removed and Ji-su was given a complete body search. Again the woman in the military uniform apologized for the intrusion and explained that everyone who visited had to be thoroughly searched. Ji-su's purse was taken from her with the promise that it would be returned. Ji-su's hood was again placed over her head, and she was escorted from the little room.

Her guide and minder told her to step up into a cart, much like a golf cart. The woman almost lifted Ji-su into the cart and secured her with a seat belt. Ji-su felt as if she was deep underground. Her ears had popped on the elevator, and she was cold. She had the feeling she might be inside some kind of cave. The golf cart traveled for several minutes, and Ji-su was certain she was heading even closer to the center of the earth. Was she inside a mountain prison of some kind?

When the golf cart finally stopped, Ji-su's minder removed her hood and replaced it with a different hood. The new hood had a slit in the front that allowed Ji-su to see where she was, but her face and hair were still covered. The minder helped Ji-su step down from the golf cart. They walked up a few steps. Ji-su found herself in an observation room with tiered seating, a kind of amphitheater similar to an amphitheater where medical personnel might sit to watch a surgical procedure.

There was a curtain across the large observation window. Ji-su and her minder were the only two people in the amphitheater. They sat and waited for a few minutes, and finally the curtain was drawn to the side. Ji-su was looking at what resembled the day room of a mental hospital, a place where patients came to play games and watch television. There was a large oval table in the center of the room, and there were chairs around the table.

One by one, a parade of unusually strange people filed past the observation window, and each one took a seat at the table. The people were prisoners or patients or both. They all wore the same clothes. Each one wore an exact duplicate of the distinctive black paramilitary uniform worn by Kim Jong-un whenever he appeared in public. Each one of the people around the table had a squared-off hair do. Clearly, the haircuts were an attempt to copy the square hair that was characteristic of Kim Jong-un's unique haircut. Some of the haircuts were more successful than others. A few of the prisoners were built like KJU, fat and puffy. Others did not physically resemble him at all. Some were skinny, and some were tall. There were even two women at the table who were dressed and coiffed like KJU. It was the most bizarre collection of people Ji-su had ever seen. This group was obviously composed of Kim Jong-un wannabees. These were all people who were trying to look as if they were the former leader of North Korea. Several of them had achieved their goal and looked exactly like KJU in every respect, including body shape. They were all Korean.

A staff person entered the room and sat at the table. He was a muscular man who appeared as if he could handle any of the inmates, or whatever they were. All the people around the table looked as if they were medicated, but not to the extent that they were unable to speak or were falling asleep. The staff person spoke, "Let's go around the table and have everyone give their name." The man said it as if he'd said the same thing a hundred times before. He pointed to the person on his immediate left and told him to stand up and give his name.

The man stood up and said, "I am Kim Jong-un, the ruler of North Korea." When he said this, the others who were sitting at the table began to mumble louder and louder and became restless.

The staff person told them to be quiet, that they would each have a turn. "All right, Kim Jong-un, please sit down." He pointed to the next person.

That man stood up and said, "I am the real ruler of the Democratic People's Republic of North Korea. That man is an imposter." He pointed to the man next to him who had just spoken.

And so it continued around the table, each inmate claiming to be the real Kim Jong-un, the true leader, the one with the royal blood line. Each one called the others who were seated at the table frauds and fakes. Occasionally, one of the people at the table would become somewhat belligerent and had to be talked down. Finally, one man stood up and said, "You are all imposters. I am the only true leader of North Korea. I am being held against my will, here in this insane asylum. You are all insane. I am Kim Jong-un, and I have nuclear weapons that I will send against you and destroy you. I am not insane, and one day I will have my power and my weapons back. You will all be sorry."

Ji-su had seen enough. She told her minder that she was ready to leave, and she stood up and left the amphitheater. Ji-su handed the hood with the slit back to the minder and stepped up into the golf cart. She willingly put on the hood that covered her eyes. She didn't say a word and let herself be transported back through the underground tunnels, into the elevator, and up to the concrete warehouse. The hood was removed from Ji-su's head, and the limousine was waiting there. Her minder gave Ji-su her purse and asked if she needed to use the bathroom. When Ji-su said she didn't and turned to get back into the limousine, the driver replaced the hood. Ji-su sat in silence through the rest of the journey back to her hotel. It had been a day she would never be able to forget as long as she lived. She had asked for it, and her wish had been granted. Ji-su never mentioned anything about this day again. The trip into the twilight zone had never happened.

Chapter 39

ST. SERAPHIM

W*hen Ji-su returned to St.* Seraphim after her debriefing, she talked with the head priest at the monastery about her wish to continue to live at St. Seraphim... at least for a while. The monks often took in those who needed help, but they took in outsiders only temporarily and on an emergency basis. No one except the brothers themselves ever stayed on permanently. It was a religious order, and the people who lived there had taken vows and were the only ones who really had the right to be there. It was an unwritten church rule.

An exception had been made for Song-gi's family. The cook who had worked for the monastery for decades was retiring and going to live with relatives elsewhere in Russia. He was almost seventy years old and way past his working prime. Now that Mrs. Ri had entered the picture and had turned out to be such an excellent cook, the monks were anxious to have her take over the kitchen permanently. The small house the old cook had inhabited at the rear of the St. Seraphim property was being renovated and expanded for Song-gi and his parents.

The fisherman would need years of rehabilitation in order to be able to use his leg. Mrs. Ri was spending all of her spare time, when she wasn't occupied in the kitchen, working with her husband so that one day he might be able to walk again. The monks could not begin to think about turning this family of three out of their home at the monastery. They had no papers to legally allow them to be in Russia, and they had nowhere else to go.

The monks had become fond of Song-gi, and some of them were talking about expanding their tutoring services to include other children. Some even talked about starting a small school. The brothers at the monastery were well-educated and intelligent people, and many of them liked to teach. They had loved the time they'd spent with Song-gi, and they thought they could take on a few more students. It would be good for Song-gi to have some classmates and some playmates.

Taking in the North Korean family had expanded the horizons of the men at St. Seraphim. Their food was unquestionably more delicious, and it now had an international flare. They'd found a mission teaching Song-gi and thought they could serve their own goals by expanding their teaching functions. Prayer was a wonderful thing, but to dedicate all of one's waking hours to prayer was so sixteenth century.

The monks were using computers now. It was time to embrace community service, and teaching small children seemed as if it might be the perfect way to do that. The monastery was well aware of what went on in Moscow. They knew all about Putin's benign neglect of the Russian Orthodox Church. The monks at St. Seraphim felt they were far enough away from Moscow that they could quietly begin to tutor and teach more students. It would be a small and low-key start, but the brothers wanted to do this. Although none of them would ever say it out loud, they'd been pretty bored with praying all day. The entry of the North Korean family into their lives had livened things up considerably and put them on a potential new path.

The one problem they couldn't figure out how to solve was the problem of Ji-su. They had assumed she would go with Sergei back to Sergiyev Posad when Sergei decided it was time to go home. It was obvious the two loved each other very much, and everyone assumed they would marry. Then all of a sudden, Sergei had flown off to the United States, almost in the middle of the night, and now Ji-su was asking if she could live at the monastery permanently. It was a whole new world, and a whole new set of issues to contend with.

They decided to tell Ji-su that she could keep her room at the monastery until Sergei returned. Then they would reconsider the options. Ji-su knew this meant that the monks assumed Ji-su and Sergei would marry and go back to Sergiyev Posad. Ji-su knew this was not going to happen, but she went along with the deal the monks had proposed. Ji-su had also grown fond of little Song-gi and his family, and she didn't want to think that there would come a point when these three dear people would no longer be a part of her life.

Computers had always been a part of Ji-su's life. As she began to enter the human race again, she realized she needed a computer. She didn't have one, and she had walked by Sergei's laptop, which he'd left behind in his bedroom, every day. She was sure Sergei wouldn't mind if she used his laptop for her work. They had no secrets from each other after all. Ji-su knew Sergei's passwords, so she decided to use his computer.

Ji-su sent most of her emails from her phone. When she opened Sergei's computer, she found that Sergei had sent a video to his computer from Skaneateles a few weeks earlier. Ji-su was curious about the video, and she didn't think Sergei would mind if she looked at it. She was curious about what Sergei was doing in the United States and concerned about Thomas. She decided to look at the video Sergei had sent to himself.

After some of the shock had worn off, Ji-su wondered if her life would have been different if she'd never used Sergei's laptop and had never opened up his email and looked at the video. She wondered if Sergei would have found the courage to tell her what he had discovered about Kim Jong-un's DNA. Would he have wanted to spare her the pain of knowing what he knew or would he have honored their agreement that there would be no secrets between them.

Ji-su could understand how making that decision would be one of the hardest Sergei or anybody would ever have to make. She could understand why he'd not wanted to tell her what he knew until he could discuss it with her in person. She respected what she thought had been his decision-making process, to keep her temporarily in the dark. She had happened on this information by accident. She hadn't gone snooping in Sergei's business. Nobody deserved any blame for any of this.

Ji-su had long suspected she must have some kind of a connection to the North Korean royal family. The story her wet nurse and adoptive mother had told her so many years ago had been one of the first clues that she might be related to the Kims who had so ruthlessly ruled the Hermit Kingdom for more than half a century. She could not overlook her resemblance to KJU, and of course, it was that resemblance which had made her indispensable to the U Group and their mission. She had suspected the truth all of her life, but to be confronted with the irrefutable evidence that she was KJU's twin was devastating to her in every way.

She needed time to absorb and process what she had discovered, although she didn't think she would ever be able to completely come to terms with this new information. She retreated to her room at the monastery and refused to speak to anyone. She refused offers of meals and said she was ill and wanted to be left alone. She stopped answering Sergei's emails from the United States. What could she possibly say to him now? She couldn't make small talk with him about what she was doing or what he was doing. Given the impact of the DNA revelation, Ji-su was scarcely able to think about her ancestry, let alone speak to anyone else about it. She was consumed with searching her own mind, for who she was now and who she was going to be in the future. There was nothing else in her life at this moment.

She had accepted the fact that Sergei had postponed revealing the information he had discovered in the video about the DNA until he could be with her. Ji-su had to admit to herself that she was also putting off telling Sergei what she had decided about their future, the impossibility that they would ever have a life together. They had both held back and delayed saying and doing the uncomfortable things and delivering the bad news until they could do it face to face. Ji-su found she wasn't angry with herself or with Sergei about any of this. She was incredibly and overwhelmingly sad—sad to the marrow of her bones and the deepest recesses of her heart.

She would eventually be able to deal with the truth about her biological background. She would be able to put it in perspective and separate herself from the evil she had despised in her sibling, her own twin, her brother. She was connected to him through genetics only. She had never lived with him or shared his life, his values, or anything about him. She was her own person, separate and individual and quite apart from anything that he was or ever had been. Ji-su would get over this and be able to rise above it. She was much less certain about her ability to relinquish her love for Sergei. That would be the more difficult task. That would be the journey she would never really complete, the journey she would struggle with for as long as she lived.

Chapter 40

SKANEATELES, NEW YORK AND RUSSKY ISLAND

S*ergei stayed in Skaneateles for* more than six weeks. Thomas was discharged from the hospital, and Sergei took him to the triplex to complete his recovery and rehabilitation. He made good progress, although Sergei wondered to himself if the man would ever regain the brilliance that had characterized his personality before the accident. Sergei was a priest and knew that God worked in mysterious, and sometimes convoluted, ways. In spite of wanting to leave things in God's hands, Sergei was angry that this gifted and creative soul had been diminished.

Sergei was going to do everything in his power to try to get Thomas back to where he'd been before he'd suffered a severe blow to the head and his heart had stopped. Sergei was also a realist and knew that sometimes you just couldn't have your old life back, as much as you might want it. Sergei was sad, but he was determined to do everything he could to provide Thomas with the best quality of life he could give him. The therapies helped, but Thomas was depressed and seemed lonely. Thomas had always been a loner, but he'd never seemed lonely in a sad way. He'd had his inventions and his computer work that had kept him busy and productive and challenged. Now he was living at the triplex. He hadn't even asked for a computer of any kind since he'd been released from the hospital. Sergei found this to be upsetting and unusual behavior on the part of his friend Thomas. The man had practically lived and slept inside his computers in the past. Now he hadn't even asked to see a laptop.

Sergei knew he'd been putting off discussing with Thomas what he'd learned from watching the video at Thomas's house, the video of the discussion about Kim Jong-un's DNA. Sergei wondered if he'd fallen into the trap of denial that so many people fall into when confronted with something they don't want to acknowledge or think about or talk about. It could be that he'd not brought it up with Thomas because, if he didn't bring it up and talk about it, maybe it wouldn't be true. He had rationalized his delay in telling Thomas about finding the video because he'd told himself Thomas needed more time to recover his strength. Sergei now realized that he was the one who feared disclosure. It was time to talk about the video.

Thomas still did not remember anything about the day of his accident, and he didn't remember anything about the video. When Sergei showed it to him, Thomas was stunned, and it was obvious he didn't remember ever having seen it before. The video was a shock. In spite of his genuine inability to remember that he'd previously watched the video, viewing it a second time had shaken something loose in Thomas's mind. Sergei could tell that there was something different about Thomas after he'd seen the video.

Sergei wondered if Thomas had blocked off the entire day of his accident because what he had discovered on his computer that day was such a terrible revelation. At some level, he might have refused to remember anything that had happened because what had happened had been so abhorrent to him. Sergei was hopeful that bringing this devastating issue into the light might help with Thomas's mental healing. Thomas might have locked up his mind and closed off part of his consciousness because he couldn't confront the truth about Ji-su.

They talked for hours and days about what to do. Sergei was delighted that Thomas seemed to be opening up and remembering things. He was becoming more like his old self. Revealing the truth, no matter how shattering, led to healing. Sergei had learned something from this dilemma. He hoped he could hang on to his courage and his belief that shedding light on problems was the only way to begin to solve them. He knew he would have to confront Ji-su with her past, and he was terrified that it would destroy her and destroy their relationship. But it was the only way, the only possible choice he could make. He loved her too much to hide anything from her, especially something this momentous. Thomas agreed that full disclosure was the way to go. There could be no more secrets.

Ji-su had stopped emailing him, and she'd stopped returning his calls. He knew he'd been away a long time, but he was desperate to get back to Russky Island to see her. Sergei didn't understand why she'd cut herself off from him. He'd even gone so far as to contact the head priest at the monastery to ask if Ji-su was all right. Sergei simply wanted to know that she wasn't ill. The reply from the priest had reassured him that she wasn't sick, but it was more what the priest hadn't said than what he had said.

Something was going on with Ji-su, and Sergei didn't know why she had stopped communicating. He needed to leave Skaneateles and return to Russia to straighten things out with Ji-su. He said this to Thomas, and Thomas understood. Thomas assured Sergei that he was going to be fine. He sadly admitted he might never be the man he'd been before his accident, but he assured Sergei that he was now able to function on his own. They said their goodbyes, a difficult time that always brought tears for both of them. It was late November when Sergei returned to the monastery at St. Seraphim on Russky Island.

He first saw her again in the courtyard where they had spent so many hours walking and talking together. It was their special place. He watched her from a distance for a few minutes. She was talking to Song-gi, and she was laughing. Sergei was happy to see her laughing. Things could not be that terrible if she was spending time laughing with a child. She finally looked up and saw him.

A cloud of tremendous sadness moved across her face for a brief instant before she smiled and began to run towards him. In that fleeting moment, as he'd read the expression that had crossed her beautiful countenance, Sergei knew everything that she was going to say to him. He swept her into his arms when she reached him. He held her and kissed her, and they had a joyful and passionate reunion. But deep in his heart he knew what she had decided had to happen between them. He knew she loved him with her whole being, and he knew he wanted her more than he had ever wanted anything before in his life. But, in the end, perhaps all of that loving and wanting would not be enough. They spent the next two days in Ji-su's room. No one dared knock on the door. Everyone stayed away and wondered what would happen when they reappeared.

Christmas was coming, and St. Seraphim was busy decorating for the important Christian holiday. Song-gi was thrilled with the preparations for the birthday of the Christ child. His family had never practiced a religion of any kind. The only religion that had been allowed in North Korea was the worship of Kim Jong-un. The practice of other religions had been strictly forbidden, but the brothers were quickly making a small convert to the Russian Orthodox Church with the Christmas story.

Song-gi asked over and over again to hear about Mary and Joseph and the holy child, the birth of the baby in a stable full of animals, and the journey of the wise men bringing gifts of gold and other unusual things. Every priest told the story a little bit differently, and Song-gi took in every word. Song-gi had learned to tell the Christmas story himself in Russian. There was a wonderful nativity scene of three-hundred-year-old ceramic figurines at the monastery, and Song-gi talked to each of the figures in the crèche every morning—in Russian. He even talked to the sheep and the donkeys in Russian. Song-gi was especially delighted when he heard that later on in his life, Jesus, the carpenter, had chosen several fishermen as his best pals.

The little boy loved the greenery and other decorations the monks had brought into the monastery. Decorating the huge Christmas tree they'd cut down and put up was a high point. The monastery smelled good, like a pine tree forest, and it looked beautiful. Song-gi had heard there was going to be a pageant and a dinner with special food. When the brothers told him there were going to be gifts on Christmas Day, he'd asked them if the wise men were coming back.

Ji-su knew that being with Sergei again would be a test of her resolve to do what she believed was the right thing. She allowed herself to make love to Sergei, and finally she told him what he already knew. She told him how much she loved him, and she told him he had to return to his life in Sergiyev Posad. She told him all the things she'd told herself in the weeks he'd been away, all the reasons why they could never have a future together. Ji-su told him not to argue with her. She said she would never be able to live with herself if she made him give up the life she knew he loved.

He protested and argued and declared his devotion to her. He said he wanted a life with her, even if it meant giving up his life as a priest in Sergiyev Posad. They went back and forth and battled it out. Then they made love again. Then they cried. They argued some more. They clung to each other as if the world were coming to an end.

Finally, Sergei realized he was not going to be able to talk Ji-su out of her decision. He was devastated. He said he didn't want to live his life without her. He packed his few belongings, booked a flight to Moscow, and left St. Seraphim without saying a word to anyone. The brothers had been worried that this would happen, and they were quite concerned about Sergei. They didn't know what to do about Ji-su. No one, except for Song-gi, was still in the Christmas spirit after Sergei had left the monastery in despair.

Ji-su knew the monks wanted her to leave. She had been welcome at the monastery as long as she had been with Sergei, but now that she had rejected him, she felt they no longer wanted her at St. Seraphim. She was going to have to leave. She spoke with the head brother and asked that she be allowed to stay through Christmas while she looked for another place to live. She had her South Korean passport now, and everyone knew it. Lack of identity and travel papers were no longer excuses for her to stay.

Ji-su suspected that the monks wanted her to go back to South Korea which was where they probably thought she belonged. She knew she was not going back to South Korea, but she had no idea where in the world she was going to go. Ji-su tried not to think about her future because she didn't want to dwell on how much she missed Sergei. She wondered every minute of every day if she had made a bad decision by insisting that Sergei leave her and return to Sergiyev Posad.

The monks agreed to let her stay until after the New Year. The brothers were men of God, and they were kind to her, even if they didn't understand why she had sent Sergei away.

Chapter 41

ST. SERAPHIM

J*i-su had never celebrated Christmas* before. Her South Korean family were Buddhists, but she made a valiant effort to join in the festivities at the monastery. Song-gi was enthralled with the wonderful holiday, and Ji-su tried hard to smile with him and share his fun. She'd made no effort at all to find another place to live. She was nearly paralyzed by her thoughts of the future she would never have with Sergei and by her thoughts of who she really was. It was Song-gi's good humor that kept her sane. Mrs. Ri was making several roast geese with all the trimmings for Christmas dinner. The Christmas tree was magnificent. Ji-su only wanted to go to her little room and sleep. New Year's Day came and went. No one said anything to Ji-su about moving out of the monastery.

She was feeling depressed and not herself. She blamed her moods on not sleeping well. She was a person who had always enjoyed good health, but now she felt as if she was coming down with the flu almost every day. When she didn't feel any better after a few weeks, she decided she needed to consult a doctor. She asked the priest at the monastery, the physician who had been an orthopedist before he'd become a priest, to recommend a physician she could consult at the medical clinic. He saw her pale face and gave her the knowing look of someone who has been down this road before. He looked at her with understanding and gently asked her what kind of a doctor she needed to see. Ji-su began to cry.

She knew and the priest knew that she was pregnant with Sergei's child. They had not taken any kind of precautions against pregnancy, so what did she expect? She thought she had confronted every demon that life could put in front of her, and now she was faced with the most difficult dilemma of all. She collapsed into the arms of the former doctor. He led her to her room. He told her she needed to rest, that they would talk later. He assured her that the brothers would not be evicting her.

Ji-su made an especially unfair request of the monks at St. Seraphim. She asked them not to let Sergei know that she was expecting his child. She wanted her pregnancy kept confidential from everyone outside the St. Seraphim community. She said she wanted to tell Sergei about the baby in her own way. She said she didn't want him to hear it through the gossip mill of the Russian Orthodox Church.

The good brothers protested and did not want to go along with her request, but in the end, they agreed to respect her wishes. They wondered among themselves, especially as the weeks and months slipped by, when she was going to get around to telling the man about his baby. Ji-su had not spoken with Sergei since he'd left the monastery before Christmas. She knew she should communicate with him. He deserved to know that he was going to be a father, but Ji-su was unable to make the important decisions she needed to make.

Ji-su was living in limbo, but she had never considered having an abortion. As far as she knew, Sergei didn't know anything about the baby. She had no idea what she would do when she finally gave birth. She was definitely in extreme denial.

One weekend, Song-gi's mother approached Ji-su and asked her who was going to take care of the baby after it was born. Although she realized the woman was already much too busy, Ji-su said she would love to have Mrs. Ri take care of the baby. Mrs. Ri prepared all the meals for the monastery, and she was spending many hours every day doing physical therapy with her husband, the fisherman. Ji-su offered to pay for a professional physical therapist to come to the monastery so that Mrs. Ri would have time to take care of the baby. But there was a language barrier to be considered because Mr. Ri spoke no Russian. Mrs. Ri said she would love to take care of the baby, and Ji-su knew she meant what she said. But Ji-su also knew Mrs. Ri didn't have time to take on the job of caring for another child. Mrs. Ri might be able to care for an infant on a temporary basis, but it was not a permanent solution to the problem.

Ji-su was going to have to step up and face the reality of her situation, but all through the summer, she procrastinated. She seemed to be excited about the baby, but she had done nothing practical to prepare for the child's arrival. She knew she was having a girl, and that delighted her. The brothers had been patient and had not said anything about her leaving as long as she was pregnant. Ji-su knew she had pushed her luck at St. Seraphim as far as she could push it. The monks had allowed her to live in the monastery for almost a year, but they would never be able to handle having a baby added to their religious place.

Ji-su had been cast out of the royal palace as an infant. She and her adopted family had barely been able to scrape together enough to eat on their small plot of land. Like many other poor people in North Korea, they had almost starved to death. When the only mother Ji-su had ever known had told her she was not her birth mother, Ji-su had felt utterly betrayed by her biological family. It was a difficult thing to accept that her biological family not only had rejected her but had also wanted to kill her.

To realize that your own relatives want to murder you is to suffer a kind of emotional death. When the North Korean government had murdered Ji-su's adoptive family, who had loved her and whom she had loved, she was robbed of the final vestige of her emotional life. Ji-su was extremely thin and small in stature because she had been deprived of food. She felt that she was also emotionally thin and that there must be something wrong with her.

Because of her background, she knew she was emotionally flawed. She had always felt distant from her South Korean family. They had been wonderful to her, but she'd seen herself as an interloper in the household, an outsider who didn't quite belong. She knew it was her own fault that she felt this way and had nothing to do with the kindness and affection her South Korean family had shown towards her. They had done everything they could possibly have done to make her feel safe and accepted. It wasn't their fault.

It wasn't until she'd fallen in love with Sergei that she realized she had the ability to really love anyone. And then she had sent him away. What was wrong with her? Ji-su began to wonder if she had made a mistake in deciding to continue her pregnancy. She questioned her right to bring a baby into the world. Did she have the ability to love this child the way that every child deserves to be loved?

In spite of the striking facial resemblance, Ji-su had found it almost impossible to find any other similarities between herself and her twin brother. He had been indulged by a sycophant mother who had babied, spoiled, coddled, and promoted him. He had been stuffed with food and had been allowed to live without limits, as those around him catered to his every whim. He was puffed up with a decadent life style and with the absolute power of a despot. Ji-su could not relate to that person in any way.

For years before she knew they were related, Ji-su had watched the monster, the flesh and blood horror that was Kim Jong-un, go about his evil work in the world. Acknowledging that she shared genetics with this man had been an earth-shattering mental and emotional hurdle for her to overcome. To admit that you are kin to someone so horrible would be a difficult thing for anyone. She knew they shared genetics, but that was all they shared.

They had been separated at birth and had lived diametrically opposed existences almost since drawing their first breaths. Ji-su had to accept that she and one of the evilest men in the world were twins, but that was all she had to accept. She was a totally separate and distinct person who had nothing to do with her biological twin. She had to find a way to live with what was true and at the same time learn to love who she was. If she did not love herself, she knew she would never really be able to love anyone else.

As she was learning to accept the fact that she shared the Kim family lineage, Ji-su found she wanted to learn more about her nephew, Kim Han-sol and her niece, Kim Sol-hui. Ji-su developed an interest in her niece and nephew in an almost desperate attempt to find some goodness in her genetic code, her family line. These two young people seemed to be good people, not corrupted by the power and violence of their elders in the Kim dynasty. Ji-su wanted to know more about these two human beings who shared her DNA, and she wanted to meet them.

Of course, she knew they had been forced into hiding and had been given assistance by the Cheollim and several nations to escape Kim Jong-un's assassins who wanted to murder them. Although there wasn't much public information about this branch of the family who had lived in Macau, Ji-su read everything she could about her niece and nephew. She watched the video of Han-sol's interview with Finnish television and the short video he had made after going into hiding, the video that reassured the world that he and his mother and sister were safe and doing well.

Ji-su wanted more than anything to get in touch with these two young people who comprised her biological family. She knew that a man named J.A. Von Kleeck, the Dutch Ambassador to South Korea had been instrumental in aiding these family members escape the clutches of KJU. She debated with herself about the best way to approach the ambassador. She decided she would write a letter to her young relatives and send it with a cover letter to Von Kleeck. She would explain who she was and why she thought she was related to them. She would give them a short account of her life. She would reassure them that she had no political ambitions whatsoever, that she only wanted to meet them.

She would not mention the U Group or anything about the role she had played in KJU's disappearance. Years down the road, if she ever really got to know these people, she would share that secret with them. But it would only confuse them to hear the story now. She never expected to hear back from the ambassador. She figured he would write her off as some kind of a nut case, a kook who imagined they were related to the Kim family and wanted something from them.

Chapter 42

ST. SERAPHIM AND HALFWAY AROUND THE WORLD

J*i-su wanted to deliver the* baby at the monastery, if possible. She did not want to go to the hospital… for quite a few good reasons. Her doctor was near-by at the medical clinic. The monks had agreed to this, after much discussion and ongoing and obvious displays of anxiety. A baby had never before been born at the monastery. They were trying to embrace new things, but this was a real stretch. The baby was due the first week in September, but sometimes first babies were late.

She went into labor on September 10th. After a long and difficult labor, Ji-su delivered a six-pound baby girl in her bedroom at St. Seraphim on September 11th. Sera Kim Ivanov was a perfect, healthy, beautiful baby with lots of dark curly hair. She had Ji-su's delicately exquisite face and Sergei's high cheekbones and blue eyes. She would be a beauty. She already was.

When Ji-su held her precious child in her arms for the first time, she was forever changed. Something inside her shifted permanently and irrevocably. She would always love Sergei, but the love she felt for this tiny human being was unique and completely new. Ji-su now saw the world through a totally different prism. Everything was transformed.

Mrs. Ri was recruited to teach Ji-su how to take care of her infant, and Song-gi was delighted with the baby. He insisted on holding Sera Kim as often as possible. Of course, he called her Seraphim, and everyone agreed she was an angel. She hardly ever cried. Ji-su was trying to nurse the baby, but Mrs. Ri ended up feeding the newborn formula more often than not. The monks were excited and happy, but they were in a quandary as to what to do about Sergei. He deserved to know what was happening. He deserved to be in on all of this and share in the joy. This was his child.

Sera Kim was five days old when they came for Ji-su in the middle of the night. They told her she had ten minutes to pack a bag. She told them she couldn't leave, that she had a new baby. Whoever had come for her hadn't known anything about a baby. They told her if she wanted to meet with her niece and nephew who were in hiding, this would be her one and only chance to do so. There was an opportunity for her to see them, and she had to leave that night and at once. Ji-su was crazy, not knowing what to do. She called Mrs. Ri who now carried her own cell phone. Ji-su asked her to come to her room as quickly as possible. Mrs. Ri had answered the phone with a sleepy voice, but she said she would be right there.

When Mrs. Ri arrived in her room, Ji-su was crying and rocking back and forth holding Sera Kim. Mrs. Ri saw the bag Ji-su had packed and asked, "What's happening, and where are you going?" She could not believe that this young mother would leave her newborn and go on a trip. Mrs. Ri ignored the two men who were in the room to take Ji-su away.

"I can't explain now. It's something I have to do."

"What can possibly be more important than your child, your baby who is only five days old? I don't understand."

"I don't think I really understand either. I'm sorry." Ji-su handed the baby to Mrs. Ri. Tears were streaming down Ji-su's face. "I can't tell you. I don't know where I'm going."

"Are you being arrested? Will you be coming back? What are we supposed to do about the baby?" Mrs. Ri was close to panic.

The two men interrupted and said it was time to leave. Ji-su kissed her baby on the forehead and walked out of the room with the two men, leaving Mrs. Ri in her wake to pick up the pieces and handle the difficult explanations to the brothers. It had all happened so unexpectedly and so quickly, no one had time to think about what was really going on. Ji-su knew she had to go with the men and seize this opportunity which she doubted she would ever have again. But to leave her child so soon after she was born was unthinkable. How could she be doing what she was doing? The men from Cheollim told her to please hurry. They said they had a plane to catch. Ji-su looked back at Mrs. Ri holding her baby. Ji-su felt sick to her stomach. She hated herself for leaving, but in the end, she left the monastery and Russky Island and went with the men from Cheollim.

They drove a Range Rover to the airport in Vladivostok and bypassed the main area where commercial passengers arrive and depart. They drove to a different entrance and also bypassed the area where most private planes arrive and depart. The Range Rover finally stopped at a quiet, almost deserted corner of the air field. It was three o'clock in the morning, and it didn't look to Ji-su as if there were any other people around. The car waited outside an aviation hanger.

She hoped she hadn't made a mistake by coming with the men who'd brought her here in the middle of the night. She hoped she hadn't become the target of a few renegades from North Korea's Kim government who wanted revenge for the removal of Kim Jong-un. Had a loyal supporter of the old regime been able to figure out that Ji-su had participated in the KJU operation?

The door of the airplane hangar opened, and the Range Rover drove inside. As soon as the car entered the hanger, the door closed again. It was dark, and Ji-su couldn't see much of anything. She was told to grab her bag and get out of the car. One of her escorts took her by the elbow and led her to the steps of a small private plane which was parked inside the building. One of the men asked for her cell phone and told her it would be returned to her after her journey. He hurried her up the steps of the small plane.

As soon as she was inside, the steps closed behind her, and the door was secured. Before she'd had a chance to take even one step towards a seat, the door of the hangar opened, and the plane began to move out onto the tarmac. The plane was dark inside, and she could barely find her way to a seat. There was no cabin attendant or anyone to tell her where to sit or what to do. She still had her bag in her hand. She sank down into the first leather seat she came to, put her bag under the seat in front of her, and fastened her seatbelt. Ji-su assumed it was still dark outside, but she couldn't see anything because all the window covers were down.

The plane taxied for a few minutes, and then without any warning, it quickly sped up and took off. In the blink of an eye, they were in the air. Ji-su was the only passenger on the plane. When her eyes got used to the dark, she could see the interior. It was definitely some kind of an executive jet, sleek and luxurious, but it didn't have the feel of a plane that was owned by a corporation. Some rich person had loaned their private plane to Cheollim to fly Ji-su to meet her family members. She would never know who that person was, but she was grateful for the flight. Ji-su was exhausted and fell asleep in the dark plane.

After they'd been in the air for a couple of hours, the door to the cockpit opened, and a young man in a uniform came to the cabin to speak with Ji-su. He spoke English perfectly, but of course she knew that all commercial pilots had to speak English. Somehow he knew that Ji-su knew English. She decided not to ask too many questions. The pilot told her they would be making two refueling stops and that there was no flight attendant or food service on the plane. He gave her a kind of crooked smile when he said this as if he were stating the obvious and at the same time making a small joke. Ji-su nodded and said nothing.

The man told her he was the co-pilot, and because of weather and security concerns, he couldn't tell her exactly how long the flight would take. He couldn't tell her where their final destination was because he himself didn't yet know what it would be. He did tell Ji-su that when they made their first refueling stop, food would be brought on board. He reached into a small refrigerator in the galley and handed Ji-su a bottle of water. He pointed to the bathroom and apologized for the no frills service.

Ji-su was tired and went back to sleep. Because she didn't have her cell phone, she had no idea what time it was or how much time had passed. She hadn't worn a wristwatch in years. She woke up when the plane was landing, and she tried to raise one of the blinds that covered the windows. It was locked. She assumed all the window covers were locked. She'd never seen that on a commercial flight or on any plane. She didn't know it was even possible to lock the window covers down so they could not be raised.

When the plane landed, the co-pilot stuck his head into the cabin and said there would be food soon. Ji-su was hungry and wondered how long it had been since she'd eaten. The co-pilot drew a curtain closed between the door to the plane and the cabin where Ji-su was seated. Ji-su was obviously not supposed to see or be seen, but she could hear voices and people going up and down the short flight of the plane's steps. After what she assumed was the time necessary for refueling, she heard the stairs being drawn up and the door closing. Carrying boxes and two shopping bags, the co-pilot opened the curtains that divided the cabin. He put the food down in the seat next to Ji-su and told her it was all hers. If she wanted to save something for later, she could put it into the refrigerator in the galley. She thanked the co-pilot, and he returned to the cockpit.

She opened the boxes and bags eagerly and found a roasted chicken, salads, sandwiches, cookies, and thermoses of coffee and tea. Plastic forks and paper napkins had not been forgotten. There was plenty of food, and she indulged. She put the food she didn't eat into the small refrigerator, and then she went to sleep again. She wondered where in the world she would end up when this journey came to its end.

It had been late September on Russky Island when Ji-su left Russia, and the fall days had begun to grow cooler. So it was a shock for her when the plane landed for the final time and its door opened. She found herself in the tropics. The air was hot and humid, and it looked and felt as if it had recently rained. Ji-su had no idea where she was, but she thought she might be some place in the Caribbean. She wanted to say thank you to her flight crew, but the door to the cockpit was closed. She grabbed her bag and exited the plane. The air was heavy and sticky when she put her feet onto the tarmac. The sun was setting. Ji-su had been sleeping in her clothes for what seemed like a long time, and she wanted to take a shower.

There was an old taxi at the bottom of the plane's stairway, and Ji-su assumed it was there for her. She climbed into the back. The driver never said a word to her; he just drove. There was no attempt to hide where they were going, but Ji-su didn't recognize anything as they traveled through the sparsely populated landscape. There was a house here and there, and Ji-su thought the vegetation resembled that of an island in the Caribbean. For all she knew, she could have been in South Africa, but the slight breeze she had felt when she'd walked from the plane to the taxi had reminded her of a West Indies trade wind.

The houses finally disappeared, and it became too dark for Ji-su to see anything. She dozed off again, and finally the taxi stopped in front of a white stucco building that looked as if it hadn't been painted or repaired in twenty years or longer. Ji-su wondered what in the world she'd gotten herself into. She opened the door to the taxi and got out with her bag. As soon as the door closed behind her, the taxi took off. The driver had not uttered a word during the entire drive. Ji-su stood in front of the run-down building and didn't know what to do. It was dark, and she assumed this was her last stop and that she was going to be staying in this place for the night.

The door of the stucco building opened, and a handsome middle-aged man came out to greet her. "Hello, Ji-su. I am

Nicolaas De Vries, and I am happy to welcome you to St. Eustatius. Your niece and nephew are anxious to meet you. Their flight has been delayed, but they will be arriving in a few hours." Nicolaas extended his hand to Ji-su. She shook his hand, and he picked up her bag. He ushered her into the door of the old building. "You will meet your family members in the morning. We are planning a late breakfast for you to get to know each other."

"Thank you, Mr. De Vries. I'd wondered if anyone would be willing to tell me what continent I was on. Everything is so secretive. I thought I might not be allowed to know where I was."

"Of course, you understand the need for secrecy. We are perfectly safe here. You are on the Island of St. Eustatius which used to be a colony of the Netherlands. We are on a secluded and private part of the island where none of the locals ever come. There's really nothing here anymore. It used to be a beautiful resort. This resort was, even in its prime, small, as resorts go, but it was quite popular with the Americans and the British. It was owned by a delightful gay couple from the United States. Tom was the bartender and quite a bon vivant. Jerry was the gourmet chef who ran the kitchen with an iron hand. Everyone loved Tom and Jerry. They ran an enormously successful hotel and popular tourist spot here for many years. When one of the guys died of AIDS, as so many tragically did during the 80s and 90s, his partner couldn't keep things going. They'd been getting older anyway.

"The thing about the property is that Tom and Jerry thought they'd been renting the resort, but it turned out they had been buying it. How anyone could possibly get that confused, I don't know. They were Americans and probably had more money than they had business sense. And laws are different here in a former Dutch colony. The men's wills left everything to each other. Then the second man of the couple who'd run the resort died. People said he died of a broken heart. Anyway, one of them had one heir, and the other man had a lot of family. Everybody wanted a piece of this place. Clarifying who legally owned the land and the hotel became a nightmare. The whole thing about who owns this property has been tied up in the courts for more than twenty years. It's a terrible mess and such a shame that it's been allowed to go to ruin. Because the American courts and the Dutch courts are both involved in the lawsuit over who owns the resort, the local courts have taken jurisdiction. Long story short... or perhaps I should say short story long because I am blabbering. In any case, we are fortunate to be able to use the resort for a few days, compliments of the Dutch government. No one will ever know we are here. We have had several bedrooms and bathrooms cleaned up and prepared for you and your family, and I have brought my own cook from Amsterdam to feed us."

"Thank you, Mr. De Vries. I'm glad to know where I am."

"Please call me Nicolaas. There is food prepared for you in the kitchen. It's a cold meal, I'm afraid, but with the humidity and the heat, I think it will be all right. We have coffee and tea and soft drinks. There is also some wine and some brandy. We don't have a full bar, I'm afraid."

"It will be fine. A cold supper and some iced tea will be wonderful. And then I am hoping there is hot water. I feel as if I've been traveling for days. I don't even know what day it is now." Ji-su followed the chatty Nicolaas into the kitchen.

She dined on delicious cold lobster salad, chilled fresh asparagus vinaigrette, and deviled eggs. She drank a glass of iced tea and sent her compliments to the Dutch cook. Then she excused herself and told Nicolaas good night. He said someone would awaken her in the morning for the family breakfast. Ji-su tossed and turned and listened, trying to hear when Kim Han-sol and Kim Sol-hui arrived. Her time zones were confused, and she dropped off to sleep before she heard anything.

Chapter 43

ISLAND IN THE CARIBBEAN

The breakfast meeting was, for Ji-su, a milestone in her life. She told her niece and nephew when she saw them in person that this was the first time since she had been an infant, that she had been with anyone who were actually members of her biological family. When she met them, both Han-sol and Sol-hui commented on her facial resemblance to KJU. They hastened to add that she was a much more attractive version of their uncle and that she had a much more pleasant figure. Everybody laughed at that. As they enjoyed their Dutch breakfast, they began to share with each other everything about their lives.

Ji-su recounted the story her wet nurse had told her about the origins of her birth. Han-sol and Sol-hui were fascinated and hung on every word she had to say. Ji-su told them that her relationship to KJU and to both of them had been definitely confirmed through DNA testing. There was no doubt that they were her niece and nephew. The brother and sister said they didn't need to have DNA tests to know she was related to them. Ji-su decided not to mention anything about her mission for the U Group, KJU's abduction, or her impersonation. She knew that one day she would tell them all about it, but there was already enough for them to absorb on this sunny Caribbean morning.

Han-sol and Sol-hui told her all about their lives growing up in Macau, and they talked about their father and his brutal murder at the hands of Kim Jong-un. Han-sol talked about his education in various countries abroad. Sol-hui talked about the family's escape from Macau and told Ji-su that she was attending university in England. They said they weren't able to tell her where their mother was living or anything at all about that. They said they had solid new identities and passports and felt quite safe at Oxford and Cambridge.

The three spoke in Korean and in English. That first day, they laughed and bonded and didn't talk about politics or any of their futures or what was going to happen to North Korea. From time to time, Nicolaas poked his head in and joined the conversation. He had known the family for a long time and had lots of anecdotes to tell about the two young people when they were growing up in Macau. It was a unique experience for Ji-su. Before everyone went to bed for the night, she told her niece and nephew about Sera Kim Ivanov. They said she should have brought the baby with her. It was obvious that neither one of them had ever taken care of or traveled with an infant.

The next day, Ji-su-made up a story about how she had met Sergei, Sera Kim's father. She couldn't tell her newly found family members the truth right now, but she promised herself she would one day tell them the whole exciting story about escaping from North Korea and about how Sergei had saved her life several times during her getaway. They began to talk about North Korea and about their own futures and the future of the country they all had in common. They allowed themselves to speculate about what their best hopes might be for their country in an ideal world. Ji-su was impressed with the intellect and the understanding of both these members of the younger generation.

On their third day together, they got down to the nitty-gritty of whether or not either Han-sol or Sol-hui felt as if he or she could take on the role of leadership in North Korea. They had a full grasp of the situation and understood completely what taking on such a life would mean for them. Sol-hui said she wanted to be a writer, that poetry and writing stories had always been her passion. She claimed to be an introvert and said she didn't want anything to do with politics. Han-sol was more resigned that he might find himself one day in a political position of importance. He was educating himself in economics and geopolitical history and finance, but he said he was not ready to take on anything so momentous at this time in his life. He acknowledged he had not been brought up or groomed to be any kind of head of state.

Ji-su pointed out that George VI, Britain's beloved Bertie, had not been brought up to be the King of England. But when his older brother, Edward VIII, had abdicated the throne to marry Wallis Simpson, Bertie had been thrust into the limelight and had taken Edward's place on the throne. Bertie had led England bravely through the Second World War, and he had inspired his people, even as he struggled to overcome a severe speech impediment. Ji-su pointed out that sometimes never intending to hold power and not being raised to take being powerful for granted might make one able to wield that power with even more grace and responsibility. They became philosophical. Ji-su shared with them that since she had found out she was related to the Kim family, her sense of duty had become magnified. She talked about destiny and the service that comes with privilege. Her niece and nephew heard her. Ji-su even paid attention to her own words.

Their final night together, Nicolaas joined them for a farewell dinner. They were all thankful that he had been able to arrange this meeting for them on St. Eustatius. Nicolaas said he felt that in a couple of years, if North Korea was able to sort itself out from its current chaos, the Kims might be able to safely come out of hiding and live in North Korea or anywhere else in the world, without fearing for their lives. Ji-su said she wanted North Korea to come back from its pariah status and join the family of nations as a full, participating member.

The three set up anonymous email accounts so they could stay in touch with each other. They planned another reunion in six months. Ji-su promised to bring Sera Kim. Ji-su told her newly-discovered niece and nephew, from her heart and with considerable emotion, what joy it had brought her to find them and to get to know them. They discussed possibilities, and there were hugs and tears all around as Ji-su told her small family goodbye.

Ji-su had missed her baby terribly. But she would never have chosen not to make the trip she had just taken half way around the world to meet and get to know her niece and nephew. They were a part of her life now, and she was a part of theirs. On her trip back home to Russky Island, she had a hundred imaginary conversations with herself and with Sergei, trying to find a way to tell him that he had a baby daughter and that both Ji-su and Sera Kim wanted him to be a part of their lives. How they worked out the details of accomplishing that would be the challenge. Ji-su felt guilty that she had been so unforgivably selfish and had kept her pregnancy a secret from Sergei. It had not been fair for her to do that, and she was feeling foolish and exceedingly sad that she hadn't included Sergei. He had deserved so much better than she had given him.

Epilogue

ST. SERAPHIM

I*n spite of sleeping on* the plane, Ji-su was dead tired when she arrived at the monastery at the end of her long journey home from St. Eustatius. It was a gorgeous fall day on Russky Island. All she wanted to do was go straight to her little room, kiss and hold her baby, and go to sleep. She arrived in the late afternoon and thought she could slip into her room and find Sera Kim there.

But Song-gi was too aware of everything that went on in the monastery for her to arrive without him noticing she was back. He ran up to her and threw himself into her arms. He had missed her terribly. She'd been gone for less than a week, but that had seemed such a very long time to a small boy. She told him she wanted to go to her room, that she was exhausted from her journey. But Song-gi was stubborn and grabbed her hand. He insisted on pulling her towards the courtyard of the monastery. He said she had to go with him and would not be put off. She gave in and allowed herself to be led to the courtyard.

She gasped and almost stumbled when she saw why Song-gi had wanted her to accompany him to the courtyard.

There, on the stone bench where she and Sergei had spent so many hours talking, getting to know each other, and falling in love, was Sera Kim Ivanov in the arms of her father. He was singing softly to her and rocking her gently back and forth. Ji-su stood and watched the two of them together. She saw how Sergei held their child with such tenderness and affection. He was completely entranced with her. Nothing else in the world existed for him as he looked down at Sera Kim's tiny face. Ji-su knew as she watched them that they were and would always be a family. The practicalities would have to be resolved, but there was no question that the three of them belonged together. Tears of joy streamed down her face as she walked towards the father and his baby daughter.

Acknowledgments

The first thank you always goes to my readers: Jane Corcoran, Peggy Baker, Nancy Calland Hart, and Robert Lane Taylor. Nancy Hart and my husband, Robert Taylor, also edited and proofread *NO MORE SECRETS*. I am indebted to their sharp eyes and critical scrutiny.

Special gratitude goes to Judith Pattison, photographer, and Sandra Mannakee, technical expert. I built the circle of skulls with Kim Jong-un in the center. Judy Pattison photographed my creation, and Sandy Mannakee computerized the photographs and helped me send them to Jamie Tipton. Jamie used Judy's photographs for the covers.

Jamie Tipton of Open Heart Designs puts it all together for me to create the amazing covers for this book. Jamie also formats the interiors of the hardcover, the paperback, and the ebook. She does everything that is necessary to turn my manuscript into a printed book. She also holds my hand. I could not possibly produce a book without her professional and patient expertise.

Andrea Burns prepared the photograph of the author.

I am very grateful to all those who contributed their help to make *NO MORE SECRETS* a reality.

The first question Elizabeth Burke, M.D. always asked me when I saw her in her office was: "What's new and exciting in your life?" I promised myself that one day I would have a good answer for her. Thank you, Dr. Burke.

About the Author

MARGARET TURNER TAYLOR *lives on the East Coast in the summer and in Southeast Arizona in the winter. She has written several mysteries for young people, in honor of her grandchildren. She writes spy thrillers, stories of political intrigue, and all kinds of mysteries for grownups.*

MORE BOOKS BY
MARGARET TURNER TAYLOR

BOOKS FOR ADULTS

TRAVELING THROUGH THE VALLEY OF THE SHADOW OF DEATH

Based on actual events that occurred in 1938, Traveling Through the Valley of the Shadow of Death is a fictional spy thriller that will captivate the reader with its complex intrigue and deceptions. Travel with Geneva Burkhart through pre-World War II Germany as she deals with an amorous Nazi minder who has been assigned to watch her group of mathematics teachers. The young American woman who grew up on an Ohio dairy farm has adventures that take her to dangerous and frightening places.

Released 2020, 428 pages

I WILL FEAR NO EVIL

This World War II thriller, set in neutral Portugal, tells the story of a courageous few who risk their lives to confront evil. The reader will get to know the cadre of international patriots who live at beautiful Bacalhoa in Setubal. Max, who faced death in Traveling Through the Valley of the Shadow of Death, joins other brave souls who have devised an elaborate and secret network to transport Jewish orphans across the Atlantic to safety and freedom in the United States. Max has his revenge on the Nazis and finds love during his journey.

Released 2020, 370 pages

RUSSIAN FINGERS

Book #1 in the The Quest for Freedom Series

Peter Gregory spent his childhood in a camp for Soviet spies. Sent to live in the United States and uncover its atomic secrets for the Russians, he soon realizes that he loves his adopted country. After the fall of the Soviet Union, Peter disappears and makes a new life for himself. But Russia wants its spy back. Sergei, now a Russian orthodox priest who knew Peter at Camp 27, is forced by Russia's neo-Soviets to try to track him down. Will Peter and Sergei be able to outsmart Putin's henchmen and disappear again?

Released 2023, 354 pages

DO YOU KNOW WHO I AM?

Book #3 in the The Quest for Freedom Series

Rosalind Parsons, who everyone believes has been murdered, and her baby have disappeared. The computer expert builds a successful life for herself as Rosemary Carmichael in Asheville, North Carolina. When Gimbel Saunders, a New York State Police detective goes undercover in Wilmington, North Carolina, to track down a Russian-run fentanyl operation, he discovers Rosemary's true identity. Old mysteries are solved and a hurricane rages.

Released 2024, 368 pages

More on following page...

MORE FROM
LLOURETTIA GATES BOOKS

CAROLINA DANFORD WRIGHT

Old School Rules
Book #1 in the *The Granny Avengers Series*

Marfa Lights Out
Book #2 in the *The Granny Avengers Series*

HENRIETTA ALTEN WEST

I Have a Photograph
Book #1 in the *The Reunion Chronicles Mysteries*

Preserve Your Memories
Book #2 in the *The Reunion Chronicles Mysteries*

When Times Get Rough
Book #3 in the *The Reunion Chronicles Mysteries*

A Fortress Steep & Mighty
Book #4 in the *The Reunion Chronicles Mysteries*

The Wells of Silence
Book #5 in the The Reunion Chronicles Mysteries

Going Home
Book #6 in the *The Reunion Chronicles Mysteries*

Available in hard cover, paperback and ebook online everywhere books are sold.

www.ingramcontent.com/pod-product-compliance
Lightning Source LLC
Jackson TN
JSHW012359230225
79469JS00003B/3/J
* 9 7 8 1 9 5 3 0 8 2 3 3 6 *